GROWING UP FILIPINO 3
New Stories for Young Adults

COLLECTED AND EDITED BY

CECILIA MANGUERRA BRAINARD

Published by PALH
(Philippine American Literary House)
PO Box 5099
Santa Monica, CA 90409, USA
Palhbooks.com; palh@aol.com

FIRST EDITION

Library of Congress Control Number: 2022905048

ISBN 9781953716163 (hb)
ISBN 9781953716170 (sc)
ISBN 9781953716187 (Ebook)

Growing Up Filipino 3: New Stories for Young Adults is also published by the University of Santo Tomas Publishing House, Copyright © 2022 Cecilia Manguerra Brainard. All rights reserved.

Cover Art by Hersley Ven Casero
Cover Design by Ian Rosales Casocot

CONTENTS

INTRODUCTION

I am happy to present *Growing Up Filipino 3: New Stories for Young Adults.*

This book follows two earlier anthologies: *Growing Up Filipino: Stories for Young Adults* published in 2003, and *Growing Up Filipino II: More Stories for Young Adults* published in 2010. The first two books were critically acclaimed by *Booklist, School Library Journal, Bookbird Journal International, Melus, Multicultural Review,* among others. Both books were featured in *National Geographic's* 2020 Summer Reading List. The books were used, and continue to be used, by educators in their classrooms. They are enjoyed by adults and young adults alike.

Growing Up Filipino 3 continues the same level of excellence that the two earlier books have achieved.

Growing Up Filipino 3 has twenty-five stories by the same number of Filipino and Filipino American authors. The authors have included short introductory write-ups about Philippine or Filipino American culture and history that relate to their stories. The stories are for both adult and young adult readership.

While universal themes of coming-of-age, angst, love, family, relationships, and other young adult issues are explored in *Growing Up Filipino 3*, which makes the book appeal to all readers, this anthology offers far more than teenage accounts. These stories reveal Filipino and Filipino American mores, culture, history, society, politics, and other nuances. For instance, Filipino respect for elders, extended families, religious practices, funereal rites, love for folklore are apparent in the stories.

Politics and history, even though in the background, are inherent in many stories. One of them, "Tall Woman from Leyte," the fictional encounter of a child and the infamous Imelda Marcos, wife of the dictator Ferdinand Marcos allude not only to the Marcos dictatorship but also to General MacArthur's landing in Leyte during World War II.

"Let Me Tell You About My Aunt Edelweiss" has a character whose boyfriend is a victim of extrajudicial killings during the Duterte presidency.

The class system in the Philippines is evident in many stories: there are the rich; and there are the poor. The brothers in the Patricia Manuel Go's story "Pig," who own a potbellied pet pig, are housed in a separate residence in a gated community by an abusive wealthy father. The story "Nilda" is about another well-heeled teenage young man whose nanny or yaya hovers over him well into his teens. The characters in the story "Narisa" attend private American universities and travel to Paris, Siem Reap, and other places.

On the other hand, the character in the story "Becoming Victoria" has to worry over school tuition. The story "Then Cruel Quiet" is about a young boy who has relatives who work overseas, an exodus (the author notes) that began under the Marcos dictatorship.

The complex historical and political connections between the Philippines and the United States are alluded to by the American presence in the Philippines, and by the migration of many Filipinos to the United States.

The story "The Fancy Dancer" allows us a peek at how it was to grow up as the love child of an American GI/Air Force Officer and a Filipina. The story "Beauty Queens" is about a young girl who tells off a predatory uncle, a former Marine. The story "The Dead Boy" is about the son of an American logger.

Immigrant experiences of Filipinos in America are topics of the stories: "It's Cold in America" "Refugees" "Dress Down Day" "Happy" "The Secret" "Pigeons for Ethel", and "Kalihi in Farrah."

Several writers have fictionalized their memories in "The Rubber Duckie Confessions" "The Kite" and "Babaylan in Playland."

One writer gives a sampling of dark short fiction in "The Child." Another writer gives us a look at what Catholic seminary life is like in "The Goat." The stories "Zombie

Queen" and "Lola Ging and the Crispa Redmanizer" tell of their characters' loss of their grandmothers.

Most of the writers in this collection are published; all are accomplished. They have offered their best. It is my/our wish that the readers would enjoy these stories.

Cecilia Manguerra Brainard

GINA APOSTOL grew up in the Philippines and lives in New York where she writes novels on revolution and language, storytelling and history. Her fourth novel *Insurrecto* was named by *Publishers' Weekly* one of the Ten Best Books of 2018. Her third book *Gun Dealers' Daughter* won the 2013 PEN/Open Book Award. Her first two novels, *Bibliolepsy* and *The Revolution According to Raymundo Mata*, both won the Juan Laya Prize for the Novel (Philippine National Book Award). Her essays and stories have appeared in *The New York Times, Los Angeles Review of Books, Foreign Policy, Gettysburg Review,* and others.

CHILD OF MARTIAL LAW -- "Tall Woman from Leyte" is an offshoot from a novel I was finishing at the time—my first novel *Bibliolepsy*. It became a story on its own because, I think, I did not want to let go of one image in a scene that I discarded in the novel— the umbrella of tongues gleefully sticking out at Imelda Marcos. All my work is shaped by my growing up in Tacloban in Leyte: the world of the Warays, of Leyte and Samar islands, for better or worse constructs me. The characters in this story are all made up, but the sense of martial-law peril and martial-law resistance, girded by a child's love of place, based on this inarticulate sense of injustice endemic to my own identity as a child of martial-law rule, are all aspects of my childhood truths growing up in Leyte.

1

TALL WOMAN FROM LEYTE

I was all bathed and well-fed, like a beloved suckling pig, and my sister, as always, was walking sleepy and bored behind me, thinking of ways to skip school without being caught by Berrer, the half-blind and one-armed school guard. We waved good-bye as Manong Ramon shot off; he was the jeepney driver paid monthly for his services by my mother, a benign and depressive woman. The day was bright and cool, perfect for rainfall, and I was anxious to get back the umbrella I'd left in my second-grade classroom. It was a gift from the Abuelita, my mother's surly mother who always smelled of lemon, a bitter and profuse scent that suitably announced her presence. I adored the umbrella. It had pale pink ruffles on the hem and red shocking lips with painted stuck-out tongues across a blue background, like a sky of scorn; I liked to walk under it even on ordinary days, thinking that my thoughts were fully expressed. My mother made a face when she first saw it. "Mamá!" she said, accent on the second syllable as old-fashioned ladies of leisure pronounced it, "Shame on you for your lack of taste!" My father, an aspiring animator, said from his magical table, "And for indulging the growing madness of that child." My sister refused to walk with me when I unfurled the umbrella, which was almost always. I forgot it the day before only because my mother rushed me home to witness the molting of her African caterpillar, a gift from her brother, Uncle Benny, who travels the world on the vestiges of his family's sugar fortune. My mother is something of a biologist, though she is happier with dead animals than normal ones, who stay alive for no good reason.

So you can imagine my anxiety about leaving my umbrella behind: on this day, too, which looked like rain. But when we arrived at the school gate, it was closed. Berrer, the ancient and inhuman guard with one eyepatch and never-used batuta, yelled at us: "No class! Go home!" My sister couldn't believe her good fortune. "Mano Ramon will come back," she said to me. "Just stay here and be good." Then she left me to walk off to the billiard hall two blocks away, where one of her boyfriends, a beautiful out-of-school youth named Ronnie, could always be found.

I pushed my way through a side gate.

"Can't go in," Berrer approached me. "Not allowed."

"But I have classes today. Miss Yrinco told me to make a report on Central Luzon, the Rice Granary of the Philippines."

"Not today. School's closed."

"But why?"

"Shut up. Go home."

Of course, I knew ways of getting in without going through the gate. But the injustice of it rankled: no classes when kids had actually been woken up and bathed for school.

I remembered no warnings of typhoons, which occurred when storms blew in from Taiwan and other pieces of the South China Sea. And I knew it wasn't a holiday: I knew all those by heart. The only one that could take me by surprise was October 20, Leyte Landing Day. The school prepared months for the event: students rehearsed dancing demonstrations in the mornings, teachers sent drawings of our costumes weeks in advance, and the school contracted seamstresses to measure our chests and waists in time for the day-long celebration of the arrival of MacArthur and his troops on the island of Leyte in 1944. "I Shall Return" t-shirts were sold on the sidewalks long before the commemoration. And when the day came, aging foreign men in uniforms took their places on the podium at Red Beach, and the President and his wife sang songs to them with tears in their eyes. Sometimes, the men would sing along; they'd say smart speeches with snippets of badly spoken Tagalog, which was not even our language. And all the schools in the city came out with their dances in the noonday sun, to the ferocious, sentimental clapping of sweating old men.

I watched all this on television; I was the only one in kindergarten who did not join the dance. During that first year in school my wayward father had pulled me out of it.

"Abominable!" my father, holding a copy of the dance costume drawing, said to Mrs. Almaden, who didn't teach me history. "Do you know what you are celebrating? Subjugation and colonial suppression and American jingoism and the fall of Manila in 1898 to Commodore Dewey's ships when our rebels had already chased the Spaniards out, only to be faced with this traitor, America, Mr. Johnny-come-lately, who stole the spoils of our war. You are celebrating MacArthur, who left the country when it was convenient in 1941, left us with a consumptive president and a traitor for his successor, and returned with that snout-faced, pig-eyed dwarf Carlos P. Romulo whose misplaced love for America is equal in stupidity only to this city's perennial celebration of that damned return, can't you stop this idiocy already?"

My father was not a man of many words. I fill up this speech only so you may get the gist of his anger.

In reality, he had not known at first about the dance. I enjoyed practicing in the sun to the tune of "The Entertainer", happily skipping arithmetic and lessons in photosynthesis, subsets, and planetary motion, as the whole school flung itself into its massive dancing fever. I missed only our lessons in geography, the fascinating bits about provinces, which had set

7

personalities, like gigantic characters in books—the stingy people in the north, or the unreliable temper of Ilonggos, which came from their habit of eating too much pepper. The costume was to be a short, ruffled blouse showing our bare tummies, with matching polka dot bloomers that I adored, although my sister Anna said we'd all look like midget clowns. When the drawings of our costumes and attached explanations arrived at the house, my father exploded and sent my teacher a note. I spent the week of Leyte Landing at home, watching my father create cartoons, one showing General Douglas MacArthur landing with the president, instead of with the pig-eyed dwarf Carlos Romulo; and a bridge's suspension ropes very cleverly strike the general and the president on the head. Pow! Zap! The city paper rejected it, as it did all of his drawings. My mom said it was because they smelled. "Politics in a work of art stinks," she declared. And my dad would grunt.

October 20 was far off. It was the beginning of July. There was no reason for a holiday, as far as I could tell. I snuck into the school by the gym area, near the Belgian Nuns' Hospital. I climbed the gate and jumped in, then rushed to the elementary school classrooms. The Divine Word Missionary School is now extinct. It used to be a sprawling complex, complete with a Museum, dedicated to wartime memorabilia and the First Lady's effects. At that time, it spanned four blocks of stone and wooden buildings. Behind the high school and elementary buildings were a creek and an athletic oval where high school students did military drills and we in the elementary school practiced our huge dancing extravaganzas. I ran to my classroom and found the umbrella where I had left it, by my seat in the third row. I held it to my chest, and when I left the building I decided to take the opposite route from where I had come—across the creek and the length of the athletic oval to the other side of the school where there were no guards or gates: just the gardens and backyards of squatter dwellers and vendors of banana and cassava cakes.

It was pleasant but strange to be alone on the school grounds. I went to the guava trees by the creek to steal Father

Hermann's fruit. Old Belgian and Dutch priests ruled our school like Martian spirits roaming the grounds. They appeared out of nowhere with their pale dotted hands and vast expanses of ghostly flesh, saying: "Plants can't be touched. Keep off the grass. Who is Simon of Cyrene?" Father Hermann was the most common priestly sight among the plants and trees. He was always watering and digging, uprooting and transferring plants. I read about Francis of Assisi, the saint in the woods, and thought of Father Hermann, except that Father Hermann had big teeth that jutted over his lower lip so that he looked constantly silly, and birds never sat on his shoulders. He was from Holland and a lonely long way away from home. At least he said as much in his sermons. Other priests stuck strictly to the purpose, as far as I could tell. They read the gospel, then talked about what they read, like the Abuelita, my grandmother, when she finished reading the paper. Father Hermann, on the other hand, didn't seem to care what was in the book. He'd talk about Holland, the way his mother cried when he had left home to go far away, to the Philippines where people didn't drink milk or plant tulips, which Dutch people do every day. He'd talk about the foreigner who carried Jesus's cross, Simon of Cyrene. In some way, he was supposed to be Simon, or Simon of Cyrene was Father Hermann. Then at the end of his talk, he would always remind us to quit climbing the guava trees, stop walking on the grass, and please never play tag on the flower beds, flower seeds are imported and expensive, his teeth protruding as if to meet the white collar of his robe, a sight that led me to distractions of pity and distress.

But I took the guava anyway, looking around for hovering priests. There were none. The fruit was crunchy, seeds gritty, newly ripe and perfect. When I crossed the creek and found myself on the yellowing grass of the oval, I discovered I wasn't alone. There were moving figures on the edges of the field. I thought it was Father Hermann with some priest-buddies, diligently separating weeds from good grass, an occupation that, for Dutch people, required proper seclusion. But these people weren't wearing the loose cotton camisas of the old pale priests; they were all in blue uniforms like school guards, except that our guards wore gray. They brushed something metallic across the grass as if looking for some lost object. I had gotten far enough onto the field to be soon in their way.

I was certain that these men had something to do with the cancellation of classes and the closing of the school gates. I knew I should throw away my stolen guava, or I should go back through the gates and brave detection by Berrer. I knew I was in trouble with these men in the field looking for a priest's dentures or a dead child.

I opened my umbrella instead. It was a beautiful defensive gesture, now that I think of it; and I decided to keep my guava, too, and walked straight across the fields as if I were a regular squatter dweller's child going home from selling cakes. This was actually a regular fantasy of mine, being someone else's kid, particularly a squatter's child who did people's dirty laundry during lunch period and had salt and rice and nothing else for supper.

I was scared but no one minded me. I walked along and even came close to one man, who was smoking a cigarette and walked about the field with a keen look. I watched him do his work; I twirled my umbrella as a sassy squatter kid should. He ignored me. Then at the entrance to the field from where I had just come, on the bridge spanning the creek, a vehicle arrived.

It came over the bridge and trundled onto the field, stirring grass, earth, and men. The nearest men in uniform moved immediately toward the car. A lady stepped out. They saluted her smartly. I saw all this from a wide open field flat as a beach. Then I saw the woman point at me.

Surprise replaced my fright. The car was all black, including the windows: like a funerary car, except that its trunk was short, so maybe if it had a dead man it would be a dwarf. Or a lost child.

When the Abuelita had last read the paper, she had spoken about the rumors going around the city.

"Ten cuidado," she had told me in her raspy voice. Lisping all the time like a damaged Spaniard, she said that children were disappearing about the banks of the San Juanico Strait. The president of the country and his lady had ordered the building of Asia's longest bridge, the solution to all the problems of Leyte and Samar. At the same time, silvery fish-like scales were appearing on the long legs of the tall First Lady; she was so tall that there were uncountable scales, each scale disappearing only at the death of a child. This was the punishment exacted by the spirits of the waters.

My mother had laughed at my grandmother.

"And who has examined Imelda's legs? Your cronies at the mahjong table?"

"In fact, hija," my grandmother said, "Dolly Enage met her last month in Manila, and she swears Imelda's legs are thin and shrivelled, like the skin of smoked fish. And that's the truth, although, claro, Dolly did not mention it to Imelda at the time."

"The spirits of the bridge aren't taking people," my father said impatiently. "Mamá, you speak like the maids. There's a war out there—"

"Shut up, Prospero," my mother interrupted. "There's no such thing going on or we'd know about it. It's your mad political plots: they'll drive you crazy."

"That's what you get from an education in Barcelona: the logic of servants," my father mumbled to Anna and myself. He liked to point out to us scrupulously the defects of my mother's side of the family.

I'd lie awake at night thinking of the children spirited to the waters. I could see myself snatched from the jeepney of Mano Ramon and whisked to the banks of the Strait, maybe with a sack over my head. In the expanse between the provinces of Leyte and Samar were the steel girders of the unfinished bridge, and on them Spirits of the Waters waved me to my doom. In the evenings, I could sense the dark movement of forces in my city, seeds of pride, terror, bravery, and greed dispersed quietly by the night before I went to bed.

*

When I saw the lady point at me, I turned to run. Unfortunately, I tripped on my umbrella. I noticed a broken spine and stood clumsily to fix it. In my other hand I held my guava. Two of the uniformed men approached me and, knowing my end was near, I bit into my guava.

They marched me to the lady. From a distance, she was very, very tall, with two feet of hair. Really. Her hair was up rice-cake style, piled moundwise like a temple or a baker's dream. Her pants were red and flared, and she wore a matching jacket.

The guards deposited me in front of her.

She was beautiful. She sparkled in the sunlight. Gold was on her arms, jewels on her fingers. Diamonds, green stones, a ruby. She seemed all dressed for mahjong. But most wondrous of all were her shoes: white large stones were embedded on the tip and sides: diamonds, diamonds on her shoes, so close to the earth they glittered like the quartz I sometimes found on the beach.

She was the queen of minerals.

And below the flared swath of her red pants, I glimpsed ankles: silvery, like fish scales.

"Are you lost?" she asked. Like a common woman, she spoke in my language.

"Yes, ma'am," I answered in English.

"English-ispeeking," the woman winked at the men. "But aren't you cute. Where do you live?"

"I'm a squatter child," I said, gathering courage. "I live in that hut—ober dere—and I was looking for something to eat."

"Stealing Father Hermann's guavas, ha."

"No, ma'am."

"Well, you can have lunch with me. If you like?"

I nodded.

"See, Brosie," she told the man who had taken me by the arm, "who did you think wanted to kill me—children like this? You're all doing a good job. But it's silly to think anyone would bomb me in Leyte: my people love me. You can all go home."

*

I sat in the front, beside Brosie the driver, while the lady wafted in back upon a cloud of immense perfume. I was now struck silent by my situation, waiting for the anger of the spirits to bear upon me. For this must all be the ritual, the beginnings of the plot to lift the fish skin from her legs. She asked me questions in Waray, my language, but I could not answer her. And I had kept my umbrella but lost my guava, in the panic of our departure.

Men in the same blue uniform guarded the gates of the lady's house. People in short-sleeved barongs with guns showing through their transparent shirts were swift to come from inside the house to the aid of the lady. Several men helped her open the door and held her arm lightly as she got out of the car.

"We were very worried," they said. "No one knew where you were."

"See? No one killed me. Who on this, my own island, would want to kill me? I grew up here, these are my people. I'm annoyed with all of you!"

They laughed. Someone pointed at me.

"A squatter child," she explained. "English-speaking. Just think of that. A product of the New Society."

I sat in the back seat wondering when the product of the New Society was going to be thrown to the waves.

"Some of the foreign reporters have arrived," the man relayed in Waray with some diffidence.

"Oh, they'll see how wonderful my people are. See that the child has lunch," the lady said. "Then bring her to me in the mezzanine. I'll show them to the president."

The men brought me to a small dining room. Don't ask me what anything was like. I was only *almost* seven. I remember the green figurines, elephants and birds scattered atop narrow ledges, and the wood paneling that had faint peeling lines about the ridges, and the hushed and ordered table settings. There was a coarse-skinned, thick-lipped woman who smelled like an entire kingdom of rotting flowers, scuttling in and out in blue, a corsage dangling from her exaggerated breasts. There was a thin man in a barong, light blue Crispa shirt underneath, a mustache scraggly and wiggling like a twitching rat's tail: he had some sort of tic about his upper lip. He, too, stank to heaven of propitiatory cologne. I've since associated all such smells gathered in closed spaces—an elevator, an office sanctum, the small traffic in a hotel lobby—with that afternoon of strange hospitality.

"Is this one of the little children?" said the wide lady in blue.

A man with gun under transparent shirt answered:

"Yes. She wants her. With the president."

"We need some more, don't you think? Oh, if only I'd been told earlier; she usually tells me when she's coming! God only knows what kinds of kids *he* brought." Her hand made a fretful gesture at the mustached man. I recognized him then as one of my grandmother's many mahjong cohorts: a judge of some sort. He didn't recognize me; he was busy biting his nails, with the air of refinement people sometimes have when doing disgusting things.

"This place is a mess," the blue lady announced plaintively to no one in particular. "Who put these cheap coasters here?"

Actually, the coasters must have come with the placemats, which had drawings representing different provinces. The coasters spelled the names of the capitals that were supposed to go with the provinces on the mats. I silently rearranged the coasters on my side, so that Bangued went with the mat of the Abra mountains, and Tacloban with Leyte and its prophesied bridge.

"Hoy, bata! Stop that! Don't touch."

I immediately stopped what I was doing; but mentally I kept rearranging the coasters, focusing with pleasure on the proper match for each city, Bayombong with Nueva Vizcaya, Tabuk with the mountains of Kalinga-Apayao.

They gave me cold empanada; the bread covering the pork was soggy, though the pork itself was rich and soft, as pig flesh should be. I saw each dish as if it were a new concoction, expressly invented for this strange day; and so the noodles seemed to be a mass of foreign textures, delicate and awkward on the tongue, and the brittle fried chicken seemed a rare treat, though a bit dry about the bone. Even the rice had the taste of far-away plains, specially delivered from great distances thus slightly undercooked, its white centers crumbling as my molars carefully crunched. And the rice cakes: I unpeeled one from its banana leaf, this treat that I had every afternoon when I got home from school, sold by urchins with wise foreheads that bulged like coconuts. A black bottom scarred the cake's green leaf. The cake was burnt but warm, dense and crumbly, my favorite meal and a suitable final reward.

I was the only one eating, as everyone was moving back and forth, moving chairs, carrying out dishes, waving dusting rags.

When I was almost done with my second cake, one of the armed men came up to me:

"Time's up," he said.

I popped the last bit of bibingka into my mouth, rudely filling it and chewing. I savored the last bit of cake before I walked off to die.

I walked through halls with gaping capiz-shelled windows, which mapped a maze of geometric sunlight as the hall turned into a room and the room into a foyer, with a curlicued wooden mirror and more of those green figures of animals that were not indigenous to my country. By a closed door stood another transparent-shirted man, who let me in.

It was a dark room, of the gloomy mahogany of the Abuelita's music room, spacious with various carved pieces of furniture scattered about. Scalloped cloth was draped over a piano, and before it was the lady, her glittering shoes tapping a rhythm, as she hummed, hummed, hummed, in a clear display of passion, but all to herself. The man I instantly recognized, because his picture hung on every classroom's wall, with the

15

insignia of stars and the symbolic colors we had learnt by heart: red for courage, blue for peace, yellow for the hope of the sun. He was dressed in shorts, too formal for basketball and too casual for dinner, and a sleeveless, fitted white shirt. He was all in white. His hair was wonderfully slicked back, like a dolphin's sleek watered flesh. I'd seen dolphins in the raw, right there in the water, when my mother took me to Mindoro, on one of her hunting trips for stuffable animals. It was a shock to see him so life-like in person; in real life, he himself looked like something ready for creative taxidermy: his skin was all red and taut, stretched as stuffed animals should be.

He looked up to see me enter. There were a few other children in the room, all looking terrified, and I was ashamed to think that my expression was like theirs. One boy looked ready to pee, from the way his bottom was angled and his eyes were desperately set. And when he looked at me I recognized him. He was a boy in my grade, but in another section, Section D, the last one, the section of the dummies and the useless to society. He was the grandson of some bigshot. At least he deserved his end: he was going to grow up to be a billiard player or a wine drinker anyway; while I had my ambitions—I might even become a cartographer! Where was the justice here; and I walked slowly toward the man and his circle of children, carrying my broken umbrella.

As I walked, lights flashed, and the room's corners seemed to liven up, like the rustling of grass when fireflies pass. And I noticed the men and women with cameras who sat or stood around, and some inched closer to the man and the kids. I sat on the fringe, behind the boy from Section D. I put my umbrella before me, tenderly tweaking its spines into place.

"Here she is," the lady announced as I sat down. "She's a child from the poor, sad neighborhood behind the school where I graduated, the college where I was a struggling but smart student, as you know, though my family is prominent and goes back to the days of Martin de Legaspi."

"Miguel de Legazpi," I whispered involuntarily and immediately regretted it.

"Yes, child? Speak up! Speak up! That's why the president is here, to speak to his young countrymen, to show them he cares."

She looked at me with great favor, and I had the sense of my grandmother's tone—for the lady spoke to me in a mixture of Waray and English—when my grandmother wished me to side clearly with my mother's side of the family: as if the Abuelita and I shared many superior traits, and my father none.

I immediately regretted what I had spoken, but I couldn't help myself. I don't know what came over me, as I didn't much like bragging in school, even when I could correct my teacher on which San Fernando she was talking about, the one in Pampanga or La Union; and I was not really a talkative person, although Anna declared me slightly insane, and my obstinacy often angered the Abuelita. Maybe it was the contented weight of rice cakes, dragging me into a confident stupor, treacherous and unthinking.

"It's *Miguel* de Legazpi, ma'am. In fact, Miguel *Lopez* de Legazpi; in 1571 he settled Manila. Maybe you mix him up with *Martin* de Goiti."

A hush fell over the room.

I knew I shouldn't have spoken, but the lady made me nervous. So, as I spoke I tinkered with my umbrella—I was speaking without really thinking—and my umbrella opened wide. It was an accident. Out in the open was an array of red tongues, scattered about in a circle of scorn, with that sudden swish of umbrella sound—whoo-hup!

One tongue, split up, gaped sadly through the lone broken spine.

Instantly, the calm was shattered and men ran to me, rushing about in fat shadows, ready to grab my ruddy weapon.

At the door, the man with the gun showing through his shirt seemed to hold on to it suddenly, alert and thoughtful of his duties.

A foreign cameraman came closer, breaking the room's intake of breath; or maybe I imagined this spell of silence.

Then the president laughed, loud and crackling like a piece of mahogany smashing in two. Some people in the room smiled, cameras flashed like crazy. The lady continued to stare silently at the piano, her fingers quiet on the keys.

Then she smiled at the entire room.

"See, look at the children we are bringing up! The children of the New Society! Knowledgeable and respectful and speaking English fluently as a second language! What more can this country want? What more can the people ask for?"

The men with guns took my guilty umbrella. I let them; it was broken, after all.

I kept my mouth shut after that and just listened. When they asked me my name, I said my maid's name: Fe; and each child in turn offered their identities: seven in all, seven little fish scales. The lady sat at the piano, and I couldn't see her legs, covered by the scallops of the piano cloth; she directed all of us with her eyes. Her avid, glittering glance seemed to settle on me, and I stayed quiet, not a muscle moving, as the man before the cameras expanded in style, declaiming with his hands a riot of proclamations as he briefly sketched what a fine history we, the future, had to look forward to, this history we were making right at this moment. And all the while he shot quick glances about the room, as if the cameras were little gods coaching him toward brilliance.

And we spent the afternoon posing with the president, while he lectured us about the need for discipline, quoting Jose Rizal, lifting high his brow serene, cameras hounding us all the while. He told us to study the teachings in his book, which he held up—*The New Revolution: Democracy*—covered in white, symbolizing honor, a copy of which he gave to each of us, signed with a flourish in advance, our receiving motions stultified accordingly by the cameras' glances.

I hadn't noticed the judge in the blue shirt who was standing in the shadows behind the lady; I kept catching him looking at me.

The photographers left the hall, the children were dismissed, and my grandmother's friend the judge hissed at me: "Psst!"

The lady looked to see him talk to me, turned to speak to him, then left us, her heels tap-tapping from the room, a distinct metallic chime.

It was he who took me home while everyone else was led out. He looked at me sternly: "You should be ashamed of yourself, tricking good people like that."

And when I got home, he told the Abuelita the whole story—how I had disowned my family, pretending to be an orphan, giving a fake name, and lying like a washerwoman. Sin verguenza! He talked about my pride and bad manners, correcting Imelda as if I were Jesus in the temple with the wise men. You should have seen her, he kept repeating—just like Jesus! I heard their gasp of shame but did not look up. I accepted his version of the events, though I waited in vain for him to mention my umbrella, the core of the matter. From the corner of my eye, I could see his skinny mustache tweaking like a mad yoyo string in the frenzy of his speech.

Que barbaridad, the Abuelita said. "She is, after all, the first lady of our country, a Leyteña: what kind of grandchild is this? But what was Imelda doing with those children?" my grandmother demanded.

My mother bit her lip, shaking her head.

On the other hand, my father was looking at me with an expression I had never seen before; he was an impassive man, and he never really looked happy.

He came to me with a large smile, his teeth showing in an unfamiliar way, and clasped me to him.

"That's my girl!" he said.

For a moment, I was happy, but I didn't know why.

Then he resumed his look of preoccupation, thinking deeply about other things, flourishing his coloring pen. As if caught on an idea, he stared at his table, his tired face lit up by his magical work.

I didn't understand what it was all about. I was, in fact, not quite seven, and I cried in my room that night, quietly, so Anna wouldn't call me an idiot: I was shaking, relieved to be alive.

*

That was it: my day in history. I remember again, blinking my eyes to see it all more clearly, the lady's silent look by the piano, for we all know what happened afterward. A man in dark clothes came on a stage in the South, where she was spreading her good news about the New Society, and the man lunged at her, but it was a knife, not an umbrella. "Who on this island wants me dead? My people love me." It's my distinction that I remember when she spoke that line. She inaugurated with triumph the speedily built bridge, with unknown people dying around the country while her legs remained smooth as a dolphin's blank fin. And later, I was to find her name in many of my history books, in fact in all my high school history texts, as we learned about her traveling bounty across the land and skipped the details about the founding of Manila or the flavorful characters of the Bicol region or tough life on the Ilocos mountains, which I knew created hardworking, penny-pinching people. I never did see my picture with the president in the photos distributed around the country in shiny brochures and hardbound books. But I do remember that week in early July, her birthday, when she arrived at my school, swept free of bombs and bolos, and appeared on a stage with overbeaten Father Hermann and many other happy foreign priests, to accept their plaque of appreciation for the honors she had showered upon the university, and on my elementary school, just for being who she was, a tall woman from Leyte, whose island geography full of natural resources creates carefree, loving people.

KANNIKA CLAUDINE D. PEÑA is a freelance writer from Bataan. She graduated with a degree in Creative Writing from the University of the Philippines, Diliman. Her short stories have appeared in *Growing Up Filipino II: More Stories for Young Adults* and other literary magazines. She is currently preparing her debut novel for publication.

EXTRAJUDICIAL KILLINGS IN THE PHILIPPINES

Extrajudicial killings, or EJK, became a widespread term in the Philippines soon after Rodrigo Duterte officially began his term as the 16th president of the country in 2016. In his first year alone, his "war on drugs" resulted in the deaths of over 12,000 Filipinos, most of them from the urban poor, and at least over 2,000 of them attributed to the Philippine National Police (PNP). Many bodies were often found with cardboard placards with the word "nanlaban" (translated: "resisted," implying that the victims fought back while being arrested and were possibly armed). In 2020, as the pandemic intensified, so did the so-called "war on drugs." Apart from these unlawful killings which increased by more than 50%, reports of attacks on leftist activists, community workers, indigenous leaders, human rights defenders and journalists have also seen an increase.

2

LET ME TELL YOU ABOUT MY AUNT EDELWEISS

Let me tell you about my Aunt Edelweiss. First of all, that is really her name. Edelweiss. With the German v sound, as she's always quick to note, though she wouldn't reiterate it if you insisted on mispronouncing it.

People, especially the older ones, would always be offended whenever she corrected them. Then they would make a joke about it. "Ang arte arte!" they would say, then they would say her name correctly, twice over, before reverting to the w sound.

"If that's how it should be pronounced, then it should've been spelled that way!" they would add.

At this, Aunt Edelweiss would just smile tightly and nod. "Choose your battles" had always been her mantra.

That was not to say that she was particularly wise about all the battles she chose. Sometimes, she did choose incorrectly. Like how one particular misunderstanding drove her away from our extended family for four years.

"Misunderstanding, sure," she said when she finally showed up unannounced one day like she'd only been gone for

23

a few hours instead of a few years. Then she flashed her Edelweiss smile, much to my parents' irritation.

Aunt Edelweiss is my father's youngest sister. In a sense, Aunt E and I were the same, in that we came to our respective families much too late. She came to their family 18 years after the one before her. By then, my father already had four more siblings – it went: my father, Uncle Don, Aunt Julie, Aunt Esther, and Uncle Ishmael. And then came Aunt E.

"An unexpected blessing," Lola Inang used to say.

"A natural-born gatecrasher," Aunt E used to add.

Meanwhile, my only sister, Misty, and I were 11 years apart. Which meant she was already an actual person by the time I arrived.

But, this isn't about me. This is about Aunt E.

*

I have never actually spent that much time with Aunt E. I only knew her from that one summer from when I was 7. We went to the beach with our relatives from our father's side. All morning long, all everyone talked about was how Aunt E had promised to show up. Aunt Julie had talked to her on the phone a couple of weeks back and told her about the outing. The two of them had always been close because Aunt Julie practically raised Aunt E. They then began to reminisce about Aunt E as a child.

"She was a genius. She was always at the top of her class. And she barely studied. She always just listened to her tapes and read her novels," my father said, clearly bitter about it. He, too, was at the top of his class, according to tales, but I knew he was the hardworking type. The rote memorization type, based on how he micromanaged the way I studied the few times he was around during the school year. He worked abroad and only came home during summers and Christmases, his vacation days often spilling over to my first few days back at school. I liked having him home, sure, but I hated how he would often look over my shoulder whenever he chanced upon me doing my assignment. He wouldn't say anything, but he'd walk away after a while, shaking his head while telling my mother why she wasn't looking at my homework.

"Remember the time Inang got called into the principal's office because the teacher found her reading Lolita in her math class?" Aunt Julie asked.

I asked what Lolita was, but none of them knew.

"The point was, she was reading in class instead of doing her seatwork," my father said.

I didn't see what the big deal was. I did a lot of my spare reading in class as well.

They all talked about her with a mixture of awe, fondness, and annoyance. Because she was a genius. Past tense. When she finally went to college, they said that's when everything went downhill.

"She was only a genius here in our small town. I guess, she couldn't keep up with all the other geniuses in that state university."

In short, Aunt E, after spending almost 8 years in college (no one was entirely sure by then if she was still actually enrolled), dropped out. By the time I was 7, she was 26, and each of her siblings had a different story about her present whereabouts.

"Either these are all true, or none of them are," Aunt Esther said.

And that's when Aunt E showed up.

It was the first time I'd ever seen her and she looked nothing like I imagined. I was imagining a wild genius, kind of like a young and female Einstein. With the hair and the irreverent stare. Instead, what I saw was a kind of chubby nerd with a permanent sneer, bad hair tied neatly in a high ponytail, and tattoos around her wrist. They were letters. She showed them to me when she saw me looking. They were quotations from books I'd never heard of.

On the left:

"…for ultimately, and precisely in the deepest and most important matters, we are unspeakably alone."

–Rainer Maria Rilke

And on the right:

"Did you ever notice that animals never kill themselves, even when they're sure to lose?"

–Thornton Wilder

I asked her what they meant, but she simply ruffled my hair and smiled. "They're not that deep. You'll figure them out someday." Then she wrote them on a piece of paper for me. The piece of paper, she tore off this tiny spring notebook that she fished out from her loose jeans pocket. I learned that she always carried one. "I always forget things, so this is how I keep track." I found it so cool, I took to carrying one myself.

"What do you need that tiny notebook for?" my mother asked when we were doing our back-to-school shopping. "Are you taking jueteng numbers for Ate Aning?" She laughed at her own unfunny joke.

"Jueteng is illegal," I said. "You should stop," I added.

She rolled her eyes but nodded. "Don't tell your father."

Anyway. That one single encounter formed my entire picture of Aunt E and still, I understood nothing about her. She sounded nothing like the wayward rebel her siblings described her to be. She was quiet most of the time, just looking and listening and observing. She only spoke when spoken to. That one conversation (if you could even call it conversation) was the only unprompted one I'd seen her make the entire day. She came late, then left early — "Just as she did in our family," Aunt Julie noted. She said she had to leave before 4 pm to catch the bus. No one dared ask her to where, but when she left, her siblings all looked at one another, expecting that at least one of them had thought to ask beforehand.

*

I had no idea exactly what went down after that. But there was a big fight between her and Uncle Ishmael, apparently.

"It probably has something to do with money," Ate Misty said. I asked her why. "It's always money with Papa and his siblings." When our mother heard her, she shot Ate Misty a look. "Don't talk that way about your Papa and his siblings. They're still your elders."

"But you always talk about them that way," Ate Misty said.

"Not around Marsha," Mama said.

"Why not?" I asked.

Our mother sighed. "Will you never really make your bed? What are you again, nine?"

I frowned then left to fix my blanket. From the room I shared with Ate Misty, I could hear her and Mama talking. Mama explained that it was about money. Aunt E had asked for a loan from Uncle Ishmael. She wanted to finish her degree, she said, but it turned out that she was just helping to pay for a friend's working visa to New Zealand.

"How'd they find out?" Ate Misty asked. "How can they be so sure?"

"Stop asking me these questions. It's their issue. Not ours," Mama said, and that was the last I heard of Aunt E.

*

Years later, Aunt E arrived at our doorstep. Looking just as she did when I last saw her, only with a few more lines around her eyes. I was 15 at that point and already taller than her. I opened the door for her. "Aunt Edelweiss," I said, shocked that I was now at the same eye level.

"Misty?"

"Marsha."

She put a hand over her mouth, shocked and pleased. "Wow. Look at you."

"Who's that?" Papa asked from the kitchen.

"Kuya!" Aunt E said as she entered our house and went straight to the kitchen, but not without dropping off her frayed duffle bag on the sofa.

Papa, by then, had been retired for two months, after working abroad for close to three decades. It had been an adjustment, to say the least. That was putting it mildly. To make the long story short, he and Mama could barely stay in one room without shouting over each other. They argued over everything. I wished I was exaggerating, but anything could set them off. It would usually start with Papa saying, "No matter what anyone says, this—" then he would proclaim his opinion as if it were the last word on anything. In the beginning, Mama would just nod, but then after a month of hearing "No matter what anyone says, this—" she finally snapped.

"Why do you always say that?"

"What? I'm just stating my opinion."

"That's it. It's just your opinion. So why preface it with 'no matter what anyone says' like my opinion automatically doesn't matter?"

"I didn't say that. I never said that."

"But you implied it!"

"There you go, putting things in my mouth."

And so on and so forth.

By then Ate Misty very rarely went home, so I had a kind of VIP access to these epic shouting matches without anyone to process them with after. Not that Ate Misty and I ever processed anything together. But just someone to make eye contact with during such fights would have been nice.

So in a sense, Aunt E's arrival felt kind of like a godsend. Finally, someone else at the dinner table. I wondered if her presence would deter my parents from fighting.

And then I wondered if she would even stay long enough for a meal.

"Edelweiss," Papa said when they saw each other at last. He wiped his hands on the apron that was too small for him.

"Edelweiss?" Mama asked from the back where she was doing laundry.

"Ate Marian," Aunt E said, peeking out from the back door.

After a short Q&A between her and my parents, Aunt E asked if she could use the bathroom. She then went straight to the one near my bedroom, taking her duffle bag with her. I went back to the kitchen where I was eating a late breakfast right before Aunt E came. Papa joined Mama in the back laundry area.

"What is she doing here? Did you know she was coming?" Mama said.

"I had no idea. Text Julie."

"Why don't you text her yourself? You have a phone."

"You do it. Your phone's right there."

"Why do you then have two cellphones?"

"Why not? Just text her. Tell her, 'Edelweiss is here. Did you know she—"

"I know how sentences work. Stop doing that."

And so on and so forth.

I finished my cereal, drank the sickly sweet milk, then dumped my bowl in the sink. I was curious about what Aunt E was doing here, and how my parents would deal with it. But I was also tired of hearing my parents them turn every conversation into an argument, so instead of eavesdropping, I just went straight to my room. As I closed the door, I could hear the water running in the bathroom as well as music playing. So Aunt E was the type to listen to music while taking a bath. It didn't matter that she was that kind of person, but it felt worth noting.

*

Aunt E ended up staying for a week before disappearing yet again without so much as a goodbye.

So, first things first. Aunt E's presence did not deter my parents from their obligatory mealtime matches. If anything, she actually made them worse. Often, whenever my father would talk about "the president", my mother would simply shut up or tell him to stop talking politics at the table. Whenever she did, my father would shrug but acquiesce with a "I'm just saying. It just needs to be said."

The truth was, I didn't really care about the president. Many of my classmates found it cool whenever he swore, and often I laughed along, though I hardly understood him whenever I watched clips of his speeches. Not because he used highfalutin words or anything complex or intellectual—that much I could gather—but because he sounded drunk. "He said it!" my classmates, mostly male, said, high-fiving one another like swearing was such a novelty.

When I made the mistake of saying what I actually thought, one of them shot me a dirty look. "You're just saying that because of his accent. That's being regionalist, Marsha." Then they all shot me a dirty look.

"We can't help it. If we want to clean up this country, there are going to be casualties. Let's face it," Papa said on Aunt E's last night at our house, after he recounted a news feature he watched about these young men found dead in random places, with placards proclaiming 'nanlaban'.

"Please, no politics—" Mama began to say.

"You really believe that?" Aunt E asked, turning sharply to my father as she put her spoon and fork down on her plate.

"Yes. Look, during Marcos's time—"

"Oh no, don't talk about—" Mama said.

"During Marcos's time, you were a child in a province that was very pro-Marcos and you had very little access to the news—"

"And you weren't even born—"

"But still. I don't have to be there to know about it. Innocent people died during that time. And we're still paying off the debts of that regime. That man was a mass murderer. I don't care if you say that he's the most intelligent president we've ever had, because I know that's what you're going to say. That man abused his power. Just as this president is doing with his so-called war on drugs. You cannot justify crimes against humanity with quote-unquote progress. That's just Machiavellian bullshit. And where's the progress anyway? This generation is paying the price for the so-called good life you had when you were a child. You lived in Omelas. So don't even—"

"Hey, I didn't vote for Duterte—" Papa began, raising his hands as if to surrender

"You haven't voted since the 80s, hon," Mama said. "I bet you're not even a registered voter anymore."

Aunt E smirked then shook her head in disbelief. Papa looked like he wanted to speak more, but Mama shot him a look that completely shut him up.

I looked at Aunt E, in awe, promising myself to ask her what the words "Omelas" and "Machiavellian" meant.

*

Look, between my parents, the truth was, I always naturally looked up more to my father. It was also mostly my mother's doing. She often made us feel bad about our grades by telling us, "How come none of you inherited your father's brains and study habits?" She would then proceed to recount how, when they were still in their courting stages in college, Papa's reputation preceded him. He was supposedly the golden boy—high school valedictorian, good-looking, tall, good at basketball, the eldest of a brood of equally good-looking siblings, no vices. In short, the perfect husband-to-be.

So, because Ate Misty and I barely spent time with him growing up, save for those vacation weeks twice a year, our idea of him largely stemmed from Mama's memories. You could probably say that Mama was the same, in a sense. Because they had only been married for two years when Papa went to work abroad. And from what I know, Papa didn't come home for two years in the beginning, because of his contract. In a way, Mama and Papa also grew older, not knowing each other.

Ever since Papa came home, Mama would find excuses to go out. Sometimes, she brought me along. Then she would talk about Papa in a way that felt wrong for me to hear. Marriage woes. I couldn't exactly tell her that though, because she looked like she was desperate to talk and let it out.

"I don't know when I'll ever get used to sharing a bed with him," she once said absentmindedly while we were at the grocery store. When I heard the word 'bed', I began to walk more slowly, just so I wouldn't have to hear what she had to say next.

31

"I wish Edelweiss would stop engaging your father in these political debates," she said on Aunt E's fourth night with us. We were browsing in an ukay-ukay that we passed by on our way to the pharmacy. Mama had picked me up from school, saying she was just in the area to pick up Papa's maintenance meds.

"But…don't you think Aunt Edelweiss's right?"

"Of course. But you know your father. Mr. No Matter What You Say. But he's just all talk. He means no harm. It's not like he's out there actively supporting the killings, right?"

"What does that mean—'actively supporting the killings'?"

"He's not out there shooting people or advocating for it."

"He's just saying they're okay."

"He says he's neutral."

"So, if I steal this dress, and you saw me but did not say anything about it, then it's okay, right? You did nothing wrong because you never actually told me to steal the dress and you weren't the one who did it."

Mama shot me a look. "Have you been talking to your Aunt?"

But I couldn't help but see a look of wonder and pleasant surprise in her smirk as she said it.

*

After a couple more political debates at the dinner table, Papa stopped offering his takes on the day's news. Instead, he felt emboldened to ask Aunt E about her life as he'd never done before. Aunt E, as far as I could tell, answered him as honestly but as sparingly as she could. She lived in Project 6 and was working as a freelance video editor. Sometimes, she took gigs as a second AD for friends directing indie films.

"But those I just do for fun. Because they mostly shoot in far-flung provinces, so I get to travel for free."

"Do you know anyone working for Ang Probinsyano?" Mama asked.

Aunt E laughed and nodded her head. "It's impossible not to know anyone who hasn't worked on that show."

She told us anecdotes about her job—and she had many—but still, there was no way to tell where her job ended and her real life began. Some of the stories even sounded so fantastical that we just listened to them without asking any questions, only because the only question in our minds was, "Did that actually happen?"

I could tell how much Papa loved listening to Aunt E talk, even when he looked like he didn't believe much of what she said. He looked the way he and his siblings looked whenever they reminisced about their wayward genius sister. The one who came too late and left too early. With total fascination and beneath that, fear. It was like when Ate Misty caught a dragonfly when we were kids. She kept it in a jar in her room, and I stared at it, entranced by its luminescent color.

"It's so pretty," I said.

"Want to hold it?"

But before I could say no, she opened the jar and let the dragonfly escape. I ran out of the room and almost fell off the stairs to the sound of her shrieking with laughter.

"But you said it looked pretty!"

"Pretty to look at, but it's still a bug!"

*

"Why are you still up?" Aunt E asked me on what would be her last night at our home. I was in the dining area and it was already way past my usual bedtime. She went to the kitchen to get herself a glass of water. Then she brought me one before sitting across from me, drinking and staring out the window behind me.

It felt odd to be sitting there with her, but it was no time to feel awkward. I had so much studying to do, and I was just so frustrated. It felt like no matter how much I studied, I would never catch up. Why didn't I inherit my father's brains? I often found myself thinking. And then a tiny tiny voice inside would say, "Really? You still want his brains?" It made me feel bad. I didn't want to stop putting my father on a pedestal. But whenever he opened his mouth and made Mama feel bad for her opinions on things or for not having an opinion, I could see notches disappearing from the pedestal. And with Aunt E's arrival, there was no way for me to keep him up there.

With this in my mind, I shot Aunt E a look and suddenly felt irked at the mere sight of her. Why did she have to make me realize that my father wasn't as infallible and all-knowing as I thought he was?

Aunt E saw the look in my eye. But instead of balking, she met my eyes and held them until I looked away. "Is something bothering you?" she asked.

I shook my head.

"Please. Don't be like everyone else on your father's side of the family."

"*You're* on my father's side of the family," I said, looking up. "And what does that even mean?"

She smirked. "Don't pretend like you haven't noticed."

"I have no idea what you mean."

I, of course, had an inkling. What she probably meant was how my father's family barely talked about their feelings. They were all about the facts and opinions. There was once a time during a family outing when my father's brothers made fun of Ate Misty for her college weight gain.

"Who are you fooling with that potato salad? That's carbs. No wonder you're fat," Uncle Ishmael said. Then he went on a tirade about all the things he'd seen Ate Misty eat throughout the day.

"Like mother, like daughter, am I right?" Uncle Don said.

Papa pretended like he didn't hear. Ate Misty, on the other hand, walked up and out of the restaurant.

"Don't force me to come on any of these family gatherings ever again," Ate Misty said.

For once, Mama had nothing else to say except apologize for our uncles. To which Ate Misty said, "Stop apologizing for them. You're a victim, too."

But what Ate Misty didn't know was when everyone found out that she wasn't just in the restroom but was no longer planning to come back to dinner, they scoffed and rolled their eyes. "So sensitive. We were just teasing." And then that was that.

I looked at Aunt E's wrists and there they were, the quotations. They had somehow already faded, but I still knew them by heart.

"Do you not regret having those words tattooed on your wrists?" I asked.

Aunt E smiled. It was the same smile she gave me when I first asked her about them.

"Do you now understand what they mean?" she asked.

"I'm not sure."

I didn't add the fact that I asked my mother about them one time when I was around ten, and she was shocked. "Those are so sad. Why would you even—" She was so shocked that she couldn't even finish her sentence.

"I still do believe that we all are unspeakably alone as Rilke said," she said. "But I wish I didn't."

"But can't you just not believe it, then?"

"I don't know. It's just that no matter where I go, I feel like I don't belong."

"What about the other one? Why did you have that tattooed?"

"It's to stop myself from feeling like a total failure all the time. I mean, as long as I look to animals as a way to respond to failure—"

"But you're not a failure."

"Thanks," she said, even though the look on her face added, "that's nice of you to say, but no."

"Everyone in the family thinks you're a genius."

She rolled her eyes and laughed. "I wish they would stop perpetuating that. It's not true. I wasn't a genius. I was just different from them, that's all."

She stood up then walked closer to the window. "It's amazing how dark it can get here," she said.

I turned and looked outside the window. I guess I never really noticed, but it was indeed dark outside. Mauve, almost black.

"You want French toast?" she asked.

I said I'd never had one before.

"Sunny used to make them for me all the time," she said as she began to look for the ingredients in the kitchen: slices of bread, milk, egg, and brown sugar.

"Who's Sunny?"

"My boyfriend."

"What does he do?"

"He doesn't do anything. He's dead." She smiled at me then started beating the eggs.

"I'm sorry."

"Stray bullet. That's what killed him. The neighbors found his body next to this young boy with a 'nanlaban' placard." She nodded, but her voice wavered.

I couldn't speak. There were no words. I knew what my father would say if he heard about this: "He's probably a drug addict, too. He wouldn't have been killed if he weren't." Which I now knew did not make sense. Then I felt bad — who was I to pass judgment on what my father would say?

"Bon appetit," Aunt E said as she presented the plate of burnt French toast in front of me. She sprinkled it with a pinch of brown sugar then watched as I took the first bite. It was delicious. She smiled, but I could tell her mind and heart were elsewhere.

*

The next day, Aunt E was no longer around by the time I woke up. And I woke up early because it was a school day.

"Where's Aunt Edelweiss?" I asked as I sat in for breakfast.

Papa stayed silent while Mama sighed. "Gone. Along with your tuition fee for the next quarter."

Papa sighed. "Stop overreacting. It wasn't a lot."

"I swear. When is Edelweiss going to get her act together? How old is she to still be begging her siblings for money?"

"She did not beg. It was a loan."

"May I remind you that you still have one more child to put through college and you retired way too early to prepare for it?"

"I told you. It's not a lot. And she'll pay me back. She promised."

"She never pays any of you back. Because you never ask her. That's why she still can't stand on her own two feet after all these years."

Papa shot Mama a look but remained quiet. It was such a weird development that I couldn't help but stop eating.

Mama noticed. "Hey, kid. You're going to be late. Finish your breakfast and get ready for school."

"She said it was for her boyfriend's burial," Papa said.

"Oh." Mama paused. "And you believe her?" she asked, tentatively.

"Yes. Of course. Why wouldn't I?"

I looked at them both, waiting for them to turn this bit into an argument. But all Mama did was do the sign of the cross. I wondered if Aunt E told Papa how her boyfriend died. Or how they even managed to talk about it. But I could see a look of worry in my father's downcast eyes, and suddenly whether he knew or not did not matter.

I looked around the kitchen for a sign of the French toast that Aunt E made last night. The plate and bowl that we left in the sink, the jar of brown sugar that she left on the countertop next to the stove. But nothing.

It was like she was never there. Like always.

JOHN JACK G. WIGLEY is the author of six books: *Kadenang Bahaghari* (Pride Lit Books, 2019); *Hantong: Mga Kuwento* (UST Publishing House, 2018), a finalist in the 2019 National Book Awards; *Lait (pa more) Chronicles* (Visprint Publishing, 2017); *Lait Chronicles* (Visprint Publishing, 2016), a finalist in the 2017 National Book Awards; *Home of the Ashfall* (UST Publishing House, 2014); and *Falling into the Manhole* (UST Publishing House, 2012), winner of the Best Book (Gawad San Alberto Magno) in the *15th Dangal ng UST* and a finalist in the 13th Madrigal-Gonzalez Best First Book Award/ He is the Chair of the Department of Literature and a full professor at the University of Santo Tomas. He finished the following degrees: AB English (Holy Angel University, 1989), MA Literature (UST, 2004) and PhD Literature *Cum Laude* (UST, 2012).

ANGELES CITY

I am biracial—an Amerasian, to be more precise. I was born and raised in Angeles City just a few meters away from the Clark Air Force Base. My father is an American GI and Air Force Officer who was stationed in the Philippines during the Vietnam War. My mother is a Bicolana who had big dreams of making it big in the city and ended up working in a bar. I was their lovechild. Angeles City is now served by the Clark International Airport and the Clark Freeport Zone but back then when I was growing up, it was the home of the Clark Air Force Base, the largest United States military facility outside of the continental America. I didn't know then that Fields Avenue, the street where I grew up, was a honky-tonk area for prostitution, and a favorite spot frequented by the U.S. servicemen who wanted to experience life outside of the military base. It was also known as an epicenter of the sex trade. This was my world, growing up.

3

THE FANCY DANCER

I was born and raised in Angeles City a few meters away from the Clark Air Force Base. My father is an American GI and Air Force Officer who was stationed in the Philippines during the Vietnam War. My mother is a Bicolana who had big dreams of making it big in the city and ended up working in a bar. I was their lovechild. Their story might have been the original source of the musical *Miss Saigon*. Except that my story's set in the Philippines, not in Saigon. Just the same, I may have been *Tam*.

I was in grade four when Mother rented a barbecue space along Fields Avenue in Balibago. When my parents separated and the cocktail lounge that Mother used to own and run folded up, she had kept connected with the bar girls and the American servicemen who frequented the area. She didn't want to run another bar maybe because Mother felt she was already too old to become a *"mama-san"* to all these girls who wanted to marry American servicemen, their own idea of the great American dream, and she didn't want to run the risk of getting herself enmeshed in a controversy because we were all growing up and studying in a Catholic school. She didn't want us to embarrass ourselves in school.

But she did not want to lose all her contacts either. Somebody suggested that she open an eatery or cafeteria, but she thought that it was a business that would be tiresome to put up. So much would be at stake. Maybe, I could think of a business that does not require too much work and too many people, she said. This gave her the idea of opening a small space where she could run a barbecue business, something that she could personally handle and was easier to manage.

She eventually opened the business during the summer vacation and obliged me to help her since I had no classes, together with two distant nieces she brought from Bicol during her last trip to Matnog. My sister had a job at that time and my brother was simply uncooperative. Every early afternoon, she would come from the market and I would help her marinate the chicken and pork meat. I would use bamboo sticks to skewer the necks of chickens, the gizzards and the hotdogs together. She would also buy bundles of sampaguita garlands and rose corsages. "Americans are very romantic. They want to give flowers to their girls so I bought these, too. It would be additional income for us," she said.

Angeles City is now served by the Clark International Airport and the Clark Freeport Zone but back then when I was growing up, it was the home of the Clark Air Force Base, the largest United States military facility outside of continental America. I didn't know then that Fields Avenue, the street where I grew up, was a honky-tonk area for prostitution, and a favorite spot frequented by the U.S. servicemen. It was also known as an epicenter of the sex trade. I didn't know that these girls, who were good to me and Mother, were prostitutes. I just thought about them as my aunts. But I sensed that they were acting rather funny and strange because of the weird sexy dresses and thick make-up they wore, and the erotic dancing and incessant cussing, the dating and kissing of different men every night. *Maybe they were a different kind of girl*, I thought.

At about six in the evening, we would go to the barbecue stall carrying two basins full of marinated meat, a styrofoam ice chest containing more meat without barbecue sticks, an improvised cash register, and some loose change. I would place a generous amount of charcoal on the grill and start building a fire. While fanning the charcoal, thick smoke would make my eyes water.

"Hurry up, customers would soon be coming," Mother said, as she instructed the two girls to wipe the tables with a wet cloth. She started counting the change. "I heard from Lydia that there are a lot of TDYs who arrived yesterday, so expect a lot of people coming in tonight."

"What's a TDY?" I asked her.

"Temporary duty. These are American Air Force men who are only stationed at Clark briefly and temporarily because their work is somewhere else," Mother said nonchalantly.

"Oh," I muttered. I was meaning to ask her if my father had also been a TDY when he met her, but I guessed Mother was not up to answering personal questions, so I continued preparing the grill.

Three hours later, the space was jam-packed with people. Mother had to call for two more helpers to assist us in serving the customers. My face felt like it was almost red because of the heat coming from the grill, as sweat dripped from my forehead. But I was happy fanning the hotdogs and the chicken breasts. There was a lot of singing and dancing. Some Americans noisily stood up and raised their beers. The girls that they were with clapped their hands and started singing. One tall blonde guy walked to the jukebox and played "One Way Ticket" by Eruption. It was a cover of the Neil Sedaka classic and was a very popular song at the time.

> *Choo, choo train a- chuggin' down the track*
> *Gotta travel on, ain't never comin' back*
> *Ooh, ooh, got a one-way ticket to the blues.*

Two Americans got up and held the hands of their Filipina partners and started dancing on the street. There was no space inside and the music was loud enough to be heard outdoors. There were bystanders who stopped to watch the merrymaking. Others went out and also began dancing.

> *Bye, bye love, my baby's leavin' me*
> *Now the lonely teardrops are all that I can see*
> *Ooh, ooh, got a one-way ticket to the blues.*

One of the girls, one that I called Tita Tess, came to my corner and grabbed my arm and gestured for me to join them. She said to Mother, "Ate, hiramin ko muna ang anak niyo ha? Let me borrow your son for a while. Inday," she turned to the helper. "Bantayan mo muna yung binabarbecue. Watch the barbecue."

I looked imploringly at Mother and motioned for her to stop Tita Tess from abducting me, but she just nodded her head with a quaint smile on her face.

"Everybody," Tita Tess called everyone's attention. "This boy is a very good dancer, and he'll teach us to dance to the song. Halika dito, huwag ka nang mahiya. Come here and don't be shy," she held my arms and shook them. Then she held my hands and put them in the air. Everyone clapped their hands and went outside.

"Show us how, fine boy," one American GI said.

"Yeah, teach us the steps, fancy dancer," another replied.

> *Gonna take a trip to lonesome town*
> *Gonna stay at heartbreak hotel*

Determined not to disappoint Mother and Tita Tess, I nervously told everybody to make a single file, just like a train. "The one who is behind should place his left hand on the left shoulder of the person in front. Like this. And then, as the music continues, we move like a train. When we take a step, we bend our knees and sway our right hand and our hips. Got it?" I was a dancer in school and got used to training and choreographing kids in their shows and programs. "Let's try it, left hand on the shoulder, everybody," I gestured. The people at my back assembled and, despite their tipsiness, followed me closely like blind servants following their master.

> *A fool such as I that never learns*
> *I cry a tear so well.*

"Ok, once we hear the chorus, we move in circles," I said in a voice growing louder with confidence. "Just follow the beat of the music, and don't cut the chain. Everybody, go!"

> *One-way ticket, one-way ticket*
> *One-way ticket, one-way ticket*
> *One-way ticket, one-way ticket to the blues.*

The line became a circle as we glided around the corner of the stall. The circle became a bigger one. Then the circle became a line again. It grew longer, extending far across the street. Some of the American visitors who were not part of the group joined in the dancing. Some of them were wrapping their arms around the waists of the girls, instead of just holding their shoulders. But everybody laughed and had a good time.

> *Choo, choo train a-chuggin' down the track*
> *Gotta travel on, ain't never comin' back*
> *Ooh, ooh, got a one way ticket to the blues.*

When the song faded, there was an uproar heard from the crowd. Some were hugging one another. Others were either clapping their hands or shaking them and offering a toast. I went back to the barbecued hotdogs, tired and perspiring. Two girls came to Mother and said thank you. It was the best of times, they said.

One American soldier who looked older than everyone went towards me and shook my hand. "That was a blast, kid. You made these people happy," he said, grinning. As he held my hand tightly, he put in a twenty-dollar bill.

I didn't know what to say. I said thank you but I didn't

think he heard it. Most of all, I never fully understood what he said.

When it was closing time and all the guests were gone, Mother and I packed the containers. She sorted the leftovers and discarded the sauces. The helpers started washing all the used bowls and bottles in the small kitchen. I swept the floor littered by beer tabs and cigarette butts. It was past midnight.

Mother tapped my shoulder and brushed her hand against the collar of my shirt. "It was good of you to have thought of leading the dance. You are a good dancer," she said.

"I didn't understand what the officer said to me," I butted in. "He thanked me for making them happy. What does that mean?"

"Well, those young boys are like you, only older by a few years. Some of them had no idea their life would be like this here. Now, they probably miss their homes and their mothers," she said, with what seemed like an irony to me. "Maybe what they all need now is real good dancing."

I frowned. I didn't catch what Mother meant. Then I had to ask her. "Did you and my father meet this way?"

"Oh yeah, we did," she said emphatically. "Only he danced too much. Until now, I still think he does. I just don't know where." She looked at the sky briefly, and then briskly untied her apron. "It's late. Hurry, we're closing the store."

I followed her as I held ready to close the accordion door.

VERONICA MONTES was born and raised in Daly City, California, and continues to make her home in the San Francisco Bay Area. She is the author of the award-winning chapbook *The Conquered Sits at the Bus Stop, Waiting* (Black Lawrence Press, 2020) and *Benedicta Takes Wing & Other Stories* (PALH, 2018). Her work has appeared in numerous print and online journals. To learn more, visit veronica-montes.com.

US MILITARY IN THE PHILIPPINES

Following its defeat in the Spanish-American War of 1898, Spain ceded the Philippines to a new colonial master and paved the way for two of the US Armed Forces' largest overseas military installations: Subic Bay Naval Base and Clark Air Force Base. Both closed in the early 1990s, but US military presence returned a few years later—and remains to this day—at the behest of the Philippines, which requested support against aggressive actions by China in the South China Sea. When Subic Bay and Clark were in full operation, local economies reaped the benefits of catering to servicemen eager to pay for adult entertainment in the bars and clubs of adjacent towns like Olongapo. There is much to consider about this fraught situation, perhaps beginning here: what toll has it taken on the mental and physical health of the Filipinas (some extraordinarily young) who performed this difficult labor?

4

BEAUTY QUEENS

I once saw a movie where beautiful, long-haired girls knelt on a golden beach grieving the loss of loved ones. They ripped out their hair and wailed while blood ran down the sides of their faces and onto the flowers they wore around their necks. My Auntie Cely is wailing like that now, wailing like her life has been coming to an end for weeks and this is her last chance to make an impression on the world. My mother glares at her and mutters an incredible string of cuss words under her peppermint breath. I keep a light hold on her wrist in case she tries to jump up and gore her sister through the stomach with the horns I imagine she keeps hidden under her thick black hair. This image makes me laugh, which I shouldn't do, considering this is her mother's—my lola's—wake and everyone is kind of sad, really.

Lola died in her sleep after emitting a loud and prolonged sigh. Someone let it slip that she was naked, a fact that thrills my cousin Girlie and me to no end. Out of thirty-eight cousins, Girlie is my favorite, my true and kindred spirit. We were born two days apart in the same hospital and often pretend we were switched in the nursery, which would actually make me her and her me. I think about that a lot.

My mother calms herself by taking deep, exaggerated breaths. She and Auntie Cely do not get along. Not with each other or any of their sisters or, less surprisingly, with any of their brothers' wives.

"You're okay?" I ask.

"I'd be fine," she says, massaging her own neck, "if your Aunt would shut up." She puts a hand to her hair, and then dips it quickly into her purse to pull out a mirror so she can check her lipstick. Without looking at me she says, "Zeny, go sit with your lolo."

This task requires walking by Auntie Cely's husband Mark, an ex-Marine who rambles off the names of islands and provinces I can't even spell and who bores Girlie and me to death with accounts of what he calls his "previous life in Southeast Asia." His conversations always begin, "Once in Cotabato…" or "My good friends in Bohol…" He used to kiss Lola's hand, sometimes raising it to his forehead and holding it there for a moment while he closed his eyes. Lola would flare her nostrils and head for the kitchen.

When I was little, I'd beg Mark to come see my turtle, my sterling silver locket, my Holly Hobbit lunchbox. Afterwards, he'd hand me five dollars. "For candy," he always said. At my seventh birthday party, he walked into our family room with a box so big it made everyone gasp. Inside were three party dresses, a fake fur coat (in white), and a Barbie doll with a large suitcase. The suitcase opened to reveal the interior of an airplane where Barbie could serve passengers coffee and tea from a rolling cart.

Mark and Auntie Cely moved to Arizona soon after, and they didn't come home until I was fourteen. I regarded Mark as a stranger. "Shame on you," my mother said. "*Look* at him when he speaks to you." So I did. I looked at his nose, his forehead, his hair—anywhere but his eyes. Twice today he has wedged himself between Girlie and me, pretending like he needs to get to the other side of the room. "What would you call this sandwich?" he says with a smile, scooting sideways and managing to press up against both of us.

*

Lolo sits in the first pew and keeps perfectly still as people whisper in his ear and place envelopes of money in his breast pocket. Sometimes he turns and stares at Auntie Cely, willing her into silence. She looks tragically lovely, what with her hair a little mussed and her eyes brimming with tears. She has planned it that way; she is brilliant that way.

All afternoon, Lolo has kept each of his hands on top of each of his knees, bracing. "Hija, who sent that terrible arrangement?" he says, pointing with his lips. He is talking about a wilting wreath of red carnations.

"I think it was the Santos family." I whisper so nobody will hear.

Lolo nods. "You know," he says, "your grandmother was a beauty queen in the Philippines."

"I know," I say.

"There was a parade and all the little pink and white flowers caught in her hair. She took them out later and kept them in a dish on her dresser."

I've heard this a million times. I want something else. I want to hear about how Lola loved to kneel in the garden and sing to her flowers. I want to hear about the time she kicked the neighborhood pervert in the balls or how she quietly gave birth to Uncle Roly as she hid from Japanese soldiers in the attic of the old house. I wait, but he doesn't offer anything more.

"Is that all?" I finally say, pulling myself up and looking him in the face. "Is that it? My grandmother was a *beauty queen?*"

He stares at me like I am the biggest disappointment of his life. I return the favor.

*

Once when I was seven years old, I woke up obsessed with the word 'biscuit' (the week before it was 'crisp'). I sat in front of the mirror saying it over and over again. I liked the sound of it as it came out of my mouth, my tongue wrapping

49

around the hard edges, hitting against the back of my two front teeth when the final 't' sounded. I was so overwhelmed that I mixed together oatmeal, flour, and orange juice and made one hundred and five small biscuits. When no one would eat them, I cried and brought them to my lola. She laid them out in her garden like a thousand gifts and held me on her lap while we watched the birds feast.

*

Girlie likes that story.

She's sitting on a couch in the foyer with her feet propped up on an ottoman. She can tell it's me by the click of my footsteps. "Is Auntie Cely still throwing a fit?" she says. She is staring at the ceiling, probably dying for a cigarette.

"Can't you hear her?"

She listens for a moment and closes her eyes, nodding. "What did Lolo say?"

"Oh, you know: 'It rained flowers,' and all that."

"If I have to hear about that one more time, I will vomit," she says. "Tell me a story."

The people who have been milling around all afternoon smiling at us like we're orphans, are drifting out. They leave in groups and pretty soon it's just the two of us sitting on the couch with the rest of the family inside, staring at Lola. Then Mark walks up.

"Hi girls," he says. He salutes with one hand, while clutching his paper cup in the other. I'd bet a thousand dollars he didn't get that cup of coffee himself. Auntie Cely brought it to him, or maybe one of our mothers. They always hover around him, making sure he's comfortable, happy.

Girlie and I raise our eyebrows and cross our arms over our chests, but Mark stays put. Mark is unfazed.

"So," he says, "I understand your lola was a beauty queen in the Philippines."

"No kidding," I say.

He smiles and turns towards Girlie. "I believe your mother can boast of a crown or two."

"Wow," Girlie says, rolling her eyes.

Girlie's the best.

"Beautiful girls in the Philippines," Mark adds. "In fact, I met a number of beauty queens when I was there. Zamboanga, Cebu, all over. And I certainly married into a family that's full of them." He smiles; he winks.

It's like I'm watching this from the other side of the room. I can see us straining our necks to look up at him and him, smiling down at us. I stand up and say it: "My lola was a beauty queen. The women *you* met were prostitutes," I say. "Why can't you tell the difference?"

"What are you saying, Zeny? What is this all about?"

"You're not fooling any of us except maybe Auntie Cely," I say. "We all know you're one of those ass-hole Marines that kept the Olongapo bargirls busy swiveling their hips." I raise my arms and swivel my hips.

Girlie stares at me with unabashed love and devotion. She stands up; she pinches my arm.

"You wait just a minute now," Mark says, not even blushing, not even embarrassed. "I treated every woman I met with the utmost respect."

"Oh, you mean 'conduct befitting' and all that? What does that even mean? You said 'thank you, Miss' when you finished your business?" He stares at me with his mouth wide open.

"Yeah," Girlie says.

Girlie's the best.

NIKKI ALFAR is a wife, mother, fictionist, dancer, kickboxer, knitter, and origami folder. While she has yet to receive acclaim for folding, knitting, boxing, dancing, mothering, or wifing—go figure—she has managed to cadge repeated recognition out of the Palanca, Nick Joaquin, and international Mariner literary authorities, as well as back-to-back National Book Awards for her story collections *WonderLust* (Anvil Publishing) and *Now, Then, and Elsewhen* (UST Publishing House).

Nikki smokes like a chimney, and has one grandbunny and two children with writer Dean Francis Alfar—Ryo is also a published writer, and Rowan is an accomplished calligrapher.

BASKETBALL IN THE PHILIPPINES

The Americans introduced basketball to the Philippines at the turn of the century when the Philippines became a colony of the United States following the Spanish American War.

The first American teachers taught basketball and baseball through the YMCA and the public school system. Basketball started as a women's sport in 1905 but by 1910 men competed in a basketball tournament. Filipinos fell in love with basketball and have been passionate about the sport ever since. One can find basketball hoops in remote parts of the Philippines, where players in flip-flops or barefoot can be seen playing

The Filipino basketball team participated in the Far Eastern Games which ran from 1913 to 1934. In 1936, when basketball was listed as an Olympic sport for the first time, the Philippines sent a men's basketball team which finished fifth in the games. The Philippines also participated in the 1951 first Asian Games where the Filipino team won the gold medal. The Philippines has participated in the FIBA World Championship, FIBA Asia Championship, and Southeast Asia, Games.

5

LOLA GING AND
THE CRISPA REDMANIZERS

During the basketball season when I was young, Lola Ging would ritually invoke divine intervention on behalf of the Crispa Redmanizers.

This was a lengthy process which required an assemblage of certain arcane paraphernalia: her hand-high stack of well-thumbed Spanish novena pamphlets, the current favored rosary out of her vast international collection, and two identical used butter cookie tins, one of which was improbably always brim-full with ivory-colored watermelon seeds for mid-game mastication, the other; was used as a receptacle for discarded seed shells. She was a masterful multitasker and could watch TV in rapt concentration without once stumbling in her muttered devotions or reaching by mistake into the wrong cookie tin.

On those PBA game nights, she would ensconce herself—seeds and all—on the living room sofa in front of the television, while I read or did homework or otherwise occupied myself at her feet. I was in grade school then, which meant that my homework did not require the same soul-devouring intensity that my high-school-aged brothers were obliged to focus on their own assignments, under the watchful eyes of our suspicious parents.

Instead, I was left in the ostensible care of Lola Ging—but even she could only divide her attention in so many ways, among so many tasks. More often than not, I found myself with ample time and opportunity to take otherwise unconscionable liberties, such as eating powdered milk straight out of the Klim can, with a spoon and the untrammeled glee of having successfully achieved the forbidden. (In our house, it was generally agreed that cookies came in 'tins', whereas all powdered substances, from milk to Tang, were in 'cans'. Don't ask me why.)

I was always careful to be very quiet when thus flagrantly flouting the laws of our land, though the reality was that I could probably have gotten away with a great deal more. Lola's eyes would be glued to the televised hardcourt—her ears, presumably, were heeding the sonorous tones of the announcer, while simultaneously engaged in spirited dialogue with God. As far as I could tell, their conversations were conducted in a polyglot admixture of English, Ibanag, a smattering of her faulty Tagalog, and robust Spanish cursing. "Diablo, Diablo, Diablo!" Lola would cry out suddenly, startling me, and for years I remained convinced that this Spanish word for 'devil' literally meant, 'Look, Lord, the ball has been stolen!' since that was generally what was occurring onscreen at these times.

Lola maintained that her intermediary intercession was invariably efficacious, despite the fact that the Redmanizers seemed to lose nearly as often as they won. She explained this to me once (after I had applied my brilliant strategy of standing on two phone books—both Yellow and White Pages—to replace the incriminating can of Klim on its just-out-of-reach shelf). "They win because of the power of prayer," Lola said—she had once been a Spanish teacher at a convent school, and retained a certain style of elocution. "But sometimes they lose, because they are stupid."

"If they're so stupid," I asked, in my most smart-alecky manner, "then how come Crispa is still your favorite?"

Lola looked at me as if my pre-teen IQ had precipitously plummeted down to the calumnied Redmanizer levels. "They are my team," she said.

She was not actually my grandmother—rather, she was a distant cousin of my mother's late mother, and had come to help my parents out, when Mom had unexpectedly given birth to twins, resulting in a household graced or cursed with no less than four rambunctious boys under the age of five. The principal of the school in which Lola then worked had strenuously objected to her abrupt midterm departure, but my mother was her favorite not-quite-niece, and Lola Ging would not be dissuaded. She had not been particularly concerned over the administrator's 'You'll-never-work-in-this-town-again' wrath, since she and her sister had inherited a flourishing tobacco plantation in their home province, and could thus actually live in perfect comfort without pulling in a salary. (Which Lola Den-den did, unless you counted running mahjong games out of her lanai six nights a week.)

Not long after the twins' surprising birth, however, some uncouth rebel soldiers (her description, not mine) expanded their territory to quite impolitely include Lola Ging's ancestral lands. Abruptly bereft of both home and income, Lola nevertheless offered to move in with her sister, once acceptable yayas had been secured for all the boys, but of course my parents would not hear of it. So by the time I was conceived (once again surprising my over-amorous parents, but utterly delighting Lola: "We will have a full team!" she cried), she had firmly established herself as the family authority on all matters spiritual, logistical, and nutritional.

When the five of us kids had exams at school, we were forbidden to eat eggs in any form, as the Holy Spirit had pointed out to her that the oval shape of eggs, when taken into our bodies, would naturally result in a test score of zero across the board. She tyrannically decreed that our beds were never to be arranged pointing toward our bedroom doors, since this would provide a clear path that was certain to be followed by the insatiable Angel of Death, who apparently would have liked nothing better than to populate paradise with the pure souls of more-or-less innocent children. And she sternly compelled me to eat every last spoonful of rice on my plate, as neglecting a single grain would be a sinful excess that might just induce God to punish me by forcing me to endure my next life as a chicken—pathetically scratching at the ground for any stray bit of rice thoughtlessly discarded by wastrel girls like me.

Reincarnation was hardly a tenet of Roman Catholic doctrine, but that bothered neither Lola nor me one iota. She was convinced that her peculiar blend of folk remedies, superstitious dread, and pseudo-Christian dogma was precisely what the Lord Jesus had intended, when He set His omnipotent hand upon Saint Peter and declared him the rock of His Church. "We are Christ's followers," she said frequently. "He can walk on water just to show off; why should we not also exercise faith to make our lives better?"

Although my own blind faith in Lola's inviolability lessened predictably over the years, I was still willing to afford her the benefit of the doubt throughout my adolescence, given the implausible yet overwhelming wealth of repeatedly occurring supporting evidence.

When my eldest brother Tony turned eighteen at last and claimed his driver's license at the earliest possible opportunity, Lola insisted that his first trip should be to the grocery store, where she claimed that she had to pick up several inestimably crucial household items. This in itself was highly unusual, as Lola Ging usually went to the grocery only on the first day of each month, commandeering a veritable fleet of household helpers in order to amass the preferred foods, supplies, and cleaning materials needed to sustain a home of eight family members and sundry. On this occasion, in contrast, not only did she unaccountably run out of Tide detergent in the very middle of the month, she averred that she required no assistance whatsoever to pick up the multitude of things that were so sorely needed from Makati Supermarket (which was then located, appropriately enough, in Makati).

Regardless of Lola's uncharacteristic behavior, Tony was so exhilarated at the chance to demonstrate his new skill and privilege that he instantly agreed. Indeed, he drove several times around the block, instead of simply parking, to wait for Lola to emerge from the store with the predictable assortment of bags and bag boys. The pair of them had traveled nearly three-quarters of the way back home, when, quite without fanfare, orange-yellow flames erupted from underneath the hood of our once-trusty family station wagon.

With admirable speed and presence of mind, Tony immediately stepped on the brakes, shouted, "Lola, get out of the car!" and ran for his barely-begun life—only to turn around, several meters away, and discover that Lola Ging was still seated placidly in the passenger's seat, rolling her most recently-acquired rosary between her fingers with maddeningly methodical calm. Gathering all his resolve, courage, and sense of familial love and duty, Tony gritted his teeth and turned back, with the intent of dragging our recalcitrant grand-aunt out of the potentially explosive vehicle.

As soon had he taken hold of her obstinate arm, however, the offending hood of the inflammable car promptly blew off and catapulted through the air, landing with an ominous thump in the precise spot where Tony had been standing just seconds prior, thinking himself out of harm's way. "Lola!" Tony scolded her later, still exasperated, although neither of them had been so much as scratched. "Why didn't you get out when I told you? You could have been killed!"

"I knew that God would watch over me," Lola told him. "So I stayed still to remind Him to take care of you also, because it is sin verguenza to address the Lord while running about like a chicken."

My second eldest brother Gene was the wild one in the family. In fact, he had taught himself to drive at the age of twelve, and only we kids and Lola Ging knew that he would sometimes switch seats with the family driver and drive us all home at the end of school days. By the time he was in his senior year of high school, he drank, smoked, habitually cut classes, and had so many girlfriends at the same time that the inner door of his closet was covered with graffiti charts of whom he had dated, how often, and whether or not he had already professed to love them.

It was therefore a great surprise to everyone, when Gene suddenly opted to go to college at the Philippine Military Academy—voluntarily shaving his head, donning the PMA uniform, and subjecting himself to the myriad hardships of cadet life at the far-off Baguio campus.

"Excuse me, cadet," Lola Ging said, tapping the shoulder of a random sunburned, emaciated, and bald young man in uniform, when we were finally permitted to visit. "I am looking for Cadet Eugene Arambulo."

"Lola, it's me," said Gene, smiling with mingled amusement and fondness.

"Dios por dios, Eugene, what has happened to you?!" Lola cried out in horror, and proceeded to stuff him with fattening lugaw the instant she managed to get a moment with him in private.

We were all surprised still further, when Gene simply disappeared from campus toward the end of his freshman year. Even Lola was mystified as to his whereabouts—although, unlike my panic-stricken mother, she was certain that Gene was fine and simply up to no good, as usual. "Once a rascal, always a rascal," she pronounced; and took one of his old t-shirts, lit it with a votive candle purloined from our parish church, and proceeded to burn it in our bedroom.

Our shared bedroom was truly an outlandish place of worship—festooned with posters of floppy-haired, come-hither teen idols on one side, and dominated by a massive altar overpopulated with saints, dried everlasting flowers, and dewy-eyed Santo Niños on the other. On the best of days, it was not the most spacious of chambers, and on that evening, I awoke from sleep on the verge of imminent asphyxiation from smoke inhalation. Teary-eyed, I stumbled across the room to throw the door open, and accidentally bumped my hip against my little bookshelf, knocking one of my old school yearbooks to the floor.

The book fell open—by what certainly seemed like sheer happenstance—to my brother Gene's high school sophomore class photo, and Lola peered at the book through the smoke, nodded sagely, and said, with a sniff, "For once, at least, he has gone to the library of his own choosing."

And it turned out that he had in fact been hiding in the ceiling of the PMA library, living on packets of crackers and Cow Label dried beef until he had judged that the search for him had died down enough to allow him to truly effect his escape. ("I guess I'm just not the military type after all," Gene decided later; for a change, he was the only one surprised by this revelation.)

Like Tony, the twins, too, were victims of a vehicular mishap. They had decided to conduct a pulse-pounding bicycle race across the flat roof of our house ("And when did you acquire the delusion that you were circus performers?!" my mother demanded of them at the hospital) and ended up pedaling their way to the emergency room at Makati Medical Center. Charlie had broken his good right arm and Manny, his left leg. These had snapped in such an alarmingly innovative way that the doctors warned my apoplectic parents that the boys might never recover the full use of their afflicted limbs.

"Good, it serves you right!" our mother yelled at them, and promptly burst into disconsolate tears. Lola Ging, of course, did not weep, but instead set to work the following Monday, once my parents had left the house for their respective workplaces. She summoned the helpers to fetch the twisted remains of my brothers' traitorous conveyances, from which she scraped the dirt on the tires, picked up from the surface of our all-too-slippery rooftop. This she blended with holy water that she had sent me to wheedle out of our befuddled but obliging parish priest, creating a muddy concoction that she then smeared on the twins' casts (over much protest from them, in stereo) and her own aging but sturdy limbs. Since the culpable dirt was now blessed, she explained, she would compel it to perform atonement by transferring some of the health from her arms and legs to those of the twins.

After many weeks of this sacred spa treatment (coupled with a cleansing ritual involving a solution of mundane water and bleach, just before my parents came home each day), Charlie and Manny recovered completely from their respective injuries, neither significantly worse for wear. But I was not the only one who noticed that, on rainy days thereafter, Lola would sometimes walk with a barely perceptible limp, and gingerly flex her right arm when she thought no one was looking. She attributed this behavior to increasing age and worsening arthritis, whenever the subject was broached.

Lola Ging was indeed getting older. She had taken to dyeing her hair a light-absorbing shade of absolute black, and I suspected that she would always be indignantly disappointed that the Crispa Redmanizers had ceased to exist as a leading team—whereas their long-time bitter rivals, Toyota, had risen, phoenix-like, from the ashes of their own temporary disbanding.

As for me, never quite as intrepid or accident-prone as my siblings, Lola helped me in a quite different way. I was getting older, too—at fifteen, my adolescent angst manifested in a vague but urgent sense of desperation for a boyfriend or at least some semblance of a notion of what I was going to do with the rest of my life. So Lola Ging taught me to cook—her way, broiling meat and baking pastry with the fire of multipurpose pagan/shaman/Christian religious conviction.

"Lola," I said to her, dragged unwillingly into the kitchen after a lifetime of being unable to so much as fry bacon, "this is the twentieth century, you know. If the way to a man's heart is through his stomach, then he's not the man for me."

"To make perfect palitaw the way your mommy likes it," she dictated, blithely ignoring me, "you must sink the pieces in boiling water for no longer than one 'Our Father', one 'Hail Mary', and one 'Glory Be'. Then they will float to the surface, and you can take them out to roll in sugar and coconut. Then you are finished, and your soul is saved from purgatory at the same time."

I remember staring perplexedly at the stove, trying to determine how to convert this culinary catechism to the seconds or minutes commonly used by the other 98% of the global population. Ancient or not, Lola Ging could have been the world champion at Rapid Rosary Recitation, if they ever held the Olympics at the Vatican. It was almost dizzying, listening to her intone the mysteries at velocities approaching Mach 1: "Hail-Mary-fool-of-grace-the-Lord-is-weeth-you-blessed-are-you-among-weemen-and-blessed-is-the-fruit-of-your-womb-Jeessous…"

I was more than old enough by then to wonder if the Blessed Virgin—who was not, as it turned out, a god herself and therefore not omniscient—could possibly understand what Lola was saying. Certainly there were times when I had trouble myself; it had only been during my confirmation ceremony, a few years earlier, that I had learned that the Act of Contrition did not, in fact, go: "Oh, my God, I am partly sorry for having offended thee," or "Oh my God, I am hardly sorry for having offended thee." This resolved a rather troubling issue for me, as I had always considered it rather a disrespectful way to petition my Creator for forgiveness.

But I could not argue that Lola Ging certainly had more experience with such matters than I did, nor with the fact that she had evidently discerned and effectively alleviated my then-growing confusion as to the eventual direction of my life. It was over the course of our curiously Catholic cooking sessions that I discovered, with some astonishment, that I wanted to become a chef. That was how my own personal, rather sedate road to Damascus ended up leading me to London after high school, studying at Le Cordon Bleu to pursue my divinely revealed dream.

And that was why I wasn't there when Lola Ging died peacefully in her sleep, in our once-shared bedroom, at the admittedly ripe age of ninety-four years and seven months.

When I returned to Manila for the funeral, I had not shed a single tear. I was elected to speak her eulogy, because no one else in the family trusted themselves not to break down crying, and I was the one who remembered to break the rosary made of dried, condensed rose petals that we had placed in her hands in the coffin. (She had done this herself for Lola Denden the decade before, roundly scolding the funeral director for attempting to condemn her sister to roam the earth in an endless cycle of mysteries.) Seeing that my mother was still in no condition to tend to practical matters, I efficiently volunteered to be the one to pack Lola's things, after the requisite forty days of mourning had passed.

While I had been gone, it seemed that my half of our former bedroom had been engulfed by a riotous melee of stacked antique newspapers ('Redmanizers win championship!'), crumbling braided palms from a dozen Palm Sundays past, and tin upon tin emblazoned with the label of a long-defunct butter cookie company. I remembered my childhood amazement at always seeing these tins full of watermelon seeds—regardless of how many Lola Ging had already consumed at any given point in time—and decided to open one of them, before storing the lot in one of my pre-assembled balikbayan boxes.

The lid stuck initially, then burst open, when I employed the twisting technique I had learned at cooking school for handling recalcitrant containers—and all of a sudden the room was filled with what seemed to be millions of floating, empty watermelon seed shells. They lingered in the air for far longer than the laws of gravity could conceivably permit; and I found myself standing amid a strangely slow ivory-colored rain, as I laughed and shook and cried at last, perhaps learning my final lesson from the multitasking maestra of my youth.

Like any good coach, she had known when to take charge, and when to simply have faith in her charges.

As for the seed shells, they eventually did drift gently down to my head, my shoulders, and the parquet floor—light as a whispered prayer; as grated coconut flung up toward the sky; as powdered milk out of an illicit can of Klim, from a high shelf somewhere just out of reach.

YVETTE FERNANDEZ has written over a dozen children's books, including *Haluhalo Espesyal* (Adarna House); the *Dream Big Books* series (Summit Books); and *Good Morning, Manila!* and *Good Night, Manila!* (Anvil), dedicated to her daughter, Safiya. Creative writing mentors include Nieves Benito Epistola, Ricky Lee, and Noelle Q. de Jesus.

Yvette currently leads the editorial team at Summit Media, the Philippines' largest lifestyle publisher. Previously, she was editor in chief at *Esquire Philippines* and *Town&Country Philippines*. She was an editor at *Bloomberg News* in New York for over fifteen years. She finished her master's degree in Journalism at Columbia University.

RITES FOR THE DEAD

Rites for the dead are extremely important to Filipinos. The wakes are usually elaborate with expensive caskets and lavish floral arrangements. Often, caterers are hired to provide sustenance to visitors and mourners.

Sometimes family members based abroad prefer to postpone a trip back home to visit a seriously ill relative since they know they are expected to be there for the funeral anyway.

Since the majority of Filipinos are Catholic, there are usually daily Masses, blessings with holy water, and nine-day novenas that accompany the wake and last till after the funeral.

During the burial, as the family members say goodbye one last time to the departed, it is normal for them to kiss or caress the body as a final farewell.

6

ZOMBIE QUEEN

The cousins were all asleep when the call came in, its ringer piercing the early morning quiet. Eloise let it ring a few more times before finally opening her eyes and reaching over for the avocado green phone on Mama's night table. In the back of her sleepy mind, she knew it was the call she had been expecting for the last few days, yet hoped would never come.

"Lola has gone home to Papa Jesus," one of the Titas said when Eloise finally answered with a tiny "hello." She didn't know exactly which Tita it was, but it felt as if someone had thrown sand in her eyes, and her tummy did a flip-flop.

"No!" she said, feeling a tiny hole poked in her heart that grew bigger by the second.

"No!"

"Shut up! Let us sleep!" yelled her cousin, Timmy, throwing a pillow at her. Timmy, 11, was eight months younger than Eloise, and had always been annoyed he hadn't been born earlier. If he had, he would've been grandchild number one, and the big boss.

"Get dressed and we'll see all of you at church," the Tita said, and hung up. Eloise stared at the receiver that now resonated with a loud dial tone, and twisted the coiled cord around her finger.

"What happened, Eloise?" asked her little brother Jorge, his eyes barely open, from the other side of the big mattress on the floor, on which all four cousins had all spent the night.

"Lola is dead," Eloise said, quickly realizing how blunt that sounded, and regretting she had not used the gentler phrase Tita Whoever had used.

There was a long silence as the news set in, and then the blubbering started. Timmy, who liked to pretend he was a grown man, and who was quite tickled that his voice had been slowly deepening, wailed the loudest of all.

Back in the summer, on one particularly sweltering day, the cousins had gone swimming at Lola's house. Well, not quite swimming, since they didn't have a real pool, just three inflatable polka-dotted ones that the driver, Mang Pepe, had set up under the shade of the santol tree, and inflated all by himself.

"Marco!" Timmy called out, his eyes closed, his arms reaching out to grab whoever he could.

"Polo!" the cousins called out, splashing in and out of the pools, as Lola watched happily from her lounging chair.

"Marco Polo... freeze!" said Timmy, as he stumbled about.

Mica, Timmy's sister who back in December had received her First Holy Communion, made the sign of the cross twice, to escape his scrutiny.

It didn't work. "Mica, do not use the sign of the cross in vain," Lola called out. "Papa Jesus will not like that."

"You're it, Mica," said Timmy.

"But I don't want to be it," said Mica. "Lola, join us so you can be it,"

"No, no, it's too hot, and I just came from the parlor," said Lola.

"Please, Lola Pola," asked six-year-old Jorge, running out of the pool and pulling her by the hand.

Lola could never say no to her youngest grandchild, the same way she never said no to her husband, for whom Jorge had been named. Lola hesitated for a few seconds as she touched her newly coiffed hair that had been teased, combed, and lacquered with a good amount of hair spray, and then shrugged as she stepped into the biggest of the pools in her floral housedress. Eloise watched as the pink flowers on her grandmother's dress turned blood red as the water seeped in.

"Let's play zombies!" Jorge said. "You're the queen zombie Lola. You're dead."

"That doesn't sound like a fun game," said Lola. "I don't want to be dead."

"But we're all dead, Lola," said Mica. "You'll be the Queen of the Dead."

And so Lola became the Zombie Queen, sticking her arms out and shuffling after her beloved zombie grandchildren in her ruined hairstyle, on that hot, sticky day.

Afterward, everyone had ice candy made from coconut milk and sugar put in deep freeze.

The cousins' teeth chattered as they bit into the ice candy, the cold shooting through their flushed skin till they felt quite like the zombies they were emulating.

Summer days were always fun at Lola's house, when the cousins were sent over to visit every day while on school break.

Mornings were spent playing piko in the driveway, habulan in the garden, or shaking the mango tree and collecting salagubang that fell to the ground. They removed the insects' legs and tied them with string, so they buzzed around like the cheap plastic birds on a stick sold outside church on Sundays.

In the afternoons, when Lola said it was too hot to play outside, the cousins stayed indoors and played jackstones, Touch the Queen, and Mother, May I? in the long hallway upstairs, while their yayas read komiks or watched grainy old movies on a black-and-white television set.

One special summer a few years back, Blackie the dog had four babies, so each of the cousins got to choose a puppy.

Kids and puppies romped about the whole summer, and all of them, two-legged and four-legged creatures, ended up with lice. A horrified Lola scrubbed them all down with pungent smelling shampoo and watered-down gasoline, and the next day they were all frolicking together again.

But Lolo didn't like the idea that his grandchildren had lice—what if the neighbors found out? What would they think?—and so he had Lola give the puppies away. Lola had no choice, she always followed what Lolo told her to do, even if it broke her heart. The cousins cried for days, till school started again, and they stopped going to Lola's house every day, till they eventually forgot about Blackie's offspring.

Summer now seemed a lifetime ago as the cousins sat in the freezing chapel that reeked with the scent of stargazer lilies, as a never-ending stream of people filed past a bronze casket holding a dead person the grownups claimed was Lola.

It didn't look like Lola at all, that waxen figure with the sunken cheeks and salmon colored lipstick attempting to hide grayish lips. And that turban. They had never seen Lola in a turban before. It made her look like a genie, a scary one.

Four days earlier, Mang Pepe and Lola's helper Corazon had picked up Eloise and Jorge in Lolo's old Mercedes after school.

"Where is Mama?" asked Eloise.

"She said she had to do something and asked us to pick you up," said Mang Pepe.

In the car, Mang Pepe told Corazon about an old lady who was very sick in the hospital. Her hair had been shaved, he said, and she had a hole in her head. It helps to have lots of money, Mang Pepe said, or she would already be dead.

"Is the old lady a zombie?" Jorge chimed in.

Mang Pepe immediately stopped talking and started tut-tut-tut-ing to himself, and Corazon down looked at her calloused hands.

"Who is this woman you're talking about? Eloise demanded. "What happened to her?"

She did not get a reply.

That evening, a very tired, red-eyed Mama sat Eloise down in her bedroom and told her that a blood vessel had exploded in Lola's brain earlier that day. She was in a deep sleep at the hospital. She was not in pain at all, Mama assured Eloise.

"When will she wake up?" Eloise asked.

Mama bit her lip and looked away.

On the rainy day of Lola's funeral, just before they lay her in the ground at the cemetery, the attendants opened the casket one last time.

The glass was removed and Lolo bent down to kiss Lola's rouged cheeks.

"Meding, why did you leave me?" he cried as he embraced his wife of over 40 years. "I should've gone ahead of you. Now who will take care of me?"

Mama and her sisters wept silently beside their father and patted their mother's legs. Eloise and Timmy, the oldest of the grandchildren, awkwardly stroked them too. They were hard as logs.

Then Lolo trained his tired eyes on Eloise and Timmy.

"Kiss her goodbye," Lolo said quietly.

Eloise and Timmy exchanged horrified looks. Kiss a cadaver? Surely, Lolo couldn't be serious?

"Kiss her."

Eloise felt grownup hands pushing her forward. No one ever defied Lolo.

But this time, this one time, surely they could say no?

"You heard what your Lolo said. Kiss your Lola," Timmy's mother said under her breath, glaring at her son. "Now."

Eloise watched as Timmy squeezed his eyes shut and bent down slowly toward the bloodless hands clasped forever in prayer, holding a rosary of crystal.

"Kiss her," his mother repeated, pushing her son's head down suddenly so his lips and nose pressed hard against Lola's pale knuckles.

When he stood back up, Eloise saw his wide eyes filled with terror, the end of his carefree days of childhood.

"Tim, don't be ridiculous!" his mother whispered loudly, yanking him away from the casket as he retched violently. Mang Pepe suddenly appeared out of nowhere, and lifted a sobbing Timmy by the waist to take him away.

Eloise's heart pounded so loudly she was so sure everyone else could hear it. She made the sign of the cross twice, the way Mica usually did, swallowed hard, then leaned down toward the lifeless shell of the once vibrant woman they had all loved so much. Her lips brushed the frigid, clammy fingers of the dead woman, this would-be zombie, Queen of the Dead, and she, too, froze inside.

It was never going to be the way it was again.

DANTON REMOTO has just published his novel, *Riverrun*, with Penguin Random House South East Asia. He has previously published a book of stories, three books of poems, and six books of essays in English. The Writers Union of the Philippines has awarded him with a Pambansang Alagad ni Balagtas (National Achievement Award). He has been a Fellow at the Cambridge University Summer Seminar and the Bread Loaf Writers' Conference. He has also translated five novels in English into Filipino. He finished his second novel during the Covid-19 lockdown and is now translating the two novels of Amado V. Hernandez: *Mga Ibong Mandaragit (Birds of Prey)* and *Luha ng Buwaya (Crocodile Tears)*. Along with his translation of Lope K. Santos' monumental novel, *Banaag at Sikat (Radiance and Sunrise)*, they will form part of Penguin Books' South East Asia classics of literature.

MEMORIES AND CHILDHOOD GAMES

My Philippine memories mostly deal with the childhood games I played in the Philippines. Under a round, harvest moon, we played hide and seek among the acacia trees, startling chickens asleep on the branches of the trees. On summer afternoons, we played mock war games, with dried papaya seeds as pellets for our wooden toy guns. And when the wind was there, we would make our kites and fly them, watching our frail and flimsy kites sail in the blue enamel of the sky.

This is my Philippine memory.

7

THE KITE

In that moment floating between wakefulness and dream, I first smelt the crushed garlic. Its heady, golden-brown fragrance sizzled in the morning air and I finally tugged myself from the depths of a dream. I knew that Ludy would be frying again last night's rice in that lake of garlic and vegetable oil, then season it with sea salt. I rubbed my knuckles against my eyes to wipe away the cobwebs of sleep, stepped out of the room and saw Mama in the dining room.

"Oy, wash your face now so we can have breakfast," she said, dressed in her sky-blue teacher's uniform.

"Where's Ludy?" I asked.

"As usual, she must be taking her sweet time buying bread from the bakery in the street corner," Mama said.

Before she could recite a litany of other complaints, I had gone to the bathroom. I turned the faucet on. The cold water tightened the skin on my hands. I washed my face.

I heard the familiar sound of our jeep. I quickly dried my face, then ran to the front door and opened it.

I reached only up to Papa's belly, which spilt generously from his black leather belt. Too much beer, Mama would often say, in a tone hovering between a complaint and a declaration. To which Papa would only answer with a grunt.

But this morning, when I raised my face, I saw a strange paleness on Papa's face.

"C'mon, Danny Boy, let's have breakfast now. I'm in a hurry," he said, then walked quickly to Mama. They talked briefly, in hushed tones, and then I think I heard Mama stifle a sob.

After breakfast, Papa cleared his throat. When I looked at his eyes, I knew something was wrong.

He said, "A C-47 plane crashed in the town of Lubao an hour ago. I heard it from the commissary. The passengers are now being evacuated to the hospital."

When I looked at Mama, she seemed to wilt in her uniform. Her shoulders were hunched and her eyes were lined with red. Papa stood up and turned his face away. In a bitter voice he said, "That C-47 plane should have been thrown to the junk ages ago!"

Sweat began to break on my back, even if it was a cool morning. I ran after Papa who was already out of the house.

*

As I sat beside Papa in the jeep, I felt the morning like a cold knife against my skin. It was already March and summer was about to begin, but the wind gusting from the Zambales mountain range made the mornings still shivery. The sun was still rising, balancing itself on the mountains. And the rest of the military air base was still asleep.

We reached the main road that forked in two directions. On the left it swerved to the main road hemmed in by big acacias and white buildings. On the right, the road led to the small, well-equipped hospital. Papa stopped the jeep. I got off, intending to kiss him goodbye.

Just then, the siren of an ambulance broke the early morning silence. Papa and I looked to the left almost at the same time. An ambulance loomed, its siren screaming. It sped past us, then wound its way into the hospital's driveway. It screeched to a halt before the lobby.

Papa restarted the engine of the jeep and I climbed back on the front seat. In a few seconds, we reached the lobby just as the ambulance doors were beginning to open.

A hospital attendant in green cotton uniform got out, then lifted a stretcher whose other end was carried by another attendant. I saw the face of Papa's friend, the one who loved to play chess under the star-apple trees in our backyard, his eyes alive to the pieces on the board, plotting the moves in his mind. But now his eyes were shut. His khaki uniform was torn to shreds around the elbows and knees.

"Pablo!" Papa shouted as the attendants rushed back to the ambulance. The next stretcher carried Mrs. Medina, Mama's friend. Her body was limp, as if all of her bones had turned to water. Blood clotted on her white dress.

Another ambulance siren wailed. Just then, I felt something huge and burning in my stomach. Bile rose to my throat, flooding my tongue. I shut my eyes and when I opened them, I saw my vomit through a film of tears. Papa bent down, then wiped my eyes and lips quickly with his handkerchief. He led me away, back to our jeep, back to home.

I had fever on and off for several days. I could only sleep when my eyelids had become as heavy as stones. In one of my dreams, broken glass panes tried to hold themselves together, their patterns shaped like cobwebs. Then when they could no longer hold back, the veins of glass finally burst, turning everything into blood.

By day, I began reading King Arthur and the Knights of the Round Table, which Papa had long wanted me to read. I was sick, I marked the pages where Merlin, the magician, appeared. After closing the book, I would sometimes scan the white ceiling, wishing I could talk to Merlin. I wanted to ask him if he could erase bad memories?

Luis visited me and filled me in on the lessons I had missed. He also told me the latest funny anecdotes in class. He would sit on the rocking chair from across my bed and talk endlessly to cheer me up, until it was time for dinner. He would then go to the kitchen, and return with a tray containing my food. He would also get another tray and take his dinner with me. My liking for Luis sharpened because of his solicitousness and care: he was always there when I was ill, or weak, or just wanted company. Sometimes we went to his house and climbed the fruit trees in their yard. We would just sit there, together, on the sturdy branches, eating the sun-ripened guavas, the green leaves and the blue sky embracing us.

Luis was like my shield, my safe and secret shield.

*

When I went back to school, the accident still burnt on the lips of my classmates. They brought to school copies of the Manila Times, which had bannered the news on its front pages. Forty-five killed in Pampanga plane crash, the headline said. I turned away from my classmates, thinking that those were mere words: they did not capture that morning's terror.

After the lunch break, my classmates talked about the wake. The countless stands of frangipani flowers smothered the chapel such that some of them were already displayed outside. A young man just stood quietly for days beside the coffin of his girlfriend, all of eighteen years old. Children with black ribbons pinned on their shirts roamed in the chapel and the grounds, wondering aloud when Daddy would wake up from his sleep. And then, my classmates talked about the dead, their faces locked in pain, this woman whose limbs were found hanging from a nearby tree, that soldier whose balls were crushed.

Papa and Mama did not bring me to the chapel or bring up the topic of the accident in my presence. Even Ludy had been ordered to keep quiet. I knew they must have slipped into the chapel when I was asleep. They must have even gone to the mass burial, but I never saw them grieving again, until I looked at their eyes and saw everything there.

When I returned to school, my classmates badgered me about my unusual silence. They asked me if I was there in the chapel as well, brave enough to look at the faces of the dead.

"No," I answered. "I stayed at home because of my tonsillitis."

*

The days went by. The wind began to die amongst the acacia leaves shrouding our house. And the heat, ahhh, the heat became so fierce it gave me headaches.

At noon, when I squinted, I could see the heat waves writhing like small liquid snakes in the air. I kept to myself, catching up with the lecture notes that Luis had lent to me. When graduation day came, I was quite disappointed, because I only got the Second Honors. Maria Theresa – a tall, lovely girl with a black mole like a five-centavo coin on her right cheek – got the First Honors. Anyway, I'll study harder in Grade Four, I thought. And besides, it was already summer. I knew I could roam everywhere with my friends, with no thought of the assignments I had to do for next day's classes.

During the days, my friends and I played with marbles the colors of a peacock's tail. Sometimes, my friends spun their wooden tops, and I could only stare at them with savage envy as they threw their wooden tops on the ground. The tops would spin with such grace and speed for all the world to see— a whirl of wood and light and air! And then, my classmates would lasso the tops and throw them right in the middle of their palms: the tops would still be alive and spinning in a blur.

When I did that, my wooden top would wobble on its tiny pointed toe, and just drop dead.

When night fell, we had mock war battles with the boys from the other side of the river. We used slingshots for weapons. For bullets, we used clay pellets or dried papaya seeds. Luis and I always belonged to the same group. I thought of ourselves as Batman and Robin. Together now and forever, for all time. Sometimes, we would hide behind the trunk of the giant acacia tree, our bodies pressed close together I could smell the fragrance of soap on his skin, or feel his arm warm against mine. And then, the cicadas would begin their one-note singing, a rich, heavy sound that would sift through the trees and float to the nearby homes, warm with light and the smell of dinner. I always felt safe and invincible when I was with Luis. I wish I could be with him until we grow old.

Sometimes, my friends and I played hopscotch or hide-and-seek, hiding behind the trees, in the pigsty, or near the bamboo cages inside which the chickens, disturbed, would cackle. And when the chaser would be near any of us, we would run away, our shadows breaking the moonlight. After this game of hide and seek, the winners' shrill voices rose in the air, and in the night sky, the stars of summer shuddered.

*

One afternoon, we decided to make our own kites. We teased the younger kids in the block who only knew bôka-bôka, the kites made of grade-school pad paper, with folded edges for wings and broomsticks for ribs. We, the older ones, used split bamboo for our kites. For the bodies and heads, we used thin paper that was made in Japan and that came in different colors. For the tails, we used long crêpe paper, a kind of tissue paper that was creased to make for a crinkly texture. Then we glued powdered bits of glass on the thread, so the thread could easily cut the opponents' thread.

"Let's play in the field near Gate One," Eduardo said. "I'm tired of running around in the fields behind our houses."

At twelve years old, he was the oldest and the biggest in our group, and therefore, the unofficial boss. This claim was confirmed in an unspoken manner early that summer, when he boasted that he had just been circumcised by Old Damaso, the barber, in the woodlands near the river. Old Damaso chewed the tender guava leaves while he cut Eduardo's foreskin with a razor blade. Afterward, the old man spat his saliva on his hand and put the saliva around the wound. He then asked Eduardo to take a plunge in the clear water. Eduardo, the now-circumcised Eduardo, also led our group in stealing the red watermelons from the fields of our neighbor, Thomas. Sure, our parents could afford those sweet, succulent fruits. But somehow, stolen watermelons seemed sweeter.

"Yes, let's do that. The fields there are wider, and the wind, stronger," said Enrique, his voice always hoarse, as if he had sung all night.

I felt my heart beat furiously. I remembered that the wreckage of the C-47 plane had been towed from its crash site to Gate One. "For investigation," said the official reason but my friends and I knew it was there because the people outside the military air base would have pried the wreckage apart, then sold it per kilo to the nearest junk dealer.

"Okay, let's go," Luis pressed on.

I thought: If I don't come with them, they'll ask why. They'll know and then they would call me a sissy. "Okay, let's go," I heard myself say, in a full-bodied voice that seemed not to belong to me.

The sun was hiding behind a belly of clouds when we reached the dirt road beside the fields. When the wind blew, the white feathery flowers of the cogon grasses began to ripple, like so many waves.

"The wind here's really stronger," said Eduardo.

Enrique smiled smugly, glad that he had been proven correct.

"O, let's have a dogfight now!" Eduardo continued.

"Yes, now! Now!" came their cry, which became louder and louder as they geared their kites for battle.

I looked at my kite: a red head, blue body, and white tail. It even had the tricolor of the Philippine flag! I noticed only now, and I smiled. I had worked on it for two straight days, buying the materials with the coins that I had saved and kept in an empty can of Darigold milk. I had with my own hands cut the bamboo from the grove near the river, then split it with my father's machete. Afterward, I whittled the wood to the shape of the kite's ribs. When everything was ready, I pasted the thin papel de japon on the ribs of my kite, body and bone becoming one.

Even if I lose, I thought, I'll still keep my kite.

I released some line from the ball of thread in my hand. And then I ran on the dirt road, following my friends who were running ahead of me. Our thin cotton shirts began to fill with the wind, like sails billowing.

The kites of Enrique and Luis rose slowly but with majesty in the air. The heads of their kites bumped again and again. The threads entwined, trying to cut each other. Finally, Luis's thread snapped, and his kite went veering to the left. Luis ran after it.

"Al-agua! Al-agua!" the boys chorused, their words rising in the air, in memory of the kite games of old done on white sandy beaches, when the kites had to be saved from certain destruction if they fell without grace into the sea.

Eduardo and I were the opponents, and this early, I was not sure of my chances. Eduardo's kite was bigger, but I knew that my thread was certainly sharper and stronger.

Our kites soared slowly in the blue enamel of the sky. I felt the wind becoming heavy on the line of my thread. Cheers rose around us while the heads of our kites tried to smash each other's body, cut each other's tail. On and on it went for minutes, the kites circling each other, bumping, and then smashing against each other: gladiators on the kill.

With a sudden and strong tug at my kite, I finally ripped Eduardo's. But his kite swung back, his thread entwining itself around my thread. Then suddenly, I felt the wind's pull beginning to go from my line. When I squinted, I was horrified to see my kite falling in a wide, aimless arc.

My kite drifted away, borne by the wind in the direction of the cogon grasses. I ran after it, my ears filling with the sound of the boys' voices in the sunlit air: "Al-agua! Al-agua!"

Everything was green and sharp. I used my arms to ward off the stalks of tall cogon that were blocking my path. The flowers smothered me, filling my nose and mouth with the spores hidden inside the thin, light strands.

Something warm began to trickle from my left arm, but I did not stop to look at it.

I only wanted to save my kite but something in the middle of the field cut the light. Its swift and sharp reflection bounced back to me. My kite had fallen near the wreckage of the C-47 plane, now a mass of twisted aluminum and steel.

My heart boomed. When I looked down, there were threads of blood on my left arm. For a moment, I just stood there without moving, not knowing what to do.

Slowly, I went to my kite. I bent down and picked it up. I thought it would have a hole, but it looked just the way it did before. It was still whole.

Suddenly, the wind blew. It sounded like a moan, like somebody in the throes of pain. The cogon lifted their stalks and flowers to the wind, heaving wildly, loudly, about me. I began to sweat. I began to call for my mother, for my best friend, Luis...

But nothing else happened.

Years later, I would know that what I had heard, if anything, was the sound of something fleeing from me. On that day, in the middle of the field, standing beside the plane's wreckage, I could only grip my kite—solid, whole, almost pure—gripping it like a shield against the wilderness of the wind.

CECILIA MANGUERRA BRAINARD is the author and editor of over twenty books, including the novels *When the Rainbow Goddess Wept, Magdalena,* and *The Newspaper Widow.* She is the editor of the popular young adult anthology *Growing Up Filipino 1 & 2 & 3.* She has received awards, including a California Arts Council Fellowship, a Brody Arts Fund, an Outstanding Individual Award from her birth city of Cebu, a City of Los Angeles Cultural Grand, a Special Recognition Award from the Los Angeles Board of Education, among others. A long-time California resident, she was born and raised in Cebu, a place she has fictionalized in her writings as Ubec.

SPANISH-COLONIAL CEBU
The Philippines is an archipelago of more than 7,600 islands. Many of these islands are small and literally disappear at high tide; only eleven islands make up 95% of the total land area, including Cebu where I was born. My beloved Cebu is a sock-shaped island in the central part of the archipelago. Cebu City is the country's oldest city, having been settled by the Spaniards in 1565. Cebu still retains a Spanish colonial atmosphere. The triangular Spanish Fort, old stone churches and houses still remain. Its antiquity has captured my imagination as a writer, and I have, in many of my writings, used Ubec (Cebu backwards) as my mythical setting.

8

THE DEAD BOY

When I was fourteen, Bill Lowry died. He was murdered one night in Magellan Hills where he and Bebop Villarama were necking. Although Sister Candida made us pray for the repose of his soul, the underlying message to the entire student body was such sinful acts merited that kind of punishment.

I had a serious crush on Bill. Before his father died and before Bill went steady with Bebop Villarama, he used to be an altar boy at Redemptorist Church where I attended many six o'clock Masses just to see him. I used to tingle with embarrassment when I stuck my tongue out to receive the Host. I was sure I appeared retarded and Bill would never love me. Once I caught him studying me in a mischievous way; and he flashed a smile that lit up that church and made me stumble on a pew. I spent all day at school writing "Mrs. William Lowry" on sheets of paper, which I later shredded and disposed of with great care.

Soon after this incident, Bill met Bebop Villarama who was seventeen like him, an "experienced girl" we called her because she reportedly had a passionate affair with a twenty-five-year-old pharmacist when she was only fifteen. Any religious devotion in Bill's heart evaporated the night he saw Bebop Villarama in her red miniskirt, doing the twist so she looked like a pretzel at Lorna Lardizabal's coming-out party. I hated Bebop Villarama. She had interfered with what I prayed would be a budding romance. I had hoped that after the smiling incident, Bill would talk to me. But what could he have said to me—I see you in church often? Do you know that your neck turns the color of coral when you receive Holy Communion? Not the stuff for romance.

I should have put Bill Lowry out of my mind, but for some reason talk of Bill's and Bebop's Saturday trysts in Magellan Hills only made him more desirable. A Catholic boy gone bad—I was torn between wanting to save him and sharing forbidden pleasures he and Bebop knew.

Bill's family was one of four American families in Ubec. I'd seen him around for as long as I could remember, not only in church, but in movie theaters and local hangouts populated by young people. I knew, through some kind of osmosis, everything there was to know about the Lowry family. His father was an American logger who fell in love with his laundrywoman, a rather ugly woman who came from the interior of Palawan. He actually married her. They had two children, Linda and Bill, who fortunately favored the father's looks. Mr. Lowry looked like a movie star, tall with red hair and a commanding presence. The Lowry family lived in an enormous sprawling bungalow on a hill overlooking Ubec City. During a rare moment, Mama gossiped that Mr. Lowry surprised them all by not being the heathen protestant they took all Americans to be; he was a devout Catholic who led his family to Sunday Masses. It was he who encouraged Bill to become an altar boy.

The times I saw them at church, I thought they were the perfect family; I had only my widowed mother and an aging German shepherd who had belonged to my father. I used to daydream that I had a father, a brother, and a lovely airy house like theirs. I daydreamed a lot.

Unfortunately when Bill was fifteen, his father died in a car accident near his logging camp. His car plunged down a steep cliff and it had been impossible to disentangle body parts from the metal. The rest of the family unraveled at the seams after the father's death. Before the traditional year of mourning passed, Mrs. Lowry started putting on lots of makeup and dressed in outrageously loud colors, prompting people to refer to her as the "merry widow." People were unkind to her except Mama, who was widowed when I was nine, and who sometimes said grief makes you do strange things. Then she would sigh and gaze away at invisible images that I could not conjure.

Linda, who was a year older than Bill, also got involved in some scandal. It was never clear exactly what happened but a story circulated that their driver raped her and she became pregnant, and her family dispatched her to the States for an abortion. Another version said Linda became involved with the driver, a version that floated around during many merienda sessions as people sipped their coffee and speculated on how a well-bred girl like Linda Lowry could cavort with someone from the lower class.

While the Lowry women became topics of conversation, Bill himself transformed from the meek somewhat aloof handsome altar boy to the playboy running around with Bebop Villarama. It had gotten to the point where people kept a watchful eye on Bebop's waistline to see if it had thickened somewhat because after all the young couple were spending too much time together, alone, in dark forbidden places. And everyone knew that sort of thing amounted to nothing else than unwanted pregnancies and early marriages.

Bill's murder came right around the time people's tongues itched for something new to wag about. In our small-town minds, his death marked the depth the Lowry family had sunk to.

It was my best friend Mildred who called at seven in the morning. "Have you heard?" she asked.

"What?" I had been rushing through my breakfast.

"About Bill Lowry?"

"What about him?"

"He's dead."

"Dead!" I gasped.

"Shot six times with a rifle. Magellan Hills."

"Dead!" I repeated. Ubec was so small you kept track of births, marriages, and deaths. Either event was Big News. "What happened?" I asked.

"I'll tell you later." She hung up.

I bolted down the rest of my rice and hurriedly told my mother what happened. Making the sign of the cross, she raced to the telephone while I took off for school.

The principal called a school assembly since everyone talked of nothing but the murder and Sister Candida figured she might as well confront the matter and put it to rest. Besides, Linda was a graduate and when Mr. Lowry was alive, he gave hefty donations to the nuns. Voice shaking, the principal announced over the microphone that an unfortunate incident had occurred last night. The brother of our alumna, William Lowry, was killed by an unknown assailant. She urged us to pray for the repose of his soul, then she led prayers for the dead. Some high school girls started sobbing, which I found embarrassing, although I felt like crying myself. We had all fallen in love with Bill at one time or another. Bill was tall, angular with brashy hair the color of some exotic fruit. He could be standoffish at times, and flirtatious at other times. He bewitched us. When he and Bebop became a twosome, Miriam, who had the most beautiful, sleekest black hair that fell below her waist, cut it to show her sorrow. She even wore dark colors for weeks.

I had laughed at Miriam then, but later I envied her for her gumption. I could never have done anything that dramatic. Perhaps it was because I grew up fatherless, but I preferred being invisible. I never told anyone that I had a crush on Bill. No one. And when Bill himself had been around, I hardly acknowledged his presence. He was too old for me, too out of reach, a demi-god. Even when Mildred told her biggest secret (she had seen Jojo Katigbak's penis when he changed into his trunks at a picnic) I never revealed a thing.

Sister Candida's assembly made no dent on our high emotions. Girls walked around sniveling and crying. They blamed Bebop Villarama for seducing Bill, for dragging him up the hills, for causing his early death. Miriam swore she'd shave off her hair; she said Bebop should have died, not Bill.

Bebop had survived. The way I tailored the shreds of information, this was what happened. After a party, Bill and Bebop had driven to the hills and parked in an area above the Police Constabulary (PC) headquarters. Someone, most likely a PC, crept toward Bill's car to spy on the couple. Catching the peeping tom, Bill called out, startling the man who started shooting. Bill was shot twice in the face and four times in his chest. Bebop managed to scramble out of the car and run all the way down the mountain to civilization.

*

After the initial shock of Bill's murder subsided, a kind of fascination gripped me. Death had always attracted me. Ever since my father's death, I'd ponder on dead animals—dead piglets and puppies—poking at their corpses, wonder how rigor mortis happened. How could they be so still? How could they be so empty? Had their souls (if animals had souls) actually gone to heaven? And what about my father? When he had that heart attack and died as quickly as the snap of a finger, did his spirit hover over his body? And did his soul fly to me to bid me farewell, as I imagined he did? There was much to consider about death.

I wanted to see Bill Lowry for the last time before they buried him. I told Mildred we should go to Everlasting Funeral Home downtown. Usually, corpses were laid out in their coffins at the Redemptorist Church, but Mrs. Lowy chose Everlasting Funeral Home. It was more Americanized, she reportedly said. Everlasting Funeral Home sat across Flower Drum Restaurant which was cheap but was considered the worst restaurant in town. After eating in Flower Drum, you were ready for Everlasting Funeral Home, people said. You weren't supposed to eat meat products at Flower Drum because there was no telling where the meat came from in the first place; it could have come from Everlasting.

Mildred dared me to eat at Flower Drum; I bounced her dare back and she accepted. We sat in a booth and she ordered a Coke and pork bao. I had a Coke and bean cake and we kidded about her pork bao. We were still laughing when we jaywalked in front of jeepneys and cars to Everlasting Funeral Home. Near the enormous double doors, our smiles froze at the sound of organ music and thick scent of dama de noche.flowers. The heady sweet smell of the flowers gave me the sensation of being back in time when my own father was laid out in his coffin at the Redemptorist Church. I experienced it all over again, that unreal floating feeling as if I were a mechanical doll. Walking down the marble aisle of Everlasting Funeral Home, I counted in my head: one-two-three-four-five. "Five years," I muttered.

"What?" Mildred whispered.

"Nothing," I said, not knowing how to tell her that I'd just realized that my father had been dead for five years.

She looked at me quizzically and shrugged her shoulders. I shrugged mine.

A rhythmic sobbing echoed in the room as we approached Bill's coffin. I glanced at the front row and located the source of the sobbing—Linda Lowry. Her face was drawn and wet from tears. Arms folded across her stomach, she heaved up and down as if struggling to breathe. Beside her sat Mrs. Lowry in absolute silence. She wore a low-cut black mini-dress and three-inch black stiletto heels. Her cheeks and lips were bright red; her hair had been dyed a terrible auburn. She was such a sight, I did not dare greet her.

When I reached Bill's coffin, I was feeling as light and fluttery as an angel. My breathing had turned so shallow, my legs felt like buckling. Bill had a magnificent coffin, bronze in the inside and mahogany on the outside. The idea was that the bronze would protect the body so it would stay intact for many years. My grandmother Filomena's corpse had not decomposed after twenty-five years, proof, my mother declared, of her sainthood. I'd heard stories about dead people growing hair and fingernails even as they lay in their coffins. The worst story was about the priest whose remains showed great distress: his fingernails clung to the coffin's lid. He had been buried alive and upon waking in the coffin, struggled to try and get out. Horror stories like these swarmed in my head, and at that moment, I was greatly relieved that my father had been embalmed; he was definitely dead when we buried him.

The two bullet holes on Bill's face left no doubt about his being irrefutably dead. One on the right cheek and the other closer to the ear. Poor Bill Lowry. Seventeen years old, and except for the bullet holes, resplendent in his dark navy suit. Even with his grotesque little smile, he was handsome. I sighed, remembering that wonderful smile Bill had given me at church. What promise in that smile. You are the prettiest fourteen-year-old, that smile said.

The oppressive feeling lifted when I remembered the times I had written "Mrs. William Lowry" while my mind traveled far, me and Bill honeymooning in Hong Kong, me and Bill in a sparkling house with our six children—three boys, three girls—and two German Shepherds, and one white cat, living happily forever after.

Mildred nudged me. "He looks terrible," she whispered.

I started to shake my head; I had not thought so. But when I studied him again, I agreed that this dead boy really didn't look like Bill. It was a mannequin—stiff, unyielding, expressionless. I could not help crying. Perhaps the contagious sobbing got to me; or perhaps I cried for my shattered fantasies. Maybe I cried for my dead father, or maybe it was for the realization that someday I'd end up in a satin-lined casket with strangers checking me over.

We left in silence, Mildred and I. We took the jeepney home in total gloom. But later, we gossiped about Mrs. Lowry's low-cut black dress, so low you could see her cleavage; and we giggled at Linda Lowry's smeared eye shadow; and we wondered if Miriam did have the nerve to shave her head; and we laughed at how shook-up Bebop was, she was contemplating entering the convent. But he hovered around, this dead boy, as a feeling of incompleteness.

A few weeks after Bill's funeral, when Mildred and I were in the bamboo grove at the back of school, we found a dead baby sparrow. It already had feathers and still felt warm. We could not figure out how it died. Mildred speculated it fell from its nest and starved, but it didn't look emaciated. We finally buried it under some leaves. Even while we stood there, ants started crawling toward this makeshift grave. I felt incredibly sad. I remained silent for a long time, then wanting to say something, I blurted out, "I had a crush on Bill Lowry."

"I know," Mildred said.

"You did?"

She nodded.

I told her how I filled a piece of paper with his name and slipped this under my pillow so he'd dream of me. I also related the smiling incident; and I told her about writing "Mrs. William Lowry" on paper. We giggled over my silly daydreams.

She confessed that she liked Bill too, and we shook our heads like two old women and muttered, too bad, he's dead. We didn't say much else.

GEORGE GONZAGA DEOSO graduated from the University of Santo Tomas with a Bachelor's degree in Literature. His fiction, poetry, and essays have appeared in a number of publications such as *Liwayway Magazine, Philippine Panorama, Philippines Graphic, Philippine Daily Inquirer*, and the *Sunday Times Magazine*, among others. He was also a fellow for poetry in the UST, Iyas, and Silliman University National Writers Workshops. He is the author of *The Horseman's Revolt and Other Horrors*, a collection of dark short fiction (UST Publishing House, 2020).

FILIPINO GHOST STORYTELLING

Ghost stories often play significant roles in the lives of children growing up in the Philippines. These stories could serve different purposes: from being tales exchanged between friends seeking thrills, to becoming ways of explaining a certain phenomenon in both rural and urban setup. Long-running series and franchises, such as *Shake, Rattle and Roll* (for the movies), and *True Philippine Ghost Stories* (for fiction) had played a key role in shaping the Filipinos' concept of ghost stories and the supernatural. The tradition of ghost storytelling in the Philippines had since evolved. Auteurs, literary fictionists, and comic book artists in the country continue to seek new ways of telling ghost tales, not only to scare readers and viewers but to also reflect on the manifold issues faced by the country and its people.

9

THE CHILD

When she told him she was going out to hear the six p.m. Mass, Sylvia Bautista was in her Sunday casuals, car keys jammed in her denim pocket. She found Max in the carport on tiptoes, fussing on a cabinet, most likely on a hunt for another pair of pliers he must have lost a long time ago and had just remembered to look for now. Between them the battered sedan sat like a silent observer, behind the car through the lifted carport door a chilly draft wavered in and Sylvia could see the approaching darkness of a summer night laying on the empty street. When she spoke Max turned and regarded her with a smile, his right cheek smeared with grease.

"Would you want me to go with you?" he asked. Maximo Bautista was a content developer for an ad agency on the weekdays, but on the weekends he'd usually turn into semipro family mechanic. Since that day they realized that Jet was gone and had no intention of coming back, Max had devoted much of the time he was off work to hole himself in the carport, Sylvia sometimes hearing from the kitchen the clatter of tools on a small wooden table, or the hood of the car slamming, or his own bicycle accidentally falling on the ground.

He liked fixing things, and because he was either clumsy or was just too sad, whatever it was he thought of doing would consume his day and it would be evening before he'd join her inside the house.

"No," she said. "You'd have to wash up and we might be late."

Relief smoothened his face. Sylvia walked to her husband and kissed him on his clean cheek before going in the car and settling herself behind the wheel. When she started the engine, Max stood in front of the hood, looked at her, and told her, "Take care." He waved a hand like an eager kid. She waved back before wheeling out of the carport.

At another point in time, she might have turned on the radio, perhaps to sing along the classics that DJs were in the habit of playing over on Sunday FM stations. Now though, as she drove over the streets of the village and out of it, she could only stomach the silence. She basked in it, the silence of the car, no music now, because that would only remind her of her son. Jet didn't like road trip conversations, opting instead for the FM dials of the old car, hunting for whatever music to distract them from small talk.

Christ the King Parish was in PhilTowne Homes, the village next to theirs. As she surrendered her license to the guard at the entrance of this neighborhood and after receiving a laminated card with a number on it, she thought back to how her husband had asked her if she wanted him to come. She knew he only asked because she was his wife, and it was the right thing to do. One of the things they have long agreed to have differences over was their beliefs. They were wedded in the church, nineteen years ago, but he had long made clear that he couldn't be counted on to be devout.

Sylvia was raised by her parents, in Iloilo, to be a God-fearing woman, so that when she came to Manila to finish college and eventually work as the secretary of a jewelry store chain owner, she hadn't questioned her own beliefs. Exhaustion in the city though had slowly drained her of motivation to attend the weekly Mass. By the time she met

Max, when her boss hired the services of the ad agency, she had completely mellowed out on the practice of her faith, or when she found reasons to be thankful and mutter a prayer. She hadn't been one to pray just to ask for something.

Even now, she reflected, as the car eased on the gravel path leading to the church.

She resumed her Sunday appointment with God a couple of weeks ago, in the morning, shortly after she read the note on the table that said "I'm sorry. Don't look for me now." When she first told Max that she wanted to hear Mass, he just agreed, although the look on his face later hadn't been without pity. Their discussion on religion from a long time back returned to her and through his eyes she had almost heard him: you're only doing that because you wanted to ask for something. Because something happened. You want him back, as much as I.

She hadn't told him anything, didn't defend herself,

Each of the parking spaces by the church front was occupied, and Sylvia had to find a spot somewhere further down the sloping road of the village, in the neighborhood which must have been used to the Sunday crowd of churchgoers. After driving past a brief line of parked cars by the sidewalk, she found one just in front of a houseless lot. She turned off the engine, stepped out the car, made sure it was locked, before approaching the faint sounds from the speakers of the church. The choir and pianist were tinkering with some notes from a hymn to be sung later during the service. She had on a blazer, worn over a button-up blouse, and yet as she walked, she felt cold. The dark sky was smudged with patches of gray that could only be clouds blotting out some stars and half of a possible full moon, somewhere above the cross at the tip of the church's ornamental roof. The wide-opened church doors revealed the pews almost filled with faithful from all walks of life, their backs to her.

When she and Max settled in the village where they now live, at the time that she had also given up her life as part of the workforce, she had learned from a neighbor that there was a church in the next village. She had resigned not only to tend to her pregnancy then, but to also prepare herself for the eventual life of a full-time housewife. She would drive on her own to this other village in their then-brand new Civic on occasional Sundays. This didn't persist though, as suddenly, after years of having not attended a service, she began to feel distant from the whole thing. At times her mind hovered elsewhere as the usually soft-voiced priest began his homily. Nonetheless, she had her son baptized in that church.

She walked up the flight of marble stairs and finally entered the church, dipping her fingers in the bowl offered by a white stone angel. The priest had just emerged along with his ministers from one of the offices at a side of the church and Sylvia knew that in a while he would take his place at the entrance of the center aisle leading to the altar, just a few feet from the bowl of holy water. She made a sign of the cross and walked over to the nearest empty seat: the rightmost seat of the last pew at the back.

When the choir, settled at a mezzanine by the entrance, began the first song, Sylvia realized that she had sat herself beside a bald kid of about six years old, in a crisp white dress that ended in the middle of her shins, the material dotted with a white squared pattern. Besides the kid, a couple of feet away, was a pair of teenagers who wouldn't stop looking at each other.

Sylvia was a bit confused at the sight of the kid. For a while she doubted the impression that the seatmate was a girl. She was bald, her head clean-shaved. The kid might be a *he*. But then after the song had ended and after the priest had settled himself between the altar and the hardwood risen Christ high on the wall, the girl smiled at her, an unmistakably girlish voice escaping out of her grin, before the kid herself turned back to the priest who had then finished the introductory rites.

They sat and the liturgy began. Sylvia wondered, and was then sure, that either of the young man or woman who still hadn't found reasons to stop adoring the other (the young man's arm was around his companion's waist as they sat there while the reader delivered the word of the Lord) were responsible for this kid beside her, and she felt pity. Perhaps the young man was allowed to go out that Sunday by the parents only if he'd take the kid with him. It didn't help that the kid looked restless. Sylvia observed, with mounting irritation, that the child's feet were swinging back and forth like a pendulum, as she sat there. Sylvia felt the bench vibrating with the child's movement.

She tried to focus on the Mass, and for a while she succeeded. She forgot the bald kid and as the chants and prayers proceeded, thoughts of her own child filled her mind.

Nineteen years ago she gave birth to a boy, whom they loved as any parent was bound to love a child, perhaps even more. Her husband had moved then to another ad agency and he earned just enough for them to live what simple life a white-collar with middling work experience could offer. There was still much to want, but at least they hadn't many problems sustaining the boy's education. They had maintained and paid for a car and had at least begun saving a fraction off their mortgage.

Jet had only been in private schools. Sylvia and Max had made sure that he would breeze through his grade and high school without having to find reasons to think they were impoverished. Wife and husband were impressed that their hard work wasn't wasted on the kid. They were proud to stand beside him on the stage when it was time to collect his "Best in," and "Most," medals and another medal, a golden one, to prove that he finished as the top student among all the fourth years. Even Max was teary-eyed upon learning that his son had finished as the class valedictorian.

So when the time came for Jet to choose among the schools the entrance exams, which he had aced, they could only nod encouragingly at his choice. Though for a few nights they had wondered how they would push through with his double degree in this private institute in Manila given what they had. They were comforted then to know that Jet had snagged a scholarship to partially defray the cost of his attempt to finish his degree in Geology and Chemical Engineering.

Despite this, they still had to wrestle with other expenses. Because the institute was in Malate, Jet had thought it would be better for him to live in the dorm on weekdays instead of having to chase PUVs every night in the choking traffic of Manila just to be home in QC. On top of this, thousands of pesos had to be shelled out to obtain the laptop model required by his course.

For the first few semesters the Bautistas found themselves on a tightrope of a budget. Costly school materials had to be bought, and every weekend when he was home Jet seemed to have never run out of requirements to ask funds for. Max and Sylvia were troubled because for the first time in their lives they were now scraping even at the savings they had for retirement. As they noticed the young man grew his own beard, grew taller than the two of them, and spoke in a voice that seemed to be much deeper than they had last remembered, they also saw how their cost of staying alive had ballooned as well without Max's income keeping up.

And then came the day, a year and a half later since the boy first enrolled in college, when he delivered the news that must have precipitated the chain-reaction of bad luck.

It had been a weekend, and he had walked in through the gates carrying his bag of dirty clothes which Sylvia had been used to washing herself. In his other hand was a satchel of school materials, the long hair he had sported in a disarray and he had looked like he hadn't slept for the past couple of days.

"I'm sorry," he said when he fell on the couch, hands rubbing his face.

The couple had sat on his either side and asked what was wrong.

"I lost the scholarship," he wasn't sobbing when he said that, just the plain look of shame. And somehow the fear that he would have to stop attending college. Some prof had given him a five, a grade the MOA for his scholarship had specifically mentioned to avoid.

"But you don't have to worry," Sylvia had said, although deep down she knew what she said was a bald-faced lie. "We have enough saved up for you to go on studying."

She caught the look of surprise on her husband then, but he didn't say anything. He just consoled his son and agreed with Sylvia.

Later that night, on the bed with their voices hushed, Sylvia expressed her intent on working again.

"We haven't much choice, do we?" Max said, always the man of caution.

"He deserves it," she said. "He, should get nothing less."

"I could work overtime, of course."

"You know that wouldn't be enough, unless we want to starve."

"I know."

"There's this daycare in the village. I think they're looking for someone. I saw something on their tarp about a 'teacher' being wanted"

He just sighed, and they had slept in each other's arms as they always did, though both of them nursed some deep-seated worry.

Sylvia was pulled out of her musing by the commentator, who had announced that they must all rise. There was another round of reading and singing. After this they sat again and the priest, a tall, solidly built man, took to the podium and began his homily.

She wasn't one to ponder on coincidences, but when they were reminded by the priest that one of the readings was about the prodigal son, Sylvia couldn't resist thinking that divine intervention was working double time for her. She thought for the first few minutes of walking out without waiting for the body of Christ and coming back to her husband, no questions asked or answered. But she decided to finally settle on her seat. After all, had she not come for this? To find refuge in someone else's stories?

Sylvia knew the parable almost by heart, and she wasn't surprised when the priest said, "As parents, we are expected to strive to forgive, for forgiveness is what God has for all of us who have sinned."

What surprised her was when the priest juxtaposed the gospel with a fable by Aesop. He said, "We must also acknowledge the complexity of our roles as guardians. There is this story of a boy who was imprisoned for theft."

The story goes that the boy was sentenced to the gallows for multiple counts of felony. There was a huge crowd watching the execution, including the boy's mother. The boy asked to speak with his mother, and when she had come nearer to him, when she thought he was going to whisper some last words, the boy bit off her mother's ear.

"And you know what the boy said?" the priest asked the solemn crowd, answered as expected by no one. "He said, 'I won't be here had she discouraged me the first time I did this!'"

The whole story brought a chill to Sylvia's entire being. Is this what I was looking for? She thought to herself.

Beside her the child's feet had grown more restless as the man behind the podium droned on and on. The bench was almost quaking, and yet the couple who was supposed to look after the child was still busy with each other. The boy's head was on the shoulder of the girl.

The gospel and the bald girl's behavior had lodged a lump of curses in her throat. She must do something about it, or else, she'd simply break down. Sylvia then turned to face the girl, not to talk to her, but to the young man and woman at her other side.

Just as she was about to open her mouth to call their attention, the girl stopped moving her feet and stood on the knee rest at the back of the pew in front of them. Before she could process what was happening, the girl walked past where Sylvia was sitting, still flashing her sweet smile. She noticed that the girl's skin was pale and that deep dark circles were under her eyes. When she walked from the pew though it didn't look as if she was suffering from anything. Just restlessness, Sylvia thinks, and she was about to proceed with her intent of saying a word or two to the couple now beside her when she realized that the girl must be going to the bathroom somewhere in the inner offices of the church, where she was walking to.

Sylvia stayed put then, letting herself immerse in the words of the man in front. It was then inevitable that she would think about Jet.

Where does one begin when thinking about what he did? If Sylvia was to go to confession, she wouldn't know what to say about him. She and Max had never laid a hand on Jet, but they had always told him when he did something wrong. She wasn't the mother in Aesop's parable who would encourage her son to steal; though she believed they have always been the parents with arms opened to welcome the son who strayed from his path.

But even that was not enough.

Perhaps she would begin by saying she wasn't aware that something was happening. Maybe their fault was they trusted him too much. The months had proceeded back then as they had before, only Sylvia had busied herself as well with some children in the nearby daycare on weekdays, and Max began rendering longer work hours. They felt more exhausted, but they didn't tell their child and made it a point to look like they had it all under control when he went home on weekends.

They would hand him the monthly payment for his dorm, and then his tuition for every semester. This went on for a year and a half during which time the couple noticed some strange behavior on the boy which they chose to attribute to the fact that he was growing up. For instance, Sylvia had noticed that his shirt had begun smelling of cigarette smoke, and after talking to Max about it, they decided to tell him how at seventeen, this wasn't the most ideal habit of all. He had said, "okay," when they confronted him. They weren't surprised when his weekly load of laundry still carried the stench of nicotine the following weeks.

There were also some weekends when he would not even go home. He would call the day prior to a Saturday and tell Sylvia or Max that they were out on some field excursion to acquire some rock samples during the weekend. He told them they'd have to go to some town in Tagaytay or Mindoro and that he would also have to pay for the trip. Sylvia would drive out of the house, buzzer beat to the three pm cutoff of a money transfer service to send him the needed amount.

On the days that he was home Jet would scarcely go out of his room. Sylvia slowly began to feel that he wasn't going home to be with them anymore but just to have his laundry done or to be handed his dorm and school money. They didn't say anything about it at first, just observed their son leave his bag in the living room, say hi to them with bloodshot eyes and a wave of his gaunt hands. He had begun losing weight. He would go out of his room only to spend some time in the bathroom, or to bring a platter of food to and from the table. He said he had a headache, or that he had to pull an all-nighter to review for an exam or to finish a plate that's why he holed himself in.

Still, the couple resolved to let him be. Max thought the pressure kids these days had to endure may have been different from their own college years. "It's all about competition now," Max had told her when she said she was worried, "he'll emerge from that and be more successful than any of us could ever manage."

Sylvia, in retrospect, thought what his husband had said had not been all wrong. She wrung her hands as the priest's words now flew above her head. She could feel herself lapse into that state when all thoughts tumble down to her regrets.

They had talked to him one day, sat him down on the couch and told him that they were there for him if he needed any help. Sylvia had even told him, "We're always here, love. Remember that, okay?"

Jet murmured a "thank you" as he sat there, obviously suppressing some embarrassment. He said, "I guess I just needed more time to do some schoolwork. Thanks for your concern though. I appreciate it." With that, he smiled at them before standing and going to his room. They couldn't help but notice how his shirt had hung on his frame as he turned his back to them, how baggy his jersey shorts had been. How restless were his eyes when he faced them.

They had terrible suspicion then. But when Sylvia inspected his room on weekdays she found nothing to incriminate his son; the Bic lighter was the only thing in his room she disapproved of.

One Saturday, this suspicion plunged into certainty when the bell buzzed and they were surprised to see a couple of young men standing at their gate. They were Jet's dorm mates. "We came here to see if Jet's around, Tita," said Stephen, whom Max and Sylvia were familiar with as they remembered him visiting the house with Jet one afternoon when they were in their first year, as they were required to finish some group work.

When they let the young men in, they looked a bit shy and had only taken a sip from the glass of lemonade she poured them. Stephen said, "We came here to check with Jet."

"Well I think he mentioned something about having to stay in the dorm to finish some project or something?" Sylvia said.

"He isn't in the dorm, Tita," Stephen said. "He hasn't been in the dorm for several weeks now."

Then Denis, the other boy said, quietly, still shy, "He doesn't really stay with us that long. He only goes twice a month, on the days when we were supposed to pay for the rent. He collects our money and tells us that he was going to pay the landlord for us."

Stephen continued, "Then just this morning we were told that we had to vacate the unit. It turned out that we were behind our rent by three months already, that Jet never made the payment. We just came to check if he's here and to get our money back. We won't make him pay for his share, Tita, we just want him to return our money. We could split the amount

Jet was supposed to pay. We just don't want to lose the space because it is difficult to find a room affordable as what we have now."

Sylvia didn't say anything for a while. When she finally found the voice to say something, she said, "There must be a mistake, I'm sure."

"We thought so too, Tita. We came here because we also thought Jet might not be well or something."

"He's been acting strange lately…"

"Why don't we call him?" said Max. He sat on the couch with a blank expression. His voice was even.

"Of course," Sylvia said, and then picked up her phone to dial her son.

When she dialed, she felt something knotting up in her stomach. She recognized this as disbelief, and as the phone rang unanswered multiple times the feeling was overtaken by dread and the need to cry. Finally, after three attempts, the call was picked up.

There was a background noise, men talking and laughing, one of them howling as if a joke had been cracked. Jet's voice came on, slurred: "Yeah? Who's this?"

He didn't even bother reading the dialer's name. "Jet, dear? Where are you?"

"Mom?" A pause, after which the background laughter was subdued. "Mom, is that you?"

"Yes. Where are you?"

"I'm at the dorm, Mom. I needed to finish some papers."

Sylvia's fingers fluttered to her throat. Her voice cracked when she said, "Jet, son, your dorm mates are here. They're looking for their money. They said you took it."

"Huh?" Sylvia recognized this double-take. She knew Jet so well to know that Jet was thinking of a lie. Which he promptly delivered: "I didn't take their money, Mom. I didn't—"

"Where are you, son?"

Silence. Even the background noise simmered down to whispers.

She asked again. "Where are you?"

Five seconds might have passed before the call was dropped.

She looked at the three people watching her in the living room. Then she said, "I guess we better head to the dorm, boys, and pay up to your landlord."

After stashing some cash they've hidden for their savings in her bag, and after calming herself down, the four of them rode in the sedan and drove to Malate. At the dormitory they spoke with Mr. Olinares, a widower with a grumpy old face who flatly told them that Jet never once spoke to him for the past few months, much less even hand him anything. The Bautistas didn't argue, as they too trusted the old man, having seen him when Jet was first settling in his room, when they helped him bring some of his things when he was in his first year.

After dropping by the dorm, Sylvia decided to check with the school, and though she was not particularly surprised, still, she felt as though she was about to sink into the office chair before the table of Ms. Ocampo, who had explained to her the meaning of the numbers the registrar had printed on Jet's TOR. The professor had handled several classes where Jet had belonged, was acquainted with the instructors in the department, and she was in a position to tell the couple that the fives and WFs had been caused by his absences and inability to pass exams. He had enrolled every semester, yes, but he would only attend his classes around three times. He has never joined any of the out-of-town field excursions because he needed to have passing grades for certain subjects to do so.

"We have also received some reports from the org he was supposed to be the treasurer of, Ms. Bautista," the professor said, taking care not to sound harsh. "I believe he was supposed to be holding the funds for their yearly activities, but no one was sure where he was or how to reach out to him."

Sylvia could still remember how she felt like someone socked her just in front of the kindly professor. She had wept, not minding anymore if the other teachers and students looking for advice in the shared office space were disturbed or had looked at them with pity. The professor was kind enough to let her weep and console her, and later, to have someone call the student organization's president and auditor to explain how much was in their org's debit card account, which they now have no access to since the PIN was changed and Jet had taken possession of it.

"You don't have to worry for now po, Tita," said the president, a young woman who had been as sorry as the professor was for what was happening. "We still had something set aside for our upcoming GA. We hope to be able to reach out to Jet though. He's a kind person, Tita. I didn't know what happened. No one knows where he is and his social media had been apparently deactivated. I hope he's safe po."

Sylvia handed to the students what remained of their savings after having paid Mr. Olinares, which wasn't enough yet to cover the whole thing. They got the student's contact number and promised to get back to them. They wired the rest of the amount a couple of months later.

In the months that followed, they had not heard from Jet. Sylvia and Max didn't fail to ring his number each day and send him text messages, but he had always been unreachable, the messages all unanswered. For the first month Sylvia cried every night in bed, and this pushed Max to sleep on the couch, though she knew he was also blaming himself for what was happening. In the mornings they would go about the business of preparing themselves for the day, but while at work Sylvia would always find the time to sit on a corner away from the bawling babies to type manically on her phone. She'd tell Jet that whatever happened, it's alright, it would be alright. Mom and Dad are there to help. No need to be afraid, they were not mad at him. Just come home please, son. We miss you. We could enroll you in another school, if you like, or if you want you could tell us what you want to do. Just please come home, or at least tell us where you are or you are doing okay. We worry about you. Are you eating? Do you have a bed to sleep on?

At night when Max was in the bathroom she would sift through messages on his phone and see the same sort of messages sent to their son's number. They would lie together on the bed, or separately, sharply aware of each other's breathing and deep sighs.

A month after they paid for all that Jet had owed to the student org, Sylvia resigned from the daycare center.

"I hope you don't mind," she told her husband one Saturday evening. They were having dinner, a part of the night when they were supposed to be comfortable with the presence of just the two of them at the table since Jet rarely went home anyway. But then the thought that Jet might be out there somewhere, in trouble, or perhaps wandering about unsure how to feed himself or where to sleep that night, this thought had worn down their meal to the sounds of cutlery against dinner plates. They grew tired of crying but they couldn't help it, and they were afraid of being unable to eat once they began to talk about their son.

"It's alright, love," Max said.

"The children," Sylvia said, voice quivering, "they remind me of him."

Max had sighed and told her he understood.

A couple of weeks after she resigned, the doorbell rang, and this brought a mute fluttering in her heart. She had always expected that one day he would come back, but after a procession of days of being disappointed by census takers and random visits from kind neighbors, her hope had flustered. Still, when she looked out the window to see the head of a boy waiting by the front gate, she couldn't help but be anxious that she would once again be disappointed. She walked out the door, and opened the front gate.

And there he stood, her son. Jet. The first thing she noticed was how shrunken he looked, how flesh seemed to have been sucked out of his cheeks. His eyes looked tired, hair tied in a ponytail, and he had on a black shirt, jeans, and flip-flops. He badly needed a shave and when she went towards him, she realized that a bath wouldn't be a bad idea. Nonetheless she hugged him and cried and cried there on the street.

"I'm sorry, Mom," he said.

She said it was fine, that what was important now was he was home. They walked into the house and oddly enough, though she had so many questions to ask, she only busied herself by cooking up an early dinner for him and watching him eat hungrily without even asking if she had eaten anything herself. She just sat, watching her son finish the meal, slurp and chew. When he was done she told him to go wash himself up.

When Max went home later that night the first thing he did was to hug his son, restraining himself from asking questions and cursing him for what he did. Max and Sylvia were just too happy that he was back, and they were much too willing to give him a chance. Though that night, after the three of them lounged in the living room to watch the evening news and when they retired to each of their rooms, Sylvia couldn't help but wonder aloud about how distant Jet had looked to her.

"Did you see him, Hon?" she said as they lay in the darkness of the room. "Like he was there but he was thinking about something else? I mean, the way his eyes shifted."

"I saw it," Max said. "And I think you know what's the cause."

She could only sigh. "I still hope it isn't what it is."

"He ate too much earlier, he looked restless, he didn't want to talk but he fidgeted like he wanted to do something he couldn't."

"I know."

"We have to be careful, I guess."

"I know," she had said that with an air of resignation, hoping that tomorrow they would find their son in a better disposition.

But that had been too much to ask.

The next morning, they woke up from a restful sleep only to find Jet's room empty. His closet and the drawer for his underthings were almost emptied as well. In the living room there was this cabinet where they had stowed money in case of emergency, thousands of pesos for sudden hospital charges. The money had been in a china jar, a teapot-like ceramic which now only contained coins, and it had been drained of bundles of paper bills, the lid just left beside the jar.

Under a mantel on the center table was a sticky note, hurriedly scribbled: "I'm sorry. Don't look for me now—Jet."

That had been almost a month ago.

Max and Sylvia went through the same cycle of pain, this time magnified by the certainty that their son had clearly refused the chance he was given. Even more, the idea that his father and mother worried seemed not to have occurred to him with that final disappearing act. Within days the wife and the husband swiveled from a vague hate for their own son, to a more persistent feeling that they were to blame. They cried, at times they would just ignore each other, and finally, they simply found things to occupy themselves.

One Sunday, she surprised Max by being up early and telling him that she would go to the 7 am Mass. He had merely groaned to her before burying his face on the pillow. When she went home later Max had already set up breakfast and he had that look that said, *I know why you're back to that faith of yours. I understand.*

That was two weeks ago. She woke up today though weighed down by a pang of sadness that she didn't get up until the last Mass for the morning at 9 am must have been over. It was fortunate that while doing the laundry she remembered there was supposed to be an evening service.

And so here she was. The priest had long ended the homily and they were now lining up for the communion, leaving the bald girl—who had returned without much fuss and who then hadn't thought of disturbing anyone on the bench by swaying her feet.

After accepting the body of Christ, Sylvia went back

to her seat and was surprised to find that the girl wasn't there as she had left her. She thought perhaps the kid had found it wise to sneak out while the brother or sister was out queuing for the altar bread. She thought that perhaps the girl was at the candle stands before the framed paintings of the Lord and His parents. As a child, Sylvia had been delighted when her own mother allowed her to light up a squat candle and watch the fire she had lit dance as they recited the Lord's Prayer. A sweeping look at the corner of the church where the almost identical pictures stood told her the girl wasn't there.

Sylvia returned to her seat, a few feet beside her the couple were now kneeling, heads down and praying, though they were still too close to each other that their shoulders were touching. The empty space between her and the couple between was glaring, with the absence of the girl. Sylvia knelt and looked up at the figure of the risen Christ behind the priest.

She believed it was her moment to talk to the Lord, this part of the Eucharist. Especially since the past few Sundays, she was wont to ask questions, and the questions had been set in the same tone. Was it our fault? What did we do to deserve this punishment? Have I ever done something wrong that I had to be sorry about for the rest of my life?

Her own life would flash before her mind's eye as she stared at the gold-painted God in front, at the wounds sculpted on the open palms He was showing as He held his arms open to everyone. Sylvia had an unremarkable life at best, and in retrospect she would like to think it was all deliberate, the choice to make everything in her life as simple as possible. She lived as a child, came of age, found work and married a man without having been hurt too deeply by anyone she knew. Nor had she, as far as she could remember, hurt anyone. She had been occasionally in contact with the same set of friends from college, she had an amiable if not too intimate relationship with their neighbors, she hadn't forgotten to call her own parents in Iloilo at least once a month, and she never felt the desire to betray her own husband, even though she sometimes thought he was too boring. She never had been one to raise a hand to correct his son, whatever mistake he might have committed as a child or as a growing adolescent.

She only had questions, though. It was not her habit to ask for favors in exchange for her prayers. Part of her had once thought of asking Him to bring Jet home, but she had long understood that prayers never worked that way. Her own conversations with God would usually end with her still thanking Him for what she still had, for all that she hadn't lost yet. Despite everything, she trusted Him, and had always been grateful.

Though that never meant she thought she was answered. At the end of her silent lists of things to be grateful for were the echoes of her own questions. She was too drowned in them that afternoon that by the time she unclasped her hand and had gone back to her seat, her eyes were blurred with tears she had to pat herself with a handkerchief just to see anything clearly around.

Then she realized that the girl hadn't gone back to her seat. And the couple seemed not to mind, still—amazingly now to Sylvia—absorbed with each other, still murmuring to each other as the choir filled the church with the words for "Behold the Lamb."

The commentator went back up to the podium to announce there would be a second collection, and donations would be appreciated as these would be used for the rehabilitation of the church in the coming months. The projector screen where the lyrics of hymns and prayer responses were flashed during the Mass showed the floor plan and draft of the church's upcoming new design as what Sylvia would like to call the "Offertory ladies" began their rounds with their velveteen pouches on each pew. That was when she noticed the bald girl in a white dress walking along the aisle to the left. She strolled as if she was wandering in a mall, the people on the seats becoming objects of curiosity for her like items beyond glass doors.

The girl skipped about, a smile on her face as if delighted with what she was seeing, her head gleaming under the white lights from the high ceiling. She had stopped beside a man with thin gray hair, caressing the back of his head. The man didn't look at the girl but just touched his hair as if ruffled by the wind.

The girl walked over to a marble statue of the Virgin by a column in the middle of the aisle, and she tilted one of the winged angels' heads at the feet of Mary as if fixing it to a proper position.

Sylvia looked at the couple beside her and was dumbfounded that they seemed not to care about what she was seeing. It was as if neither of them saw, first, that the girl wasn't beside them, and that the girl was walking about as if the aisles were her playground.

By the time Sylvia gathered her resolve to silently confront the couple, her attention was brought back to the podium when a woman came up behind it after a solemn introduction by the commentator. The woman was holding a handkerchief close to her face. Behind her was a man who looked just as sad.

From her stance and the way she was dressed, Sylvia had surmised that they must be of the same age. The woman had on a shawl and khaki pants, hair trimmed short. The man behind her looked like any balding married man in his forties. Sylvia looked around to see if the girl would finally stop her prancing about and was surprised that she was nowhere now to be found.

"We'd like to thank you for your help," the woman said, her voice hoarse and tired. She sounded like she had wept for the past few days, and like she was still trying to stop herself from crying. The church plan on the screen had disappeared and in its place was a picture of a young girl in a jumpsuit and pigtails, smiling at the camera. The girl had a rosy flush on her cheeks, complementing the blurred backdrop of what looked like a playground. The woman said, "As some of you might have known, our little Angela had been diagnosed with chronic lymphocytic leukemia and had to undergo a series of chemotherapy. My husband and I had asked for your help, and we are blessed to be given enough to cover a part of the hospital bills. Though now we regret to inform you that almost a month ago, our dear Angelica went home to our Lord.

"It had been difficult for our family to face her loss. But we are standing now in front of you to thank everyone who offered their prayers and assistance to us…"

At that point, Sylvia willed herself not to hear the woman anymore. The woman was crying now as she spoke, her face turning red, dabbing her eyelids with the handkerchief. Behind her the man whom Sylvia supposed was the husband ran the back of his hand at the side of his own wet cheek.

Sylvia had been planning to stay and wait for the priest to give them his blessings, to light a candle and say a little more prayer. But it had been too much. The woman and the man in front.

Sylvia stood from the bench, leaving behind the young couple and the empty space between them. She stepped out the wide-opened church doors, almost sprinted down the marble steps, and it was all she could do to ram her palms on her ears just to block the voice of the weeping woman from the speakers.

The night was even colder now. As she made her way to where she had parked her car, she cursed herself for having failed to find a nearby parking space, for having to come at all. She could hear the muffled steps of her flats on the asphalt, and a night wind rustling the dark trees that stood at the roadside lots unoccupied by a house.

Suddenly, Sylvia felt the sensation that she was being followed. Her back felt weighed by someone's gaze. She stopped in her tracks and looked back at the path she had just crossed. The road was empty and the parked cars looked back at her with their dead headlights and black windshields. The few houses around were equally silent, lights on the windows seemed to have been toned down. Murmurings from the bright church she left were unintelligible at this distance.

She made for her car with a quickened pace, heart racing. Sylvia felt an odd mix of fear and sadness in her. How she had been reduced to this woman too confused to process another's suffering.

When she reached the car she eased herself in and leaned her head on the wheel. She could feel her heart beating, and for a moment she felt the urge to just pass out and let the morning find her that way. A crazy woman. A sad and crazy woman. She wanted to weep but she felt dry as an ancient well.

She lifted her head and gazed at the silent road beyond the hood. Thoughts of her husband came to her, like a pleasant memory. By now, Max would have washed himself already, perhaps had already cooked something for the two of them. He wouldn't ask about her day but that was fine, they knew each other well enough now to know what questions mattered. And what answers they were better off not knowing.

She had turned on the overhead light and Sylvia now could see her own clammy hands on the wheel. When she started the engine, she thought she heard the laugh of a child beside her. She stared at the shotgun seat, which of course was empty. When Jet was in middle grade, she had often glanced at him sitting on this seat before red lights when she drove him to and from the school. He had always been that smart and quiet kid who disliked conversations.

Sylvia sighed. She lifted her hand to fix the rearview mirror, and a cry escaped from her.

She had just moved the mirror with a slight tilt when Sylvia caught something in the reflection: the eyes of a bald girl sitting in the middle of the backseat.

Their gazes met through the mirror. In the split second that she moved to turn her head the thought that the seat might be empty, and that she was alone, crossed her mind.

But the girl was there. She still had that smile and crisp white dress with square pattern all across.

"Hi, there!" the girl said, beaming. Her little hands were clasped before her chest, the bald head still gleaming.

For a while she was frozen in her seat. Sylvia wondered if she forgot to lock the car, but was at once certain that she didn't leave it open. How then…

"How come you're here?" She asked, shaken.

"It's boring in there." The girl's hand pointed at something behind, and it took Sylvia some time to realize this was the church the kid was referring to.

Sylvia swallowed. "And you came here because…you're bored?"

"I don't know. There's too much crying and singing."

Sylvia turned back to the front of the car, leaning her head on the rest. She closed her eyes, gripped the wheel, felt the engine vibrating through it. She thought, *this isn't true*. This isn't true.

When she looked in the backseat, the girl was still there. A confused look in the child's eyes.

Sylvia then asked, her voice shaking, "What's your name?"

"Name?" the girl thought for a while. "I don't know. I just woke up in there today. I don't know what to do." She pointed again at the church.

That was when something clicked in Sylvia, like a puzzle she didn't know was there was suddenly being solved in front of her.

She turned off the engine. She thought of her son and wondered, as always, where he was. Although a part of her now had tired of wondering. She thought of her husband, and was sure that he would understand if she was a bit late tonight. He might have questions, perhaps the unasked ones would now be asked. Why bother now when back when all the things were good you didn't? What was in there you couldn't find somewhere else? She could answer them now, perhaps.

"Let's go back," she said without looking at the girl.

"Why?" the voice from the backseat asked.

"The Mass isn't finished yet."

Sylvia went out of the car and opened the door of the backseat to let the girl out. After making sure that all the doors were locked and all the lights were out, she took the bald child's hand beside her and was not surprised that the little fingers were freezing, as if they were dipped in a bowl of ice.

"I don't want to go back," the girl said, although the two of them were walking down the silent road.

"So do I," Sylvia said. She could hear the music from the church, and she couldn't help but notice how the clouds had cleared and had made way for the bright stars above the steeples. There was now a certain warmth in the lights that flooded from the opened doorway.

Holding the cold hands of the dead child, she let herself be engulfed by the warmth as they made their way up the steps.

PATRICIA MANUEL GO was born and raised in the Philippines by her British mother and Filipino father. She has an MA in Psychology from the Ateneo de Manila university which she credits with helping her remain reasonably sane, since she can usually find a way to explain why people behave the way they do. She started writing last year and this is her first published story.

GATED COMMUNITIES IN THE PHILIPPINES

Gated communities are usually referred to as villages in the Philippines. This can be confusing to people who live in the US and Europe where the word village conjures up images of rustic towns or lovely little hamlets. In the Philippines, villages are often guarded by an armed security force and can be annoyingly difficult to gain access to when visiting friends or dropping things off.

Makati has the largest number of the country's most expensive villages. Forbes Park, Dasmarinas, and Urdaneta are three that may sound familiar.

In the Ortigas and Greenhills area there are a lot as well. Wack-Wack, Corinthian Gardens, and several Greenhills villages from East to West. There are also a number on the other side of Ortigas, several incarnations of Valle Verde and Greenmeadows, to name a few.

Given the desirable locations of these villages and Metro Manila's traffic problem, stickers that give access to the villages and allow people to cut through them are in great demand and very expensive.

People have even been known to buy fake stickers and endure embarrassment, hefty fines, and maybe even jail time because of the fake documents.

10

PIG

I am worried about my pig.

He lives in our lanai and his name is Pompeo. His nickname is Pompy. He's not officially my pig—my brother Miko ordered him from teacuppiggies.com without telling anyone, and the next day there was a tiny black and white pot-bellied piglet in our living room. He was pretty scared and kept running around on his hoofs that look like high heels, but then he calmed down and it was like he'd always been here.

Miko has never fed him, taken him to the vet, or given a shit about him since he got here, so I took over and now he's mine. Pompy is still black and white, but the dude who sold him to my brother was definitely lying when he said he was a miniature. We watched him go from 18 pounds to 35 ... 67 ... 110. He's at least 165 pounds by now and he's not going to stop growing anytime soon. Which is kind of a problem.

See my dad, who pays for everything in this house and is NOT an animal lover, has no idea Pompy exists. Dad lives in our other house in the village across from this one on Ortigas Ave. He comes to visit us every day for about five minutes, ten max.

It hasn't been easy keeping Pompy a secret, that's for sure. It helps that my dad is the least spontaneous person I know. We always know when he's coming. Which is probably one reason my mom left him. That's why my brother and I live in this house by ourselves. Well, there are two helpers, a driver, and two houseboys so we're not really "by ourselves." But there's no adult supervision. Yaya Remy is supposed to be in charge, but she usually lets us do what we want, and now she can't even say "I will tell you to your mom," like she used to.

So when Dad says he's coming, we hide Pompy next to the dirty kitchen and turn the music up to cover any grunts. The other day we had a scare, because I left my phone upstairs and didn't hear Dad calling. I walked into the living room and almost choked on the protein shake I was drinking when I saw him sitting in his emperor chair.

He yelled at me in his usual fatherly manner, glaring at the piles of dirty clothes that hadn't made it to the laundry room, dumbbells, and other random stuff sitting on the opium bed in the middle of the living room.

"Putangina Jaime, this house is one big garbage can! How can you and your brother stand it here?! You're twenty years old na, when are you going to start acting like it?!" I kept my cool. I thanked St Anthony (patron saint of pigs) that Pompy was asleep near the pool, out of Dad's sight and not snoring, which he does sometimes.

"I know Dad—I'm sorry. When are you moving in with us? I know you'll fix everything up in no time." Whenever I need my Dad to leave ASAP all I have to do is bring up him moving in here.

Pompy stirred, got up, and headed slowly toward us. My heart was clanging like a gong in my chest, but my face showed nothing. Pompy stopped to smell the yellow flowers Yaya planted near the pool. A vein throbbed on the side of my dad's shiny head. Pompy began his trek again. He was three feet away. I remembered St. Anthony just in time, shut my eyes, and sent out an SOS. I opened my eyes. Pompy was in the lanai!!! Fuck!!! I prepared myself for the wrath of Jose Policarpio Martelino III.

But then…my dad suddenly did that thing where he looks at the ground while talking to me. "Jaime, I forgot I have a meeting with your Tito Boy in the Pen lobby. What time is it? Five?! Putangina I'm late na. I'll see you tomorrow." Dad got up and zoomed out just as Pompy plopped on the floor with an extra loud grunt.

When my mom left, my dad got us this house. So we could have a fresh start he said, and he would join us soon. But I think that was just a way to get rid of us without actually getting rid of us. Then he bought a Maserati a.k.a chick magnet which says it all.

Our fresh start is pretty stale, but I thought I'd keep a record of things anyway. Maybe no one will ever read it. Or maybe my mom will. You never know. I do know we can't keep this pig secret much longer.

Of course the dude responsible for this whole situation, Miko, doesn't give a shit. He just thought it would be cool to have a tiny black and white pig from Vietnam in our lanai. He doesn't care that Pompy is lonely.

When he was little, Pompy was best friends with Chimmy the stray cat we adopted. But now he's so big Chimmy doesn't like him anymore. I try to make up for it. I take him for walks sometimes, early in the morning (2 am early, not old people early) when there's no danger anyone will see him and squeal to my Dad. Yes, I see the irony in squeal. Whatever.

Miko and I have the same argument every month. "Why are you always making such a fucking big deal about everything Jimbo? So he goes to a farm—so what? If I'd known the fucker was going to grow like that, I never would have bought him in the first place."

Stupid asshole—and my name isn't Jimbo. He just wants me to have a nickname as lameass as his. Mom called him Miko instead of Marcelino, but always called me Jaime.

Anyway—about her leaving…I haven't ever talked to anyone about it before. It was May 18th, the day before her birthday. I still wonder why she chose that day.

My mom was kind of famous for being beautiful before she got married (I've seen magazines and stuff) and she still is the kind of person you stare at for a while when you first see her, until you realize what you're doing and look away. I've seen people do it a lot, it doesn't matter what gender they are. You'd think that someone who's been stared at and told how good looking she is all her life would be full of herself, but my mom isn't. She's so not full of herself that sometimes she's there and you don't even notice. She's quiet and still, like a beautiful ghost who doesn't want to be seen. Maybe because the way she looks has brought her more bad things than good, so she thinks it's better people don't see her at all.

My dad, who is ugly, is way full of himself. He fills up every room he's in, slams up against your face, doesn't give you a choice in the matter. He still doesn't understand that by never giving us a choice, he makes us choose the thing he's most afraid of.

I was sitting at my desk when she came into my room. She sat down on my bed and I knew she wanted to say something but she didn't, she just sat there. I saw that she had two photos in her hand.

"What are those Mom?" I was getting a weird vibe from her, it scared me a bit.

"I was going through the drawers in my bedside table and look what I found," she said with what I guess she thought was a smile, but was just her lips stretched as far as they would go. She held up a photo of me. I am about two in it, laughing, stuck on top of a table I had climbed up on with no clue how to get down. She'd told me the story before, how she had lost track of me in the house, had run to Yaya Remy and how they had both run in panic everywhere they could think of. Until she found me. Apparently my dad had just bought a new camera, which explains the photo. He'd been right behind her.

Probably yelling at everyone for losing me. No, definitely yelling at everyone.

"I should have known that I didn't need to worry," she said, shaking her head. "Even at two you were already a good boy. And so smart. That's why I know I can always count on you." She held up another photo. One of me and Miko. He's a baby, in a Mickey Mouse t-shirt and a diaper, sitting on my lap. He's holding onto me with one hand and his bottle with the other. I didn't realize why she was showing it to me then, but I do now. She stood up and gave me a big hug. And then she was gone.

We don't know where she is, but I do know my dad made sure she couldn't come near us after she left. He changed our phone numbers, got us this house, and made us get off social media. "Your mom doesn't want you na," he said—matter-of-factly. "Don't try to call her—it's stupid."

So anyway, not to change the subject too abruptly, but you may be wondering if I'm employed or if I spend all my time hiding my pig from my father. I do have a job actually. I work for my dad. I'm in charge of Business Development which means I don't do anything because we already have more orders than we can fill. So lame, I know, but once my dad decides you're going to do something then that's what happens. I remember the first time he told us his plan for our careers, right after he had told us which majors to choose.

"Jaime, you will finish Business Management at the Ateneo, then you'll come work for Martelino and Sons. Miko will join us when he graduates, two years later. He will take Chemistry so we can stay current with industry standards." He saw our faces and his round, semi-googly eyes narrowed. "What's wrong? The business your Lolo spent his whole life building is not good enough for you?! What's wrong with making cleanser and detergent? Everything you eat, drink, wear, drive, every trip abroad you've ever been on—are paid for by Kislap cleanser and So Bright detergent! So don't get all fancy with me, putangina!"

We looked at my mom who was right there, but she was in ghost mode. I don't know if she was even listening.

I tell myself it's ok, it helps with the whole Pompy situation because I know where my dad is on weekdays. I can text Jep or Jing and let them know when they need to take Pompy out back and turn on Spotify.

It's 2 am and time for our walk. Pompy is lying on his cushion but looks up as soon as I open the sliding door. "Hey buddy, ready to go?" I hold up his leash and he runs to me. His round piggy snout is a vacuum cleaner hose, always pulsing, like he's trying to suck the whole house into it. Pigs can't see very well but Pompy's sense of smell is two thousand times better than mine. Check Google if you don't believe me.

I bend down and put the leash around his neck. His coat feels like a giant hairbrush except the bristles are stuck into leather, not rubber. He nuzzles my arms while his skinny tail wags.

People say that pigs are as smart as dogs, but they're wrong. Pigs are smarter. They're the fourth smartest animal on the planet, after chimps, dolphins, and elephants. Pompy is way smarter than any dog we've ever had. And he smells better too. No offense to dog people.

We walk through the living room and out the front door, through the pedestrian gate. I say hello to Danny, our security guard. He's cool—he'd never tell.

Pompy is snuffling his way down the sidewalk, his tail wagging faster than I've ever seen, his butt wiggling in a way that's hard not to laugh at.

Pompy and I are on Duke St. We see a car driving toward us. Two girls are in front. They are staring. The one who isn't driving opens her window to stare some more. Fuck. It's Alicia. What the hell is she doing in my village at 2:05 in the morning?!

I think about her a lot so I wonder if I might be hallucinating. But she is real, and the look in her eyes as she shuts the window and tries to pretend she wasn't staring, is definitely not something I imagined.

Alicia was almost my girlfriend. She was supposed to come over and meet Mom on her birthday but you know what happened. I didn't know how to tell Alicia about it so I ghosted her. It felt like shit but I was already feeling like shit anyway. I just hate that she thinks I'm an asshole. Well, maybe I am. The car heads down the street. I think of running after it but that would be weird. And lame. I think of my mom. I guess I believed it when Dad said she left because she didn't want us. I think that was why I never even tried calling. Also, I was sure he'd changed her number. But what if he didn't?! She wasn't there anymore for him to grab her phone and rip out her SIM like he did ours.

My heart starts to pound and I tap out her number on my phone. 0917 775 7557. It's the only number I've ever memorized. Crap—wait, it's almost 2:30 am. I call anyway. She won't be angry no matter what time I call. At least I hope not.

"The number you dialed is not yet in service." Fuck— I guess we were on a family plan. So Dad could and did cancel her number. I am sadder than I can say. I also want to call back the Globe bot lady and tell her nobody dials anymore.

"What if I email?! I search my address book, type out two lines and send them to mlm@gmail.com. Mom are you ok? I miss you. Jaime

I know it's stupid but I check again after three minutes. Pompy is staring at me like he knows something is wrong. He punts my shins with his snout and grunts louder than usual. Maybe that's how pigs hug people, I don't know. I see a new email! I almost drop my phone, my hands are shaking.

Mailer Daemon is sorry that they were unable to deliver your message to mlm@gmail.com. Requested mail action aborted; mailbox not found.

Of course he had control of her email. He controlled everything he could about her. I am such a fucking dumbass. I look up at the sky and the place we all think we know about and say a prayer for her. I ask my Papi and Mima to pray for her too.

My Mom is an only child. I have no idea who might know where she is.

I'm glad she got away. Maybe I was mad before, but not now. She stayed as long as she could.

Pompy and I head back home. We've been out longer than usual and he looks a bit tired. I'm exhausted. I put him to bed and go upstairs. For once I fall asleep in a few minutes. And I dream.

In my dream Pompy is as big as an elephant but still a pig. His snout is elastic—it expands to as long as a trunk or as short as a snout. My dad comes in and starts shouting. Miko is standing there laughing like his sides will split open. Pompy is trembling. He nuzzles me with his trunk/snout and then lifts me off the ground and onto his back. He starts to run (he really is a fast runner IRL) and we bust out of the front door. We make it down the street and through the guardhouse. He heads toward EDSA.

I hear a roar behind us and I see my dad! Putangina! He's in his black Maserati and looks like Dr. Evil in his grey shirt, his bald head glinting in the sun. We detour onto Florida Street weaving in and out of cars while people gawk. Fuck— my dad is behind us again! I see the empty lot at the corner of EDSA and Ortigas and direct Pompy there. He sails over the gate like he's been doing it all his life. But instead of solid ground beneath us, we find ourselves falling into a giant hole. Pompy is too heavy to fly back up. We fall into blackness and crash.

I wake up, my shirt is drenched with sweat. I drag myself out of bed and run downstairs. Pompy is right where I left him, dozing peacefully. I lie on the floor next to him, my arm around his neck. "I'm not gonna let him get you buddy," I whisper into his ear. "We just need a plan." He gives me what looks like a smile and goes back to sleep.

I start looking online for somewhere to go with Pompy. By the beach hopefully—La Union maybe? Which car do I take? They're all in my dad's name. If I bring mine, he can say I stole it and have me arrested. He would totally do it too.

I need to buy a cheap one that won't break down. It has to be big enough for Pompy. Crap this is way more expensive than I thought it would be. It's ok though, I've got that dollar account my grandfather gave me for "emergencies" before he died last year. Thank you Lolo.

I take out $15,000 which gives me P739,250. I secretly open an account at Union Bank and get a new prepaid cell number. I feel like I'm in a DIY witness protection program. I measure Pompy from tip to tip and side to side. He is forty-eight inches long, thirty inches high and twenty-four inches wide. I can't afford a 4x4 on my budget so I settle for a Honda Jazz. I find a 2014 model for 380k. I have to drive all the way to Fairview (Farview)—it takes me two and a half hours and it's not even rush hour, WTF.

I close the deal, drive home, but park on a different street. I can't risk Miko catching me in my getaway car. Except that's exactly what happens. Fuck. I get out, lock the door, put the key in my pocket, look up and see him staring at me. I forgot his friend Pepeton lives on Northwestern. I am so screwed. I ignore him and start walking home. Of course he follows me.

"Jimbo! So, what's with the cool new car? Not!" He laughs like he's the funniest guy in the world. I keep walking. "Jimbo! What the fuck—answer me! Who the fuck do you think you are?!" I don't reply. This time he gets in front of me so I have to stop. "Jaime, what the fuck is wrong with you?!" Fine, he used my actual name, I'll answer.

"I can't tell you."

"What do you mean you can't tell me?" he says, making his annoying chimpanzee face with the fat lips and the teeth.

"I mean I don't want to and I'm not going to."

"Fine, you leave me no choice but to tell Dad."

"Miko trust me, you're going to be so happy when you find out the plan, but if you tell Dad now, you'll mess it up for yourself." He doesn't take the bait.

"I don't give a shit Jaime, tell me now or I'm calling Dad."

Fuck. I don't see any way out of it. "Ok fine. I am taking Pompy and we are moving somewhere far. Up in the mountains." I don't usually lie, but this is almost a matter of life and death.

His face kind of sags because his mouth drops open. Then it crumples up and the words just burst out of him. "You're just gonna take off and leave me?! What the fuck, Jaime! Pompy's not even your pig! I can have you arrested for that!"

I stare at him. This is so freaky and not what I was expecting.

"First Mom and now you?!

Crap, the last time I saw Miko cry was when someone broke the new PlayStation Mom gave him for his tenth birthday. He ran into his room and didn't come out for the rest of the party—even though Mom kept trying to get him to.

"Dude, I thought you'd be happy! You hate me! And you could care less about Pompy! You were going to send him to the farm, remember?!"

Miko drags the back of his hand across his eyes and sniffs. "I don't really hate you, stupid! I just pretend I do. And I like Pompy. I was just trying to piss you off about the farm. The only reason we even have him is because I wanted him, right? I can't believe you want to leave me with Dad! You know that's a fate worse than death! You're supposed to be a good person—Mom always said how good you were. Not me—she never said that to me. So no one cares about me because I'm not good. She doesn't care, you don't care. And we all know *he* doesn't care." He's sobbing now.

"Miko, I thought you'd like being an only child! It's not like we're friends or anything!"

"We don't have to be friends—we're brothers! You're the only other family I have! You don't get to just leave me with our fucking asshole dad, Jaime!" He starts to cry again. "I can't believe you would do that. I would never do that to you!"

I feel like I should touch him but it's so fucking awkward. I try to pat his head but he bats my arm away. "Don't touch me! Fuck you Jaime!"

"I'm sorry man, geez enough already!" I realize we have been yelling at each other all the way home and are now outside our gate. "C'mon, I said I was sorry. Let's go in the house and figure it out." He eyes me warily. "As in, I can come now? For real?" I think of Mom and the other photo and sigh. "Yes Miko. I would have asked you. I didn't think you'd want to."

"You thought I'd be ok staying because you think I'm like him. Why—because I look like him and you look like Mom?! Do you even know how much that sucks?! Of course not!" He pauses to catch his breath. "I know I've been an asshole to you. And Pompy. I'm not a full-fledged fucker yet but if you leave me with Dad I will be."

We go inside. Yaya Remy looks weirded out seeing us together. She comes to tell me dinner's ready and I ask her to call Miko. "Ano bang nakain ninyong dalawa?" she says. "Why Yaya, don't you want us to get along?" I ask innocently.

She raises her eyebrows. "You are doing something! You can't fool me!" She bangs the door on her way out. Poor Yaya. It's frustrating to know you're right and not be able to prove it.

Miko has already checked out tons of places to stay. He's always wanted to go to La Union but Dad never let him. I shake my head—there are other kids whose parents wouldn't let them do stuff or go places but they usually had a reason aside from "Because I pay for everything and I said so." Which reminds me that I've never asked Miko how he's been doing with school. I know he's smart but Chemistry is tough shit.

"Dude, I'm sorry I never asked but ... how are you doing at school?" Miko looks at me in shock. He is so unprepared for the question that all he can tell me is the truth. "I haven't been in school since last sem Jaime. Please don't tell Dad! Chemistry is some tough shit and I never even wanted to take it anyway!"

We stare at each other and start to laugh till our sides ache. "Well I guess that's one want ad that Don Poli will have to take out after all." I say to Miko. "Head Chemist wanted. Must be able to keep up with industry trends and always say yes to the Supreme Leader." I pause as I realize something. "Dude—if you'd never found out we were leaving and we'd gone without you, you would have been so screwed!"

"Oh yeah," Miko says, nodding. "I got hives just thinking about it after we got home. Here, look!" He shows me his arms. They are covered in red blotchy mounds, some of which are bleeding a little. "WTF Miko—don't scratch them!" He's such a dumbass. On another note, geez—I thought *my* anxiety was bad.

We look at what's for rent in La Union, but decide just to wing it when we get there. I don't think we can explain Pompy in an email but when people get to meet him, I know they'll see what a good pig he is.

We agree to leave on Sunday, two days from now, because that's Dad's day for coming late in the afternoon. I'm not sure how my dad is going to react but I think the fact that we "outsmarted" him, and that he can't have Martelino and Sons with no sons, will make him very mad. We should warn Yaya. He's never liked her because of who she was to Mom. Miko thinks it's risky but we owe it to her. Next to Mom, Yaya's loved us more than anyone else has. We agree to tell her tomorrow and then we go to bed.

Today is our last day. There's not much left to do. I'm a minimalist. I pack light. Miko on the other hand is kind of maarte. He whines when I tell him to only bring two pairs each of shoes and slippers and that he has to buy a prepaid SIM.

He is starting to piss me off and we haven't even left yet. We finish dinner and go into the kitchen. Yaya Remy is making puchero for lunch tomorrow. The kitchen is hot and she is perspiring under her blue uniform.

"Yaya come to the dining room please." She looks at me, intrigued and follows me into a room she has been in hundreds of times but has never sat in before. I pull out a chair for her—she sits awkwardly, close to the edge. I continue, "Yaya Rems, Miko and I can't stay here na. Pompy is so big we can't hide him anymore. So we are taking him somewhere far away. We won't tell you so you'll be safe." I stop for breath. "Yaya can you please leave also? You know Dad doesn't like you, matagal na siyang galit sa'yo."

We watch her take it all in. She stares at her hands which are folded in her lap and raises her eyes to meet ours. She nods, "Tama yan ginagawa ninyo. Your father is bad." I'm a little stunned at this and I know Miko is too. It's strange to hear it out loud. I almost want to defend him but there's nothing to say. She keeps talking. "I have money for you, may naipon ako."

I say no at the same exact second Miko asks how much. I kick him under the table.

"No Yaya! That's your money! We have enough. Right Miko?" I say, kicking him again. He glowers at me but says "Yes Yaya Rems, we have lots of money don't worry. I look at Yaya again, "Where will you go Ya?" I am ashamed. I don't know about her family at all. I think she's from Leyte but I'm not even sure. I've known her all my life and I hardly know anything about her.

Miko looks at her and says "Better if you go to Dondon, diba na sa Negros na siya ulit?" WTF. Who the heck is Dondon and why does Miko know anything about him? And why is Yaya from Negros and not Leyte? I can feel Miko's eyes on my face. I ask Yaya how she plans to get away. She agrees to take a cab to the pier with Glenda tomorrow and see what tickets are available. "And don't come back Yaya ok?!" I say anxiously. She speaks slowly, patiently. "No Jaime don't worry, I will never come back here! I just promised your mom to stay with you. Now I can go."

"Maybe you'll find her Yaya!" Miko and I say together without meaning to. "Jinx, you owe me a soda!" he yells as he bangs on the table. Yaya makes the sign of the cross and says "Awa ng Dios, that is what I pray. Every day."

I realize we may not see her for ages after we leave,

maybe ever. My throat feels funny. "Yaya, what was Mom like when she was our age?" I ask.

"Your Mom? She was funny. Always making us loko and telling jokes. She had many friends. The phones wouldn't stop ringing, always people calling for her."

Miko stares at her in shock. "Mom was? Then why the fuck did she marry Dad?!

Yaya's face gets very red. "Because he tricked her! Your Papi and Mima were so strict, it was hard to make your Mom ligaw. The others got tired. But he never stopped. So kind, always try to make her happy. Sending books every day because he knew she loved to read. Never get angry. Hayop, peke! He was just waiting. The day after the wedding, the real Poli came out! The one we always see!" She shook her head. "Your Mom could not understand. She thought she did something wrong to make him change." She looks at our faces and quickly says, "She was happy because she had you. But something inside her ... was broken."

We are quiet. I think of my dad and how we're so excited to leave him. I feel sad that we're happy. I turn to Miko. "Are you sure you're ok with this? We're going to be poor. If you stay, you'll get everything."

He laughs. "Fuck you Jaime, nice try, you're not getting rid of me that easy."

"Dude I just want to be sure you're making an informed decision! Don't blame me if you don't like how it turns out. And bring all your watches—I'm bringing mine. So we can sell them if we need to."

I keep turning from left to right like I'll never fall asleep but I do and now it's 5:30 am. I run downstairs and see Yaya coming in the living room with two big bags and the brown Louis Vuitton handbag Mom gave her for her 60th birthday. "O ano, sosyal ni Yaya diba?" she laughs, embarrassed. She gives me a serious look. "Where is your brother?" Crap, I should have gone to his room first! I run upstairs and barge into Miko's room. His doorknob is broken and he never got it fixed. It reeks of beer. I look under his bed and see ten bottles

of Red Horse. I shake him awake. I think I even slap him—
I'm so mad. "You fucking stupid selfish dumbass! I'm not
going to let you mess this up for Pompy! What the fuck were
you thinking?!"

He stares at me for one second and then closes his eyes
and falls back on the bed. "I couldn't help it, Pepeton came
over and wanted to drink." I get up and shake him again.
"Pucha Miko, did you tell him anything?!"He groans and
covers his head with a pillow. "Of course not, stupid! Why
would I do that?!"

"You'd better not be lying. And if you aren't
downstairs in fifteen minutes, I'm leaving you! I don't care if
Dad kills you because you flunked! You won't know where I'm
going because I can go anywhere!" I turn and see Yaya. "It's
ok Jaime, ako na bahala."

I walk to Northwestern St. and get the Jazz. Glenda
and I use up a whole bag of snacks to get Pompy into the trunk.
He looks so comfy lying on his cushion, his head on a travel
pillow. Shit, I was supposed to take Yaya to Shoppesville to
get a cab! I run upstairs. Miko is sitting on his bed looking
almost human. I glare at him. "We are almost an hour late and
it's your fault! And now I can't bring Yaya to get her cab!"

"Dude, chillax. Mang Tirso hasn't gone home yet. He
can take her straight to the pier." I ignore him. Yaya and
Glenda bring the bags downstairs and put them in the car. We
hug Yaya, say bye to Glenda and the boys and start the car.
We've moved two houses down when I see a black Maserati
turn on to our street. WTF is he doing here?! Fuck, fuck, fuck!
Miko and I duck as I turn off the engine.

I call Yaya. "Dumating si Daddy! Get your bags!" In
her hurry she leaves the phone on and we hear her and Glenda
shouting. "Putangina—nandyan si Sir!" We've never heard
Yaya swear before and we can't help laughing.

A minute goes by and we hear my Dad. "Remy! Where
are sila Jaime?"

"Sleeping Sir!" Yaya says. Pompy suddenly lets out a
super loud grunt.

We hear my dad—"Putangina! Is that a pig?!"

Crap! I forgot we were on speaker! I turn off the phone and away we go. Miko and I laugh till we're out of breath all the way to EDSA. "Putangina! Is that a pig?!" We've said it at least twenty times and it's still really funny. I pick up my phone to check on Yaya and see a message from Dad sent at 6 am. WTH?! "Jaime, my GCs for the breakfast buffet in Circles are expiring already. I'll pick you and Miko up at 6:45." Crap— here I was yelling at Miko and I'm the one who nearly fucked us up. Which reminds me to block Dad's number. I tell Miko to do it too.

Twenty minutes later Yaya texts. "Glenda and I will go already to the pier. I told your Dad you didn't wake up yet. He got mad and left already. You boys please text me when you arrived. Yaya loves you."

Pompy is behaving really well. We're making good time. He's going to need a pit stop soon though. We're on the NLEX. Waze says La Union is three hours away.

Miko takes out his phone with the prepaid SIM and makes a new IG account. "I'm not gonna post anything! This is strictly for research." I roll my eyes but he keeps talking. "I'm only following public accounts and checking out stuff in the rest of the north. You know, for when we get bored in La Union." He's happily trawling through his feed then suddenly stops. "WTF—Jaime, pull over now!" The color has drained from his face. He hands me his phone.

I see a photo of a woman. She doesn't know her photo has been taken. She's standing in front of a shelf holding a book she has just taken down from it. She is beautiful, the kind of woman that people stare at when they first see her, the kind that people take photos of without asking, like the camera is an extension of their eyes that don't want to look away.

The name of the bookstore is on the feed. The Pink Cloud Bookshop, Baguio City.

I look at Miko and he nods his answer to the question I didn't have to ask. It's a couple more hours in the car for

Pompy, but we can stop along the way. I guess we're going to the mountains after all.

MIGS BRAVO DUTT is a writer and researcher who has published work in several countries, regions, and cultures. She is the author of the contemporary novel, *The Rosales House*, from Penguin Random House SEA and has published several essays, including one in the Washington Post. She has contributed poetry and short fiction to anthologies and journals in Asia, Europe and the USA. Migs has co-edited *Get Lucky: An Anthology of Philippine and Singapore Writings* and its sequel *Get Luckier*.

HOUSE BLESSING

In the Philippines one does not fully move into a new house unless a priest has blessed it. This common tradition is meant to ward off any negative spirits. During the ceremony the priest leads the homeowners and their guests in a ritual of prayers. Then the priest visits every room in the house and blesses it with holy water. The participants follow him around, holding a candle to bring in light to the new house. After the blessing, homeowners often scatter coins as a symbol of prosperity. Other rituals include bringing in a pot of rice, a jar of salt, and a pitcher of water with rose petals. Some families also choose an auspicious date, like those ending in eight, for the move-in. The homeowners and guests then conclude the ceremony with a feast in celebration of this milestone.

11

BECOMING VICTORIA

I had been waiting by the white cane chair on the porch while Mama was inside the house fitting bed covers for Señora Cordova when the swing door opened. I caught a glimpse of the Cordova's drawing room and even saw Emma in a ballerina costume, gliding from one end of the room to the other. Two other girls in similar outfits followed suit. A piano sat next to the wall, and above it, a large landscape painting of a red brickhouse surrounded by a field of sunflowers. A huge sofa and plush armchairs were arranged neatly around a coffee table that had a vase of purple orchids. The Cordova's house was the grandest house I had ever seen. Or at least partly seen in that sliver of time. I wished the door had stayed open longer than the four times it swung back and forth, when a helper in uniform had rushed in, before it shut firmly again.

On Sundays at the church, I would watch the Cordova family on their way to the front pews, with Emma somewhat bemused but without looking at anyone in particular. She typically dressed in stylish clothes similar to those worn by popular celebrities. And like a celebrity, Emma seemed to not have repeated the same outfit ever. Five years earlier at an

Easter Sunday tableau, Emma had been selected as the angel who announced Christ's resurrection. She had been an unforgettable vision standing on top of a makeshift tower in her flowing white gown. Last year Emma also stood out as the Reyna Elena at the Flores de Mayo parade featuring 'beauties' from the town's most prominent families. I watched from the sidelines with other onlookers who suddenly shushed each other when the biggest four-poster arch, decorated with pink and white roses, emerged at the tail-end of the parade. Four young men wearing barong Tagalog, off-white embroidered formal shirts, carried the arch. In the center, Emma marched gracefully in a regal gown embellished with buds and petals made from delicate fabric. The other 'queens' in the parade had been stunning on their own but when Emma appeared, they simply faded to the background. I mentally called these occasions 'Emma's public appearances.' She had several of them each year.

*

I lay in the dark on my narrow bed with a mosquito net shrouded over me like a veil. I was wondering what it was like to be Emma, always dressed in lovely fashion and living in luxury, when I heard my door open. "Are you off to sleep, Toyang?" Mama asked from the doorway.

"Yes, Mama. I've finished all my homework. Ma, how come I don't see Emma Cordova anymore?"

"Maybe she's in Manila. I also haven't seen Señora Cordova for some time now. They could be together."

"Do they also have a house in Manila?"

"I heard they do. Señora once complained about how lax security guards were at their gated community. Why the sudden interest about Emma, though?"

"I walked past their house today and I've been wondering since what the rest of the house looks like. I only had a brief glimpse from their porch while waiting for you that one afternoon."

"It's grand, like the houses of rich people in the movies," Mama said. "Anyway, go to sleep, Toyang. The

Cordovas live in another universe whereas ours is here, our feet on the ground, even if this lot is no longer our own. But one day, who knows, you could redeem it and make it ours again," Mama kissed my forehead before leaving.

A shaft of light slipped through the gap under my door, but even that disappeared as Mama switched off the living room light and the sound of her footsteps soon receded into their room. It wasn't that late but none of our neighbors had a TV and though they had radios, they turned them on only for morning news and weather advisories. This extreme quietness in the dark brought back my anxieties. What if I couldn't move up to high school? Or maybe I could but would have to settle for the rural high school? Students there worked in the fields, rain or shine, and hardly stayed in the classroom to learn basic literacy. I wondered about Emma again. She probably didn't need to worry about a single thing in her life. She simply sat prettily.

*

A few years ago the National Tobacco Administration manager had tried to recruit Papa to their new tobacco program, upon Señor Cordova's instruction. Papa had rejected the initial proposal, but Señor Cordova met him personally and ultimately convinced him to change from the reliable corn crop to a new variety of tobacco that could triple harvest. Señor Cordova's company and the NTA would provide everything from training, seedlings, fertilizers and other support. At harvest time they would then buy the tobacco leaves from the farmers at a 'preferential rate'. He also promised Papa a commission if he could form and lead a team of farmers. He just needed help with recruitment to kickstart the program and it would be smooth sailing from there. Papa left his regular job as messenger at the municipal office to focus on this.

The first few harvests were successful and we celebrated each season with a trip to the city to buy new implements, kitchenware, and new clothes. After shopping, Papa would treat us to a cold refreshment, halo-halo topped with ube ice cream at a popular snack parlor. But we enjoyed only two or three seasons like that. Soon seedlings and fertilizers arrived late. Prices of tobacco started to drop and its popularity faded. I thought this was due to either flooding or drought, but apparently farmers incurred far more losses than expected. I also read from an old newspaper, used to wrap dried fish from the market, that the government had signed an agreement that was supposed to address the tobacco problem. But the paper was torn apart so I couldn't read the rest of the article.

In time Papa lost his team of farmers to yellow corn leaders and was left with unpaid loans. "How come we still owe NTA that much when they took all our harvests in the past two or three seasons?" Mama asked once again.

"I also don't understand, Flora. They said it was because of the seedlings and fertilizers, including for seasons lost to either El Niño or La Niña. They said they're not a charity."

"I wish we hadn't gone into this contract with them."

"I shouldn't have listened to Cordova. His proposal had sounded too good to be true even from the outset. I should have trusted my gut and not given in to his sales talk."

Papa and Mama bickered more often these days and once Papa even blamed Mama for her connection to Señor Cordova. I had yet to learn the nature of this connection aside from Mama's sewing the Cordova's bedsheets and curtains.

*

I had since passed the entrance test for a highly selective program at Valleviejo National High School in Santiago City. I should be excited about this but then I'd have to pay higher miscellaneous fees and need greater daily allowance. "Toyang, why don't you just attend the rural school here, that way we don't have to worry about your daily fare," Mama suggested at dinner.

"But Ma, I've qualified to the science section of VNHS. Mrs. Cruz said I'm extremely lucky to have gotten in and that I'm the only one in San Mateo who made it." I had jumped with joy when my homeroom adviser had happily shared that news to me a few weeks before. But now I couldn't finish my dinner. I put my spoon down.

"We shouldn't throw this rare opportunity away," Papa nodded in my direction.

"I know, Ben, but we both don't have permanent jobs. How can we manage with our measly and unstable income?"

"I will talk to Agnes. She once promised to pay for Toyang's tuition."

"But Agnes will again say that she has yet to hear any good news from us and that every time we write, it's to ask for some help or another. And I can't blame her. Even if she's your sister, one can get tired of giving, you know."

"Did Tita Agnes really say that?" I was surprised. I remembered Tita Agnes as generous.

"Your Tita must have said it jokingly. But, as you know, your Mama is too proud and wouldn't ask for help even when it's necessary, as in this case," Papa shook his head.

Papa eventually wrote to Tita Agnes who now lived in America. Every night, I said an extra prayer for Tita Agnes to be more generous so that I could also buy new school supplies. High school students carried more books and I badly needed a new backpack as my old bag was already tattered from three years of heavy use. Every morning I woke up with high hopes, eagerly waiting for the postman. Every afternoon I ended up disappointed.

I'd been holding my breath for nearly a month now. Then this morning a motorbike stopped at our gate. I ran to meet the postman who handed me a long white envelope. It had the VNHS logo. I showed it to Mama. It was a notice for the last day of enrolment that also sounded like a warning. If I didn't enroll in the next two weeks, the school would cancel my place and award it to someone else in the long waitlist. Papa read the letter as soon as he arrived. "I'll go to Santiago tomorrow and will place an overseas call to Agnes," he said. I nodded though I doubted that the much-needed help could still make it.

I couldn't sleep however hard I tried. In the dark I put my palms together and prayed fervently until I could feel tears pooling at the corners of my eyes. I blew my nose as quietly as possible. I wiped off tears with the sleeves of my shirt and resolved to attend the rural high school if I had to. Their enrolment period ran until the end of May. I still had time.

*

Papa slumped into the nearest chair when he arrived from Santiago. "I did my best, Toyang. I begged Agnes like never before, but she's in a tight situation."

"I hope it's nothing serious?" Mama stopped pedalling on her sewing machine.

"She didn't tell me the details."

"But what happened to her earlier promise?" I asked as I handed Papa a glass of water. How could Tita Agnes take something back so easily?

"She wanted to help but a check paid to her bounced or something. Let's wait for a few more days." Papa skipped dinner and went to bed early, which he rarely did in the past.

Mama came over and lifted my chin while I was clearing the table. "Toyang, it's not the end of the world. You still have the rural high as fallback."

"I know, Ma." Though I'd come to accept this fate last night, it still pained me to think that all my earlier efforts were wasted. "But after graduating valedictorian at SMCS, this is so unfair. And to think I was the only one from the entire San Mateo school district who qualified."

"I can borrow money from people I know. But that would only get us through the enrolment. We'd face the same problem every day for the fare and other expenses."

"I'll check if I could do some work at the library. I could earn extra money."

"I don't think that's allowed, anak, because you're only thirteen. Toyang, if it means so much to you, I'll borrow money from the Cordovas." Mama held my hands now.

"But Ma, you know how much Papa hates that family. And don't we owe them and NTA still?"

"The farm account is a different matter. I could ask for advance payment for future sewing commissions."

"Aren't they in Manila?"

"I still see Señor's car around. I'll talk to him."

"Ma, I don't want you to do that knowing Papa hates them. I'd rather attend the rural school than owe them more favor." My voice was breaking by then.

Mama opened her mouth, but pursed it again. She hugged me tight. Things would be better in the morning, she said.

*

"I told you not to be anywhere near that family ever again," Papa's voice rang clear from the kitchen.

"Nothing happened, I couldn't borrow anyway," Mama replied. They were preparing dinner while I was waiting for them by the living room window.

"What did they say this time?"

"They weren't at home."

"Oh well, that's a good excuse. They could be hiding in their rooms to avoid beggars like us. Some people really do that and I wouldn't be surprised if the Cordovas resorted to it too."

"No, it's not like that. The helpers said that Señor Cordova followed his family to Manila. They haven't heard from him since. In fact they're worried because they'll be running out of food soon."

"That's his problem then," Papa emerged from the kitchen holding a bowl of vegetable soup, Mama trailed him with a plate of rice.

Mama looked dejected while Papa tried to cheer us. "It's a blessing in disguise that the Cordovas are out because any help from them carried unfair conditions," he said.

*

I just wanted to stay under my blanket all day, but we had to be at the rural high school before nine o'clock this morning. I heard a motorbike and so I rushed out from my room. Papa had already stepped out to meet the postman and returned just a few minutes later, holding a notice from a remittance company. "Toyang, it's from your Tita Agnes." Both Mama and I were by his side instantly. "This should be enough for the first month at least. We can worry about the rest later."

*

We reached VNHS just a day before the enrolment deadline. We filled out the form and paid the minimum amount for miscellaneous fees under the instalment scheme. "We made it, Toyang," Papa could smile genuinely now.

"Thanks Papa. I know you'd swallowed your pride again, asking for Tita Agnes' help like that. Someday this begging will come to an end."

"I have no doubts about that," he squeezed my hand.

"Toyang, let's ask if there's any grant that you could apply for," Mama reminded me.

We approached one of the counsellors after the orientation. She signed an orange stub and told me to bring it to the Students Welfare across the hall. The receptionist gave us a two-paged form. As I filled it out, I realized that the provincial government awarded a monthly stipend to deserving low-income students. But first we must get a local government official to attest that I was indeed an indigent. The assistant at the counter also gave me a blue card that provided a twenty five percent discount on food and beverage at the cafeteria. I shot a glance at Mama who seemed relieved for the first time since the last three months or so.

*

Before I started high school I visited Bong, my grade school classmate, who lived in the farther side of our village. I took the longer route past the Cordova's block, which had a smaller gate from this side. The wrought iron gate was padlocked. A white notice board beside it had a *For Sale* sign with a telephone number that buyers could call. I peeked through the gaps in the fence, but I couldn't see any movements inside the yard. I checked once more to be sure. The scenery remained the same. Only tall grasses swayed now and then. A barn and a small house, likely the staff's quarter, blocked the main house from view. I looked at the sign once more before returning to the road, walking more briskly in my eagerness to break the news to Bong.

"Oi Toyang, what a surprise. I didn't expect to see you," Bong waved from their narrow bamboo gate. "Come." He led the way along a patched-up cobblestone path. I left my slippers by the door and could feel the rough cement under my feet as we entered the dimly-lit living room.

"Good afternoon, Auntie Tasing," I greeted Bong's mother who was in the kitchen.

"Kamusta, Toyang?" Tasing wiped her hands and drew the striped pink and blue straw curtain fully open. "I'm sad that you and Bong won't be classmates anymore," she said standing by the kitchen doorway.

"I know, Auntie. I'm going to miss Bong on weekdays."

"I wish Bong could also go to VNHS. But we can only afford rural school."

"We also couldn't afford on our own. Tita Agnes is helping us."

"You're blessed to have kind relatives. Anyway, I must get back to my cooking."

"Bongga, do you know that Emma Cordova's house is up for sale," I asked as soon as Bong's mother was out of earshot. We moved to a bench by a window that looked out to a dirt road.

"You came all the way to share this not-so-recent news?" Bong pretended to roll his eyes. "That sign has been there for a few weeks now."

"I didn't know. I was busy with the entrance exam. Why is it for sale? Or maybe I shouldn't wonder. It's common sense. Why would one choose San Mateo over Manila, right?"

"In case you've forgotten, I've never been to Manila. One day I'll see it for myself." He shifted on his seat and crossed his legs almost primly. "So, are you excited about your new school?"

"I'm more anxious than excited. I'm not sure how those city kids will react to me, small-towner that I am."

*

At Valleviejo National High School my classmates hardly paid me any attention. I became less anxious when this dawned on me. I should have realized sooner that to them I was a nonentity, not even worthy of being judged. This reception soon made sense as I had nothing much in common with them. While female students wore uniform white sailor-cut blouse paired with a blue pleated skirt, my classmates found ways to be distinct either through trendy shoes, funky accessories, or cool backpacks. I owned none of these. Though VNHS was a public school, Mrs. Cruz said that doctors, lawyers, and other influential parents now enrolled their children to its science section. At the orientation, a teacher had told us that each year, thousands of sixth graders across the province took the test, but the school selected only a handful. The science group was an elite class of thirty students taught only by the best teachers from the large school district. Admission to this group had become a huge pride or even a status symbol for families. Parents spent considerably on private tuition to prepare their children for admission.

I found a welcoming classmate in Stella, another 'out-of-towner', but this one wore shoes and accessories even finer than those by the so-called 'cool' crowd. The group could smell this and attempted to recruit Stella to their clique, but she preferred her independence. And to my surprise, my company. Lunchtime became an oasis in the middle of the day when we could talk and laugh freely. We became Ella and Toyang, best lunch buddies.

*

In the first few weeks at school I'd been mostly quiet because my teachers and classmates seemed to be speaking in a foreign language, even during our English and Literature classes. I wasn't aware of the books and topics they discussed. Ella came to the rescue. She took me to the library and led me to a section that had all the references. "How did you know

146

about all this?" I was surprised that she seemed to have read all the books by Austen, Dickens, Twain and other authors.

"I have them at home," she said as though it was the most normal thing in this world. She pulled out *Great Expectations.* "Read this, it's my favorite."

I spent late nights and weekends catching up with what my classmates had already read earlier. Even in algebra, the concepts were all new to me while my classmates reacted as though they were as basic as MDAS. I'd sought the help of Mrs. Cruz and every Saturday afternoon since, I had been solving Math exercises in her living room until I levelled up to my classmates.

I took a break from schoolwork to visit Bong. Once again I checked the Cordova's property along the way. A new *Private Property* sign was now painted on the fence. I couldn't wait to tell Bong so I practically ran the remaining distance to his place. "How's school?" We hadn't met in weeks because of my sessions with Mrs. Cruz.

"As you can see, my skin is darker than ever." He stretched his arms to show the lines above his elbows. "We spent more time cutting grasses than studying in the classroom. We hardly have reading time," he shook his head.

"It's just a few more years. Soon we'll be out of high school."

"Which is going to be tougher because we definitely can't afford college."

"I'm sure we'll find a way. We have time."

"It's the story of our lives. Bahala na si Batman," Bong moaned exaggeratedly.

"Can we talk about something else? Do you know who bought Emma's house?"

"I heard it's a family from San Antonio."

"San Antonio? What's their family name?"

"How does it matter?"

"My friend, Stella, happens to be from there. San Antonio is a small town, too, like ours so it's likely that she's heard of the new owner."

*

"Ella, I heard that someone from your town has just bought this grand house in San Mateo," I asked Ella at lunch.

"Is that the one formerly owned by a tobacco company manager?"

"Yes, that's the one."

"As it happens my uncle now owns the property."

"Seriously. Wow, your uncle must be super rich." My jaw simply dropped.

"They own gasoline stations," she said in an attempt to explain the source of their wealth.

"You're so modest. You didn't tell me that you come from a wealthy clan."

"We're just the poor relations. My uncle's family is the affluent one."

"Still, you are related to someone that rich. Have you been to their new house?"

"No, not yet. But I'll definitely be there for the housewarming."

*

A few weeks later Ella came rushing to tell me that I was invited to her uncle's housewarming. When the day arrived I donned on the belted maxi dress that Mama made for me from a floral fabric that my grandmother had sent in her last care package. It looked formal enough, befitting the occasion. I checked my reflection again and suddenly felt conscious. I wasn't used to new clothes anymore. I took out our biggest umbrella to avoid being noticed by my neighbors who could be nosy at times. Holding the umbrella low to cover my face, I walked briskly to the Cordova's block. I almost retreated when I reached the entrance, but several people were behind me and I didn't want to attract their attention by suddenly turning around. I took a deep breath, absent-mindedly crossing the fingers of my free hand. I recognized the mayor's car and some congressmen-plated SUV along the driveway. The van of San Mateo's parish priest was also parked along with dozens of other cars. A second wave of anxiety hit me and I hesitated about ascending the stairs, suddenly overwhelmed by the thought of meeting influential people. But before I could run, Ella came out of the swinging door. "Toyang, the blessing is about to start," she led me into the Cordova's house—in my mind, it was still the Cordova's house.

Smartly dressed and perfumed people greeted each other with hugs and air kisses. Some of the faces, like that of the mayor's and his family, were familiar, but obviously the reverse could never be true as none of them knew my family at all, socially anyway—they might know my parents as registered voters from Precinct 117A. I moved past the crowd somewhat awkwardly that I almost bumped into two elderly ladies. One opened her fan wide to cover her lips as she whispered to the other. I heard her mention 'Cordova'. The second lady stopped in her tracks, her eyes widening. "He could go to jail, you know. Swindling like that," she replied in a low voice, but still loud enough that a few heads turned to their direction. They kept quiet after that.

I carefully stepped to the side and looked around the house. The walls and windows had been repainted and the interior had changed vastly; the piano and the large landscape painting above it were no longer there. The décors were now oriental and the furniture characteristic of the local designs. I moved closer to Ella who pointed to an unassuming couple, her uncle and auntie, leading the guests. They soon gave a tour of the house, stopping at each room as the priest blessed it with holy water. I saw the master and three other bedrooms for the first time. I imagined one of them to be Emma's and how it might have been painted pink and had an elaborate dresser on one side and a shelf for her doll collections on the other. But now the three rooms had identical beds and nightstands, and devoid of personal touches. The twin beds were covered in embroidered white spreads. Only the color of fitted sheets and pillowcases made the rooms distinct from each other—blue in one, yellow in another, and pink in the last room.

Ella and I stayed back and looked out to a small pocket garden. "Such a lovely view. Who will get this room?"

"It's a guest room. Uncle Andy and Auntie Julie don't have children," Ella said.

"But this house is so huge for just two people."

"That's what they do. Buy a house and when they get bored of it, they buy another one." Ella turned to re-join the other guests.

"Your aunt is so different from Señora Cordova."

"In what way?"

"For one, your aunt isn't wearing any jewelry."

"It's funny that you say that. One time customers mistook her for a gas station aide because she dressed so simply."

"I thought rich people must always wear fabulous designer clothes and dazzling jewelry."

"Not my aunt. She's far too busy to worry about those things. In fact she claims to be allergic to jewelry."

"Wow." I made the hats-off sign. "Do you happen to know why Señor Cordova sold this house to them?"

"I never asked. I've heard whispers though."

"Like what kind?" I turned to face Ella fully now, not wanting to miss any of her words.

"They said the previous owner, your Señor Cordova, committed 'stuff', but they never elaborated what sort of stuff."

*

"Ma, I've finally seen the rooms." I pulled a stool and sat beside Mama.

"I made a pale pink curtain for Emma's room back then," Mama paused from her sewing.

"That's exactly what I'd thought while in one of the rooms. Did you make any of her dresses?"

"No. I only did fabric covers, fitted sheets and drapes. Señora Cordova used to go to a famous couturier in Santiago for their dresses."

"But why did they sell their house?"

"I don't know the entire story. Someone said that Señora Cordova is unwell and must stay in Manila for treatment." Mama glanced at the wall clock. "Toyang, after changing into your housedress, please wash the dishes. I have to finish these pillowcases for Mrs. Cruz."

"Okay, Ma. Let me just check on something first." I pulled out a tattered Spanish-English dictionary from a small bookshelf. Earlier at the party the lady with the fan had whispered the word "stafa". I thumbed through words that started with the letter S, but I didn't find what I was searching for. Then it occurred to me that there could be a vowel, perhaps an 'e' or an 'I', before it. I turned the pages to letter 'e'. Then I found the word. "What? No way." I read the translation and its meaning carefully.

"What is it, Toyang?" Mama looked up.

"Oh sorry, Ma. It's nothing. I'm just checking the meaning of new words I've just picked up," I returned the dictionary into the shelf and went to my room. I sat on my bed still shocked by what I had heard and read. I couldn't wait to tell Ella that it was *estafa* that Señor Cordova had committed. And that he could go to jail for swindling his company. "What about Emma? What will happen to her?" I absent-mindedly voiced my thoughts. I got up reluctantly and changed into my housedress. I straightened my new maxi dress, patting away any dust or dirt before hanging it back in my closet. I could wear it once more before washing.

I decided to tell Mama what I'd heard. She didn't seem surprised. "Indeed that's the talk of the town. Señor Cordova is going to be tried in court. And yes, he could be imprisoned for what he did," Mama looked sadder for some reason. "Anyway Toyang, you shouldn't concern yourself with those things," she said before turning to her sewing machine.

In the kitchen my hands became busy with the motions of cleaning, soaping, and rinsing the dishes, but my mind kept on wandering back to Emma's earlier public appearances. It dawned on me that they were, merely that, appearances. Suddenly I felt cheated. Emma and Señora Cordova were delusional and they had projected their delusions so well that I had believed, and at one point even yearned for, that illusion.

I couldn't help but compare Señora Cordova to Ella's aunt, Julie. What a huge contrast. Auntie Julie who owned several gas stations hardly displayed her wealth. I rinsed the soapsuds off the last glass in the sink and placed it on a tray for drying. I wiped my hands on a dishtowel, a patchwork that Mama had sewn together from fabric swatches. I heaved a big sigh, less because my dishwashing was over, but more because characters like Emma and the Cordova family were no longer part of San Mateo's ongoing narrative. I was glad that Auntie Julie had taken their place and could now add a better turn to our town's story.

IAN ROSALES CASOCOT teaches literature, creative writing, and film at Silliman University in Dumaguete City, Philippines where he was Founding Coordinator of the Edilberto and Edith Tiempo Creative Writing Center. He is the author of several books, including the fiction collections *Don't Tell Anyone, Bamboo Girls, Heartbreak & Magic*, and *Beautiful Accidents*. In 2008, his novel *Sugar Land* was longlisted in the Man Asian Literary Prize. He was Writer-in-Residence for the International Writers Program of the University of Iowa in 2010.

COMING OF AGE IN THE 1990S
When I was writing "The Rubber Duckie Confessions," I knew full well that this was my first time to mine my memories of growing up and coming of age in the 1990s—and I wanted very much to reflect the landscape of that time, informed very much by the popular culture we were shaped by, hence the specificity of movies and power rock ballads. But I also knew that I wanted to touch on two very specific things many teenagers, then and now, are concerned with: the volatile fluidity of friendships and the awkward grappling with body issues.

12

THE RUBBER DUCKIE CONFESSIONS

In memory of Jacqueline Piñero-Torres, high school best friend

Lately, in that brief limbo of evening time between dinner and homework, in the solitary sanctity of my bedroom, door locked, curtains drawn, with only the night light on, I've been listening to power rock ballads again.

Sans headphones—just the way I like it.

I make sure the volume of the cassette player is always turned up high, but not too high to attract Mother's show of passive aggression. The track's on constant rewind, the naked reverb of the music bouncing off the bedroom walls and enveloping me where I lay in bed, in paroxysms of pure emotion. It is the bittersweet bliss of being understood, as only music can:

> *In my life, there's been heartache and pain*
> *I don't know if I can face it again*
> *Can't stop now, I've traveled so far*
> *To change this lonely life…*

There is nothing foreign about Foreigner, I swear. This is intimacy, something like ESP.

At fifteen, a shave closer to sixteen, I'm allowed to think that nothing else matters in this moment in the world, except music that *gets me* perfectly.

You must understand: I have unanswered questions. I have impressionistic feelings that roller coaster. And I know only that whatever it is that plagues me at the moment syncs somehow with this plea:

> *I wanna know what love is,*
> *I want you to show to me...*
> *I wanna feel what love is,*
> *I know you can show me...*

My lips curl deliciously to the words and music, my body a vessel of whatever spirit exists in the song—and the world is lost to me in that instant. And for many instances, and for many evenings, I have my serenade parade of REO Speedwagon ("Can't Fight This Feeling"), Journey ("Don't Stop Believin'"), Phil Collins ("Against All Odds").

But it isn't really *love* that I really wanted to know, although in a way it kinda is. Love—the way I see it in the movies or read in books—feels too much like an abstract thing that happens to *other* people.

But heartache I do know. Also pain. Also loneliness.

Especially loneliness.

You see, it has been eight days since my friends—my beloved barkada—last spoke to me. I could feel their avoidance of me like it was the Great Wall of China: from up in space, astronauts could probably see the outlines of my hurt and bewilderment.

What have I done to deserve this? For answers, I could only get their awkward silence, their averted eyes, their quickened steps in the corridors as I trailed behind them from period to period, from classroom to classroom. My school days are long.

My evening commiserations set to music, however, are short.

"Antonio Christian Sanchez," someone soon intones. This is Mother outside my door, her voice frightfully even— and loud enough to conquer Bonnie Tyler singing "Total Eclipse of the Heart" to submission. Mother is an overworked college professor currently in the purgatory of teaching freshman composition and saddled with the task of raising six boys of varying degrees of temperament. As a result, Mother can be scary as shit.

She'd be scarier if she didn't vent what frustrations she had into her gardening. (Needless to say, our house is a jungle, with potted plants everywhere—and the garden outside teems with immaculately considered vegetation that the word "hobby" *is* an understatement.)

Mother does not knock to signify her presence—we just know she's there like a poltergeist waiting to pounce. "Antonio Christian Sanchez," she repeats my full name again, which is code for irritation. (I can hear my brothers snickering in their rooms, the bastards.) "I'm sure your nightly journey through these frivolous songs mean something to you," she says. "But don't mind me. They're not a disturbance at all. I'm sure these essays I have to grade can take care of themselves."

Then she goes away. Chastened and guilty, I allow the last refrain of the evening's chosen power ballad to fade away to 8:45 PM silence.

I weep inside and think: *No one understands.*

*

I never understood the quickness of my world turning as it did that Monday morning eight days ago, shortly before the flag ceremony. One minute, I was getting down the tricycle at the school gate in an immense hurry to get to the morning formation in order not to be marked "tardy" and ruin my homeroom grade, and the next minute I could feel the sting of my excited "Hello!" to my friends—Gerard, Leah, Wendy, and Monica—being returned with two distinct things:

(a)   a deliberate silence, which could cut you; and

(b)   backs being turned to me, signaling indifference.

It burned, a void in my guts opened, and I knew instantly what was up.

I was confused. Didn't we just enjoy a weekend together, having watched the new flick *Pretty Woman* at Park Theater, which immediately led to all of us descending merrily on Pelrico Record Bar along Real Street to buy a cassette of the film's soundtrack? (At least Wendy, anyway. She alone among us had the generous allowance to burn. And she didn't buy a cassette; she bought a *CD*. I checked my envy.) Later, at Wendy's apartment on Luke Wright Street, we whiled away the Saturday afternoon listening to Roxette singing "It Must Have Been Love" on endless repeat. We swooned to the music.

By the fourth repeat of the song, we knew the lyrics by heart. By the sixth, I was performing it with gusto in front of my friends, mimicking every nuance. I sang like there was no tomorrow, my mouth wide open for that full emotional belting to rival Marie Fredriksson:

> *It must have been love*
> *But it's over now,*
> *It must have been good*
> *But I lost it somehow...*

Oh, indeed I have lost it, in retrospect, and it was so clearly over now.

*

What happened between Saturday and that terrible Monday is lost to me. I remember all of us bidding each other a long, chatty goodbye at Wendy's—and then it was Sunday, Mother's one day in the week where she was a barking general, reminding us of the requisite importance of church-going. What could have led so suddenly to the silent treatment

Monday brought? Did they have a clandestine meeting on the Lord's day to decide on banishing me from the group forever?

When Tuesday came, my still hopeful smiles returned nothing from them.

By Wednesday I learned to no longer say hello, accepting the cold silence towards me—even as they gabbed animatedly among themselves—as purgatory I had to endure.

I was getting paranoid, and from the fringes I collected what morsel of conversation I could to explain why I was suddenly an outcast. I combed for clues. I heard them talk about new movies they were excited to watch together. About new songs they loved from Wilson Philips and Bon Jovi. About whether they had copied Jacqueline's math homework. No clue at all. They talked about Rheina's new Econo motorcycle, and Wendell's nonexistent girlfriend, and the latest gadget trend among the privileged young: *walkie-talkies.*

They all had new, expensive walkie-talkies, and apparently every night for the past week they'd been radioing each other late into the night, delighting in this instance of a new communication device. They even had a word for it: *kit-kit*, as in "Let's kit-kit later tonight!"

Mother would find walkie-talkies and kit-kit frivolous.

Which means I was never in on any new gadget trend. Ever.

By Thursday, I learned to be inconspicuous. Or I tried to anyway. Because occasionally, I'd spy them looking at me with cruel intentions and giggle.

Then I heard them say this:

"Rubber duckie!"

Rubber duckie?

Were they calling me a rubber duckie?

I wept inside, the cruelty of the world more than I could bear.

I know the world can be cruel, and that this cruelty can be infuriatingly random, and that often it is a fight that's fought in the solitary. Mr. Mister says so in "Broken Wings":

Fight the fight alone
When the world is full of victims
Dims a fading light
In our souls ...

Once I heard Mother—in a rare instance I attributed to an incredibly long work day, a lean paycheck, my brother Matt being beastly about his JS prom suit (he was insisting on a tailored three-piece ensemble you could get at Gaisano Metro in Cebu), and grading three sections worth of new "compare and contrast" essays—commiserate to me: "You young people have the mercy of cobras. You are capable of such intolerable cruelties." (This is how she talks to me, really. She's a fatal combination: an English major and a big drama queen.)

But I suppose Mother is right. When I was in first year, cruelty was a classmate named Karen Villarin, a petite girl given to fashionable jewelry who was also our batch's undisputed No. 1 in the honors roll. She carried this distinction around like royalty, expecting the rest of us to kowtow—and when we didn't, she unleashed fury in the subtlest ways, like a ninja assassin. So when I gained the highest grade in English in our class—*helllooooooo*, my mother is an English teacher, and I've been voraciously reading all the classics since the third grade—Karen took that as an affront, and accused me of being Miss Torres's "pet." I rolled my eyes then. But later in class, when she casually said in a singsong, "Feed the children of Negros"—evoking the tagline of a national campaign from a few years ago (was it 1985?) to combat child malnutrition in our province—she looked straight at me with a barely-there amused look. I smoldered in quiet anger, and shame.

I've always been so painfully thin—"wangkig nga mapalid sa hangin"—and when I really think about it, my skeletal frame has been a festering source of deeply felt embarrassments. I've learned various coping mechanisms that got me through the day. And I learned even more ways to cope after Karen's "malnourished" remark directed at me.

But I also learned to become body conscious. The mirror became a witness to an increasingly long list of physical shortcomings I had. The occasional breakout of acne. The slightly bulbous nose (but only very slightly). The weird discoloration of skin you could mistake for sideburns.

And the uni-brow.

Near the end of freshman school year, I finally noticed said uni-brow on my face. The male models in the issues of *GQ* I've been devouring had no uni-brows. One night, arming myself with Mother's tweezers—which she was using for armpit maintenance—I plucked the unwanted follicles of hair straddling the area between my eyes, and soon marveled at the new look of having two distinct eyebrows!

Come early the next morning in school, while milling about in the corridors waiting for the flag ceremony to start, I saw Karen dragging Leah and Wendy by their hands and snaking her way towards me, gabbing to the two girls excitedly.

What is she up to? I thought.

And when they were finally in front of me, I heard Karen tell Leah and Wendy in a fit of giggly certainty: "This is *what* I was talking about, this is what I *mean*. This, girls, is a uni—"

Karen pointed to the spot on my face where my uni-brow used to be.

When she turned to look at the point of her demonstration, I could see her face change shade—from certain, unashamed giddiness to one of sudden confusion. She looked at me. And it finally dawned on my soul what she was up to.

I grinned.

Karen backed away, dragging Leah and Wendy along with her.

*

It wasn't the last time Karen was cruel to me. It was the first time, however, that I keenly felt what could be done to fight cruelty. But what divine intervention happened though that made me pluck my eyebrows *the night before* she could unleash her cobra intentions?

I have no idea.

But now it isn't just Karen that vexes me. I feel abandoned by friends—and there seems to be no divine intervention this time around. Is this cruelty, this collective silent treatment?

The more vexing question is this: what did I do to deserve it? Was I cruel to someone in my barkada without my knowing it, and this is my punishment? My questions find no receptacles—*talk to my mother? forget it*—and my only comfort is the nightly power ballads belting out answers. Eurythmics, for example, promises hopefulness:

> *And we were feeling very small*
> *Underneath the universe.*
> *And you know that I'm gonna be the one*
> *Who'll be there when you need*
> *Someone to depend upon,*
> *When tomorrow comes...*

I weep at a universe without answers, without tomorrows.

*

But what is a "rubber duckie"?

It is a toy duck—yellow and empty and squawks when squeezed—that you can find floating in a bathtub, decorative and entertaining, with no use at all in the actual act of bathing. I know this for sure.

During recess at the canteen, I've taken to Jacqueline as my constant companion, both of us having a go at our favorite snacks of pandesal asado, and sitting far enough from my former friends to give me breathing space.

I like Jacqueline. She is way smarter than Karen, is the sharpest in math class in fact—but she is inexplicably ranked No. 2 in our batch. She is a voracious reader like me—and soon became my main source to borrow the latest *Sweet Valley*

High book, and anything else of that confection. (This includes *The Nancy Drew Case Files* and Christopher Pike horror novels and the occasional Enid Blyton.) One time, I made her read Katherine Neville's *The Eight*, which I loved—and soon she became my source for the latest Neville novels as well. She is also kind, and good-natured about the way we often tease her about being a klutz—she is always tripping over something, which does not dissuade her at all from walking faster than the rest of us seemingly for a destination only she can see.

"But why are they not talking to you?" Jacqueline says between bites of her pandesal asado.

"That's just it, I don't know."

"Even Gerard, Ton?"

"Even Gerard."

"But you've been best friends since grade school."

"Well, yes—and no. We weren't grade school classmates, but I know him since before because of Sunday school."

"In church?"

"Yep."

"Like Bible stories and stuff?"

"Like Bible stories and stuff."

"Isn't it un-Christian to unfriend an old friend? Unfriend. Is that a word?"

"Unfriend? I don't think so," I say, gobbling the last of my pandesal asado, and knowing what to ask Jacqueline next. "By the way, you know what a rubber duckie is?"

"It's a toy duck, for bath time."

I hesitate. "What do you think it means?"

"Means?" Jacqueline scowls, looking at me like I am a puzzle. "It doesn't mean anything, Ton. It's a toy."

"I know, I know … But if it's a … a metaphor, what do you think it'd stand for?"

"Well … it's yellow."

"Usually yellow."

"Yellow means a coward, right? And it's empty …"

"Which means …?"

"Empty means it has no substance."

"And it squawks when you press it," I say, hiding the unease creeping in my voice.

"Which means ... It has no voice of its own, can only squawk when someone else is pressing it. And such an irritating sound, too. It's not even a duck's quack. It's like a shrill horn," Jacqueline says.

I sigh.

"But I like rubber duckies though," she says. "I know because I remember watching Ernie."

"Ernie?"

"Ernie, from *Sesame Street*. Don't you remember the song? The rubber duckie song?"

"There is a rubber duckie song?"

Jacqueline laughs and nods excitedly, and clearing her throat, sang in a low register to escape notice from everyone else in the canteen:

> *Rubber duckie, you're the one*
> *You make bath time lots of fun.*
> *Rubber duckie, I'm awfully fond of you*
> *Rubber duckie, joy of joys*
> *When I squeeze you, you make noise.*
> *Rubber duckie, you're my very best friend, it's true ...*

"Anyway," she finishes, giggling. "It's about friendship. Rubber duckies can mean friendship, friendship that brings joy." She smiles. "And don't make me sing more, Ton. You know I have a terrible singing voice."

"You do have a *terrible* singing voice," I say, and we both laugh.

We laugh and laugh, at everything and nothing—a silly, private joke between friends we scarcely knew could be a wellspring for endless, nonsensical mirth.

Laughter, even silly laughter, is a sound better than weeping. But it does not keep my paranoia a bay.

*

Days pass, and then still more days—and one soon learns that no one actually dies of heartbreak. Not to say the pain of losing friends vanishes—but somehow I've learned to consider the persistent dull aching that pain becomes as a symptom for wanting to live. And as a reminder that we should treasure, more and more, the idea of connection.

Mother, who could see through me like an x-ray, looked up from her lecture notes one breakfast time, took my hands with such contemplative care, and before I could say anything, she blurted out: "Antonio, you know, of course, that the very fragility of things like friendship actually reminds us to be careful, and to always be on the side of nurture."

I panicked. "What do you mean?"

Mother sighed. "I know what's going on with you."

I was silent.

Did my nightly power ballads reveal too much? Did one of my bastardly brothers squeal?

"It's best if you think of things in this particular way...," she continued. "All the things we love are living things. Be nurturing."

See what I mean that Mother can be scary as shit?

But I suppose she's right.

And after a while, I did get used to the new dynamics of things.

The silence no longer intruded like a bull I had to be wary about. In the school corridors, I learned to pass by my former friends as if we were ships in the night, still afloat but bound for different destinations. In "I Won't Hold You Back," Totò gives me a similar reminder:

> *Now you're gone, I'm really not the same,*
> *I guess I held myself to blame.*
> *Time can erase the things we said,*
> *But it gives me time to realize that you're the one who's sad...*

But the song also continues with this:

Now that I'm alone it gives me time
To think about the years that you were mine.
Time can erase the love we shared,
But it gives me time to realize just how much you cared…

The evenings of power ballads still have their purpose, I suppose. For entertainment mostly, and no longer on nightly repeats. And because Jacqueline and Eliel and Rosewell and Niña—new friends who have come to be possessive of my room as headquarters of sorts—find the songs incredibly on the nose, wearing their sentiments on their sleeves without restraint, their heightened melodies ripe for emotive lip syncing. "They can be a bit much," my friends tell me.

*

It is Gerard from my old barkada who breaks the silence first, and Jacqueline who brings him in one Saturday afternoon in my house. "Guess who I brought over," Jacqueline says cheerfully.

Gerard and I look at each other, and my bedroom suddenly feels small. "You guys talk," Jacqueline says. "I'll help your mom make some snacks, Ton." She quickly disappears.

Silence is awkward.

"Is that Foreigner you're playing?" Gerard begins.

"Yes."

"I miss your room."

I don't say anything. I wait for him to say something.

"I'm sorry, Ton," Gerard finally says, after a long beat. "You must be mad, with us not talking to you at all. It was all so silly at first. You know how we talk to each other every night via radio, right?"

"I don't have a walkie talkie."

"Right, right …" Gerard nods, and then: "Well, anyway, you were the only one in the group not in our kit-kit circle, and you know what happens when one of us is not there. Some of us began talking about you."

Really now.

"What did you guys say about me?"

"That when you get excited when you sing, or talk, you … spray."

"Spray?"

"You spray when you get excited."

It soon dawns on me what it means. "Oh," I say.

Gerard continues: "And so one of us said over the radio, 'What if we don't talk to him for one day, so we don't get sprayed on.' We laughed. It was meant as a joke, a prank. And then one day became two. And then three. And you know what happened next. It just tumbled out of control. I'm sorry, Ton. It was all so silly."

It is all so silly.

But I am remembering my uni-brow again. And my occasional acne. And my slightly bulbous nose. And my weird skin discoloration. And my thin frame. And now this: apparently I "spray" when I talk and get excited. I feel the shame of all my shortcomings bubble up from inside me—and I burst into tears.

"I'm so sorry, Ton," Gerard says.

I cry harder, and Gerard lets me—and I feel a twinge of gratefulness for that.

All the things we love are fragile, living things.

When my tears subside just enough, I ask Gerard: "And rubber duckie? What did you guys mean when you called me a rubber duckie?"

"A rubber duckie?"

"Yes, I heard that. You called me a rubber duckie."

A beat.

"I don't remember us calling you a rubber duckie."

"You did. I heard you."

In my paranoid scrambling for answers, I heard you.

"Ton," Gerard says, "a rubber duckie is what you call the antenna on a walkie talkie."

"Oh."

And then another one from me: "Ohhhhh …"

It was like a switch turning on in my head.

And then somehow I find myself beginning to laugh at my old paranoia.

And after a while, I laugh even harder—*the silliness of it all.*

And soon Gerard begins laughing, too.

It is an infectious sound that begets more laughter, roaring far above the power laments of Foreigner on my stereo. And when Jacqueline comes back bearing snacks, she starts laughing as well, never mind that she has no idea what it is we are laughing about.

We all laugh. It does not take much to realize laughter can be a ballad, if you let it ring, and is the most powerful of them all.

JAMES M. FAJARITO grew up in Gloria town of Mindoro Island, Philippines. He works as Associate Professor at the Communication and Languages Department of Holy Angel University, Angeles City, Pampanga. He finished a PhD in Literature from the Philippine Normal University. His poems, essays, and stories were featured in Philippine publications, including *The Philippines Graphic, Sunday Times Magazine, Ani, Philippine Panorama, Liwayway, Health & Home, Philippine Daily Inquirer, The Philippine Star,* and *Manila Bulletin.* A poem of his was included in *Sustaining the Archipelago: An Anthology of Philippine Ecopoetry.* He lives in Angeles City with his wife and child.

THE PHILIPPINES AND CATHOLICISM

In a country of 109 million, where about 8 of every 10 individuals are Catholic, religion is very much a part of the people's way of life. Introduced by the Spanish colonizers who ruled the archipelago for more than 300 years (1565-1898), Catholicism is evident in religious festivals, colonial-era edifices, private schools run by religious orders, and in the values of the people. Catholic priests serve not just in the Philippines, a good number of them can also be found spreading the good news, so to speak, in foreign territories. Typically, aspiring Catholic priests begin their journey to priesthood as college students taking up Philosophy. To many fresh seminarians, being away from home to study and live in a cloistered institution could pose innumerable challenges, homesickness being just one of them.

13

THE GOAT

We called him the Goat. When we uttered the word to refer to him, it was with derision and contempt. We hated him more than we hated our holier-than-thou schoolmates. But *they* were another story. Between them and the Goat, they were saints. We could have found meaning in this world even with their presence. But with the Goat, there would have been no meaning at all. Hell, none!

"We," of course, referred to my classmates and me, twenty-eight freshmen seminarians collectively known as the Unity Class of Saint Ernest Seminary. A bunch of provincianos from across many Luzon provinces, we were wide-eyed on our first month in that seminary located in the heart of the metropolis. Though many of us had vague ideas why we had chosen the path of priesthood over other beaten tracks, we had vaguer ideas of the treatment we would get from our Filipino Language professor, whom every old-timer seminarian knew as the Goat.

We freshmen seminarians were housed in the Sacrificial Lamb Building, the oldest edifice in the seminary that featured structures ranging from medieval-looking to pretentiously modern. The three-storey building clustered offices and classrooms on the first floor, classrooms, study halls and clinics in the second level, and dormitory rooms for seminarians and priests in the third. Thus, we found it too convenient to come to our classes from our third floor rooms.

Days before our first session with Fermin Uban (a.k.a. the Goat), we received a subtle warning from upperclassmen. The only problem was that, back in the day, we had no inkling of the concept known as "subtle."

It was over lunch when an upperclassman named Candido opened up a conversation topic—the Goat.

"Brace yourselves for a year of Saturday torture, guys," he warned his freshmen seatmates in the dining table. "The Goat is the type who doesn't take 'no' for an answer."

We didn't really believe the swagger of Candido, for we couldn't accept that a professor of a minor subject as easy as Filipino Language would even pose any challenge. But *that* was our undoing. Our own pride would lead to our fall, or something like that.

The Goat's manner of arrival on the first day was exactly how it had been described days ago by Candido. A stainless owner-type jeep stuffed with borloloys and reflector stickers parked itself nonchalantly just outside our classroom. Though the vehicle was screaming for attention, the driver was not. He was a fortyish man of average height with a paunch. The only distinguishing mark on his face was his goatee.

"Must be the Goat," a classmate whispered to me.

To some upperclassmen's disappointment, four uneventful Saturdays passed by, and our discussions with the Goat were, at best, hum-drum. Routine attendance-checking. Routine lectures. Routine assignments. Even his constant reminder that on weekdays he was a full-time teacher at some famous school became routine. Surprisingly, his sanitized version of claim-to-fame eventually turned into routine: that he had joined the longest funeral this country had ever witnessed—with a snapshot to boot! He would always shove to us the coffee-table book about the fall of the dictator: one snapshot of the longest funeral caught him atop a vehicle with a raised clenched fist. A classmate remarked once that the Goat didn't look like an anti-Marcos activist in the picture, but actually resembled a man too furious because he couldn't drive his pathetic, attention-seeking jeep into the sea of people.

But the jarring illusion of a routine awarded us with a false sense of complacency and comfort, with a tinge of smug self-confidence. The carefree subculture dulled us that we never saw the arrogance of the Goat coming.

It was a boring July Saturday morning of lecture about the significance of communication when, out of the blue, the Goat posed a question so silly but just enough to galvanize the class: "Do animals communicate using languages?"

Instantly, the class became animated, an observer could have surmised the professor had inquired if Marcos was a hero. The question polarized the class—the half insisting that animals had their own language, while the other arguing animals couldn't possibly utilize language. It was a heated debate, triggered perhaps by our restlessness for some form of action. I, for one, was uncharacteristically animated, even stressing my lungs out that Ernie Baron, a popular media personality, always believed in the "language of monkeys." But none beat the boldness of Rodolfo, a flamboyant classmate, who stood up unceremoniously and raised his voice on his untenable belief in the language of animals—moments *after* the Goat had categorically declared that language was exclusively a human trait. Rodolfo's boldness received loud cheers, which were the last that could be heard from that Filipino Language class. For the Goat spoke—with authority—the final words: "Animals have no language, and those who believe otherwise are free to withdraw this subject!"

It was the lowest point of our first semester at Saint Ernest. If at all, we learned humility, tact and clarifying the definition of a term before impulsively jumping into a fight. But I never knew things could get any lower, for when I saw my grade in the subject at the end of the semester, I was disheartened I got only 83. I thought I deserved way better than 83. To add insult to injury, my seatmate who had never recited even once for the entire semester received 84.

That the Goat harbored a grudge against half the class was apparent all-semester long. That he would strike back by handing out unfair grades was really unexpected, at least for us freshmen seminarians. We really thought he had no place in the seminary. But we were too afraid to rock the boat, so to speak. So we were resigned to accept our fate to be yes-men in the Goat's class until March, the end of the semester for the second and last Filipino Language subject.

I decided to be a more diligent student, but a yes-man, nonetheless. I hated his subject, but I had no choice but to follow the whims of the Goat. Interestingly, I topped our quizzes and exams, giving me the faint hope that my grades for the second semester in Filipino would be definitely higher than 83.

But as the saying went, life happened while I was busy making plans. A chicken pox outbreak hit the seminary, and a two-minute hurried conversation with a convalescing seminarian was enough for me to receive the unfortunate baton to be the next chicken pox victim.

The morning I felt unwell and saw small red dots in my hands, I knew I would spend the next drudging two weeks in the infirmary. I innocently prayed three Hail Mary's to every red dot in my body, but I later realized that sudden religiosity didn't translate to sudden miracles.

It was late February, the worst time to sport chicken pox marks in the body, with the academic requirements fighting out for attention of a diligent student's time. I was afraid of losing a slot in the Dean's List. But I was more afraid of getting another 83, or lower, from the Goat.

Our infirmary was a six-meter-by-five-meter room in the Sacrificial Lamb Building's second floor. Each patient was allotted a cot, even as our population swelled to fifteen. Chicken pox patients like me had nothing to do for two weeks except eat, stare at the ceiling, sleep, wash ourselves, and listen to FM radio. The constant promotion of a Rick Astley song made me memorize the lyrics of "Cry For Help." As the days wore on, I was getting sick of the song, especially that I noticed that we patients were getting disinterested to take care of our looks, which, because of facial hair, ridiculously resembled the appearance of goats.

Francisco, our class president, was sympathetic of our plight that he spoke for us with the concerned professors. As a result, we were required to write reaction papers, reflection papers, position papers, and other papers our teachers could conjure. It was fine by me, as long as my grades would not experience any nosedive. I began writing them as soon as I became capable. But the Goat didn't give out any requirements. When he was asked by our president, the Goat responded with a blank stare. Which made me extremely worried: did he want a new book, reflection sticker for his jeep, or something better?

My two classmate-patients had an idea, however pragmatic. They held a brainstorming session between the two of them on how to pass the Filipino subject without the Goat specifying any requirement in lieu of our absences and the Final Test. I overheard them conversing during the second week of our confinement.

"My uncle said there are really, really good reflection stickers in Banawe," said Maximo, the most pious in our class. "Do you think the Goat will like it?"

"Probably not," Simplicio responded, the thinner of the two. "Every inch of his jeep is tattooed with stickers. Brand-new pocketbooks from Cubao might do the trick. Remember: our previous project was an individual review of a new romance pocketbook, and the pocketbook had to be submitted to him—without any scratch and without expecting to be returned."

They tried to sell me their idea, which I meekly refused. I was too principled—and broke—to buy my grade from the Goat.

What I did was I studied for the examination like crazy, with the help of Francisco who had tipped me off about the exam's scope. Meanwhile, Maximo and Simplicio pushed through their plan: to be sure, they purchased reflection stickers from Banawe *and* romance pocketbooks from Cubao. However, we were not allowed to meet the Goat come examination day. He was too afraid to catch the disease and had relayed strict orders that we did not see him. Thus, we expected to receive Incomplete (INC) grades.

The following Saturday, days after my return to normalcy, word got out that the Goat had arrived supposedly to submit grades to the Dean's Office. I zoomed from the third floor dormitory to the ground floor, hoping to inquire how I could have my grade converted from INC to something better (preferably higher than 83). Fellow seminarians who saw me immediately gave way, one could imagine I was Moses effortlessly parting the Red Sea. Either they were still afraid to get chicken pox, or I was running too fast to endanger one's safety.

But the Goat had just left, the Dean's secretary informed me. (She was not afraid of me, having suffered from chicken pox in her teens.) Cognizant of my situation, she took the list from a brown envelope, and peeked at a bond paper. Her face suddenly lit up, smiling when she said, "Wow! You have a grade here. 97!"

I was so surprised and delighted. Still skeptical, I asked to see the list myself, and there it was, my name with a glowing 97 printed across it. I thanked the secretary profusely and left the office in cloud nine.

The word immediately spread. I got the highest grade in the subject without taking the Final Test *and* submitting other requirements. Most of my classmates, including some schoolmates, were happy for me, seeing vindication in the grade.

"You should thank the Goat," Francisco suggested. "He sympathized with you."

I thought about the comment and decided that the Goat was not worthy of *any* expression of thanksgiving. I ought to have received a grade higher than 83 the previous semester.

His recent awarding of a high grade was only a belated payment for the injustice of the past.

As for Maximo and Simplicio, they received final grades, all right. But they were barely passing grades, which I reckoned they deserved, considering their sub-par classroom performances. I didn't ask what they had done to the reflection stickers and romance pocketbooks. I wasn't sure how they felt about their grades. What I was sure of was that my latest grade would go down in the annals of Saint Ernest Seminary's history as just another dubious entry in the checkered career of Fermin Uban, Filipino Language professor, grudgingly known in the seminary as the Goat.

ANGELO R. LACUESTA has won three National Book Awards, the Madrigal Gonzalez Best First Book Award, the NVM Gonzalez Award, and numerous Palanca Awards and *Philippines Graphic* Awards. He has written several books of fiction and non-fiction, as well as a number of films. He is Editor-at-Large at *Esquire Philippines*, Senior Editor at *Panorama: the Journal of Intelligent Travel* and a Member of the Board of the Philippine Centre of International PEN.

YAYA OR WET NURSES
The yaya is a wet nurse hired to take care of a baby in a mid-to-upper class Filipino home. The yaya basically becomes the surrogate mom since she takes care of the child's needs, from eating, bathing, potty-training, and so on. Oftentimes, the yaya sleeps in the child's room so if the child should wake up, she can take care of him or her. Sometimes the yaya continues her service even when the child is no longer very young. As the following story "Nilda" illustrates, sometimes middle-upper class Filipino boys experience their sexual awakening with their yayas.

14

NILDA

My first kiss, it was full of tongue. It felt like a sliver of flesh from a stony green mango, one of many I plucked that summer from my perch on the lowest branch of the tree in our front yard.

My yaya Nilda stripped the skin off with a rusty old peeler and made deep parallel cuts with a knife, the blade making clean, bloodless wounds in the whitish flesh. She sat me down in the kitchen in the warm afternoon, my mouth wet, my hair and body hot and smelling of the sun. She handed me the knife, and I sliced close to the seed, with what force I could muster, so that in one labored, uneven stroke the slivers came away and apart, falling like white fingers into the palm of my brown hand. In three round bowls she prepared three kinds of dippings: rock salt, sugar in dark soy sauce, and red-brown bagoong. I dipped and brought the slivers to my mouth, tasting the sharpness of crystal, the sweet and salty mush, the briny mulch against the mango sliver, hard rind and tender flesh meeting teeth and tongue, making the inner cheek swell and pucker with pleasure.

During the kiss, we were sitting wet by the pool. She tasted my mouth with hers and pressed herself against me and I smelled the surge of pool chlorine, coming off clean and sharp from her skin. She slipped the straps of her bathing suit off and her shoulders were like white wings. I looked down and saw her breasts, small and pale, in front of me, and then pressed against my body.

It was the 80s and I was thirteen. My father was an attorney who worked for the government. He was tall, thin and handsome, but he was also tense and hunched, like he was listening for a signal or poised to make his next move. He had small alert eyes and wore his lips in a constant curl, like he was about to make a quick comment or a hard order.

The dark suit was his trademark. I suppose he liked the way he looked in it, bigger and meaner, with the shoulder pads becoming his shoulders, the dark, shiny shell his skin and flesh. To cover his large ears, he styled his hair in a big bouffant. Moroy told me large ears meant a long life. From their size and the way they stuck out you'd think my father would live forever. To complete the look he wore a blank expression on his face that was so impenetrable it scared both acquaintances and strangers. But what really made him scary was Moroy, who was always a step behind him, like a big solid shadow.

I liked Moroy. I was fascinated by the way he talked and the way he thought. He had a kind of thinking you could trace with a firm straight line. He was wide and solidly built, moonfaced and foul-mouthed, with squinted, slanted eyes and crooked teeth. Whenever he kidded me around, he turned his big body with startling quickness, reaching out with a fat hand to throw a fake jab or flick an ear.

Moroy's trademark was a small shallow crater on the back of his neck, the size and shape of an old ten-centavo coin and colored a dark, violent purple. I was sure it was from a bullet. Whenever I asked him about it he would promise me that one day he would tell me all that I needed to know.

It made sense to hire someone who knew what it felt like to take a bullet. But even then I knew it was foolish to have a bodyguard who was also your driver. Still, my father insisted on just having Moroy around as minder, chauffeur, errand-boy and right-hand man.

Moroy did enjoy driving our 1976 Mr. Slim, solid, swift and heavy, from its three-point chrome star, to its extended rear bumper. The engine started with a deep shudder as though it were shrugging off sleep, and its heavy, bulletproof body moved with a low roar.

Moroy told me about my father's hidden life, his secret schedule. Sometimes he would need Moroy to drive him to the airport for the next flight to Hong Kong or Jakarta for an overnight trip. Or he would be at a five-star hotel, drinking and talking with businessmen and ambassadors. Or the Floating Casino, coming out in the morning hours wearing that same snarl on his face. And when he sat in the car and told Moroy to head home, or to the next thing, he said nothing. There was no good news or bad news. There was only, Moroy supposed, the business of the day.

Whenever he had to go somewhere my father would call for Moroy from the garage. He would then pick up my small presence, perched in my mango tree, in the corner of his vision, and send me scurrying into his room to retrieve his clutch bag. I remember it, black, heavier than it looked, with an evasive smell that dared me to open it while he wasn't watching. There were papers, checkbooks, thick bundles of dollar bills and a gun.

My father wanted me to become a lawyer like him. He spoke to me about how much trouble he had gone through for me. I knew the way to make a kid serious was to warn him of the consequences. He told me if I didn't study I'd end up like Moroy, whose meager future depended solely on his master, and whose job, ultimately, was to be expendable.

Moroy handed his gun to me once. There was so much to touch, so much to feel. There were ridges, incisions, screw heads, crisscross patterns, pinholes, nipples. It smelled of oil and metal. My hand could not refuse its shape. I held it the only way it allowed, tightly embraced around the grip, pointer finger slipping into the trigger's hollow. I went further and aimed it at the sky and pulled the trigger; he had second-guessed me and it was empty, but the force felt so real. Something clicked and the gun vibrated with a tight metallic sound that startled even Nilda, who just glared at us. "One day," Moroy whispered, "you'll shoot a loaded gun, with real bullets."

Nilda's duty was to pay attention to me, to take notice of me, every inch, ever part, every blemish and scar, from the sunbaked hair she shampooed every day to the toenails she clipped every two weeks. She was fresh from the province, pale and very young, hired by my mother to replace the old woman who had been wet nurse, maid, and servant for several years.

I spent most of the summer climbing the mango trees at the edge of our front yard. They were tall and thick enough to spread over our concrete fence, and gave our house a dark, imposing presence.

But from my low branch, the light was gentle and I found I could feel the breezes that glanced off our small swimming pool in the middle of the terrace. As the day advanced I saw the tree's shadow grow longer on the grass and the dogs bark in relief, before everything quieted down toward the evening.

At dinnertime my father had Nilda fetch me from the tree, and I opened my arms to let the afternoon's bounty tumble into her outstretched skirt. In the twilight her legs looked very white, against the mango tree's dark bark and my own skinny brown legs.

Nilda had come from a province overgrown with mango trees. She taught me to climb our tree and pick its fruit. She taught me how to peel the mangoes and how to eat them. She taught me how to make the three sauces that made three different flavors. It was Nilda who tasted of the green mango we ate, both of us sitting by the pool in the sun and the heat. It was her tongue in my mouth during that long kiss. On that first hot day by the pool, she opened herself to me and her thighs held on to my small body. The sun beat on my head like a hammer, and as I grew hard I felt a headrush, as though the impossible length and girth of my manhood had dissipated me.

I couldn't move. Only my knees moved—they trembled uncontrollably. Moroy had demonstrated this movement to me by pumping a middle finger in a tightly rolled fist. "One day you'll do this!" he had told me, and when I stuck my own finger in my fist he laughed because I didn't get it. But once from my tree I saw two dogs turning around each other in what I had thought was a heat-crazed stupor as they struck and mounted, joints frozen as the male pumped into the female.

Nilda moved with me and around me. Moroy promised me I would feel like a man after my first time, but I felt I had been swallowed whole, a small boy with salty, sweating skin sliding into her opening. I had thought it would make me stronger, but I could predict nothing. The rush came, from nowhere and from everywhere. She was silent as she held me and only whispered, yes, as she guided me into her, dark and wet, smelling of the sun and the pool chlorine, like nothing else I had ever seen or felt.

*

Over lulls in my father's schedule, Moroy would drive me around aimlessly. We ventured through tight roads, into tough neighborhoods, their houses dark and cramped, their street corners and sidewalks packed with people. Moroy was a policeman once, and this had been his beat. He knew people wherever we went, the security guards at warehouse gates, the bums that hung out in front of gambling dens and sari-sari stores, the tough guys guarding the beer garden doors. Sometimes we got out of the car so he could buy cigarettes or gin, and when he walked he squared his shoulders and walked a little slower than usual. It was like a killer's walk. He enjoyed the moment. I tried to match his stride.

Though he was silent most of the time, I knew my father enough to know when he was worried about something. I knew enough about the times to understand that things were changing. Political tides were shifting, he said at the dinner table evening, to no one in particular. He had to learn to work with the system.

One night that week my father went out into the yard, in his pajamas, in the middle of the night, and fired his gun into the sky. The first shot woke me up. Through my window I saw his thin, hunched form snapping back with every shot. It looked like his body would break apart. The muzzle flash burst like tails of comets crashing into earth. I ran into his room and saw my mother crying, her face in her pillow. The clutch bag lay on his bedside table. The shots deafened me and I could hear nothing in the silent pauses in between. Then there was a long pause before it started again. Nilda came up behind me and pulled me back into my room, holding me tight and talking to me. She was used to this, she told me. In her town they had domestic disputes, police rubouts, exchanges between the military and the NPA. They would sit quietly and wait it out, wondering who'd been killed. In the morning the news would come around, a vice-mayor or a barangay captain dead, or a group of soldiers, or ordinary townsfolk.

My father must have used up four or five clips that night. I tried not to think of the possibility of the bullets returning to earth. Every Christmas season we heard stories about bullets being fired into the air and lodging themselves into young boys' skulls when they fell back to the earth. We all pretended everything was normal when he appeared in the kitchen the next morning, in his thin, dark suit, cradling his clutch bag. He fixed Moroy with a hard look and told him to prepare for a long drive.

The summer had ended. After my first day back in school, Moroy drove up to pick me up at the gate, slapping on the horn excitedly. He greeted me with a grin, like there was something he couldn't wait to tell me. When I entered the car he drove, slowly, letting the engine's slow churn fill the silence. Outside the sun had begun to turn a darker yellow.

We drove out the high school road, past the football fields. Outside my window the buildings slipped by, the gym, the chapel and the grade school. He turned into the side road that led to the seminary. He was still grinning, tapping his thumbs on the wheel to an Ilonggo tune he was humming that he had taught me once: "Lumalabay nga daw aso, aso pa lamang…"

His grin was different, like he had suddenly become clever and was planning to do something really terrible this time. The blood flowed from my arms and legs and I imagined he could bash my head in and bury me under the bushes without anyone ever knowing.

Deep into an empty road deep in the campus, he made a quick three-point U-turn. He stopped the car, pulled up the handbrake, opened the door and stepped out. He came over to my side and gestured to the driver's seat and the wheel. I scooted over and gave the gas a few hard pumps. On the dashboard the needle rose past the red mark as the buzz of the engine drilled into my back. I drove the clutch to the floor with my left foot and released it slowly, allowing the rest of my strength to creep into my right. The car moved, back toward the main campus road. Moroy reached over to the back seat and put his gun on the dashboard.

We passed college students walking to their classes. If they looked closely they would have seen it, blue-black and tinted orange from the late afternoon sun. Moroy pointed to another side road, telling me to take it. It opened into a hidden clearing, covered by an undisturbed layer of dead leaves.

I stopped the car and shut off the engine. When I opened the door, the sounds of the school had gone. Moroy took the goon and slid out the clip to inspect it. He slid the clip back into the grip, producing small, startling sounds, a low sliding screech, a snap, a click. Then he drew the stock back and released it. He handed the gun to me and I held it with both hands, close to the center of my body. I could feel it against my groin. In my lap it sucked up the lines and folds of cloth.

We stepped out onto the leaves and the grass. He motioned me over to the edge of the clearing, where the trees began. I held the gun low, thinking of where it was pointed.

"OK. Here," he said. We had gone some distance into the trees, where the only things I could hear were our own movements disturbing the fallen leaves and the brown undergrowth.

"Now aim it at that tree and shoot." Moroy pointed at a tree at random.

I raised the gun, looking at my hands like they weren't my own. He gripped my hands and taught me to hold it with my right hand taking aim and squeezing the trigger, my left hand cupped like a cradle to keep steady and cushion the recoil. My arms trembled with the weight.

"Now shoot."

Something in me refused. Maybe it was the image of my father shooting into the empty air, his thin frame snapping back with each bullet he fired.

"What's the matter with you? Squeeze the trigger!"

Nothing happened. Moroy's moon face broke into a fat smile. "I won't tell your yaya," he said. I saw in his face that he knew about what Nilda and I had been doing.

I fired fast and blind, imagining myself emptying the clip into Moroy's big skull. My arms flung upward wildly with each shot and the force forced me to shut my eyes until they hurt. When I opened them, the smoke had cleared, but the smell of gunpowder stayed in the air.

Moroy smiled and put his hand on my shoulder. It was his way of telling me everything was all right, my secret was safe with him. We walked to the tree so I could look at the exploded bark and the clean round holes in the white wood underneath. Out of the corner of my eye I could see Moroy looking at me. When he moved toward me I swung around and kept him in sight. He flashed his signature smile, took the gun and congratulated me for a job well done.

We returned to the school parking lot, where Moroy asked me to treat him to fish balls and Coke.

Moroy prided himself over once being the mayor's "trigger." But when his boss lost the next election there was only his old police detachment to return to. Then he started working freelance for government officials and big businessmen.

I asked Moroy about the kind of trouble my father was having. Things were changing, he told me. He was even in danger of losing his job.

"Where would you go?" I teased him. "He made you too comfortable. Now look at you. You're fat and spoiled."

He smiled and turned to me, hunched his shoulders, bobbed his big head and threw slo-mo jabs at the air. Then he sat down and gave a thoughtful smile. He looked down at his shoes and I saw the ten-centavo scar on the back of his neck.

"And you're slow," I added.

*

That night, Nilda held me inside her by twisting her legs around mine. I felt unnatural. I couldn't stop. I came, my body jerking uncontrollably. It must have looked funny, my small body plugged into hers, my eyes rolled up inside their sockets, my lips curled and trembling. It took all the energy from me.

While Nilda and I spent the long, rainy after-school hours together, my father's secret trips with Moroy grew more frequent. One night in September, on one of those trips, a van sidled up to the car as it sped along the coastal road. The van door opened, guns poked out and opened fire. A brief chase followed, then the inevitable crash. The scene was littered with blood, glass shards and spent shells. They even showed it on TV. Policemen and reporters crowded over the wrecked car.

That was the one encounter Moroy didn't survive. As the van gained on them, Moroy swung the car from side to side. When the van sped ahead and spun to block their way he tried to sweep it to the side. When the twisted metal of the van locked with the car's fender and did not let go he steered and drove the car's bulletproof bulk into it. Then he threw himself to the backseat to cover my father's body with his own. Five or six men stumbled out of the van. They fired pointblank at the windshield until the bulletproof glass gave way and then poked their guns through the holes. But the bullets couldn't poke through slow, fat Moroy. The TV cameras showed him lying with his arms outstretched, spreading his body out, his hand gripping his unfired gun.

The few bullets that had found their way around Moroy's body punched through my father's legs and narrowly missed his windpipe. The emergency doctors at Makati Med thought he was dead on arrival, but eventually discovered a weak pulse. Hours later he was lucid enough to recount the ambush in vivid detail. At Moroy's funeral the mayor came and spoke gravely about how this bodyguard had once taken a bullet for him, too.

Months later, my father could walk again, only with a very stiff limp. He looked like a hollowed-out tree. He had taken a long vacation and spent most of his time at home. He had a nurse who pushed him around the house in a wheelchair. He spoke with a raspy, exhausted voice, but told me how he still wanted me to become a lawyer.

He bought me a second-hand car for my graduation. It rattled and the air-conditioner sometimes didn't work. The week before school, Nilda and I rode the Marcos highway fast and hard, all the way to Fairview, where there was a huge empty mall where nobody visited but they still played movies, even to empty theatres. We bought ice cream and we watched a Tagalog movie. Five minutes into it she leaned against me, took my hand and brought it up her skirt, between her thighs. It felt warm and very tender to be touching her there. It felt as though what had happened between us had been ages before.

Yayas become redundant when their wards are grown. Nilda left at the end of that month. I was fourteen, entering high school at the end of the summer. My mother gave her a ticket for the boat ride home, along with a month's pay.

Nilda's eyes were red and wet with tears while she undressed me, slipped her uniform off and joined me for our last bath together. I planted my feet on hers and kissed the hollow of her shoulder. It felt good to know her body. I knew where she liked to be touched and kissed, and how her many different parts tasted. I pressed myself against her, covering her body with mine, from the skin on my face to the soles of my feet.

Nilda laid out her bags and her boxes in the living room and opened them in front of my mother for inspection. I saw her uniforms, her bathing suit and her pink underwear and noticed that she had snuck in two of my old sport shirts, folded tight and small. There was also a photo of me as a boy, in an old silver frame. My mother wordlessly put it back on the piano where it had belonged.

I put her bags in the back of the car and we drove in silence to the port area. On the way I asked her what she was planning to do back home. She said she didn't know. She turned to me and said she wanted to stay with me and go with me wherever I wanted to go. "Ubani ko nimo," she said, in the language she had taught me, what they spoke at home. I smiled and told her I would visit her one day. She laughed bitterly and asked me if I even remembered where she lived. Of course, I said, it's where there are mango trees all over.

DOMINIC SY teaches Philippine literature and Southeast Asian literature at the University of the Philippines Diliman. His stories have appeared in *The Transpacific Literary Project*, *The Literary Apprentice*, and *transit: an online journal*. His book of fiction, *A Natural History of Empire*, won the Kritika Kultura / Ateneo de Manila University Press First Book Prize.

OVERSEAS FILIPINO WORKERS

In the Philippines, it is common for one or a few family members to leave the country in a desperate search for decent income. This exodus of Overseas Filipino Workers (OFWs) first began under the dictatorship of Ferdinand Marcos, but continued to accelerate even after the country transitioned to democracy. Support for dictatorial rule, meanwhile, though initially muted after the People Power Revolution, has seen a resurgence in certain sectors over the last decade. These large social forces manifest everywhere, but they are often felt more sharply in the most private of settings: at home, with family, at the dinner table.

15

THEN CRUEL QUIET

"Welcome, O life!"
–James Joyce

Rufino's bakeshop stood, like a sentinel facing east, between the neighborhood and the advancing commercial district. For the first time in the boy's memory, someone had painted the road. A white strip ran along the asphalt to the orange X of the intersection and began again on the other side. When the road was widened, the builders removed the shrubs and trees and paved over the grass. The boy in his uniform stood still at the sidewalk, red and new, watching as a cement truck roared by. He watched it spin slowly and inevitably away, before walking up to the tiled porch of the bakeshop and pushing open the door.

Sunlight poured in through the large dust-stained windows. Rufino, the baker, sat on his swivel chair behind the counter. He was tall and solidly built, with a blue shirt and a white apron. A pair of wiry, oval glasses slid down his oily nose. In three rows, beneath the display, an assortment of bread and pastries lay in individual baskets. In another display were the muffins, mamons, and loaves of raisin bread. Nearest to the counter sat the cakes. The boy eyed the pan de sal, soft and supple in one of the baskets. He resolved to buy a pack after the cake, for old time's sake, with his own money.

When the boy entered the bakeshop, Rufino jumped. Five stacks of five colors in varying degrees of smallness lay upon his desk. He grabbed the bills and sorted them quickly into the register. Then he turned to the boy, furrowed his eyebrows, and smiled.

"Samuel? Samuel! You're so tall!"

"Good afternoon, Tito."

"Look at you now! You must be in third grade now," said Rufino looking at the boy up and down. "No, I'm sorry, you must be in grade four."

Samuel replied that he was in the fifth grade, which was very near the sixth—itself almost high school.

"Oh, yes, yes. Soon you'll be like your brother. If I remember right your brother ..." Rufino looked at the ceiling to search his memory.

"He's in college now," the baker declared.

"Yes, Tito, he is."

"Wonderful. And you too, Samuel, after high school. It'll happen sooner than you think. Sooner than you think." Rufino stared out the window. Samuel beamed up at the baker, and said that he wouldn't mind. He asked how the shop was doing.

"Hmm? The shop," said Rufino. "It's moving along, the shop. Yes, moving along."

"And how is Tita Rita?"

"Back in the province with her mother. Please pray for her." Rufino pushed his glasses up his nose. "As for Celing— you remember Celing? New Zealand now."

"What's she doing?"

Rufino cleared his throat. "Wait, I'm sorry, there's something I need to check first." The baker turned to one of the displays and pulled out a tray of mamon, inspecting them one by one. Samuel watched him sort them out meticulously, his face slightly colored. Samuel's stomach faintly rumbled.

"I'm sorry," said Rufino, as he put the tray back. "Where were we? Right, Tita Rita's at the province, Celing is in New Zealand. But anyway, how are you? What'll you have?"

"It's Mama's birthday," said Samuel, heaving out his chest. "I'll have the caramel cake."

"Today? No, no. We don't have any caramel left."

Samuel blinked twice as though he hadn't heard.

"I'm sorry," said Rufino. "You should've called. We don't make them as often as we used to. As often as I'd like."

Samuel's shoulders fell. He asked if there was nothing similar.

Rufino shook his head. "Impossible. People used to come for them from all across the metro." He stood up and paced behind the glass display. Samuel followed from his end, searching anxiously for another cake. But in their wrinkled walls of icing he saw only disappointment.

"Maybe the mousse," said Rufino. "Or the black forest. Yes, your mother, I remember she enjoys black forest."

Samuel had no memories of his mother liking black forest. But perhaps she did. He couldn't be sure. He considered his options, looked at the card by the cake, and balked.

"I'm sorry, but that's really how it is now," Rufino gave him a kind look. "The caramel would've cost even more."

Samuel calculated quickly and knew that he would not be able to buy the pan de sal. Rufino put the cake in a white cardboard box with a green cover labeled "Rufino's." Samuel was twenty short. He asked if he could pay it at another time.

"Well, I don't normally. You see it's not good for business." Rufino ran his fingers along his hair and shrugged. "Well, I know who you are. Okay."

"Thank you," said Samuel.

"Your mom will love it," said Rufino as he handed Samuel the cake. "It's not as good as the caramel, and it doesn't sell as often. But it's a fine cake. A fine cake."

"I don't think she'll complain."

"No, she won't," said Rufino. "But next time you must call me. Your brother always calls. But, of course, this is your first time, isn't it?"

They walked together to the door. Samuel, holding the box with his two hands, pressing it to his chest to distribute the weight, nodded to Rufino and thanked him as he exited.

"Say happy birthday to your mother for me," called Rufino. "And for Rita and Celing!"

Samuel walked down along the newly painted street. Just a year ago, the mayor had decreed that their road was to be turned into a thoroughfare, after which the contractors descended. Now there were neither clouds in the sky nor trees by the road to block the heat. The sun swept through the emptiness unopposed. Perhaps, thought Samuel to himself, such things were not meant to last. He thought, briefly, of returning in triumph in his forties to a landscape of glass and fiber optics. But in the intersecting streets, things were as they had always been: dirt, grass, a mango tree before a pastel-painted wall; a dozen gates of varied colors, all of them crowned with spikes; walls laced with broken glass.

Passing Sto. Domingo Street, he heard a babble of familiar voices. At the edge of the road, not far from the intersection, a group of Samuel's classmates had gathered around something on the ground. The boys, like Samuel, wore khaki pants and white polos with short sleeves. The girls wore white blouses with long, blue plaited skirts. The former were crouching near the center of the circle, one of them with a stick to poke at whatever it was they had captured. Another took photos with his phone. The latter, Samuel saw, was Billy. Around him were Mae, Gina, Ricky, Diego, and, nearest to Samuel, leaning back from the group, her slender arms stretched into the air, Estrella. She saw Samuel in the distance and called him over.

On the ground, at the center of their circle, lay a large frog, its hind legs crushed, its pelvis flattened into the dirt. A cacophony of colors spilled forth from its mouth. A car had rolled on the frog's lower half, driving out its guts—intestines in the dirt, crumpled lungs and tender tissues, a pink tongue lolling in the sun. A column of black ants stretched out from the grass to these entrails, their legs pitter-pattering on the flesh. Diego, who held the stick, poked one of the bloated organs, spilling yellow ooze onto the road. Samuel felt his stomach lurch and a bit of acid hop up into his throat. He stepped back from the group and turned to face the asphalt. He counted to ten.

Estrella walked up to Samuel while he counted and ruffled his hair. The sunlight through the shivering leaves danced on her face while the tips of her short brown hair tickled her jaw. Her plaited skirt fell just above her shin, the open air grazing her caramel skin. She had removed her bowtie and loosened the first button of her blouse. Of all the girls in their batch, she had been just the fourth to wear a bra. She asked about the box in Samuel's hands and saw that it was from Rufino's. Gently with long light fingers, she pulled the cover up. A whisper of cool air wafted up to their faces. In the sunlight glistened the icing, the chocolate shards, the five supple red cherries.

"I love Black Forest," she said, gripping his arm.

"My mother loves it too."

"Can I have a slice?"

"Oh, I can't give you a slice."

"Why not ... How about a shard of chocolate?"

"I can't, Ella."

"Please ..."

"No ..."

At the circle, the children were laughing. Diego, with his stick, had burst what was now a shriveling lung. Amidst the chortling, Billy turned and looked in Sam's direction. He called Estrella.

"A cherry," she said.

"I really can't, Ella."

"Just one?"

"I can't. How will it look?"

"It'll look perfect."

Before Samuel could respond, Billy popped up between them, breaking Ella's hold on Samuel's arm. He wrapped his arms around their shoulders and grinned. He had a round face with a faint line of fuzz on his upper lip. Although he wore the same polo as Samuel, it always appeared to the latter that Billy's was neater and crisper. His shoes were never scuffed and were pointed at the tips. Samuel's were bluntly boxed.

"Have you seen the frog, Sam? You should get a close look. It's something to see."

"I've seen it," said Samuel.

"What? From here?"

"I was nearer earlier."

"Were you? I didn't notice. I'm sure you didn't see the liver though. It's like a balloon."

"I've seen that in the lab."

"The lab? That's nothing. And weren't you sick that day?"

"I wasn't sick," said Samuel, his cheeks coloring.

"Ricky," called Billy. Ricky was a thin boy with a long face. He limped as he turned. He had a wound on his left knee that he got from a race with Billy. Dried blood coated the frayed fibers of his khakis. More covered his nose from a pimple that had burst when he fell.

"Was Sam there," Billy asked, "when we were dissecting?"

"Who?"

"Sam, Sam." said Billy, holding an open palm beneath Sam's chin.

Ricky looked at Sam, squinted, and shrugged. Billy sighed and asked Diego, but Estrella interrupted.

"He was there, Billy. I remember."

Billy turned to Estrella and they stared at each other. After a few seconds, Billy looked away and shrugged, licking the sweat off his upper lip. He let go of their shoulders and walked back to the circle. Estrella went over to Samuel and replaced the cover of the box, their fingers grazing.

The ants ran rampantly over the frog. Billy watched them for a moment, and then turned.

"I dare you, Sam" he called out loud, "to touch it."

Samuel turned to Billy. "You want me to touch you?"

Diego and the girls snickered. Billy's mouth twitched, but he stood his ground and pointed at the frog.

"Touch the tongue. Come on. If you can."

A tricycle roared past the adjacent street. Samuel stood by the road unmoving, feeling the tribe's collective gaze. He thought of those blood-filled, rubbery guts hanging about his palm, the ants crawling to his fingers, their feelers tickling his skin. He had excused himself at the lab due to a bum stomach, and had stood for an hour in the boy's cubicle, reading the same lines of graffiti over and over with his pants around his ankles in case anyone peeked beneath the door.

"I'm not touching that," he said.

"You want gloves? We can get you gloves."

"I don't want gloves," said Samuel flushing brightly. "I'm not touching it." He had the urge to rush over and punch Billy in the face. But Samuel was holding the cake, Billy was bigger and faster, and between the two of them was the frog, its cornucopia of pink, purple, and blue.

"I'll do it," said Estrella suddenly. Samuel turned to her to say it wasn't necessary, but she shrugged him off. She walked towards the frog without looking at either of them. Billy, startled at first, made no move as she approached. Then he uncrossed his arms and glanced at Samuel smugly.

They gathered around the frog while Samuel turned away, his face hot and red. The cake was warm now. He strode towards the intersection and turned. Children, he muttered. He could hear Billy snapping photos with his phone. Samuel stomped the ground in rage and almost dropped the cake. He hurried down the street until their laughter faded into echoes in his mind, until they vanished, softly, into the air.

But where Estrella had held his arm, his skin still tingled, seething in the heat of the sun.

*

Tito Ramon stepped into the house, holding by its neck a bottle of Châteauneuf Du Pape. His blue polo, buttoned down, bulged boldly, while his coat hung limply across his shoulder. Wobbling slightly as he walked, Tito Ramon blinked and stretched out his arms to relieve his jet lag. This was only his third time to come home, only his second time to visit them.

"I have returned!" he declared, raising the bottle in the air. He looked around and saw a boy standing before him, holding open the door. Samuel embraced his uncle, his brow reaching the older man's shoulders. Breaking their embrace, Tito Ramon held his nephew out in front of him, and peered into the boy's face—those large, bright eyes. He drew a total blank.

"Okay, let's see. You can't be Christian," he muttered, tilting his head right and left. "No, he'd be in college now, so that's impossible. There are only two of you left, I think. Yes, since Rissa's gone. So that makes you... Sol? Solomon!"

"Samuel, Tito." He had changed his shirt to the red-checkered polo that Tito Ramon sent two Christmas's ago.

"Samuel," he exclaimed. "Yes, yes, it's Samuel. You must be, what, wait, let me guess." He paused to rub his chin and looked at Samuel up and down. "Grade four."

Samuel said he was in the fifth grade, which was very near the sixth—itself almost high school. Tito Ramon slapped him on the shoulder and concluded that that was splendid.

At the sound of the doorbell, Mrs. Gregorio hurried out of her room. She wore her favorite blouse and old office pants. She hadn't worn the latter since she resigned, twenty-six years ago, after giving birth to Rissa. Two years back, however, she had found them again in the closet, crumpled behind her wedding dress. Getting them on had since become the standard with which she judged her wellbeing, and the many months that followed had been equal parts shame and disenchantment. But now on her fiftieth birthday, she could finally say, after the grueling effort of having to zip them up— and though the pants still cut slightly into her thighs—that Mrs. Luisa Gregorio was in all manner of the word contented.

Tito Ramon embraced his cousin and they exchanged greetings. Mrs. Gregorio apologized for not having been able to pick him up at the airport. Tito Ramon waved it away. He handed Mrs. Gregorio the bottle, which she brought to the dining table. On the lazy susan, two platters of kangkong and broccoli flanked a bowl of Mrs. Gregorio's spicy beef tapa. Beside the broccoli sat a container of steaming rice, while beside the kangkong was an empty space to be filled with the pancit malabon Mr. Gregorio would bring home. Mrs. Gregorio set the bottle down beside the pitcher of water and showed her cousin his seat. She told him that it was actually Rissa's seat, but of course she would not be able to make it. Tito Ramon removed the cover of the beef tapa and savored the smell, until Mrs. Gregorio slapped his hand and replaced the cover. Feigning injury, he asked about his aunt.

"Mama's sleeping," said Mrs. Gregorio. "She fell asleep waiting. You better say hello."

"Duty calls," said Tito Ramon to Samuel, rolling his eyes and then chuckling. They went into his grandmother's room, while Samuel sat in the sala, his feet propped up on the coffee table, and waited.

Christian came shortly after sunset. He wore a red collared shirt, untucked over his jeans, the ends of the latter fraying around his sneakers. Pockmarks from years of acne covered his cheeks, while a pair of thick, square glasses sat on his fat nose. He held a pink package wrapped with yellow ribbon. He quickly scanned the room.

"You got the cake?" Christian asked.

"Yup."

"Quick, sign the card." He gave Sam the package and a pen from his breast pocket. Samuel opened the card: a baby bear with a long snout held up a parchment at the center of the page. It read, "To the Best Mother in the World."

"Is this for Mother's Day?" asked Samuel.

"It's ambiguous," said Christian. "Just sign it."

Samuel signed his name in print. Christian walked to the dining table and surveyed the food. He poured himself a glass of water.

"Tito Ramon is here," said Sam.

"Does he still think he's funny?"

Samuel laughed.

"This is obviously his," said Christian, holding the Châteauneuf-du-Pape by its shoulder. He unwrapped the paper, inspected the label, and placed it back it on the table. He took the present back from Samuel and they made their way into the kitchen. The cake box lay on the counter.

"Why isn't this in the fridge?" said Christian. "The ants will get at it." He opened the box and grimaced.

"It's Black Forest," said Samuel.

"Why didn't you get the caramel?"

"He ran out."

"Didn't you reserve one?"

"He, he didn't have them anymore. He said they've been out for a week."

With a groan, Christian opened the refrigerator, rearranged the Tupperware, and fit the box inside. He opened a cupboard and hid the present, while Samuel tried to keep out of the way. Just then, they heard the front door swinging open.

Upon entering his castle, Mr. Gregorio, bearing a bilao of pancit, barked out for his sons to free his hands. The lamplight glinted on the gray strands of hair that swept across his scalp, while his thick, oval glasses covered the wrinkles beneath his eyes. He pointed his large nose at an acute angle to the roof and called again.

Samuel took the bilao and brought it to the table. His hands freed, Mr. Gregorio stretched out his arms and settled into his chair. In his old, short-sleeved barong, the medium-rise apartment sales-manager looked almost like a politician. Christian sat at the chair opposite his father. They didn't speak. Seeing the wine bottle, Mr. Gregorio held it up by the body and read the gothic impress, his eyebrows furrowing, his mouth slowly forming the words. He dropped it back into place.

Looking around, Mr. Gregorio found the remote control for the air conditioner and lowered the temperature by a few degrees. He waited a few seconds while the aircon adjusted before turning to his sons.

"Where's Tito Ramon?"

"He's with Mama and Lola," said Samuel.

"Call them to dinner. Let's get started."

Coming out of her den, Lola Gabriella tottered forward with a cane in one hand and Mrs. Gregorio supporting the other. Lola Gabriella's silver hair, long and lustrous, was combed back behind her head and held together with a red hairband. She advanced with her back bent low, her cheeks sagging beneath her chin, the flaps beneath her arms swinging left and right with every step. Tito Ramon came out of the room just behind her.

"Good evening, Robert," said Tito Ramon.

"Let's eat," replied Mr. Gregorio with a nod. "You brought the wine."

"Me? No, not at all," said Ramon. "It brought itself. It sang to me as I walked past the duty free, and, well, you know. Who can resist a sirène? 'Raamooon, buvez avec moi …'"

"Was this the wine you brought before?"

"Before? Let me think. Well that was some time ago, but, no, that was chardonnay, Talley Chardonnay. Not French, to be sure, but when you're in a pinch, eh?"

"In…a pinch?"

"If you ever need to pick some wines," said Tito Ramon smiling sweetly, patting Mr. Gregorio on the back, "then you just let me know." Mr. Gregorio stiffened his shoulders.

"Or any drink at all, of course," Tito Ramon bantered on. "Nothing like getting drunk together after all these years, eh?"

"Ramon," said Mrs. Gregorio sternly, tilting her head towards Samuel.

"Oops," mouthed Tito Ramon, taking the seat beside Mr. Gregorio. Then he leaned in and whispered:

"Just tell me when."

Samuel pulled a seat back for Lola Gabriella and, once she sat in it, pushed it back into the table for her. Christian sat beside his grandmother. Samuel sat between Christian and Tito Ramon, while Mrs. Gregorio sat between her husband and her mother. When they were all settled, Tito Ramon spun the lazy susan until the tapa was in front of him. Then he clasped his hands and smiled at no one in particular, looking around the table.

"Who wants to start," said Mrs. Gregorio, happily. Everyone cast their eyes down to the table.

"Samuel?"

Samuel closed his eyes and made the sign of the cross. Everyone bowed their heads except for Lola Gabriella, who stared at the edge of her plate. After the prayer before meals, Samuel added another prayer of thanksgiving for their mother, who he said was the very best of all their gifts. He requested that she have a happy birthday, and a happy fiftieth year ahead of her.

"Amen!" said Tito Ramon. "Good job, Samuel." He removed the cover of the tapa and began to help himself, while Mrs. Gregorio beamed at Samuel and mouthed "thank you."

The lazy susan was spun counterclockwise until everyone got a bit of everything. Samuel got a pile of tapa and jammed it into his mountain of rice. He avoided the kangkong and the broccoli and waited until the pancit came before him before heaping a load onto his plate. On top of the pile, he squeezed a calamansi with his fork beneath it to catch the seeds. He placed those on the rim of his plate before tossing everything together and digging in.

"So how are you feeling?" asked Mr. Gregorio, when everyone had gotten their food. "Readjusting to the climate?"

Tito Ramon grinned. "Those first few seconds outside the plane were horrible. I thought I was going to choke from the heat. But I cooled down eventually. It's actually pretty cold right now."

"That's good, that's good. How about your work? These aren't good times where you are."

"Only when you think about it," said Tito Ramon laughing and sticking a spoonful of rice and broccoli into his mouth.

"Are you doing all right?" asked Christian.

"Well, I've had to hop around between jobs a bit. But I think, and I'm crossing my fingers here, I think I finally have a good one."

Tito Ramon beamed at the table. Mr. Gregorio raised his eyebrows.

"What're you doing?" asked Mrs. Gregorio quickly.

"Tutoring children at the local library. Math and reading mostly. A bit of science. I just put out an ad online and people started calling. See how the world is changing?"

"Do you earn a lot?" asked Samuel. He winced as Christian kicked him on the leg.

"It's enough. Not like my old job, of course, and there are no securities"—Tito Ramon paused to swallow his food—"but at my age, having to scout around… the important thing is that there are a lot of stupid kids out there. Rich, stupid American kids with rich, worried parents. So there's a market.

"And I figure…" he continued with a forkful of pancit in his mouth, "I figure when we finally recover and everything picks up again, I can get my old job back. I mean the economy probably won't get worse at this point." He knocked three times on the table.

"A teacher," said Mr. Gregorio. "So we'll have two in the family."

"Two?" said Tito Ramon. "Who's the other?"

"Our own Christian," said Mr. Gregorio. "A truly generous spirit, planning to teach at the university like every good communist."

Christian put down his spoon and glared at his father.

"How noble of you," said Tito Ramon, his face lighting up. "That's truly admirable."

"It is noble," said Mr. Gregorio. "All those years of tuition so he can never leave school."

"Robert, please!" said Mrs. Gregorio. The man turned to look at his wife.

"Well anyway," said Mr. Gregorio, turning back. "So you're doing well enough."

"I am, I am, yes. How about you?" asked Tito Ramon.

"The industry is doing better. Booming now, especially for condos."

"So you must be meeting clients all day."

"Well, that depends. Right now, for the past week or so, I've been focusing on networking, building up contacts."

"I see, but how about when you meet up with clients? How many do you usually get?"

"When I do? It really depends. But when I do, when I do talk to clients, around seven."

"Seven! Seven sales a day!"

"Potential sales."

"Right, but sales are up in general? Across the board?"

Mr. Gregorio shrugged and drank from his glass.

"That's great, that's great," continued Tito Ramon. "I mean, it's great to see the industry picking up. You've been doing this for so long."

"Yes, well, you have to try and be the best at what you do."

Tito Ramon nodded, his mouth full of pancit.

A brief silence fell upon the table, punctuated by the tapping of metal on plastic. Samuel watched as Christian pushed around a grain of rice at the center of his plate and tried to stab it with his fork. On the other side of the table, Mrs. Gregorio held her mother's hand and guided the spoon to her mouth. Mr. Gregorio spun the lazy susan for a bit but didn't get anything.

"Well now," said Tito Ramon after a moment, reaching

for the Châteauneuf-du-Pape. "Perhaps we can have the wine, eh? Do we have a bottle opener? Shall everyone drink? Luisa? Christian? Samuel?"

"I'd like some," said Samuel.

"None for Sam," said Mr. Gregorio frowning.

"What harm, Robert? What harm?" He popped the cork and poured into Samuel's glass.

"I won't have any drunkards in the family."

"Drunkard? He's not a drunkard," said Tito Ramon. He stopped pouring into Samuel's glass. "Only a bit for you, Sam. That's all you get now. Savor it."

Samuel thanked his uncle and held his glass close, avoiding his father's eyes. Tito Ramon poured wine for four more, and gave a little bit to Lola Gabriella. She furrowed her eyebrows and leaned in for a closer look.

"It's wine, Tita," he shouted into her ear. "Good wine. Great wine."

Lola Gabriella looked up at her nephew, blinking once, and then turned to stare at the glass.

Samuel took a sip. The wine was hot on his tongue and burned its way down his throat. He pressed his eyes together and wheezed.

"You okay, Sam?" said Tito Ramon, slapping him on the back. Samuel said he was. "So how is Rissa?" asked Tito Ramon. "I was told that this was her chair."

Christian looked up from his plate.

"She's fine," said Mr. Gregorio.

"Where is she now again?"

"She's in Dubai," said Mrs. Gregorio, glancing at her husband. "She called me this afternoon to say *happy birthday*. She's so busy there."

"What does she do?"

"Clerical work," said Christian.

"A clerk? Well, that's not too bad, not too bad."

Tito Ramon tipped his glass into his mouth and poured himself more wine.

"At least she's in Dubai," he said. "Not in the, the what, what is it, Syria?"

"She's not in Damascus," suggested Samuel. He had learned the name a week before in class. His face was getting hot.

"Yes! Imagine all the fighting if she were there. And I mean, you know how a lot of people are refusing to leave."

"It's terrible," said Mrs. Gregorio.

"They've lost Damascus though," said Christian.

"You mean the rebels?" said Tito Ramon.

"Of course he does," said Mr. Gregorio. "He follows all rebellions, our budding communist."

"If you notice, Tito," said Christian, "leftists tend to gather wherever there are despots, especially those who cry out 'communist!'"

"Perhaps we should bring out the cake," said Mrs. Gregorio suddenly. "Samuel, could you please bring out the cake now?"

Samuel hurried over to the kitchen with a little wobble in his step. He took the cake box out of the fridge, removed the cover, and took a deep breath. Then he brought it over to the dining table and placed it between his mother and Lola Gabriella.

"What's this?" said Mrs. Gregorio.

"Black Forest," said Samuel, blushing.

"What happened to the caramel cake?" said Mr. Gregorio.

"It's all right, Robert. Black Forest is lovely," she said, squeezing Samuel's hand.

Mr. Gregorio pulled a knife out from the utensil drawer along with a pack of small candles. Mrs. Gregorio stuck five of them into the cake's rim, beside the five shining cherries. Samuel took some matches from the cabinet while Christian got the camera. Reaching for his phone, Tito Ramon offered to take the pictures so they could have a family photo. Mrs. Gregorio thanked him and handed him her old digital camera instead. When everything was finally in place, they gathered around the cake—Mrs. Gregorio sitting beside her mother, the boys standing behind them. Samuel stood between his father and his brother, the former's heavy hand weighing down on his shoulder.

Tito Ramon steadied the camera. Seeing the camera lens, Lola Gabriella blinked for a bit and smiled. Christian began to sing "Happy Birthday" and everybody followed suit until the song's crescendo, when Mrs. Gregorio blew out the candles. Tito Ramon took a picture of the candle blowing, and then took another one of them all smiling. Mrs. Gregorio called him to come join the photo, so Samuel went around the table to be the new cameraman. Tiptoeing slightly, he took three more photos that all had the same pose. Afterwards, Christian went to the kitchen and took their present out from the cupboard. Mrs. Gregorio crowed delightedly as she read the card. "The best mother in the world," she said, smiling with delight at her sons who looked down at their shoes. She unlaced the ribbon and opened the box.

"Is it a wrist watch?" she said holding up a red rubber strap.

"It's a calorie counter," said Christian. "It counts how many calories you've burned as you walk."

Mrs. Gregorio fiddled with the buttons. A black zero blinked incessantly on the screen.

"Thank you," she said, looking up and smiling. "I'll use it tomorrow."

"Come, come, let's get this over with," said her husband with the knife.

Mr. Gregorio cut the cake and put them into small plates, distributing them around the table. Tito Ramon poured himself the last of the wine to eat with his slice, tilting the empty bottle into the glass for just a little bit longer, just in case. When everyone had gotten a plate, Mrs. Gregorio gave a slice to her mother.

"Why are you giving her cake?" said Mr. Gregorio sternly.

"It's all right, Robert."

"All right?" said Christian, "How is it all right?"

"At this stage, it's just about easing them in."

"You mean killing your own mother."

"Well, she's my mother, Christian, and it's my cake, so I will handle it."

"When you're old," said Christian frowning, "You won't get any cake. Even if you beg."

Mrs. Gregorio didn't respond. Lola Gabriella cut a bit of the cake with her fork and brought it to her mouth. She closed her eyes and let out a low *mmm*.

"Do you remember, Luisa," said Tito Ramon suddenly, reclining into the chair, "the last time I celebrated your birthday?"

"It was a long time ago, Ramon."

"I think it was the year before I left. You were fourteen, right? I didn't know yet when I was coming back. I'm not sure I wanted to."

"You shouldn't have left, Ramon," said Mr. Gregorio. "You left us at the best we ever had."

"The best?"

"The best and the most peaceful."

"Oh. Well, perhaps."

"Things were orderly then, remember. When a man could live and work in peace."

"No truer words have been said," said Christian, "from the apathetic middle class."

Mr. Gregorio dropped his hands onto the table. Mrs. Gregorio winced, and Samuel sunk back into his chair.

"And who are you to say so?" said Mr. Gregorio.

"An educated man," replied the son.

"Oh, and do you pay for your education? Do you work your ass off to be a man?"

"Robert!" said Mrs. Gregorio.

"What we had was rule of law. We had everything we needed to earn our way. If I did it, then anyone could have done it. And if they didn't then it was their own damned faults."

"I think," said Tito Ramon putting a hand on Mr. Gregorio's arm, "I think we should all just settle down—"

"Brainwashed by your own luck," said Christian.

"Were you there?" cried Mr. Gregorio. "Were you there?"

"I'm over here, at your table, while Rissa slaves away in the desert so Samuel can go to school."

Mr. Gregorio stood up and banged his fist onto the table.

"The blood of your countrymen waters the soil," continued Christian, "while you sit here thinking about your 'self-made' bank accounts and air conditions."

"'The blood of your countrymen!'" said Mr. Gregorio. "And where did you get that line?"

"From the mothers of the dead, from the brothers of the tortured!"

"Christian, Robert" said Mrs. Gregorio weakly. "Can't we please just finish dessert?"

"They should be shot," screamed Mr. Gregorio. "Leftists and communists, they should be shot!"

Christian, trembling, gripped the table's edge, his nails digging into the wood.

"They've broken the contract! Society should destroy those who wish to destroy it!"

"It is the right of every man to spit into the face of his oppressor," screamed Christian.

"We were a real country then! A country to be proud of!" And from the top of his lungs, Mr. Gregorio sang:

> *May bagong silang! May bago nang buhay!*
> *Bagong bansa, bagong galaw, sa bagong lipunan!*

Christian stood up from the table, flinging his chair aside. He stormed out of the dining and into his room, slamming the door behind him.

Mr. Gregorio sang a few more lines and then trailed off into silence. Mrs. Gregorio sat in her chair, her legs crossed, facing the opposite direction. Samuel said nothing. Tito Ramon picked up the Châteauneuf-du-Pape, shaking it in the air and tipping it into his glass though he knew there was nothing left.

"Do you have another bottle," he asked.

Lola Gabriella ate the last piece of her cake.

*

Samuel stood outside the bathroom door, waiting for his grandmother to finish. In the dim light of the corridor, he watched colorful and shapeless patterns mesh and meld on the wall. When he turned to the left, they vanished. He stared at the wall and held the forms before him as best as he could, holding them together until his pupils began to twitch. Mrs. Gregorio came out into the corridor and stood beside Samuel.

"Thank you for getting the cake," she said. Samuel mumbled a "you're welcome" and a "Happy Birthday," while Mrs. Gregorio kissed his brow and waited with him in the corridor. When Lola Gabriella left the bathroom, Mrs. Gregorio held her mother's arm and brought her to the bedroom, where she settled her mother in bed, tucked her in, and wished her a good night. Then she went to her own room.

Samuel locked the bathroom door behind him. The tiles on the floor were cracked and stained, and the smell of medication emanated from the toilet bowl. Dark yellow spots lingered on the toilet seat. He hung his clothes on the towel wrack. Grabbing a tissue, he wiped the urine off the seat. After undressing, Samuel walked to the sink and looked at himself in the mirror. He touched his fat nose and ears, and his clean upper lip. He looked into his pupils, the right eye first and then the left. For now, they were working perfectly, but he knew they would soon degrade.

Samuel looked down at his body, at his scrawny arms and legs. He tried to flex the former before dropping his hands back down over the non-existent muscles on his chest. He ran his finger through a field of tiny black pinpricks at the bottom of his pelvis. Like stony sand, or gravel. He held his genitals and let them go, before stepping into the shower area and turning on the water.

He closed his eyes. The warm, sultry water came over him and slid down his body. Heat emanated from his skin, from his chest and legs and feet. He felt waves of agitated heat falling upon him, spiraling around him over his head and back, curling and swirling at his toes. He remembered the heat from Estrella's hand, hot like the water trickling down his skin, falling across his legs and swirling around his toes. Slowly and surely, he submitted to the heat welling within him, to its strong, burning release.

He opened his eyes, blinking and peering through the water that clung to his lashes. Stretching his arms out before him, he reached for the soap and rolled it thickly in his hands. He soaped himself and let the bubbles fall to the ground while his eyes got used to the steam. His vision returning, he saw a thin black line curling behind the smoke. It was a trail of ants, long and cursive, running along the pipes. Samuel blinked. The ants had burrowed into the cracks in the tiles, excavating where nobody could see them. Following the trail with his eyes, Samuel pulled aside the shower curtain and watched as the ants crawled behind the toilet bowl, up the base, and onto the toilet seat. They gathered around the faint yellow outlines where the dark spots of urine had been, their little legs pitter-pattering on the seat, their feelers rubbing together.

Samuel stood in the shower, silent and horrified. He grabbed the pail behind him and filled it to the brim. He splashed it at the wall, at the column of ants. They fell to the ground in little drops and scattered to all directions. He flung water at them again and again until black corpses swirled about Samuel's feet. Half blind, he threw water at the wall, at the toilet, at the floor. The ants swarmed and swirled and retreated into the cracks.

After the initial carnage, Samuel bent down to peer into the cracks in the tiles. He could see nothing within them, just a dark and hollow tunnel stretching into unknown caverns within. Samuel stood beneath the hot shower, the dead swirling about his toes. He threw water into the wall again to no avail. Deep in the cracks of the tiles, the ants crawled about in glee, waving their thin feelers in the darkness and biding their time. Trembling and crying, Samuel Gregorio swung the pail of water with all his might, with all of his will and desire, at the marching of the ants.

EILEEN R. TABIOS has released over sixty collections of poetry, fiction, essays, and experimental biographies from publishers in ten countries and cyberspace. Most recently, she released her first novel *DoveLion: A Fairy Tale for Our Times* and first book in French translation, *La Vie erotique de l'art*. Her award-winning body of work includes invention of the hay(na)ku, a 21st century diasporic poetic form, the MDR Poetry Generator that can create poems totaling theoretical infinity, and a first poetry book, *Beyond Life Sentences*, which received the Philippines' National Book Award. More information is at eileenrtabios.com.

NEVER FORGET, NEVER AGAIN

"Negros" was written in 1995-1996 as a protest-story against Ferdinand Marcos' martial law dictatorship in the Philippines. I am saddened by how the story continues to have relevance over twenty-five years later due to the ongoing corruption and governmental abuse imposed by Filipino political leadership on a long-suffering populace. Relatedly, I am stunned that many younger Filipinos apparently are not well-informed about Marcos' martial law regime. It is difficult for a people to progress forward if it doesn't know its past. "Negros" addresses this need and serves as an ever-timely reminder for Filipinos to be vigilant against political abuse.

16

NEGROS

"***DAAAAA-deeeeeeee****! Daddy, daddy, Daaaaa-deeeeeeee!*"

My mother did not look dignified yelling down the mountain. Her hands flapped like wings of chickens we chased for dinner, her blouse escaped from the waistband of her skirt, her hair streamed in all directions from her loosened bun and her mouth thinned around a circle of prominent teeth. She screeched from the balcony of our house which stood on top of Mount Asawa. She, most assuredly, would have been dismayed if she realized that her voice topped that of Auntie Feling's whose water broke when she was visiting the previous month. Clutching her belly, Auntie Feling's exhortations to call the doctor had been audible even to the traffic on the road circling the bottom of the mountain.

Mount Asawa was actually a hill, but everyone was accustomed to calling it a mountain because of its name. The other thing about its name was that "Asawa" could have meant "wife" in Tagalog. Thus, my father's friends always enjoyed a rollicking good time discussing the many ways to "Mount Wife" when they first heard of it.

Anyway, there was my father's asawa ordering me and my father as we were half-way up the mountain to hurry in a voice loud enough to carry to Manila. We broke into a run, wondering what disaster had befallen the household. My father had gained weight over the years but he easily ran ahead of me—his quivering backside, encased tightly in brown polyester, looked like the rump of a fat water buffalo.

As we burst into the house, the servants were running through the living room, much like the time Mama stood barefoot on the sofa and screamed with regard to the unexpected visit of a neighbor's pet monkey who slipped in through an open window. "Ayyyyyyyyyy-sussss! Everyone get that lice-ridden creature before he tracks his diseases through the house!"

This time, my mother was instructing all servants, "Black, black, as much black as you can find!" before dashing off towards the servants' quarters.

"What's going on here?" my father demanded as we followed my mother. We entered Manang Inday's bedroom where we found the maid lying on her bed, clutching her knees to her chest, mumbling and shivering despite the heat.

"Ayyyyy-sussss!" we finally deciphered some of Manang Inday's mutterings. "I am freezing!"

My mother started layering the clothes bundled in her arms over Manang Inday as was my father and I watched, open-mouthed with amazement. I reached for my father's hand which returned my clasp firmly.

"Her body has been taken over by mamau," Mama explained, her perspiring face looking back at us and inviting us to share in the horror of the matter.

"Mamau—a ghost?" I repeated, concerned and moving behind my father. My father closed the cavern of his mouth and snorted.

"Another ghost? Why did we move to this place?" my father complained, releasing my hand as he disgustedly flung both of his up in the air. "Ever since we arrived in this city, I've been haunted by floods, neighbors who eat the evidence of their depletion of my chickens, a roof that won't stop leaking and a different ghost showing its pathetic presence every month! Are these mamaus breeding behind the chicken coop?"

Then my father laughed at the ceiling, apparently thinking he inadvertently displayed some wit. I smirked, too, as his lack of fear made me unafraid.

"Well, and what does this ghost want this time?" my father asked after he stopped barking to himself at the sight of Mama's frown.

"Have you no respect? The body of Inday, who could never hurt a soul and undoubtedly was just minding her own business, has just been invaded by an unwelcome visitor from the other realm!" my mother, her hands on her hips, chastised my father.

"The other realm?" my father mocked in high-pitched tone.

As the warning look became murderous on Mama's face, he calmed himself, smoothing back the sparse strands over his glistening scalp. He sat in the lone chair of the room which, next to the servant's bed, allowed for a direct look into Manang Inday's grimacing face. He pulled me to his side and whispered, "We're in this together, buddy. Let's discover the surprise du jour!"

Du jour was French and meant "of the day." My father loved to teach pieces of trivia that he thought I would not learn otherwise from the nuns at my elementary school.

"All right, let's hear it," my father said, sinking his chin into his chest with demeanor of preparing for a long, tedious story. His profile was that of a multi-bellied Buddha in a yellow, short-sleeved golf shirt. "But first, why did you cover Inday with your slips? Isn't it better to cover her with a blanket then your underwear?"

My mother dropped her eyes and blushed before she responded, "My slips are black. Nana Sitang said that if ever a ghost takes over the body of someone in our household, we should cover the body with black material because black feels more comfortable to a mamau."

I remembered Nana Sitang's visit to our home and the conversation turning to the nature of ghosts. Nana Sitang could not explain, however, why black was more comfortable to mamaus or why the comfort of ghosts was significant, only that she had managed to pick up these gems of wisdom from her village's witch doctor when she was a teenager. Of course, she had cackled through tobacco-stained teeth, this was before Nana Sitang's parents discovered and put a stop to her visits to the witch doctor who also dabbled as the bookie at local cockfights. Before my father could remind Mama of these points, we heard a slight scuffling noise behind us.

"Oh, good, Neta, you found more black," my mother said to one of the servants who stood just beyond the doorway, her head tilted away from the room as if there was a disease she could catch by just looking. Manang Neta blindly held out a bundle of clothes. Sighing, Mama allowed Manang Neta to avoid entering the room and went over to take the pile from her hands.

"Hey, that's my jacket," I piped as I noticed one of the articles of clothing my mother was layering over Manang Inday from the results of Manang Neta's forage through the closets.

"Shusssh, boy," my father ordered. "Why do you need a jacket when you live in a tropical country?"

"But it's American and from Uncle Cosmos," I mumbled to myself ignoring his lesson that I lived in a "tropical country" and wishing only to retrieve the jacket my favorite uncle had sent me for my tenth birthday. My jacket was black with a picture of Captain Kirk, Mr. Spock and Dr. McCoy on the back.

"Okay, Gloria, what does this ghost want?" I could tell my father was losing patience by the way he emphasized his words. Since we moved from Manila to Baguio City three months ago, we had been visited by three ghosts, including the one who inhabited Manang Inday's body.

The first one was a dark shadow that hovered outside my parents' bedroom window and pleaded for old clothes that they could spare. The ghost made its request in what my father called a "whining, toadying tone that no self-respecting ghost would ever use because real ghosts should have no reason to behave towards humans in a servile manner!" In disgust, my father threw out his old bathrobe but refused to let my frightened mother empty the drawers for more clothes to dispense out the window.

"It's only a loko-loko from the neighborhood trying to stiff us," he said, waving at her to return to bed and slamming the shutters closed. However since my parents' bedroom overlooked the air over a steep-sided valley created by one side of Mount Asawa, we have never determined how a person could have managed to throw a shadow from right beyond my parents' bedroom window.

The second ghost appeared a month later and took the shape of my father's old bathrobe floating beyond the bathroom window when my mother had to exercise an act of nature in the middle of the night. With one frayed sleeve pointing at my mother, the mamau chastised my parents for their selfishness. The tunnel-like darkness of the empty sleeve reminded her, my mother later said, of the throat of a shark that had opened its jaws at her when she was a little girl swimming in the seashore by the fishing village where she was born. My mother decided to make a generous donation to the local orphanage the following day, much to my father's dismay.

"You weren't there!" Mama replied heatedly over breakfast after my father berated her for confusing dreams with reality. I sneaked a forgotten mango slice from my mother's plate as I waited for my father's response.

"Of course I wasn't there! Since when have I ever accompanied you to do your Number 2? It does not smell sweet, Madam!" my father roared back, stabbing his fork in the air and breaching one of my mother's rules of never pointing an eating utensil towards the direction of another. But my father's anger did not accomplish anything as my mother proceeded later that day with her gift to the orphanage.

"Susmaryosep! Don't use that tone of voice with me," Mama snapped back at my father as they discussed the third ghost. "You can listen, too, with your elephant-sized ears as I question the spirit."

By expressing "Susmaryosep" instead of the shortcut "Ayyyy-susss," I could tell my mother was really agitated. "Susmaryosep" is short for "Jesus, Mary, Joseph" whose names my relatives frequently invoked in moments of stress.

My mother bent over Manang Inday's quivering face. Poor Manang Inday, I thought as I always did whenever I happened to pay attention to her. Her face bore a distinct resemblance to Uncle Fillmore's bulldog: the same mournful brown eyes surrounded by drooping lids; the slack multi-layered folds below the chin; and a bulbous forehead. Uncle Fillmore also had noticed the resemblance upon acquiring the bulldog and so named it after Manang Inday, much to the distress of his wife, my Auntie Feling who sure must have busted one of Uncle Fillmore's eardrums with her views on the matter.

"Now, now. You should be warmer now," Mama crooned, her face about an inch away from the bump protruding from the tip of Manang Inday's nose. "Who are you and why are you visiting us through poor Inday's body?"

Manang Inday started to act like a fish, disconcerting my mother and causing her to move closer to us. The servant's lips kept shifting as she breathed through her mouth. Finally, the ghost discovered that one can breathe more easily through a nose and after a few times of becoming accustomed to this notion, used Manang Inday's mouth for speaking.

"Is that you, my little garbage can?" Manang Inday, or rather, the mamau, asked. It had to be the ghost because the voice did not sound like Manang Inday's voice. The voice was melodious instead of Manang Inday's that had reminded many listeners of the braying of a discontented goat.

"Is that you, my little garbage can?" the ghost repeated lovingly.

"Yes," Mama could manage only one word through the surprise, then prolonged wince contorting her features.

"Mama, why is she telling you a garbage can?" I asked the question as well on behalf of my father as, both wide-eyed, we looked at her.

The mamau laughed with Manang Inday's face: soft rolling peals that sounded like the hymn being outlined on air whenever the bells tolled from the church another hilltop away.

"My little garbage can, this must be your son, Matthew," the ghost said. "Well, I'll tell you why, my sweet boy."

I scowled at being called "sweet" but leaned closer with my parents toward Manang Inday's body. The mamau's voice was full of mischief, courting us with the manner of sharing confidences.

"When your mother was a little baby, I helped take care of her. We would spend many afternoons in the shade of the biggest star apple tree in your grandmother's yard. There we would sit, I rocking her back and forth while I feasted on little bags of sweets.

"Oooohhh, I had such sweet tooth," the ghost said with an air of self-congratulation. "I always carried around bags of churros, susporos de casuys, palitaos, polvorons, maja blancas, maruyas and bibingka. My favorite was puto maya; I loved to watch my mother make it with sweet rice, coconut milk, brown sugar and grated coconut meat. My, my, they were so delicious!"

Here, the mamau interrupted with a few choice smacks with Manang Inday's lips. My mouth also started to water.

"One day, your mother started crying and crying. I kept rolling her and patting her on the back but she would not stop bawling. Then I noticed her small chubby hands reaching into my bag of sweets. Your Mama wanted some, too.

221

"Well, she was just a baby and couldn't have eaten the snacks with her soft, little gums. So, after much thought, I chewed and chewed a tiny piece of my favorite puto maya and then fed the result to her. She loved that so much. And that's how she became my garbage can. Because I would chew sweets and feed them to her, directly from my mouth with a kiss."

"Eeeeeeuuuuuuuwwwwwwwhhhhh," my father cried out before we both burst in laughter and pointed our fingers at my mother who stood frozen, a pained look on her face. Mama tried to hide her embarrassment by starting to straighten her blouse and smooth her hair back into her bun.

"That's why you're a garbage can, because you ate her leftovers when you were a baby?" I wheezed between my laughter.

"Aaahhh, but Matthew, she was *my* little garbage can and so I loved my honey honey bun bun," the ghost noted, screwing up Manang Inday's lips into a grin wide enough to display the blackened fillings in all of Manang Inday's cavities.

My father elbowed me to look at him. Cross-eyed, he started whispering in a sing-song, "honey honey bun bun." Choking on my laughter, I bent and crossed my legs as I felt my bladder begin to expand.

My mother cleared her throat and asked in as business-like a demeanor as she could manage, "Auntie Lina, why are you there? What can we do for you?"

"I'll tell you, my darling, but before I do, could you bring me something to drink? I am so co o o o ld," the ghost replied and made Manang Inday's body shiver exaggeratedly.

Mama quickly called for Manang Neta. Manang Neta showed the back of her uncombed head again as she still refused to look into the room. "Yes, Ma'am," she squeaked.

"Heat up some Campbell's," Mama instructed.

"Yes, Ma'am," Manang Neta squeaked again and ran away to the kitchen.

"Campbell's soup? How kind of you to share such luxuries as American food," the ghost said gratefully. "But now, let me tell you why I'm here. Do you remember, my little garbage can, your distant cousin, Eliel?"

"Only vaguely, Auntie Lina. Doesn't he now live in Negros?" Mama asked, referring to Negros Occidental, the country's primary sugar-growing province.

"Yes, yes. Things are bad in Negros for your cousin's family. My heart breaks to see Eliel so skinny. He refuses to eat because his children do not receive full sustenance from the little that he can offer them. Yet he's the one who must remain strong to be able to feed his family," the ghost nodded Manang Inday's face up and down as she sighed.

"That is sad," Mama said. Solemnly, my father and I nodded our heads in agreement.

"Well, you and Andrew are doing so well here in Baguio City, two well-educated professionals that you are," the ghost continued. "Congratulations, Andrew, on your recent promotion to Senior Vice President at Banco Baguio! My goodness—you've become such a big-shot banker! And Gloria, to be principal of Baguio High School—what a coup!"

"You don't have to explain, Auntie Lina. We will be more than happy to help," my mother quickly interrupted. Mama later told me that hearing the mamau recite our family's good fortunes made her uneasy. "Never take blessings for granted, Matthew," my mother warned.

Unlike the situation with the other two ghosts, my father did not utter a single word of complaint over my mother's offer to provide assistance. He only pulled me closer and looked sadly at my mother.

After my mother agreed to assist Uncle Eliel, the mamau did not speak again, despite mother's questions and other attempts to engage her in conversation. She only indicated her presence by intermittently making Manang Inday's body relapse into a fit of shivers until Manang Neta brought the soup. The ghost still uttered no words as she finished a bowl of Campbell's noodles in chicken broth. After she emptied the bowl and emitted a loud burp, Manang Inday's body sat up on the bed with a startled look on her face, the layered clothes flung off disarray around her. When Manang Inday brayed at us familiarly like a goat, then we knew the ghost had departed.

*

Before we immigrated to the United States three years later, Uncle Fillmore and Auntie Feling agreed to my father's request that they provide assistance to Uncle Eliel and his family. But until we left, Mama dispatched a servant with packages of food and money every six months to travel the hundreds of miles to Negros which was located on the Southern part of the Philippine Archipelago.

As I helped my mother the day after the incident to pack the first set of provisions to Negros, Mama mentioned that she doubted that the mamau was actually Auntie Lina because she inhaled and drank the soup loudly.

"Your Auntie Lina never would have slurped. She was a lady," my mother emphasized, her hands patting the bun on her head to ensure that it had trapped all the stray strands of her hair.

"Yes, Mama," I agreed dutifully and then asked, "But Mama, why did you consent to helping Uncle Eliel if you didn't believe that the ghost was Auntie Lina?"

"Because Negros is Negros, my son. And I had no doubt that Eliel's family needed help. The ghost was just reminding me, that's all," Mama replied before turning aside and bending down to look at something in the rug.

She would have been upset if she knew I saw the teardrop sliding down her nose, I thought as I allowed her to pretend to rub away at an invisible stain on the rug.

Later, as we were packing to leave the country, my mother stumbled across a shoebox of correspondence from Uncle Eliel. She read from some of them and gave me the first letter Uncle Eliel wrote to her. Mama said I should bring the letter with me to the United States so that I will remember those who are left behind. My letter said...

We are so grateful for your help. We ate meat that day, the first that we have had for over a year. We usually eat only rice and vegetables, sometimes with fruit, and, of course, we have our water and salt.

The last time we ate meat, we found some frogs in the fields. We put on pieces of old clothes—of course all of our clothes are old, heh-heh— and kerosene in a bottle to make a light. Then we went frog-hunting at night. But, more often than not, we are too tired to hunt at night. When we get back to our barracks, it is late and we are so tired that all we can do is sleep.

My Uncle Eliel's letter mentioned other things but I usually thought about how his family did not have much to eat. Many years later, I conducted some research as an aide to a United States Senator who was being lobbied by Amnesty International regarding certain labor incidents in Negros.

I learned that about seventy percent of the province's sugar growing land was located in haciendas, a remnant from the Spanish colonial days which has been compared to American southern plantations before the American Civil War. The workers' houses were typically rough-hewn wooden shacks with no more than twenty-five square yards of floor space. Most families possessed only sparse furnishings such as thin straw sleeping mats and a few utensils. Many haciendas also contained barracks that were partitioned by cardboard walls to house sacadas, seasonal farm workers, from the poor of neighboring provinces. The sacadas were treated the worst among all workers, usually assigned the most menial and hardest jobs such as cutting cane. I remember my mother telling me that Uncle Eliel originally moved to Negros as a sacada and never managed to earn sufficient money to leave what he thought would be a one-year posting.

I learned that most hacenderos belonged to a tight-knit political oligarchy. Some were absentee landlords, enjoying the fruits of their wealth in Manila, Hong Kong, London, New York and elsewhere outside of Negros. Some paternalistically defended the hacienda as the best way of life for the people of Negros, who, some hacenderos said, were unable to become self-sufficient. At this notion, the representatives from Amnesty International scoffed before adding that in any event truly benign dictators would have been less inclined to ignore the widespread hunger and illiteracy surrounding them.

I learned that the landless comprised as much as ninety-eight percent of Negros' population and that the province's poverty rate exceeded eighty percent.

I learned that the land reform promised by Corazon Aquino when she overthrew Ferdinand Marcos never materialized and that the landless and impoverished continued to provide fertile ground for labor and political agitation, driven not only by communists but also local priests and nuns responding to the grinding poverty afflicting their flock.

I learned that Negros Occidental was a microcosm of the extreme economic and political inequities that affected the entire Republic of the Philippines. I grew to picture it vividly in my mind as a place where dark-windowed luxury cars drove around malnourished children too hungry and deprived of energy to do anything but mimic puddles on the dirt.

Finally, to finish my research, I tried to live on water and salted rice for as long as I could. I did not last long—a failed experiment that also made me recall the aftermath of the ghost's visit to my home in Baguio City. I remembered once more my consternation over how Uncle Eliel and his family would have hovered on the brink of starvation without my parents' aid. My childhood sense of security had been uninterrupted until my exposure to Uncle Eliel's dilemma as he worked the sugarcane fields of Negros. It was the first time in my life that I felt the ground shake beneath my feet. Uncle Eliel was not a stranger to my family; he was family. I never met him but for a long time after the mamau took over Manang Inday's body, I felt Uncle Eliel's presence every time I sat down at our dining table.

Ahhhhhh. Delicious, isn't it, my little garbage can, my honey honey bun bun? I would hear his voice behind me as I ate. When I turned around, there would be no one there or only one of the servants looking quizzically at my frightened expression. I came to imagine Uncle Eliel as a diaphanous, floating face with elongated chin exaggerating the size of his mouth, an open chasm trickling saliva from one corner as he coveted my food. I lost weight that year. It was also the year when, with hunger as my teacher, I first learned how to faint.

MARIANNE VILLANUEVA was born and raised in the Philippines. Her fiction and memoirs have appeared in The Santa Fe Writers Project, Café Irreal, Necessary Fiction, ZYZZYVA, Witness, and Gulf Coast, and in anthologies such as ms. Aligned 3: women writing about men, and Manila Noir. Her novella, Jenalyn, was a finalist for the UK's Saboteur Award. She has received fellowships from the California Arts Council, Banff Writers Studio, and the Bread Loaf Writers Conference.

MY SISTER-IN-LAW

Stories are the way I mourn the people who meant the most to me. I wrote Narisa after my sister-in-law passed away from leukemia, at thirty-seven. She and I had been on so many adventures together. She was the closest to a soul sister I ever had.

It is a dark story in mood, even though my sister-in-law was the sunniest, happiest person imaginable. Narisa was really about my rage at the unfairness of fate.

The heart of it is a trip my sister-in-law and I took to Angkor Wat. The trip had a spiritual significance for both of us. I remember how reverently she touched the stone panels that told the story of the Mahabharata. We would go early in the morning to be there at sunrise. We even stayed through the most punishing noon to early afternoon hours. Afterwards, we'd crawl back to our little pension and collapse!

17

NARISA

Her husband's side of the bed was empty and had been for some time. He was visiting the farms in Iloilo. She did not expect him back for at least another week.

She could hear the children stumbling downstairs for breakfast. They had to leave the house in near dark: Manila traffic was terrible—and getting worse. Even leaving at dawn, it would take the driver over an hour to get them to school. She debated whether to go downstairs and have breakfast with them; she was still thinking about it when she burrowed further into her pillows and closed her eyes.

Suddenly, the room was bright. Serafina glanced at the clock by her bedside and was surprised to discover that it was past 9. Already the house had settled into the languorous somnolence of a warm day.

Something had wakened her. A strange cry, like a child's. The last echoes of it were still there in the silent room.

Serafina lay in bed, willing herself to stay still.

The sound had seemed so close.

Suddenly, as if an hourglass had turned, the years began to fall away, began to shed, like skin. And there, before her, was the face of someone she had not thought about for a long time. They were together, in Siem Reap. She could feel the extraordinary, dizzying heat. She could see the crowd of little boys who waited as each tourist bus pulled in, disgorging its load of Japanese and Korean tourists. She saw the saffron-robed monks, smiling and chatting with people and posing for pictures, in complete indifference to their vows of silence. She saw the four gigantic stone faces of Buddha, rearing above the temple plain. She saw the frieze of stone panels engraved with *apsara*. And there was Narisa herself, a healthy, radiant Narisa, her delicate arms outstretched in invitation.

Don't be sorry, Narisa said. *I have no regrets.*

Somewhere, a peacock shivered. A panoply of colors beat in the still air. One, two. The peacock opened its mouth.

Narisa cared about things. About the environment. About clean air and clean water. In fact, about everything. When they were girls, she could never pass a beggar—and there were many in the streets of Manila—without giving something, anything. She collected stray cats as easily as other girls collected earrings and hair ribbons. She gave the maids English lessons.

The vultures are multiplying. That was how she referred to the developers. She said they had destroyed everything, even Siem Reap.

Narisa was the daughter of No. 3 Man in the Cambodian consulate. She and Serafina had met in third grade, in the convent school in Manila.

She was thin—almost extraordinarily thin. At first, Serafina had wondered if she were ill. Serafina had an active imagination, from reading the Mills & Boon paperbacks her aunt lent her. Serafina had taken a chance and peeked into her lunch bag one day. The contents of the bag, it disappointed her to learn, were shockingly ordinary: egg salad between two slices of white bread; a banana; two small, dry-looking cookies.

By the time she and Narisa were in fifth grade, they were spending all their weekends together. They shared dolls and birthday parties. They liked the same sort of books—*Nancy Drew* and *Little Women*—and music and television shows. They shared the same anxieties about grades. They even had the same skittishness about boys.

And then, one day, Narisa told Serafina that her father had been posted to Paris. The news was devastating. There were tears, tantrums, periods when Serafina thought the whole world was conspiring against them, all to no avail. Narisa had gone. A month later, Serafina received Narisa's letter, which broke her heart. Narisa loved Paris and was learning how to be happy there.

Serafina grew up. Her friends were the normal sort: girls who loved clothes and parties, who dreamed of being married one day. Her high school grades were good enough to get her into several small, private American universities on the West Coast: the University of California at Santa Cruz, Claremont, Mills. Her parents said no to Santa Cruz, fearing the pernicious influence of American morals and recreational drug use in a public university. t was so apparent what those Americans brought with them to the Philippine islands: there was always that bitter smell seeping out of their clothes.

Serafina did not choose, her parents did. She ended up in Mills. Towards the end of her freshman year, she happened upon Narisa again. Naturally, on Facebook.

From reading Narisa's wall, Serafina learned that Paris had not been the biggest adventure in her friend's life. Narisa had lived in Hong Kong and New Delhi, Rio de Janeiro and Tel Aviv. She had attended the University of Virginia in Charlottesville but at some point had dropped out. She had dated a Malaysian-Chinese boy, a boy her parents had approved of because he was the son of a business associate of her father's. She had been faithful to this boy, for years. But soon after they had set a date for the wedding, she met a Dutchman named Alexandre and ran off with him to Amsterdam. After several years, Narisa and her Dutch husband moved to Paris. The reasons for the move were rather vague, so Serafina simply assumed that the move was job-related.

Narisa's parents were dead. Her mother and father had died within a month of each other, both felled by lung cancer. Since Narisa was an only child, she was now completely alone in the world. Serafina left a message on Narisa's wall. A few days later, Narisa responded.

Serafina spent her days giving instructions to the help: Have you watered the plants? Are the children's lunches ready? Each passing year seemed to bring her closer to a great blankness. The lumbering buses, crawling like beetles and clogging up traffic, the surly policemen, always with their hands out for the shakedown; the pall of brown smoke hanging like fluorescent mist over the EDSA—all of these were coming to seem particularly oppressive.

Narisa was going home to Siem Reap. By herself. Serafina didn't feel like asking about the Dutch husband. All she knew was that Cambodia was not far.

Serafina had never been to Siem Reap. Had never, in fact, traveled around Asia, except for shopping trips to Hong Kong. But she had seen pictures of the temples of Angkor Wat. She had been fascinated by the enigmatic Buddha faces, draped by snaking vines. Yes, she decided. She would go. Yes, she would join Narisa in Siem Reap.

The peacock wandered around Narisa's garden, resplendent. Its feathers shivered slightly as it walked. It would pause at the pool and remain in the same spot, looking down at the murky green water as if entranced by its own reflection, for long minutes. Now and then it would emit a thin, wailing cry, a cry that sounded like a baby's thin wail. It never failed to startle Serafina.

"My crazy peacock!" Narisa would say, laughing. "My crazy, crazy peacock!"

Apart from the peacock, there was an Australian emu. And two feral brown monkeys who kept up high-pitched chattering and thumped around on the roof as soon as the sun was up. A gaggle of ducks waddled around a stone fountain, sometimes chased by a thin, black cat. Serafina accepted this eccentricity—after all, Narisa did not have any children.

She was still the gentle spirit Serafina had known, except that now her large, dark eyes were full of wry humor. Why had she not found anyone to love her and take care of her?

Not a day passed without Narisa looking directly into Serafina's eyes and asking, "Are you happy? Here, right now?"

Every morning, they had breakfast on a balcony that overlooked the garden. A young man in a white shirt and dark pants poured them rich, dark coffee. Narisa spoke proudly of her kitchen, run by the young man's mother. "His mother worked for my mother. I grew up on her curries and fish cakes," Narisa said. "But now, Tia Dith is old. She holds the stirring spoon like this." She demonstrated with her right hand, simulating a claw.

Serafina threw a quick glance at the youth, who was at that moment setting a basket of warm croissants on the table. His face remained still, pure, untroubled. He didn't understand English, probably. Serafina was relieved.

Narisa continued:"His mother is teaching him how to cook. He lived with his father in Pnomh Penh for a while, but two years ago he returned. He hates the city. No one told him that Siem Reap had turned into a city as well."

How beautiful her life is, thought Serafina. She tried to staunch the feelings of envy; Narisa would have been horrified to learn of them.

Along with croissants, there was always fruit—guava, star apple, papaya—accompanied by tall glasses of frothy watermelon or mango juice. For dinner there was steamed fish or roasted chicken, pumpkin or eggplant stews, prawns baked in banana leaves, cilantro-flavored salads. Serafina found herself unexpectedly happy and content. It was not something she was used to feeling.

The two women made it a point to rise early. The driver was instructed to take them to the smaller temples, away from the masses of tourists. Cambodia, Narisa said, was fast becoming what she contemptuously referred to as "a Disneyland." She was upset, profoundly upset. She had grown up in Siem Reap and knew what it had been like, before. Before the Chinese and Korean tour groups and the humanitarian aid workers and the Raffles Hotel.

"The people are thieves," she said. "They are excellent pickpockets. Tourism is a sickness. A fucking sickness."

Serafina raised her eyebrows. She had never said that word, never. Even now, though the women were alone, she wondered at Narisa's saying it. Was this Narisa's way of telling her, "You don't really know me?"

Or was it simply a form of bravado?

Narisa's English was fluid, excellent. There was just the slightest suggestion of an accent. Her sentences had a peculiar lilt: they always ended softly, even when Serafina knew Narisa was trying to be her most emphatic.

There was a small rundown building right by the main causeway. It may have been a temple once. Here the orange-robed monks gathered to chat with tourists and pose for pictures. It made Narisa angry to observe them.

"It is not right," she said, shaking her head. Her small head, bound with a light blue silk scarf. "They no longer care about the vow of silence."

Inside one of the temples, water bubbled up from some ancient spring. The whole of Angkor, Narisa told Serafina, had been constructed over an underground reservoir. She laughed when Serafina scooped up a handful of the water and splashed it over her face. "Now," Serafina said, "Will I be lucky?" The water was slimy. Serafina felt a twinge of fear as it ran over her eyes. She thought of waterborne blindness, disease, death. What recklessness! But Narisa always had that power, that power to make her forget herself.

During Narisa's childhood in Siem Reap, she told Serafina, she had rarely encountered foreigners. The town was a backwater. The ruins of Angkor Wat lay in isolated and resplendent decay, only the shriek of monkeys disturbing the quiet. Narisa and her friends were free to climb to the tops of the old temples, to smoke cigarettes and drink beer there. Sometimes the yellow-robed monks smoked with them. Then they would lie back against the mossy old stones and gaze at the long rows of buildings, buildings that had stood there forever.

"There was one monk," Narisa told her. "He had the most beautiful, delicate ears. Sensitive, too. He was not made to be a monk. His family had given him to the monastery, because he was the third son and the fifth child. They thought, at least in the monastery, he would be fed."

Those days, Narisa told Serafina, people were more respectful of the temples. Their lives were oriented around the river, about what could be taken down the river to Phnom Penh, or what could be brought upriver from there. Later came American cigarettes. American jeans. News. Wars were fought far away: in Vietnam, in Laos. What evil there was in Siem Reap was of a different sort.

Now, of all the old buildings, the only one that remained was the School for the Blind. Narisa told Serafina that she still went once a week to the school for the blind, where you could have an hour-long massage for the equivalent of 50 US cents. Narisa said she loved the feel of hands, tentative, against her skin. The room where she lay, on a narrow wooden table covered only by a thin mattress, was very large, plain, with windows that had no shades. All that shielded the bed from prying eyes was a flimsy bamboo screen.

"The boys are very good," she told Serafina. As she spoke, her face became remote and sad. Serafina had never met the Dutch husband. All she knew were the handful of pictures on Narisa's Facebook wall. She couldn't even recall his name. Alex? "I am not married anymore," Narisa finally admitted. "We have been divorced a number of years."

There had been, Narisa told her now, a baby, a death. Serafina could feel the despair behind Narisa's words. She didn't know how to respond. She tried to switch topics. She pretended that she hadn't detected Narisa's unhappiness.

"What a beautiful bird that is," Serafina said, gesturing toward the peacock, who was at that moment strutting awkwardly on the lawn. "Oh, that," Narisa said. "Her name is Angsana."

"Does it stand for something?" Serafina asked.

"I don't know," Narisa said. "The houseboy picked out the name."

Serafina had turned her head to look at Narisa, but Narisa had her head lowered, and Serafina couldn't see her eyes.

Shortly Serafina had returned to Manila, she received a message from Narisa. She had not slept in six days. She'd just been told that there was cancer in her liver.

She said, "I asked all my old friends to come, everyone is juggling commitments."

Serafina responded quickly: "I'll come." She wondered what she was escaping from.

The line for passport control was longer than Serafina had remembered. A military officer yelled, "Hold your passports up! High up!" The soldiers were cold, businesslike, unsmiling. One yanked Serafina's hand so high she felt she was making a salute. Serafina shrank from him. "I'm sorry," she stammered. "I'm sorry."

The heat was alive, an animal licking at her skin. Narisa was just outside the building, standing in front of a small white car. She waved at Serafina. Narisa said, "Well, let me tell you, you look exhausted. You must bathe," she said. "Rest. Thank you for coming back again so soon."

Instead of replying, Serafina hugged her friend close. She could feel the ribs through the back of Narisa's blouse.

Again they walked around the ruins, again they chatted on the balcony while the boy served lemon grass tea. His face was beautiful, Serafina decided. She watched his hands as they arranged plates on the gleaming white tablecloth—the fingers were long and delicate. He moved so carefully, as if the plates—sturdy, earthstone—were precious.

Narisa wanted to talk about mutual friends: the girls who'd been their classmates in the convent school in Manila. "Remember Jinggay?" she said. "And Pete? And Gina? Jinggay's husband is some kind of diplomat, I ran into them in Phnom Penh. I invited her to visit—anytime! But that was a year ago and I never heard back from her."

And what about Sandy, Serafina asked. "Ah yes, Sandy," Narisa said, her upper lip curling in amusement. Sandy's father was American. She went into the backs of cars with boys, all the time. "She is a doctor now, I heard," Naris said. "She has her own clinic in Tucson. She's actually crazy about her husband. She sends me pictures. Looks a little like George Clooney."

Narisa's voice always had that tone of gentle amusement, but now she spoke haltingly, and her hands were veined and knotted, not like the hands Serafina had known before, not like the hands that stroked the keys of whatever piano Narisa happened to be near. She had studied for many years. The playing went away, like smoke.

Narisa described for Serafina the blood, the pain, the stillborn baby.

It was many years later. Serafina lay alone in her bed. "Where are you?" she said softly, to the silent room. "Tell me, have you turned to smoke? What do you think: shall we see each other again?" Serafina waited long, but the only other sounds she heard were the beams of her old wooden house, settling slowly into its foundations.

When Serafina saw Narisa again, that time in Siem Reap, her long black hair was a memory. Her head was wrapped in a light blue silk scarf. The bones of her neck and shoulders stood out, like the bones of a young bird. Or a baby chick. There was fear in her eyes. That look hurt Serafina, worse than any knife wound.

Narisa said, vaguely, "Perhaps the water—"

"Do you mean here, in Siem Reap? Some chemical contamination?"

"No, no," she brushed away the supposition. "Paris. I was living there when I was diagnosed."

Serafina had four children, an indifferent husband, and two enormous black poodles who sat on the couch and kept her company while she watched TV. Narisa thought she was lucky.

At some point, there seemed to be a glut of articles about Angkor Wat in the glossy travel magazines. The articles talked about the feelings of wonder evoked by the first sight of the temples and of the Buddha faces, so squat and serene, facing the four directions. People lined up at 4 in the morning, taking light readings with their expensive cameras, waiting for the first rays of sun to strike the causeway, the limpid pools of standing water. It was like a veneration, like a gathering of pilgrims. Angkor Wat had been designated a World Heritage Site by UNESCO. The biggest donors to the restoration program were the South Koreans, followed by the Japanese.

One day, Narisa and Serafina had decided to hire a boy and his elephant to take them to the top of a nearby hill. Serafina listened: Narisa was in the kitchen, speaking to the young houseboy. His voice was rough and angry, which surprised her. She peeked in the door and saw the boy and Narisa standing very close, Narisa practically leaning into him. And then the boy pushed her friend away. Serafina quickly backed away from the door.

In a few minutes, Narisa emerged. Her eyes were red. "Let's go," she said. Serafina was filled with disquiet.

The elephant that took them to the top of the hill was an old female. Her flanks were painted with bright red diamonds. Was this some kind of good luck symbol, Serafina wondered? Tiredly, the animal plodded upwards. When they stopped and looked at the temples on the plain, Serafina was spellbound. Was this what those ancient priests must have seen, as they looked at the vast network of temples and spires?

The boy who led the elephant was bored. After a few minutes, he began making clucking sounds, which Serafina guessed was his way of telling the elephant to turn. But the elephant seemed too exhausted to even turn. The boy grabbed a long stick and began to prod at the elephant's eyes.

"No!" Narisa shouted. "Stop! If you don't stop now, we will not pay you."

The boy stopped. Eventually, the animal turned. They rode most of the way back in silence. When they were almost back at the temples, Serafina asked, "Does your animal have a name?"

"Bongkatmas," the boy said.

Narisa exclaimed, "That is a Thai name!"

The boy said simply, "My mother was Thai."

Afterwards, when the ride was over and Narisa was paying the boy for his services, he produced a small wooden elephant from the pocket of his ragged shorts.

"You like?" he said. "For you, special price. Only US$7. It's good luck, see the trunk? Pointing up? Always good fortune for the owner!"

"Don't!" Narisa cried. Serafina had been reaching for her purse, thinking: $7 was not too big a price to pay if it would feed this boy's family for a few nights. But she stopped when she saw the anger on Narisa's face.

"$7 is a lot for that," Narisa said.

"Please," the boy said. "I am poor. Very poor."

"Don't beg!" Narisa admonished him. "You must never, ever beg. Begging makes you no worse than an animal."

The boy shrugged and turned away. Serafina watched his back for a few moments. Something about the droop of his shoulders made her want to call him back. "Hey!" Serafina said. "Here's five dollars for you. I know that's more than it's worth. But I'm doing it because I like you. Okay? So you'll remember us."

The boy's face broke into a wide grin.

Afterwards, in the car, the little wooden elephant on Serafina's lap, Narisa said, "The people are ruined. Absolutely ruined."

Narisa did not die in Siem Reap. She was desperate to live, so when she heard about a healer in Mexico, she went. She was almost not granted a visa, the consular official knew at once that there was some kind of problem. He said, not unkindly, "You may not have the strength to return. Do you know anyone in Mexico?"

"Yes," she lied. But she didn't.

There was also the matter of her traveling companion, a young man. He was almost not granted a visa. But Narisa appeared so distressed at the thought of traveling alone, and was so obviously ill, that the immigration officer relented and let them both through. That was what she told Serafina.

Serafina sent Narisa a private message. "That boy—he is your lover?"

"No!" Narisa said. "I think I am in love with him, but I'm too old. He is married, he has two little children. His wife feels sorry for me and lets him care for me."

Within a month it was over. At the very end, she was not alone.

The young man returned to Siem Reap. Serafina could not remember his name. She was sorry she had no way of contacting him.

Later, there were all the usual recriminations: what was Narisa thinking, and so forth and so on.

She wanted to live. Who could blame her? Serafina understood her desperation. As regards Serafina's own health, she was fortunate: Thus far, she was 39 and had never suffered anything more troublesome than a vague pain deep in her belly during her monthly periods. What Serafina considered luck, Narisa called a blessing. Serafina resisted such a notion; she didn't think she owed thanks to anyone.

Narisa was not a religious person, but she was spiritual. In one of her last e-mails, she had mentioned the name of a famous healer. Serafina googled him and found a picture of a dark-skinned man with penetrating eyes. He had begun healing while still a Catholic priest. Eventually, his healing had created a rift between himself and his superiors. He was asked to leave the priesthood.

He still had many followers. They built a house for him in a small town in Oaxaca. Sick people began traveling to Mexico just to see him. The authorities discouraged it, on the grounds that he was taking money from people who were desperate. But more and more people came, every day.

Serafina imagined Narisa kneeling, offering her face to the man's healing touch, her eyes closed, her slender hands clasped together.

Serafina wrote to the healer, not really expecting anything, but after several weeks, he did respond. "Your friend was already very sick when she arrived here," the healer wrote. "There was nothing I could do for her. Except help her to endure the pain."

At the very end, when Narisa was at her weakest, he helped her out of her clothes, wrapped her in a soft grey robe, and lowered her into a warm pool of bubbling spring water. She gave a soft, contented sigh and lowered her head. After a while he noticed that she hadn't moved at all. Her eyes were still open. So she passed. So she slipped away.

"She was at peace," the healer said.

But, Serafina thought: the trauma of experiencing the senses shutting down, one by one.

All the body knows is life. It will not yield until made to.

The previous night had been bad. Serafina was close to finishing her 30-day allotment of Ambien, but she'd swallowed two little pills, praying they would work. Lying on her bed, on soft down pillows that annoyed her, pillows she used only because her husband has developed an irritating tendency to want to be surrounded by the most expensive accoutrements, Serafina imagined Narisa in the water.

What was it about desire? It gnawed at her heart. Age and time did nothing to quench its intensity.

The little wooden elephant Serafina bought from the little boy in Siem Reap, the one who caused Narisa's eyes to flash in anger, a rare and unsettling anger, was on her desk, next to her computer.

One cannot have everything. One cannot live as Narisa did, insatiable. Serafina knew this with pure certainty.

But, gratitude. That, one should feel. Every day.

She began to plan the night's dinner.

MARILYN C. ALQUIZOLA was born in San Francisco, California to Juvencio C. Alquizola and Sofia Caballero Alquizola, both from Cebu. Her life-long interest in literature was instilled in her by her father, Juvencio, who wrote poetry. Marilyn has taught Asian American Literature at several universities and has published articles on Carlos Bulosan, Asian American Literature, and Asian American Studies. Currently, she has broadened her scope to the areas of multi-media arts such as painting, sculpting and assemblage, video, and creative writing.

BARRIERS BY LAW

The original communities of Filipinx Americans were very much unlike what you see in the States today. The immigration of Filipinx to the United States, minutely varied, was predominantly limited to one of young working-class males who contributed their labor to the work of agriculture and food production, generating a community of bachelors during the 1920's and 1930's. The gender imbalance in these communities was exacerbated by legal barriers such as the anti-miscegenation laws that enforced racial segregation and criminalized interracial marriage. Thus, the establishment of a family and other rights of a normal life were limited especially when compared to the dominant culture population. The historic beginnings of the Filipinx American communities that were systemically constrained in terms of access and resources is reflected in the characters of "It's Cold in America!!" Although the actual story takes place in the 1950's setting of the Cold War, the residual effects of racism resonate in the interaction of the characters involved.

18

IT'S COLD IN AMERICA

Once a week or so, a small party would gather in the Abadias' flat in San Francisco's South of Market district. Some years later, the modest working-class neighborhood would be transformed into the SoMa district peopled with hipsters and pretenders frequenting trendy shops and restaurants. But for now, it was a blend of industrial buildings and flats. And in one homey flat, Mr. and Mrs. Abadia were waiting for the staggered arrivals of their weekly guests. So, it was a good thing that their third-floor flat, with so many stairs, had a workable lever that remarkably opened the door from the upstairs perch. Their front door, made of wood, framed an all-too-transparent rectangle of glass that Sylvia Abadia, with delicate strategy, covered in cream-colored lace. Cream was her favorite neutral, and she deftly disguised the flat's cold atmosphere with skills she learned in 'industrious' classes during her early school days.

The industrious homemaker once made her own living as a single woman in commerce and midwifery in the Philippine islands. Shortly after arriving in the States, she set upon a new life and changed her name from Sylvia Fernando Delgado to Mrs. Sylvia Delgado Abadia, eventually becoming a reluctant stay-at-home wife of the 1950's. She spent her daylight hours crocheting doilies and bedspreads, sewing dresses, skillfully manipulating her old-timey, paddle-operated Singer sewing machine that she had acquired from a comadre who lived a few blocks away. She systematically painted the walls and then the bare, uncarpeted wooden steps with a mustard-colored paint she wistfully referred to dark gold. Her peculiar palette of colors, a cream on the wainscot and a light green above the lower panel, worked in the totality. A pale yellowish green in the kitchen, the almost hot pink in a bedroom, and the aubergine patterned rug all worked to counteract the ascetic and cold atmosphere of the flat.

The guests would begin to arrive in early evening, making their way up the wooden stairs in staggered arrivals. A slender woman was first to arrive, not having far to travel since she lived in the downstairs flat. Jean Johnson was the Abadias' tenant. (Mrs. Abadia, through her practiced frugality, managed to acquire the building they lived in.) Usually coming with husband in tow, she was alone this evening. With her lie-gap smile as a bright accessory, she climbed the stairs. Laughing gaily, she started her chitchat before reaching the top, her husky-voiced English dotted with Visayan accents and heavy footfalls. She made a lot of noise for one so slight.

Other more sedate arrivals would watch their footing in silence, afraid that any misstep may result in a painful tumble on the hard bare "dark-gold" stairs. More often than not, outsiders to the community would arrive empty-handed. Those culturally adept would bring something, some foodstuff or something to drink, to add to the bounty.

From week to week, the visitors varied. Some guests were regulars, and others appeared then disappeared. They were a mixed assortment of folks that didn't seem to fit together, and yet they were there in one room. All were warmly welcomed by the hosts, Sylvia and Benigno Abadia, referred to as Manong Benny and Manang Sylvie by those who were younger. For the peers, elders, and outsiders, the honorific title was dropped.

The guests gathered around the entertainment center of the day, not a cumbersome cabinet with a large-screened TV, but a red formica table with curved chrome-colored legs. Brazenly mimicking marble, the tabletop was a far cry from that in cost and appearance. The slightly padded vinyl chairs were matched and colored with the same red hue, resonant of the group's vibrant spirit. These people did not come to relax and make small talk. They came to play hard, make noise, and make big talk! The Abadia cluster of friends was a blend of strays. There were single folks without families and there were also couples. Most were from the Philippines. Some were "Americans," which was a synonymous with white. Other comers and goers were from nondescript foreign countries. They were an odd assortment.

The kitchen with its shiny table adjacent to the stove, was favored by all over the living room, which lay at the polar end of the long hallway. This room, the living room, housed a green sofa, heavily padded, adorned with crocheted green and yellow doilies on the headrest and arms, and far more comfortable than the hard vinyl chairs. The room had a view of the wide alley seen through its bay window, a functional architectural signature in the overcast city of St. Francis. Even though the living room offered more physical comforts, it could not compete with the kitchen as the place to mingle.

On both sides of the long hallway were more rooms: the bathroom with the claw-foot tub and a sink, and separate commode in yet another room. There were also two small bedrooms on the same side, opposite the stairway leading downstairs to the front door. Other than that, it was a straight path from the kitchen and dining room to the living room and master bedroom at the other end. On the mustard floor in the hallway lay a long, floral-patterned, runner rug that evoked the images of octopus or squid tentacles more than it looked like flowers. This illusion was bolstered by the rug's color, a shade similar to the color of pusit, a dish Manang Sylvie often cooked. It was like squid in su tinta, in its inky aubergine sauce, similar to a Spanish tapa or a comparable dish made in Cuba.

Instead of the hallway runner, Sylvie, in her daydreams, pined for wall-to-wall carpeting, a luxury craving cleverly marketed that made her current carpet less desirable to her. For Sylvie, an already Americanized consumer, less was not more. More was always more. She would have appreciated better what she had on hand if only she recalled that the hallways of the first and second-floor tenants were pitiably covered with worn-out patchy linoleum, remnants of previous days and previous dwellers. Wall-to-wall carpeting was never to be installed in the flat, another daydream among many unrealized.

Characteristically, Sylvia Delgado had what her relatives back home called "high-hat" thoughts. Her cousins and nieces said she always sought after "society," as they called it. Sitting in her living room with a carpet that matched the hallway carpet that was also not wall-to-wall, she adorned the rounded glass coffee table with more hand-crocheted, flower-laden doilies that she starched so the floral decorations would stand up proudly. In short, she made do. That was her fate. Bahala na. Her current society was waiting in her kitchen that evening. It was not the society of earlier dreams. The members of this social group did not bring prestige such as that was. Instead, they brought laughter, gossip, good times, loose change. and crumpled dollar bills to stake in a card game of winning and losing.

Back in the kitchen, the noise level rose and the little party started to bubble as dinner was served. "Seelbia, he called her, "That dish reminds me of when I was young," said Pedring, their gentleman friend. Tonight, the ever-handy chicken and pork adobo was one of the viands, a term used in lieu of entree. And of course, there was the compulsory steamed white rice, a staple made properly on the stovetop by the miraculous measurement of water that reached the joint of the first knuckle, no matter what amount of rice was being cooked. There was a definite technique to cooking rice, as these were the days before the rice-cooker became a kitchen fixture. Sadly, the advent of the rice cooker subtracted something vital from the rice: the brown crust at the bottom of the pot, delicious when doused or soaked with a flavorful soup. In the Abadia household, it was called dukot, both a culinary by-product and humble delicacy of the past, a culinary casualty and collateral damage of smart technology in the kitchen.

Other dishes followed in tow, among them a sautéed mixed vegetable and pork dish, mostly made with chopped chard and flavored with garlic, onion and toyo. The hosting couple borrowed or stole a name for this dish, and called it chop suey, after the dish that was really more Chinese American than Chinese. Calling the Abadia dish chop suey was a small fiction borrowed from another fiction. It was just pretend chop suey, an invention on top of invention. Not to belabor the listing of the night's menu, let's just say that it was longer, more varied, and plentiful than most "American" menus, characteristic of provincial hospitality.

After dinner was served and eaten, a more boisterous interaction was yet to begin after the dinner dishes were cleared by Sylvie and the female guests as they played their putative traditional roles. Now the cards and the beer came out, and maybe even some whiskey, brought by a guest as a cordial offering. It was a simple game they played. Only three pairs took the pot, and the joker was wild. The spelling of the game's name remains a mystery, but it was pronounced like "pie— oot" with an emphasis on the second syllable. The name of the game became the victory cry of the winner. Sometimes a winner would actually slam their six cards on the table and shout "pie-OOT!" Obviously, this winner had drunk a lot of beers. Like the stovetop predecessor to the rice cooker, the beers were simple and non-pretentious in spite of their fancy sounding names: labels like Pabst Blue Ribbon, Budweiser, Falstaff, and Schlitz would occupy shelves in the Frigidaire. Crafty beers and San Miguel had not yet made their entry into accessible popularity. Nonetheless, these frugal beers did their job, juicing up the revelry of the players. There were those present who did not drink any or much beer. Nonetheless, they too were animated participants in the spirit of the effortless card game that prompted salubrious laughter.

A panoply of different sounds permeated the evening in the third-floor kitchen: losing or winning card hands slapping the shiny red formica, a hand or a fist thumping the table, beer cans banging after a refreshing quench, Visayan or Tagalog curses and blessings added to the soundtrack of the evening. "Yawa!! Putang ina!" A man named Loy loudly invoked the devil, simultaneously insulting someone's mother as he slammed his losing hand onto the table a split second after Benigno Abadia declared his victory. As much as he was mixing languages, Loy had been anxiously awaiting a deuce card, ironically calling on the deuce himself in a single apt Visayan word: Yawa!!

If there was chaotic noise above and upon the table top, there was also a peculiar sound beneath the table. Below this sundry pandemonium, another sound was heard—that of a slight jingling: jingle, jingle-jangle. What was it? Above the din, nobody really heard it. So, no one took notice. Beneath the table someone was pulling a chain attached to a mechanism that enabled the placement of an additional middle panel designed to increase the table surface. Beneath the card players was another player, playing another game. Who knows what this player was doing with that chain? Perhaps the player used the table as a toy. Whatever the case, the game had only one requirement: Imagination. Beneath the table was a sneak, a hider, a lurker, who for all intents and purposes was invisible to the players above the table.

The Abadias had an only child, an additional person Mrs. Abadia had neither expected nor planned. Yet there she was, a younger being in the midst of an adult world. Mr. Abadia had resided in the U.S. since the age of seventeen, having himself escaped what his parents considered to be an untenable situation. He did not meet his wife-to-be until he was well into his thirties. Sylvia Delgado, also in her thirties, had led the life of a very small businesswoman in her provincial town, had become a midwife, and later a nanny or self-termed governess for a diplomatic family with five children. She had only planned to visit the States with them for ten days. The diplomat's wife was perhaps a distant cousin either fictive or real, but never verified. Benigno Abadia met Sylvia Delgado during her visit to the States, and the rest was history, as they say. Sylvia's stay of ten days became the stay of a lifetime. She was to return thirty years later, and only for a visit.

If her parents were strangers in a strange land, this child was stranger still. She was a child of a different climate, born in the United States in the overcast unsunny city of San Francisco. (According to her mother who often shivered in her flat with no central heating, "It's cold in America!!") Wide-eyed and controlled with strict discipline, the child seemed to take no offense at the adults who laughed at the American speech and pronunciation she acquired from programs watched on her parents' winged Natalie Kalmus television honed out of blond wood. She did take some offense, however, at her mother's friend who pinched her cheek quite severely outside the church after Mass on Sunday, as she squealed in a high-pitch voice, "Sooo cute!" Not only did this dreadful woman pinch, she shook the child's tender fold of flesh while she pinched. Was this passive aggression, or was it just child abuse? The child said nothing, was mute because her mother firmly enforced the notion that children should be seen and not heard, especially when they could not be polite and pleasant. Being one of few children in her parents' mostly adult society, she was certainly conspicuous, which is why and how she learned that becoming inconspicuous was a very good strategy indeed. Aurora Delgado Abadia often kept quiet and did not speak until spoken to. If other children did come around to her household, they like normal children would seek their own society, play in other rooms, making up their own games on the side. They would sneak about leaving the noisy adult society to their own devices. Sometimes, during card games, there would be a companion child, and they would also play underneath the red formica table. They were small enough, and certainly quiet enough, especially given the high level of noise made by carousing gamblers.

Aurora or Aurie, for short, became a watcher of people before people-watching became a thing. She reviewed and judged the parade of characters that came into her parents' flat. The red-topped table became the roof that hid her presence. At other times, she lurked behind a door, or in a closet. She became a spy, a watcher of people. She also became a judge, a judger of people.

Aurie's favorite regular was the fictive aunt she called Auntie Jean, the first-floor tenant: Jean Johnson (a married surname). Jean was not her real name. It was her adopted American name, somehow derived from her birth name that remained a mystery to Aurie. Other things about her were also a mystery. When speaking about Jean behind her back, Aurie's parents forgot that their daughter had ears, even though Sylvia often expressed dismay at the largeness of her daughter's ears. It didn't matter. Often, she did not completely understand the things she wasn't supposed to hear in the first place. For instance, she had heard that back in the Philippines Auntie Jean had been a "bar girl,' a euphemism for something more adverse. Auntie Jean had lived in Angeles, Pampanga, a town with a military base, and its myriad attendant corruptions. She came to the U.S., after marrying an Air Force, master sergeant, a very handsome African American man who became Aurie's Uncle Charles. It was from Charles that Jean acquired the surname Johnson. There was also talk of Auntie Jean having a daughter left back in the P.I., whose father was an Italian American military man. Auntie Jean also bragged about having a boyfriend name Jackson, but he never materialized in her parents' home, although Auntie Jean did show Aurie a black and white photo of the man.

Aurie admired Auntie Jean's glamor and humor. She thought it interesting that she acted very differently from the rest of her mother's women friends. Watching from her listening post at the open bay window in the living room, Aurie once espied Jean yelling loudly at a truck driver in front of the flat because he was saying something disparaging about her driving. She yelled at him vociferously. "Don't shout at me!" She yelled some other things as well. That scene tickled Aurie. It was also a source of amusement to her parents as well after Aurie gleefully ran from her post to relate the incident to them. Auntie Jean was yelling at a white truck driver! And, he was quite entertained by her as well, as one could discern from the benign chuckle and smiling face.

Mr. and Mrs. Abadia were well aware that Auntie Jean was a feisty character, but how feisty, they didn't know. One night, she was baby-sitting Aurie and another older girl, a fictive cousin if you will. She had come to visit when the Abadias took their routine journey to Reno for some gambling. Late at night, the sleeping children were woken by Auntie Jean's loud shriek. "Don't you tell me that! I'm going to kill you dead!" Even in the dark room, both the startled children could see Auntie Jean's reflection in the glass window of a door, and she was wielding a very large kitchen knife, pointing it threateningly at her handsome husband. The older girl began to sob. When Aurie saw her "cousin" crying, she also acted accordingly. After all, wielding big knives was far from a good thing, and it seemed like a dire situation altogether. While the older girl was sobbing like a "big girl" into her pillow, Aurie was not yet a big girl. Sitting up in the bed, she let out a big bellow followed by a piercing wail. "Waaaah!" Witnessing the impromptu duet of sobs and wails, Auntie Jean took the opportunity to further berate her husband, assigning guilt and blame to the already castigated spouse. "Now look! See what you did!! You made the children cry! See there! See!" See!!"

Auntie Jean was gutsy and had a lot of nerve. She placed all blame on the quiet man in front of her when it was really her antics and her shouting that woke the girls up in the first place. Moments later, her rage turned to sympathy as she sat on the edge of the bed, rubbing the children's arms and backs, comforting them in dulcet tones. No one was stabbed, slashed, or even nicked in the flat that night. Did the girls' weeping and bawling diffuse the situation? It's hard to say.

Even Aurie knew that Auntie Jean had a penchant for acting up or just plain acting. An addict to drama, Auntie Jean was Aurie's favorite.

Another couple who often visited the Abadias were the Romeros. Both were from the P.I., their only congruent characteristic. Their stark dissimilarities were much more glaring. They were quite the odd pair. Mellie Romero was much older than her husband. She looked like his mother rather than his wife. Aurie had been instructed to call her Auntie Mellie. She too was not her real aunt. Mellie was very small in stature, with greying hair, and a rounded body. Aurie thought of her as Mrs. Potato Head, although it was her body not her head that resembled a potato. And this Mrs. Potato Head smoked cigarettes just like women in movies and television! Aurie's proper mother never smoked. Even the improper Auntie Jean didn't smoke! The strangest thing about Auntie Mellie, Aurie observed, was her custom of rolling down her nylon stockings below the knees. She must have used rubber bands to hold them up. Why she made this strange and unglamorous fashion choice was a mystery to Aurie who knew better with the fashion sense she acquired from watching television dramas on the small black and white screen. Auntie Mellie wore red lipstick and make-up like the women in the Technicolor movies. But smoking and red lipstick were where Auntie Mellie's attempts at glamour began and ended.

Auntie Mellie's husband, a fictive Uncle Loy was significantly younger than she, and appeared to be at least a foot and a half taller. He had oily, jet black, curly hair. He was out-going and loquacious, and described as handsome by some, although Aurie didn't agree. For one thing, he smoked smelly cigars that Aurie couldn't stand, and he would stick a toothpick into the soggy end that went into his mouth, so he wouldn't have to stress his lips. He also saved his partially smoked cigars for later use. That was simply disgusting to the child. The word her mother used to describe Loy was palikero, a playboy with a soggy, used cigar. Being so tall, and talking down to the child, he sometimes annoyed her. In spite of this, she had to be polite to him per her mother's mandate. She did not want to incur any more nagging lectures than she had to.

One Christmas, Aurie had asked Santa for a doll with pale green hair. This request on Santa's list was not as odd as it sounded. Aurie spotted the doll in JCPenney's store window and had coveted it ever since. Identical dolls had pink hair, blond hair, and even blue hair. The array of hair colors was like candy! Aurie set her heart on the green-haired one and got it. She named it Mary Jane.

During one of his frequent visits to the flat, Uncle Loy caught Aurie tightly clutching her beloved Mary Jane, scurrying quietly past him on her way to another room. Soggy tooth-picked cigar in hand, he called her over to him, foiling her narrow escape. Attempting humor, he seemed to mock her. "Aurora, what in the world are you doing with that doll with green hair. People don't have green hair! They have brown hair, black hair, blond hair, and red hair." But no one in the whole world has green hair!" She merely looked at him. There was nothing she could say. He was right. People of that era did not have green hair, but the green hair was what called to her. There was no argument from her as she stared at him in silence. To her credit, she never forsook her green-haired doll, but loved her all the more in spite of the oily man's rude intervention.

But, another one-way conversation with Uncle Loy at another time actually made some sense to Aurie in spite of her prejudice against him. In fact, it made a life-long imprint. Again, during one of his visits, Uncle Loy called Aurie over to him. "Aurora, come over here," he imperiously commanded. She responded this time with a short quite logical "What?" Loving to give her lessons in life about hair color and manners, he retorted, "Don't say 'What?' Say 'Yes' instead. 'What' sounds rude. 'Yes' sounds much better and so much more graceful." Cigar prop always in hand, he proceeded to demonstrate his point as he said, "Oh Aurie!" Pretending he was her, he immediately responded with a curt and tough-sounding, "Whut?!" To bring his point across, he accentuated the "whut" with an arrogant stance and a haughty look. (Jean Johnson was not the only actor.) Continuing his lecture, he again said, "Aurie!" Then with a sweeter tone and a drawn-out short e, he said, "Yeeess? You see? It sounds more 'classy' and more graceful!" After that day, a short and abrupt "whut" from anyone else always sounded rude and graceless to Aurie. Such are the valuable lessons in life that stick with you, and the messenger was Uncle Loy.

No one seemed to know the genesis of the odd pairing of Mellie and Loy Romero. If they did, Aurie never heard it even with her big ears. Was Uncle Loy looking for a mother, or was it a bonding of real love in spite of the generational divide and discrepancies in personal attractiveness? Also, there was the issue that she, not he, was the older of the two, thus changing the configuration of the typical May/December coupling. Or maybe it was a union of a practical matter, a way for him to stay in the U.S., the land of the Yankee dollar. Not even the lurker knew, not then and not later. Like many children, she took things at face value, having not yet reached the adolescent stage of prejudicial judgment. Auntie Mellie and Uncle Loy seemed to get along, never arguing or contradicting each other like her parents often did. Mr. and Mrs. Romero were a married couple, and to Aurie that was that.

Even if, much of the time, Aurie was the sole child amongst adults, there were other children spread throughout the city in a community unbound by borders. A younger male child with a single divorced mother from Japan and a father from the P.I. was sometimes cared for by her mother at their house. At other times, his childcare took place at the household of Mr. and Mrs. Martinez. The boy's name was Justin. His parents were actually divorced, which was unusual in the Abadias' sphere. His alternative babysitters, Melchor and Edita Martinez, were parents of her then best friend Belinda, a girl of the same age. When together, Aurie and Belinda would engage in mayhem. Once, a coke-drinking contest was initiated by Belinda. At a party attended by both adults and children, they began to bolt down cokes. When they kept asking for more coke after coke, the indulgent smiling adult in charge of coke dispensing never thought to stop them. It was a wonder that neither of them got sick. It was also no wonder that neither of them remembered who won the contest. At another time, clever Belinda thought up a biting contest, whereupon they would bite each other's fingers and faces. Although it hurt, Aurie was game. She always was. In the aftermath, she left a long-lasting scar on poor Belinda's face.

On one ominous day, an incident at Auntie Mellie's house actually involved Belinda's mother, Auntie Edita (fictive) in absentia. Three women present were partaking in a discussion of a serious nature. This was not a social get-together. That was clear. There was no food or drink, and no gambling. But in spite of the gravity of the subject, two of the women were their usual *viva* and cackling selves. Justin and Aurie were the only children present. Aunt Mellie of course was present in her own home. So was another woman, ostensibly a friend of Aunt Mellie unknown to the children. The third participant was Aurie's mother, Sylvia, who had the younger boy as her charge that day.

Auntie Mellie was sobbing profusely. She was the one person who was not *viva* and not cackling. Although Mellie was not normally an effusive woman, this behavior was quite unusual. With her open palm, Auntie Mellie was hitting her bare knee directly above her strangely rolled-down nylon stocking. Between sobs, she repeated the words, "I don't know why he's doing this to me! I love him. I need him. I love him! I need him!" Her voice became louder and louder as she accentuated her words with rhythmic thumps on the knee above her rolled-down stocking. Aurie wide-eyed with wonder could focus only on the rolled-down stocking with its lumpy ring at the top around her leg.

This time, the usually invisible lurker voluntarily stood in front of the adults, squarely in full view. Being inquisitive, she was deeply interested in the drama unfolding. She did not have to hide under a table or behind a door to spy on these histrionic adults. Surprisingly, she was invisible to them without her even trying. That was because they were focused on poor, little Justin. So they did not notice her at all.

There was some big mystery afoot. And Justin became the object of interrogation. At first, they treated him like a key witness to a major crime. That lasted but a moment. The tension escalated as they began to interrogate him as if he were actually a suspect, not just a witness. It was like a scene out of *Dragnet*. Dum tadum dum. The two women attending Auntie Mellie seemed to be enjoying themselves, but poor Justin was not having a good time of it all. He was truly put upon. "Justin, did you see Uncle Loy and Auntie Edita kissing?" the unidentified woman asked. (Loy, remember, was Mellie's baby husband, the oily man with the wet cigar, and Edita was her best friend's mother.) "Who would want to kiss him?" Aurie thought.

The pathetic boy was bewildered. Why in the world would they be kissing each other? That did not sound right to the boy. After all, Auntie Edita and Uncle Loy weren't the ones that were married to each other. They were both married to other people. This question was confusing to Justin, but the two women pressed on. They were almost twice the height of the boy, standing so close to him that he could feel their body heat. He was sweating, and maybe even shuddering a bit. They were looking down upon him, and he, neck craning, was looking up at them, eyes and mouth stretched open. He couldn't run. At first, he felt like he was glued to the ground. In the moments to follow, he began to feel that he had left the ground floating upwards as the two women grilled him, flipping him over and over like a hamburger until he was done. Finally, out of the mouth of the terrified child, the probing women got the information they were lusting after. When Justin told them that the duo in question, Uncle Loy and Auntie Edita, "went into the bedroom and closed the door," he unknowingly dropped the big bomb. Boom… From the women came a chorus of gasps, sobs, and cackles. Two cackled, one sobbed, and all three gasped. "Poor Justin," Aurie thought. "He really should learn to stay out of sight, or keep his mouth shut."

Although these two children, given their lack of life experience, did not know exactly what was happening, they felt its import. If Aurie understood even a little of what was going on in this real-life scene of love and betrayal, it was only due to the repertoire of romantic dramas she had seen on the small and big screens. As for Justin, who knows? The human vise comprised of the two women who ensnared him surely caused him some dreadful moments. Certainly, the child-centered, empathy-driven, ethics of the current day could have spared the boy some grief. But the time was not so evolved. Like a proverbial small town, this tightly woven community involved characters with intertwining lives. And in this case, perhaps two of them intertwined a bit too much.

Aurie and Justin did not speak of the incident afterwards. There was a difference in their age, and neither had the life experience to edify each other on the matter. The Romeros stayed together, and no more was heard of Loy's transgression. Perhaps it was easier for the Romeros to stay together. Divorce was not as typical in those days especially in a Catholic community, and who could afford the bother and a lawyer anyway? Also, there was symmetry in that odd pairing, and it suited their needs for the time it lasted. Eventually, circumstances for Justin and his working single mother changed, and they both disappeared from the scene. Aurie did not miss Justin, having always considered the younger child an interloper anyway.

In spite of the interlacing of lives, the cohesion of the group was not to last over the years. It was a movable community. Many people did not stay in the same house or neighborhood, unlike those who dwell in permanent forever homes. Those that could afford to moved up. Others even acquired new families and circumstances. Others merely moved on. The Abadias also relocated a couple of times thereafter. The red kitchen table went with them and continued to be a magnet that drew other players, as the first set of players had already scattered in different directions. The red table eventually became the worse for wear in the subsequent moves, and later the chairs had to be patched up with red plastic tape in order to extend their life. The faux chrome became coated with a film that was perhaps an accumulation of kitchen grease.

During those passing years, the Abadias' kitchen was only to be a temporary stopping-off point at the time for those uprooted from their homelands. And those who partook in its hospitality and gaiety might well remember the kitchen with its shiny red table as a warm, welcoming, and convivial place that felt like community in an otherwise strange land.

BRIAN ASCALON ROLEY has received fellowships and awards from the University of Cambridge, Cornell University, National Endowment of the Arts, Ohio Arts Council, Djerassi Foundation, Ragdale, the VCCA and others. His books include *American Son: A Novel* (W.W. Norton), a Los Angeles Times Best Book, New York Times Notable, among other honors. *The Last Mistress of Jose Rizal and Other Stories* (Northwestern University Press) appeared in 2016. *Ambuscade* (2021) won the Finishing Line Press Open Chapbook Competition. He is currently Professor of English at Miami University of Ohio. More info at brianroley.com.

DUTY IN FILIPINO EXTENDED FAMILIES

One widespread aspect of Filipino culture is the importance of family, and in particular the sense of kinship obligation that includes relationships beyond the nuclear household.

For example, we usually had several Filipino relatives living with us or staying with us for extended periods of time.

My lola lived in a small room in back, which she shared with my tito when he arrived. My mother's sister lived with us before she married. Another Manila-based brother came for extended months-long stays with his wife and three daughters. There was a constant influx of extended family and friends staying with my lola in her small room, eating with us, sharing tsismis and laughter.

A lot was expected of family members. My tito was my lola's caregiver. Other grown children delayed or gave up romantic relationships and marriage in order to care for their parents, sometimes even at the cost of never having their own children, an arrangement that began long before the parents became elderly enough to need it.

19

REFUGEES
1980

I
MANNY

From the school desk at the back which had been raised up on books to accommodate his wheelchair, he watched the students file out of the classroom, chattering and laughing with their bags slung over their shoulders. Then he rolled up to the teacher's metal desk. She looked up from her lesson book.

Thanks for staying behind, she said, smiling at him.

Sure.

Don't look so worried, she said. It's not about a grade.

I was wondering.

No, I had a suggestion I wanted to make to you. I do work at an animal shelter, volunteer work.

I know.

She paused. How did you know?

Kids talk.

She considered that thought and nodded and said, Look here, we take in dogs, other animals. But I also do some training of service canines.

Service canines, he said. You mean like the ones for the blind?

Not just for the blind, she said.

I think I see where this is going.

She laughed. Now, I don't know what your parents—your mother in particular—thinks about pets. They can be a lot to take care of. So if she might have a problem with a dog, don't go telling her I said you should have one. She looked at him, to make sure he understood. But you might consider one.

What can they do?

Come by and I'll show you.

Over the next weeks, he went to the shelter several times. The room, loud with barking, had cinderblock walls and a narrow aisle between chain link cages that almost brushed his shoulders as his wheelchair passed. The humid air possessed a strong bitter scent, of piss and fur and sweat, which he pretended not to let bother him. She showed him a pit bull, scarred and missing an ear, abandoned in Venice, whom she said had been used in dog fights. Does he bite? Manny said, keeping back.

Don't worry, she said, scratching it vigorously beneath the chin and setting her cheek close enough to the dog's mouth to make him nervous. This guy wouldn't be the one for you.

Good.

It would freak out your mother, I'm sure. Here, let's go further back.

She showed him an Australian Shepherd. This one, she's sweet and nice. Not trained as a service dog, but she could be. If you bought one trained already, it would be costly and there's waiting lists.

He scratched her beneath the chin like his teacher had. It felt soft here and the hair was long and the dog licked his hand.

What can she do?

She'd be a constant companion. She could also wear a book bag, for school supplies and such. And nobody would mess with you. She paused. If your condition ever got worse, regressed, she'd be able to open doors for you, get objects, even dial 911 for help.

She looked uncomfortable at what she'd just said, so he smiled to show her it was fine. She seems great, he said.

Aie na ko! his mother said. No way.

But mom—

What do you need a service dog for? You can carry your own books and you can see. All that's going to happen is I will be the one to clean up its messes, no matter what you say—

No matter how much he argued and pushed, Inay would not budge. But he continued to visit the animal shelter. He liked working with his teacher and came weekly to help out, which counted towards his community service requirement.

They helped nurse an owl with a broken wing, recorded its progress in a little book. You're a natural nurturer, Manny, she said, observing him with a smile.

Nurturer? he said.

She laughed. Protector, she said. He pretended not to be pleased. She volunteered at a hippotherapy horse riding center and arranged for him to ride. She would walk in front as he rode, handling the rein, petting and stroking the horse to keep it calm, talking to it in her cheerful voice. She was different than at school. She seemed younger, wore shorts that showed shapely legs, fit from hiking—and flannel shirts. She chatted with him cheerfully as she led the horse's reins, smiling back, asking him about his social life at school and his family. He warned her about problem kids, what they said in private, not in a way that was tattling but to help her ward off potential dramas and conflicts, to preemptively plan. But he kept any taunting aimed at him to himself.

One day he noticed a pregnant horse. She helped him to set his hand against her warm belly, to feel the skin, sense the shape and movement of the incubate being inside. He kept his hand on the belly as she watched him.

What? she said.

I'll probably never be a father, he said.

Don't say that, she said. You'll find someone. There's plenty of girls who will like a boy like you.

No, it's not that, he said. My disease is probably in my DNA. If I had a kid, it might get passed on.

Oh. She turned red. I'm sorry Manny.

She seemed awkward and he changed the subject to help her.

My Tito Pepe used to care for animals, including pregnant ones.

Your tito?

Uncle—my mother's oldest brother.

He told her about his Tito Pepe and how he used to manage the animals on a coconut hacienda in the Philippines, which seemed to interest her. As they talked, the boy was surprised to learn that she had no boyfriend. He felt his heart rate kick. Without revealing that Tito Pepe lived in their apartment and slept in a sleeping bag on his mother's floor, he told her how his uncle had delivered carabao calves, fixed broken bones, stitched wounds and did surgery, using techniques he'd learned as a boy soldier during the war.

His teacher raised a brow. A soldier?

During the Japanese occupation. He lived in the jungles, for his uncles that ran guerrilla units.

How old was he?

Twelve or thirteen, he said.

Younger than you, she marveled.

He nodded.

The horse jerked forward, the belly moving beneath his brush, and he pat and stroked her warm side, at his teacher's direction, to calm the animal down.

The bus driver lowered his wheelchair on the lift and then unhooked the belt, shaded her hands and said, Isn't anybody here to get you?

My uncle had an appointment with the doctor today, Manny said.

She frowned, looked up and down the empty alleyway, the trash cans and dumpsters behind the apartment buildings.

But I can get back inside on my own fine, he added. I have a key.

She looked at him skeptically, but nodded and mussed his hair, as if he were still a boy, and let him go. His physical growth had stunted, compared to other boys, due to his disease, which affected the way some people responded to him.

At home, the apartment was empty and he could feel his pores bursting with sweat from wheeling himself in, his nostrils still acrid from the smell of alleyway urine and trash. His heart was pounding, with hope perhaps, and he went straight to the backroom where his lola and tito lived, knocked. No answer. He eased the door open, settled down, and felt the dread seep in.

Manny looked around the little room, dim and cluttered, where Tito Pepe slept on the floor beside Manny's grandmother's tiny bed. Everyone still called it "Lola Camille's room" though Pepe had shared it—or rooms like it—with her now for years. His orange sleeping bag lay rolled up in the corner. Sometimes, when Manny had friends over, the friends would learn this and look at him with disbelief. *Your uncle and grandmother sleep in THAT little room? He sleeps on THAT space of floor? How can he even get his feet stretched out?*

And his twin sister's new best friend, a tall redheaded volleyball player from school (whom Manny had a secret, involuntary, aggravating crush on), had been even blunter, stepping into the doorway last week and gawking: *He sleeps in that sleeping bag?* she pointed. *Yeah*, Tessie looked down, tried to step further back into the hall to draw her friend out. *But how long has he lived here?* said Trish. *Two weeks or something? No*, Tessie replied, *like six years*. The friend said: *Six fucking years? Why?* Tessie: *It's like a Filipino thing or something, common there for people to live crowded into their rooms with everybody else. He takes care of my grandma.* The friend: *He lives with his MOTHER? But he's like, OLD.* Tessie: *Sure, it's like a Filipino thing, I guess. Sometimes one child is assigned to take care of their mother. She can't walk anymore*

267

without help. Can we go to the movies now? Friend: *But wait, you're saying he lives on her floor so he can walk her up and down the stairs?* Tessie: *Well, not just. She also has to have help to go to the bathroom, to take a bath. And at night her legs get stiff from sitting around all day, they get cramped up, so he has to massage them. And he helps out with my handicapped brother.*

The way Tessie cringed and blushed, trying to back into the hall, Manny wanted to grab her shoulders and shake her. Wanted to tell her to stand up for their tito. Not to look so ashamed.

He held his tongue all day, but that night his rebuke came out in a loud voice—almost a shout—which surprised her, his twin who'd always stuck up for him, fought his bullies and badgered them with her sharp tongue, and had once seemed to adore Tito Pepe too. He accused her of changing, that the further they got from emigrating from the Philippines, the more Tessie seemed to look down on Pepe for devoting his adult life to caring for them. She'd denied it, angrily, and the twins hadn't spoken much since then.

But now, looking at the tiny room in which Pepe slept on a sleeping bag, it was hard to picture his tito ever in charge of anything, no less a thriving coconut hacienda back in the Philippines, including managing the farm animals as a mere teen, interacting with older men, in actual charge of them. He'd been followed around by his admiring little brother. Bino, now an uber-successful Swiss-educated businessman in Manila.

It's still hard for me to imagine Tito Betino following Pepe around, Manny said. Pepe's such a humble person.

Remember, your Tito Pepe fought in the jungles against the Japanese, and was said to kill men with his bare hands, Inay said. Don't be surprised that he managed teams of men. You need to respect him.

I do respect him.

She looked at him and smiled, Of course you do, she said and leaned forward to kiss his forehead.

II
PEPE

She arrived at the apartment. She saw the candles on the table and along the windows and stopped in the doorway. She wore casual clothing, denim blouse, Burmese earrings—not what Pepe pictured of a teacher.

Wow, she said. Candles.

Come in, Pepe called from the kitchen.

Did you set these out?

He paused, looking at her.

Look, she said. I'll be upfront with you. This is a little awkward.

Pepe nodded.

It seems that my friend, your nephew, put out candles. But he failed to tell me that it was fancy dress.

It's not fancy dress, said Pepe.

She gestured towards her own clothes: frayed knee holes in her jeans, an outdoorsy shirt. Yes, but we're not on a safari.

Pepe reddened. No.

She studied him carefully, the clothing he wore was much nicer than his usual wear—a button down shirt and pressed black slacks. But she looked uncertain. She seemed about to say something, but seeing him blush made her stop.

She looked around the apartment.

So this is where Manny lives.

Yes. He lives in the room with his sister and brother.

All three? Like the Walton's. They seem a bit old for that.

We only have three bedrooms.

She studied him.

We, she said. You live here too?

Pepe's ears burned. She could obviously see by the way he kept holding his wrist and looking down that he wanted to say more, but was too embarrassed. Suddenly, her awkwardness was gone and she smiled and came near.

Where is everybody?

He shrugged.

I believe Manny set us up on a date, she said. But I believe you weren't in on it. Am I wrong?

No.

She touched his elbow. We can relax, Pepe, can't we? Let's just have a nice meal and conversation, like Manny hadn't lit these candles, ok?

Sure.

Pepe felt himself relax a bit, but he was still uncertain if she had really put a stop to the idea of this being a date. It was as if he were set to perform a speech in front of a large audience and someone told him, to his relief, that he wouldn't have to give it at the last minute. But the possibility that he had misunderstood and he was being observed after all nagged him.

Still, they managed to have a good conversation over dinner. She thanked him many times for the dishes, and seemed interested in Filipino food, and especially in learning about any Spanish origins or influences. They got to talking about the coconut hacienda and how Pepe was once in charge of the animals and implementing modern agricultural techniques. She knew a lot about animal husbandry methods and seemed impressed. It also became apparent, to Pepe, as she gabbed and did much of the talking, that his nephew had told her a lot about him: she knew he had birthed carabao calves and nursed weaklings from a baby bottle: ministered to sick animals with antibiotics; made makeshift splints to heal their broken bones. She knew he'd designed the fish farms, then helped the peasants dig its complex labyrinth of trenches, construct the seawater dikes, install the nets that caught fish and crabs in receding tides.

His mind began to indulge a wonder if there was some possibility here, a way to marry an outside life with his obligations here in his sister's home.

After dessert, she wanted to see Manny's living quarters and bathroom, to see what wheelchair modifications they'd made. This was ostensibly why she'd been invited to come, after all: to see if a service dog could help out his nephew. She seemed much more relaxed now as she stood and followed his gesture towards the hall. Pepe showed her the accommodations he'd made, happy to have a practical task; she seemed curious about the mechanics of things, handy. He thoughtlessly mentioned that he'd made similar modifications to his mother's toilet, which was a mistake, because she asked to see it. Entering her room, she noticed the orange sleeping bag rolled up against the corner, bungee cord bundled, and the single bed.

Her mind seemed to be working, and something clicked.

She turned to him.

You sleep in here?

Yes.

In that sleeping bag?

Yes.

She avoided his eyes and went up to the bookshelves, with their mixture of Santos and Marys and books and photographs of relatives' children. She didn't talk for a while. She touched one framed photo of Manny, the largest, smiled, and proceeded to run a finger over the titles of several books.

St Teresa of Avila. Your mother's?

He shook his head. Mine.

She was a reformer. A revolutionary.

You know of her?

She nodded. I once went on a Buddhist meditation retreat in Thailand. It turns out that the monks there were big fans of Thomas Merton, and we were admonished for turning our backs on our own Christian mystic tradition and romanticizing eastern variants. They accused us of superficiality.

She paused. Your mother, I heard the story from Manny, that she was a Carmelite nun.

A novitiate. She ran away to join it at fifteen when her farther arranged for her to marry. The nuns took her in. Her father kidnapped her back out and forced her to marry my father before she could take the vows.

 Lucky you.

 He nodded.

 Shall we eat? she said.

III
MANNY

 The next day the boy was in the classroom and felt his teacher's eyes on him. She caught his eye and he lowered his, blushing. All class he had difficulty looking at her without turning red. His fingers on his pencil jittered.

 Afterward, he was about to leave when he heard his name.

 Stay after a minute, Manny, she said.

 He nodded, and they waited as the other students left the room.

 Did I do something wrong? he said.

 Wrong? Oh no. No, you didn't. She smiled at him and he tried not to look away, but her gaze went to his hands, which were folded on his lap tightly. I enjoyed talking to your uncle.

 Good.

 She was looking at him.

 He takes care of you, doesn't he?

 He cares for my lola—grandma. That's what he came here for, to America.

 I know. But you too.

 He helps with me too, yes.

 How long has he been living in that room with her?

 A while.

 And that means. Months?

 If you include our time in Texas, Singapore, and other places we've lived?

 Yes.

 About eleven, maybe twelve years.

 His shoulders and neck tensed. She nodded and walked

to the window and looked out. Then she came back. You worry about him.

He's a good man.

I know he is. You're right to think so. He's— admirable. Have you ever thought about suggesting he see someone?

Manny frowned. You mean like a shrink? There's nothing wrong with him.

You said he was a boy soldier—a guerrilla against the Japanese. Does he ever talk about it?

No.

Maybe he needs someone to talk to, is all.

He looked at her accusingly. I was hoping you would.

She studied the boy and took his words in.

We talked about animals and saints, Manny. Thomas Merton's friendship with the Dali Lama, and parallels between St Teresa of Avila and Tibetan monks. War isn't exactly the sort of topic you broach with someone you barely know. Not unless they volunteer it first.

I've tried, he said, nodding and fighting back the welling in his eyes. But I can't. It doesn't work. None of us can.

That's why I'm suggesting maybe a professional.

He sighed and looked at his hands. He nodded. But shook his head. He won't do it, he said.

Then he felt her hand set on his shoulder, and squeeze. I know, she said. He's like my dad's generation, he'll try to just soldier it through. But you're the one closest to him. Maybe someday he'll talk to you. Just keep your eyes open, look for the chance. Maybe you could help him.

He said nothing. He could not look at her.

She kept her hand there. He felt her want to say something more. Then she spoke again.

My father was a vet from the German war. Lived in east Texas. Seemed like a tough old nut, never one to talk. He hunted deer with a bow, skinned them by his own hand. He was fine with people when he had something to do with them—a task, like playing cards or chopping wood for the holiday family gatherings. But when everyone gathered inside and he ran out of chores, he'd just sit in his room, door shut and lights off. He seemed pained by the noise.

After Mom died, the relatives still came for Christmas for several years, but less and less people showed up. He'd sit in his living room with the tv on all year, no visitors. Once he put his arm through a window and cut up his hand and arm up to the elbow, after he'd fallen trying to close the drapes. Refused to go to a doctor for help. A neighbor noticed the arm and called my uncle, who called the local deputy, but even with a police officer they couldn't drag him out to get treated. When we visited, we were shocked at what it looked like. That arm. It had healed up with the bone crooked under the skin, so that you could tell where it must have broke, even beneath all the dark blue swelling.

He'd killed Germans with that arm and we owed him something. Maybe we didn't try hard enough.

After he died on that lazy boy in front of the tv, the doctor said he'd likely died of cardiomyopathy due to anxiety and stress. The Germans couldn't kill him back then, but something took root. All that pent-up emotion, she shook her head. It put a strain on his heart.

*

He tried to get Pepe to talk about the war. He studied his uncle's face as they worked on his father's rusted Indian motorcycle in the carport, as Pepe carried Manny into the bath, pushed him to school. But the right moment never came. At Manny's first awkward words, his uncle would stiffen, and his knees shake, and Manny backed off.

Leave him alone, Tessie said.

It's obviously eating him up inside.

Then I guess he just isn't ready yet.

We need to help him.

Manny, she said. Mom and Tita have been trying to talk to him for years about that stuff. What makes you think you're any different?

Still—

Manny, I heard about how you set him up on that date with your teacher. That was cruel.

He stared at her, stunned.

Did you really think that could work? she said.

He fought back a flush. She told me afterward that he's a good man, he said.

That was a consolation prize.

How would you know?

Did she say she wanted to date him?

He looked at her harshly. He went to the window and stared out. You don't think a pretty woman like her would want to date a kind man like our tito? You don't seem to have a lot of regard for people.

I just don't think we should embarrass him. It's humiliating enough for him to live off Dad in Lola Lumen's room.

In Manila our relatives live crowded into rooms.

We're not in Manila now, are we?

He said nothing. He heard her come up behind him. I know you love him. I know you think the world of him. I'm just trying to be realistic here.

Pepe's a handsome man.

Handsome isn't enough in a man, not for a woman like that. Can you imagine how embarrassed he must have been?

He tightened his lips and looked away. But inside, he felt like his body had sunk, after a sudden blow. She touched his wrist. I see what you see in him, Manny. I do. But it's not apparent to other people. You told me that we need to protect our uncle. You were right. That's why I dropped Trish.

You're not friends with her anymore?

We need to make sure he isn't hurt.

Don't you ever wonder what happened to him, during the war?

Of course I do. But it's something we can't change. We can't take it back, wars have consequences.

He returned two days later and found his tito alone in the carport, working on Manny's father's motorcycle, kneeling on a crinkly green tarp, which collected a fine mound of sanded rust. Pepe looked up, surprised.

Who's this?

Sadie, Manny said. Go on, pet her.

The dog went up immediately to Pepe and let him scratch ardently beneath the chin.

Your mother let you have a dog?

Manny shook his head. She's for you, Tito. She was wounded last year by an abusive master. She needs your help.

His tito opened his mouth as if to speak, then stopped himself; he knelt and faced the dog's eyes and immediately knew, felt at old wounds beneath its fur, unseen, faint, scabs and lumps whose textures and depths delineated a subtle history of scars.

PATRICK JOSEPH CAOILE was born in the Philippines and raised in New Jersey, U.S. He received his bachelor's in English from Saint Peter's University in Jersey City, NJ and his master's in English from Seton Hall University in South Orange, NJ. He is now pursuing a Ph.D. in English with a creative writing concentration at the University of Louisiana at Lafayette. He enjoys cooking and eating, watching all kinds of movies and television, and taking spontaneous hikes or explorations of a city. His previous work can be found in *Porter House Review*, *storySouth* and elsewhere.

THE FLAG OF THE PHILIPPINES

The Philippine flag was first flown on May 28, 1898 at the Battle of Alapan where Filipino revolutionary troops fought off the Spanish forces. It sported the same design as today's flag with the same red, white, and blue colors, three yellow stars, and a golden, eight-rayed sun. However, during the Philippines; struggle against Spain and soon afterwards the United States, the red stripe was featured on top to represent wartime. However, the flag was then outlawed for some years under the United States' occupation of the Philippines. As more Filipino representatives were elected into office, the Philippine flag was reinstated in 1919 and used throughout the Philippines' status as a Commonwealth under the United States. During this time, the Philippine flag was flown alongside the American flag, until July 4, 1946 when the United States recognized the nation's independence and the Philippine flag could be flown on its own.

20

DRESS DOWN DAY

In the second grade, the Catholic school had us bring home Manila envelopes each week, full of notices and forms for the parents to peruse. The specific flyer Mama held in her hands was for an upcoming "dress down day," a day when students were excused from wearing school uniforms. I had no care for the clothes—a white button-down, black necktie, and khakis. But I dreaded the shoes. I can still feel my feet resisting their own bend after years in those black leather Oxfords, which held my toes in tight like a bundle of stems in a ceramic vase.

"Wear red, white, *and* blue," Mama said reading the flyer aloud. "Does that mean all of them at once or separately?"

"We paid for his uniform," Papa said. "Now we're paying again for him *not* to wear it?"

"It's for Veterans Day," Mama explained. "And it's only a dollar."

"Veterans Day?" Papa said, continuing his tirade. "We're paying tuition. And where does the church collection go? We already do our share of charity work."

"It's only a dollar, Ronaldo," she insisted. "Heck, I paid a dollar for him to wear his Halloween costume last week. Did you want him to be the only one without a costume then?" She had bought me a ninja costume from the dollar store, a black jumpsuit and bandana made of thin fabric, which, for some reason, had glitter all over it. I wanted to be the Blue Power Ranger, but Mama decided thirty dollars at Party City wasn't worth one day of dressing down in a costume I'd never wear again. Being a ninja for a day was good enough.

"Well, now we've given them two extra dollars two weeks in a row." Papa walked out of the living room and into the bedroom. "We're not rich," he said under his breath.

"Red, white, and blue," Mama said to herself, giving up on her husband who offered no useful input. She turned her attention to me, a seven-year-old boy in overalls. "Did they say anything else at school? Does it matter which color exactly?"

I shrugged my shoulders.

"I'm sure we can find something."

She began rummaging through the closet in the living room. I kept all my clothes there in plastic bins and cardboard boxes. We didn't sort much of our things when we first moved into the apartment. After all, the apartment was small and there wasn't a lot of room for things to go into anyway. Most of them were clothes with faded colors, shirts and shorts that I owned even before we immigrated to the States. Basketball jerseys with misprinted numbers of famous NBA players, polo shirts with logos that resembled higher-end brands but were slightly tilted or curved at odd ends—imperfect clothing for those who couldn't afford fashion, but close enough that they could have easily fooled at a glance. My dollar store ninja costume reemerged, only to be thrown carelessly onto the floor.

"We should send some of these back home to your cousins." Then Mama clapped her hands together in a moment of epiphany.

She tossed out some more clothes onto the floor, over the sofa, and some even on me, moving other plastic bins out of the way. "Grab me a chair," she told me, and I followed. I placed it in front of her so she could climb it. Then she reached toward the top compartment, moving her arm into a mystery box like a magician into her top hat. But when she finally pulled back her hand, there wasn't a rabbit. Instead, Mama had retrieved another off-brand polo shirt, but this one was the specific shirt she had in mind.

"What's all that noise," Papa said, returning from the bedroom. "And what the hell is all this doing on the floor?"

"Look, Ronaldo," Mama said, spreading out the shirt to show him and me. "It was Lola's going-away present for Marcillo when we first left."

It was exactly what the flyer asked for—red, white, and blue altogether. Each color had a row layered on top of one another. A logo was stitched just under one of the polo's lapels: a golden sun with three rays spreading out from its curves. It was clearly a shirt meant to represent the Philippines, its own flag the same red, white, and blue with a golden sun.

"All this mess for a shirt?" Papa said. He looked at me with disappointed eyes, eyes that had just woken up from a nap, eyes that crucified me onto the floor. "You help your mother with *that*." He pointed out the scattered piles of clothes throughout the living room.

I nodded like a dog.

He continued to the kitchen where he fetched himself a bottle of beer from the refrigerator.

"Come here," Mama said to me. "Let's see if it still fits." She lifted the shirt open for me so I can slip my head through it. It was a little snug, my seven-year-old baby fat proudly protruding. Still, Mama said, "Perfect fit!"

"That's not American enough." Papa sipped his beer.

"What do you mean not American enough?" Mama replied. "It's red, white, and blue isn't it?"

"Those veterans didn't die for you."

"We fought alongside the Americans."

"But we are *not* Americans," Papa declared.

"Marcillo's got every right to wear this shirt to school," Mama said, brushing away specks of dust up and down my shirt. "We'll iron it out and you'll fit right in with the rest of them."

Papa had already finished his first beer when he reached into the fridge for another. Before he retreated into the bedroom again, he said, "A dollar to be American for a day. How I wish."

Mama was right, though. On Veterans Day at school, I wore the polo, even though the Philippine sun marked it. I couldn't help but feel too formal than the others. They merely wore T-shirts with American flags or bald eagles. But it didn't matter if we wore all three colors at once or a selection of any one of them. We all eventually blended into each other, hands against hearts as we recited the morning pledge of allegiance in the auditorium. That my shirt represented an entirely different country never crossed anyone's mind. "A dollar to be American for a day," Papa had said.

*

Years later, when Papa's liver could no longer catch up to the bottles in the fridge, the day eventually came when we were to take our citizenship test without him. It was July, a slathering of heat against the skin. But even as the sweat started seeping through my pores as I stepped out of the shower, Mama peeped her head into my room to remind me, "Wear red, white, and blue. And a nice pair of khakis." Even in late adolescence, I was still her boy, dressing me up to fit her ideal image of an American son. There was no arguing with her demands. Mama knew best.

I opened my closet to find everything I own was blue, black, and gray. Blue was still my favorite color. But Mama said to wear something more patriotic. It was, after all, the day of our citizenship test, and that meant more to her than it did to me. When Papa died, she had doubled her efforts to become American. She invested in a proper immigration lawyer by working odd jobs, from babysitting to dishwashing, before finally landing a stable job at my same childhood Catholic school serving lunch meals to the children.

"Make sure you iron your clothes, too," Mama said, poking her head in again. "We're going to take pictures after."

I owned nothing red, and the original Veterans Day polo with the Philippine sun had already been shipped back to the Philippines in a cardboard box years ago. So I picked out a plaid blue and white shirt, a pair of khakis that had belonged to Papa that I had grown into, then took the time to iron my outfit.

I looked at myself in the mirror when I finished and saw his reflection. I was seventeen, but my father's features had already made their way to the surface. I paused at his haunting, the man who ran away from his homeland but never from his vices. He embraced the liquor bottles wherever he went and took me and Mama along with him. Even after his death, he continued to embrace me, his face masking mine somewhere lost beneath.

I wanted to tell him how Mama and I made it without him. I wanted to tell him how it costs more than a dollar to be American, more than the years waited and forms signed and dated, more than the questions about the government's three branches, more than some simple written English test I could have passed when I was seven and he was still alive. I would have wanted to tell him that wearing red, white, and blue wouldn't have made any difference at all—not to them, but most of all, not to me—that he was right to say, "That's not American enough." No holiday, no dress down day, could have made me feel patriotic. When my passport came in the mail weeks later, I felt no such change.

But all that was still ahead of me. The test was a few hours away.

"Ready?" Mama said. She, of course, had bought her outfit weeks prior. She began planning as soon as the interview date was set. She wore a long striped dress—three stripes of red, white, and blue—which flowed freely down from her torso to her waist, then was pleated from there to her knees, so that when she spun around, her dress blossomed into an American spiral.

Then out the door we went, Mama and me, to become citizens.

R. ZAMORA LINMARK

Born in Manila, Philippines, R. Zamora Linmark spent most of his growing up years in Honolulu, Hawaii. In addition to *The Importance of Being Wilde at Heart*, his first novel for young adults from Delacorte/Random House, he has also published two novels, *Rolling the R's* (Kaya Press) which he'd adapted for the stage, and *Leche* (Coffee House Press), as well as four poetry collections, most recently, *Pop Vérité*, all from Hanging Loose Press. He divides his time between Honolulu, Hawaii, and Baguio, Philippines.

FILIPINOS IN HAWAII

Filipinos make up the second largest ethnic group in Hawaii, after Caucasians, or "Haoles." Though the arrival of the first Filipinos in Hawaii dates back to 1853, not much is known about them or their purpose in the islands. The first big wave of migrants took place in 1906. These were the "Sakadas," mostly men and unmarried, who were contracted to work the sugar and pineapple plantations. Contrary to their dreams, many did not return to the motherland; instead, they made Hawaii their adopted home.

21

KAHILI IN FARRAH

Everybody in Kalihi wants to be Farrah. *The name itself sounds sultry and expensive. Who doesn't want to be the reigning queen of pin-up posters thumbtacked on every wall of the house? A swimsuit goddess with long and graceful legs, pearly white teeth, glossy lips, roller-derby hips, and a million-dollar smile on a king-size waterbed next to none other than the Six Million Dollar Man himself. Who doesn't want that full-volumed, sunshine-gold man: side-combed, feathered at the top, then curled along the sides? Who in Kalihi doesn't want to be Farrah?*

*

Ernesto Cabatbangan, a freshman at Sanford B. Dole Intermediate, doesn't want to be Farrah; he wants to be inside her. He bought all her posters on discount from DJ's Record Store because his calabash cousin manages the Pearlridge branch.

He says he can't get it up unless she's there watching over him, smiling. At times, it gets so bad that he sprays the room, bull's-eyeing Farrah's mouth.

*

The two-hour season premiere of the hit series *Charlie's Angels*, starring ex-Rookie Kate Jackson (Sabrina Duncan), commercial model Jaclyn Smith (Kelly Garrett), and newcomer Farrah Fawcett-Majors (Jill Munroe) attracted 5,483,097.99 households, according to the Nielsen Ratings. A week later, Edgar Ramirez formed the Triple-FC, the Farrah Fawcett Fan Club, with him acting as the President, Katherine Katrina-Trina Cruz (1st Vice President), Caroline Macadangdang (2nd Vice President), Jeremy Batongbacal (Secretary), Judy-Ann Katsura (Treasurer), and Loata Faalele (Sergeant at Arms).

The Triple-FC's primary goals were to keep the TV show on the air and the blond bombshell's career alive. This meant watching every episode including reruns, wearing T-shirts with Farrah Fawcett iron-on stickers, buying the Jill Munroe doll, playing the *Charlie's Angels* board game, trading *Charlie's Angels* cards, and praying the novena every Wednesday with Father Pacheco at Our Lady of the Mount Church.

Once a week, the club met at Edgar's house to: 1) write letters to Farrah Fawcett c/o ABC Network; 2) show off their collections of Farrah memorabilia, including cutouts from glamour magazines and Farrah's latest swimsuit poster; 3) role-play scenes from *Charlie's Angels*; and 4) discuss sociopolitically charged issues raised by the show, such as prostitution, lesbian undertones, and Orientalism.

When Farrah left the top-rated show, they continued their Farrah piety, anxiously waiting to see her movie *Sunburn*. Unfortunately, it got scorched by bad reviews and a month later, Triple-FC wrinkled up.

*

Orlando Domingo's favorite letter is F, not F for Filipino, but F for Farrah, and he won't answer to his friends and classmates who call him Orlando, his teachers who address him as Mr. Domingo, or his mother who nicknamed him Orling.

"Just call me Farrah," he says, "as in Far-Out Farrah, or Faraway Farrah."

It all started with *Charlie's Angels* and his addiction to Farrah's blond mane. One night he borrowed his mother's box of curlers and did his hair before going to bed. When he woke up, he propped himself in front of the vanity and blow-dried, at extra-high speed, the rows of hair caged in pink. Then he removed the curlers and began the arduous task of styling his locks into the million-dollar mane covered by Farrah wanna-be's and Flip queens.

"Farrah, Farrah, what's the secret to your hair?" the Filipino Farrah wanna-be queens ask him. And all he says is, "Once a Farrah Flip, always a Farrah Flip." Or, "A Flip is a Flip is a Flip is a Flip." Or, "Secret."

"He's flipped out," Orlando's classmates at Farrington High tell each other the moment he enters the classroom sporting Farrah's hairdo. "The next thing you know, he goin' be packin' on makeup and dressin' up like her, too."

Sure enough, the day after the *Charlie's Angels* episode titled "Consenting Adults"—the one where Detective Jill Munroe (Farrah Fawcett) goes undercover as a high-priced call girl and delivers her immortal line, "I never give anything I can sell"—Orlando struts into class wearing a fire-engine red polyester long-sleeved shirt tied around his 24" waist, yellow bell-bottoms, and Famolare platforms. His face is painted, courtesy of Helena Rubinstein's The Paris Boutique Kit, which includes lipstick and nail lacquer, and Aziza's Shadow Boutique. Twelve shimmering eye colors for every occasion.

"What next?" the teachers ask during their lunch break. "Principal Shim must do something about this. Ahora mismo!" The following week, after Orlando views the episode called "The Death of a Roller Derby Queen," he wheels onto campus on black leather Cobra skates, wearing see-through Dove shorts, red Danskins, and red-and-white knee and elbow pads. And, as always, fully made-up with Farrah's hairdo that withstands the Kalihi breeze with the aid of an entire can of unscented Aqua Net hair spray.

"We gotta do something before our boys catch this madness and start huddling in skirts and pom-poms," the football coaches Mr. Akana and Mr. Ching tell Principal Shim. "You gotta do something. Pronto. Suspend him, expel him, we don't care, but you gotta keep him away from our boys if you want the team to bring home the OIA title."

Leaning back in his vinyl chair, Principal Shim considers the possibility of expelling or suspending Orlando on the grounds that he is endangering the mental health of other students, especially the athletes. But he can't. Not after he examines Orlando's file:

Born in Cebu in 1962; Immigrated to Hawaii at the age of ten; Lives with mother in Lower Kalihi; Father: Deceased; Speaks and writes in English, Spanish, Cebuano, and Tagalog; Top of the Dean's List; Current Grade Point Average: 4.0; This year's Valedictorian; SAT scores totaling 1500 out of 1600; Voted Most Industrious and Most Likely To Succeed four years in a row; Competed and won accolades in Speech and Math Leagues, High School Select Band, Science Fairs, and Mock Trials; Current President of Keywanettes, National Honor Society, and the Student Body Government; Plans to attend Brown University in the fall and eventually take up Law.

Principal Shim closes the file and throws it on his desk.

"I can't expel him. Maybe suspension." He squirms at the thought of Orlando turning the tables and charging him, Mr. Akana, Mr. Ching, and the Department of Education with discrimination against a Filipino faggot whose only desire is to be Farrah from Farrington, as in Farrah, the Kalihi Angel.

LINDA TY-CASPER was born in Manila, Philippines, grew up in Malabon, and has lived in the United States since 1956, remaining a citizen of the Philippines.

Her short stories have appeared in three collections; in anthologies and literary magazines in several countries. Her novels, historical and contemporary, trace the "troubled moments and movements" from the 1750s (*The Peninsulars*) to the 1980s (*DreamEden*). *Awaiting Trespass* was selected one of the Top 5 Women's Fiction in England, 1986.

She has degrees from the University of the Philippines and Harvard; received the SEA WRITE Award, ALIWW Parangal, Pamana, UNESCO/P.E.N., Rockefeller (Bellagio), Radcliffe Fellowship; and is a member of the Boston Authors, UP Writers, Society of Radcliffe Fellows, Restoring Sight International, and Birthright.

WE ARE OUR MEMORIES

As with all my stories, a first sentence occurs to me. In "Happy", it is about Sausolito Bay which I saw one night after a Wheatland Conference dinner. This was 1990. I had forgotten to reply to the invitation so the staff called me. I was in a fog. My father had just passed away after weeks in the hospital. The story therefore, is about loss—of family; and also of country: the assassination of Ninoy, the People Power Revolution must have impelled the rest of the story. In "Happy", Velvet tries to forget her parents' death in a car accident, the stories Pinoys exchange in the US, trying to know who they are. Somehow, however, because we are our memories, Velvet remembers her mother telling her a star came to life when she was born. Hopefully this will help her recover/discover who she is.

22

HAPPY

During the week she clerks in the craft shop where, looking across Sausalito Bay to Angel Hill past the marina and houseboats floating no higher than eight feet above mud-bottom at low tide, she thinks of going to Muir Woods. But she never goes.

It's only ten, fifteen minutes away by U.S. 101 or California 1. Twelve miles north of the Golden Gate Bridge, it's open all year round, up to sunset.

Four days a week she answers questions about vases edged with pumice, pink stoneware throats fleshlike, quietly alive. *No, it will not separate; the rocks are part of the process,* she tells customers, and thinks of the fog that waters the needles of redwoods rising up to 367 feet along the upper coast, a narrow strip indicated by a red gash in the map on the information booth by the entrance to the marina; imagines the Stellar jays scolding the wind sweeping over silver salmon and steelheads that populate the sorrel carpet of the Woods.

It's been only months since she moved to Sausalito from the barrio in San Francisco which hangs about Saint Patrick, where Mass was celebrated after Ninoy Aquino was assassinated in '83, and where her mother used to take her until she learned to make excuses so she would not have to walk home Sundays with people who, since emigrating to the West Coast, had only hard-luck stories to exchange.

Sausalito is a different mindset. Safe from common memories, she can call herself Velvet there. *Just Velvet? Just!* And wear her hair thick and long, a rippling dark shawl; or shaved to the ear on the left. And stand beside vases taller than herself, drawing stares with her silence. Stand almost without moving, without blinking: someone posing for the light, allowing it to move about her the way cameras move around a model, picking out flattering shadows.

Barbara hired her on first impression. She went to the shop in a long cotton cape with bright yellows and greens, strange windows on a purple field. *I'm Velvet,* she said. Very ethnic with her straight bluish black hair and broad, high cheekbones; a tiny mouth stained coral red, open wound-like; stark.

People look in, see the vases and her—shadows of each other—and enter to see if she speaks; if so, what she might say. Some days she wears tartans, the badge of clans in Scotland where she has never been. Instead of a gold safety pin she lets the skirt fly. On her dark skin people see cultures in collision; coalescence. They come in to see if her flesh is warm. Some days she wears a *saya* with butterfly sleeves; other days, unrelieved white, like white-on-white paintings, with a Tausug belt of many beads, and bells from Mindanao.

Where do you shop? Customers ask.

Here and there, she answers.

Barbara wears jeans and loose Madras. Beside each other, they appear to impersonate the architectural collage of different-style houses side by side along highways, like continents that have slid into each other. In Manila they lived on a street named Santa Barbara where the Spanish barracks used to be, very close to the old Spanish walls beside the bay. It amused Barbara to be told her namesake is the patron saint of artillerists.

Since moving to Sausalito, a year after her parents died in that car crash heading for Big Sur past Monterey, she has not gone anywhere. When she's not working, she sits all day by her window, watching boats that appear anchored with concrete bottoms to Sausalito Bay, making distance slowly toward Angel Hill.

Still not been to Muir Woods? Barbara asks her Mondays when she returns to work. *Go. Go see trees the height of five-story buildings with no taproots to the water table. It's coastal fog that waters them. Some are a thousand* years *old. Go with Stanley. Don't waste weekends.*

No hurry, Velvet thinks. The trees will be there longer than forever, with towering white fog to feed them. Fog running along the coast like the faint capillaries of color on the tender vases Barbara fires.

She does not want to go; or talk about her great grandfather who jumped ship when he saw her great grandmother passing by the Luneta, along Manila Bay, in a two-wheeled *quelis*. Long ago in memory not hers. Why ever mention her cousin in Metro Manila who trains pigeons to race? His birds land on trees or electric wires, and not until they get down to the ground are they judged to have returned.

She is weeding out all memories from her life, fighting them when they come unbidden while she stands, darker than the bark of redwood, shimmering inside a caftan beside a vase slashed across by stones that mimic riverbeds dried out by summer. She thinks many things in their place, things she will not say while waiting for Sunday, any Sunday, to see if she'll go to Muir Woods across from Mt. Tamalpais on U.S. 101.

She likes to think of the redwoods which have been covering much of the Northern Hemisphere since about 140 million years ago. According to the tourist map, three noted species remain, each within a limited range with roots no deeper than thirteen feet into the soil. *Spend the day,* the brochure suggests. *Walk past Cathedral Grove to Fern Creek. Take a different trail each time. It's mostly level. Mostly paved, except for trails that lead to Mt. Tamalpais. In a rainstorm the creeks become torrential, running down to Muir Beach...*

There's poison oak and stinging nettles, according to Barbara who named a vase Nettles. Once you get the rash, you get it for seven consecutive years whether you brush against them again, or not.

All of Barbara's vases have names. Saragh is radish-white with purple veins. *Anglo nude,* Velvet calls it. Muir has redwood cones along one side; rough as bark hiding heartwood. A couple from Seattle bought Muir, ordering a birdbath to match. Customers think the vases are Velvet's creations because she explains the technique without consulting the catalogues, breathlessly; while in the backroom Stanley fashions crates for each vase.

Barbara thinks Stanley is *tres* creative. *With him it's instinct. Look at his hands. Did anyone teach Van Gogh? You're creative, too, Velvet. Right now, with yourself. You look like my vases.*

She lets Barbara talk on and on, just like the radio in her apartment spinning songs and talking just like another person in the bathroom; turning the place vibrant with its staccato. She keeps the radio on day and night. *Yah, yah,* she talks back to it from time to time. Depending on how she feels, she'll throw it a smile; or crack a joke back. Repartee in the dark. With strangers.

She calls it "Happy", sits across it while she paints her toes the pink color of Barbara's Zamboanga vase, winking back at the faces on the wall tiles, marble veins giving the impression of photographs in a gallery.

Her favorite is the one with downcast eyes, lower lip hanging like a cigarette. It reminds her of Markham who works as a guide in the Hess Winery built into the old Christian Brothers monastery carved out of the hills, with the sky stretched over the vineyard. State-of-the-art equipment; galleries of modern Swiss and American artists. It's $2.50 to taste the wine.

She never took his invitation to tour the winery. She has no strong desires though she's nineteen when hormones supposedly peak and move coffee breaks into bedrooms. The other girl who worked for Barbara, but left after she trained Velvet, talked of tussles among white lace pillows. She told Velvet she comes from a wealthy Shanghai family. *How about you?*

I don't remember, Velvet answered. She is all she wants, with her own apartment and the birdbath into which Barbara pressed ferns and berries; which sits on her deck like a guest enjoying the view of the Bay and the Hill. Nothing else worth stealing. No rugs on the floor. Just clothes in the closet. And shoes.

Heading up to her apartment after work Friday, Stanley asks her out for a drink in the bar two flights up from the shop which is six flights down from her place.

"Fine," she says. She can stand an hour or so talking about work, or Muir Woods, or crates for vases.

Right away Stanley says, "What matters is being happy. It does not come from being married. My parents are divorced but they're happy."

"Oh!" The lights on Angel Hill are like fireflies, dimming/brightening in her forest of hair.

"And happiness certainly does not come from perfection." Stanley reaches for her hand, counts her fingers.

The stone in her ring sparkles. It used to fit her mother's finger but it feels too large on hers, though it also fits.

"With a car I could get a job on Nob Hill. Stanford Court, the Fairmont. Been to the Sky Room? Tourists spoil it. It used to be the haunt of those who can afford to rent artists for their amusement. You know, tax shelters, cattle ranches and the like."

The Campari has made her feel weightless. As if she has been confined for days, she wants to stretch up to the stars; but it might mean something else to him.

"You always this quiet when not working?" His ears are pressed to his head like a child's hands. "That's a pretty ring. From someone?"

"What kind of car do you have in mind?" she asks, thinking how tight his face looks, eyes slashed against the glare of the lights reflected on the window behind her. Perfect for one of her bathroom tiles. She's light-years older than him in their thoughts.

"So what's happiness?"

She lets him talk, lets him pull statements out of the air like shoppers rummaging through boxes of miscellany, while she sips her Campari and thinks of going to Muir Woods, returning by Bohemian Grove along Redwood Creek; thinks of the women who talked and talked outside the shop that morning, then after one left, the other two entered saying to each other, *I wish we can remember her name*; thinks of her mother saying happiness was all about resilience and overcoming. Or was it life; was it her own mother saying ... or some woman overheard? Or Stanley?

"Won't probably happen," Stanley is saying.

"What won't?" she asks, feeling rude for sailing away in her thoughts. The lights on Angel Hill are sticking to his hair. Barbara says Stanley knows how to carve space, can hollow it out like another Henry Moore if he gets the chance to earn more than just a living.

"Life can still come to nothing. People move out of their lives all the time. Shall we check the tide?" he asks.

"I'll sit awhile, then turn in. I'll see you tomorrow, no, Monday. Maybe Monday, we'll check the tide. Thanks for the Campari." She could like him, but she doesn't want to like anyone just now.

"Not Monday. Gave Barbara my two weeks' notice. Slipped it under the door for her to see. Hasn't mentioned it to you yet? I hope it's not under some throw rug." He pushes in his chair, waiting for her mind to change.

"Oh." For a moment briefly he makes her think of the poet from Mill Valley where redwoods were milled until 1910, who wrote poems to her on paper napkins: White bird in her head/peach fuzz between/breasts...She slips off the ring. "Take it."

"Are you serious?"

"Get your wheels."

"Start paying you back from the first paycheck." He closes his hand on the ring. "Sure you won't come?"

"Next time…" Promises. She never liked promises, never made them. She stares into her drink while he walks away, slowly as if he might come back and pull out the chair to sit with her again. No promises, she thinks. Promises list what comes after dying; list memories. Does he think it's a piece of glass!

When she looks up, the stars are white ants that have dropped their wings. She makes her own poem: No promises/ intention enough/ No sister, no brother/ Parents not yet born/ No one to pray to or for/ Just dropped/ Out of no generation. *So!* The napkin is too soiled to write on; soiled dark like the ache inside her.

She runs up the remaining four flights to her apartment. Out of breath she turns on the radio. Two quick tugs loosen her pantyhose. Winding the legs about an arm, she leans out the window to look down on the marina. He is nowhere below.

But more stars have come out. She looks for the one that came to life when she was born. Her mother said there is such a star…

RENEE MACALINO RUTLEDGE'S debut novel, *The Hour of Daydreams,* won an Institute for Immigration Research New American Voices Finalist award, Foreword INDIES Gold, and Powell's Top Five Staff Pick. She also wrote the children's books *One Hundred Percent Me* and *Buckley the Highland Cow & Ralphy the Goat,* with a third children's book releasing in 2023. Renee's stories and essays are published in *The FilAm, The Tishman Review, The Margins, Mutha Magazine, The Ford City Anthology, Literary Hub, Maganda Magazine, TAYO Literary Magazine, The Timberline Review, Mabuhay,* and others.

THE LOLA AS CAREGIVER

The Filipino American household often consists of three generations, and grandmothers, or lolas, play a pivotal role in helping to raise their grandchildren. Grandkids who don't live with their lola often get taken to her home during the day. This enables their parents to go to work without sending the kids to day care, a preferable arrangement to save money and because their lola can be trusted to be invested in their care as only family can be.

While under a lola's protective guidance, Filipino American children enjoy traditional meals, customs, and language, increasing their likelihood of growing up speaking or understanding Tagalog or another native tongue. While "lola" is the most common Filipino word for "grandmother," the variation of "nanay," meaning "mother," is a frequent substitute. My own nanays chose to watch not only my siblings and I, but some of our children as well. It was a chance for them to stay active and engaged with the family, and to send their earnings from caregiving to loved ones in the Philippines.

23

PIGEONS FOR ETHEL

Before a party, everyone in the family got a chore, and for a whole day, we vacuumed and scrubbed until the house looked new. It felt that way again, frantic and full of anticipation, except we'd been getting ready for weeks and instead of a party, Nanay was moving in.

Mama was so busy preparing Nanay's room that she told me to eat cereal for lunch. Kuya Fredo yelled at me to get out of the way as he carried all of our parents' things from the master bedroom to the den, which would be their new bedroom. My job was usually dusting. Papa would've remembered that—if he were home. But he was out buying the fish Nanay likes, all the way at Economy Market because Safeway doesn't sell the smelly kind. I quickly gulped down the remaining milk from my bowl to follow Kuya's command to get out of the way before anyone remembered to stick me with a can of lemon Pledge and an old rag from under the bathroom sink.

In the front yard, where the wooden deck and potted palms are accented with river rocks, I made a discovery. At first, the rocks all seemed the same blue gray, but when you rinsed them under water, new colors emerged. I was squatting in front of the hose, rocks in hand, when Kurt and Gina found me.

"What are you doing?" Kurt asked, a skip in his step as he approached.

I gave him some rocks and put his hand under the running water. Instantly, the dusty surfaces gave way to sparks of orange, fields of red, and oceans of blue green. "Even rocks have secrets," I said, almost in a whisper.

"Oh. Um. Yeah," Kurt replied, his cheerfulness replaced by hesitation. He quickly passed the rocks to Gina.

"I don't see any difference," Gina said. She threw the rocks across the driveway. "This is boring. Let's play tag."

Kurt declared that Gina was "it." She bolted after him, a high-pitched shriek trailing behind her like a kite's disappearing tail.

I rinsed the single rock in my hand, a small, undiscovered planet, its smoothness and warmth returning my palm's embrace. Unlike Gina, I didn't run right away, knowing that inevitably, their chase would circle back to me. Soon enough, Kurt returned, catching his breath, his cheeks pink, and this time I was ready. Tag turned into hide-and-seek, then two-square, then wall ball against Mr. Chang's garage door until we saw him glaring at us from his kitchen window. As we kicked the playground ball up and down the street, the only driveway we avoided belonged to the witch.

The witch's house was dark gray and the stones in her yard a uniform gray to match. Interspersed in the colorless expanse were cacti, twice my height, with double the arms and a thousand menacing thorns to keep us at bay. Once, Kurt, Gina, and I built up the nerve to throw rocks at one of the cacti and the witch erupted from the front door, shaking her fist: "Get off my property, you little hooligans!" she yelled. We scattered in three directions, taking heed of the only thing more severe than the house itself. The witch was covered in black trousers, a black turtleneck, and pointy black shoes, revealing only the pale white of her hands and face, the salt and pepper gray of her curly, shoulder-length hair. It was almost like she'd answered a newspaper ad for "witch" and moved in.

When the sky's colors deepened, I knew without looking at a watch that Mama would come out to find me, an embarrassment I preferred to avoid.

"I have to go," I said, turning toward home. "It's getting dark."

Kurt and Gina snickered. Unlike them, I couldn't ride my bike to the liquor store for candy. Instead, I'd give them my money to bring back Now-and-Laters and Lemon Heads. I couldn't go into their houses without letting Mama or Papa know first, even though Kurt and Gina lived on the same block. And finally, I had to go back inside before "dark," which meant well before sunset.

"Right," Kurt said, something between a chuckle and a snort escaping him. "Better give yourself a head start before the ghosts come out."

Kurt's sarcasm didn't escape me. It only revealed how little he cared for my family's rules.

*

After Nanay moved in, the buzz around the house didn't stop. Mama cleaned more than usual and Papa was always off buying okra or pan de sal or more fish. My aunts and uncles came to visit all the time, especially on weekends, which meant having cousins over. While Kuya Fredo listened to records and mixed tapes in his room with Bernard and Jojo, who were also in middle school; I spent most of my time outside with Irena, Jay, and Manuel, who were in elementary school like me. Sometimes Kurt or Gina joined us.

We played two-square in courts we drew with chalk in the street or on the sidewalk. Since our driveway was typically blocked by relatives' cars, we played wall ball against Mr. Chang's garage door, betting against the possibility he'd complain to my parents, yet again. But when I dared them to throw rocks into the witch's front yard, Irena shook her head "no way" and neither Jay nor Manuel attempted to convince her.

One night after everyone had gone home and my parents were in bed watching TV, I found my grandmother in the backyard, smoking a cigarette alone. She put a finger to her lips and said, "Shhh, your Papa doesn't know I still smoke. I'm too old to quit now."

"You have a funny name, Nanay," I told her. "It means 'Mother.'"

"Gaga, you silly girl," Nanay said. "That is not my name. My name is Pilar. Did your parents not teach you anything? Nanay is what everyone in the family calls me. I am 'everyone's mother.' That is why I get passed around from house to house. Bahala na! We will see how long it takes until your parents get tired of me too."

Learning my grandmother's name at nine years old was like discovering the first word of a new language. "Pilar" felt familiar even though I had not heard it before. I imagined Nanay as a young girl then a young woman in the Philippines, the name "Pilar" engrained in her skin, a musical note keeping time during every footstep of her journey.

"Nanay, do you believe in ghosts?" I asked.

"Ghosts? Hmm, I believe there is something more. I am saying that the world is too interesting, diba? Look at the sun, how strong it is. Look at the trees changing by themselves all the time. And you know when your neck is tingling or your body is suddenly shivering? Ooooh-weee! Maybe it's something from the other side, crossing paths with us."

After that, I started paying closer attention to Nanay, especially when she was alone and said things like "gaga," "bahala na," or "ooooh-weee." One Saturday morning before the house filled up with relatives, while I was still dressed in pajamas, I found her smoking in the driveway, feeding handfuls of raw rice to two pigeons. "A happy pair," she called them. "They always fly in together." She gave me some of her rice to feed them.

Several weeks later, the happy pair was joined by a flock of pigeons bobbing their heads around us, some perched on cars nearby and others bold enough to stand on my or

Nanay's fingers while they pecked at the rice in our palms. We got to know each bird by the colors and patterns on their feathers. One pigeon had two missing toes and bullied the others, puffing up his neck and chasing them away no matter how many times they circled back. My favorite pigeon was black and sleek, the first to feel comfortable enough to hop on my hand; he seemed to know me and I came to love the weight of him, the quick motions of his beak stabbing at each grain, the slant of his head when he glanced up at my face. As with the rocks, I came to see hidden colors in his black feathers, a streak of magenta in his neck, a hidden sweep of green in his right wing.

Pigeon-feeding became a ritual Nanay and I shared. The birds knew exactly which day and at what hour to come. If Nanay and I had to go to a family party or a road trip during that time, I worried that the pigeons would feel forgotten, but they never failed to come back the following Saturday.

One morning, I came out in my pajamas as usual, but Nanay was missing. The pigeons were already feasting on a meadow of scattered rice, so I knew she had been there. I could smell her Newport menthols nearby. Then I heard her voice— and someone else's. A few houses down, I saw her with the witch, the smoke from their combined cigarettes floating above them like a conspirator. My first thought was that Nanay was in danger. When she rejoined me on our driveway, I asked her why she was talking to the witch, my tone like my mother's when I was on the brink of getting into trouble.

"Gaga, you silly girl! Ethel is not a witch. She is a very nice lady…and she could use a friend!"

Nanay arranged for me to be just that. A few days later, she stood on the sidewalk in front of our house and watched me walk five houses down to Ethel's place. I lost sight of my grandmother as I made my way up the driveway to Ethel's front door. The towering cacti frightened me like scarecrows deliberately placed to fend off children. My heart raced as I waited for Ethel to answer the doorbell and I nearly turned around and ran home. "Not a witch, not a witch!" I repeated to myself. Nanay knew and trusted Ethel, I reasoned. Nanay had learned her name, and in so doing, had made her a real person. I trusted my grandmother and the thought of letting her down scared me more than anything else. So I did my best to replace my fear with curiosity about the "very nice lady." But just in case Nanay might be wrong, I had placed a sharp rock in my pocket as a weapon and kept my fingers wrapped around it.

Ethel seemed different close up—I could see the wrinkles on her face, the mascara over her blue-green eyes, the hairclips tucked in place behind long ears. She didn't wear any jewelry. The dark colors she wore transformed to a kind of elegance. I noticed the ribbon at the top of the collar, the subtle pattern in her blouse's stitching, the ruffled hems at the ends of the sleeves. She held a pack of cigarettes and a gold lighter in one hand, said "Pilar's granddaughter" in greeting, then invited me in.

Her voice too, sounded fuller, unlike the time she'd yelled at us to get off her property, when all I heard was an angry old lady. She spoke slowly, as if weaving each syllable together, and had a smoker's rasp. When she said Nanay's name, "Pilar," someone far beyond 'everyone's mother,' it reassured me Ethel was not a complete stranger, and I followed her in with more confidence.

"I like Pilar very much. We laugh together," Ethel said as she led me further into the house. I wondered when the two of them ever got together to laugh. Did Nanay come over to visit when I wasn't looking? Did my parents know? The mystery surrounding both women only seemed to deepen, as if the longer I spent time with them, the more secrets they'd be certain to reveal.

Where my grandmother was round, Ethel was slender, and she walked as if she could keep going and going. Inside, her house was identical to ours except for the antique furniture and faded wallpaper. It looked as old as a silent movie and smelled like attics and ashtrays. A guest among her things, sharing the space where she felt most comfortable, I remembered what I'd called her and felt chastised by guilt. For a while the two of us stood awkwardly in the dining room, neither one of us speaking.

"I have a turtle," Ethel said finally.

"Where?" I practically yelled. I had only seen a turtle once at the zoo, and that hardly counted.

Ethel led me to a sunroom where the backyard should've been. It was brighter and hotter here than the rest of the house, and the turtle was easy to find. It was bigger than I expected it to be, the size of a large basket walking in slow motion along one corner of the room.

"Her name is Retta," Ethel said.

"Can I feed Retta?" I asked.

"I named her after my sister, Henrietta. I think they're the same age."

I let go of the rock in my pocket and sat cross-legged in front of the turtle, which immediately ducked into its shell. The hard bumps felt alien against my hand. Even the turtle's legs felt scaly and unwelcoming. I ran my fingers along the scales I could reach, down to the tips of the nails, and the turtle's head reemerged for a brief moment. I looked proudly at Ethel, who watched me from the doorway as she smoked.

"They have the same name, but Retta and Henrietta are opposites. Let me show you a picture of Henrietta." She turned toward the house, but I was not yet ready to leave Retta.

"What does she eat?" I asked.

Ethel pointed to a piece of lettuce on the patio floor, its edges serrated with little bites. I tried to win Retta's affection by waving the lettuce back and forth. This did not persuade the turtle to come out of her shell. By then, my heartbeat had slowed, in rhythm to a more gradual time that unfolded in Ethel's house. Ethel too, came further out of the shadows, beyond the outlines I'd constricted her to. She didn't answer questions the first or even second time you asked them. She smoked more than she spoke. (Like Nanay, she told me she was too old to quit.) She was not eager to please. With Ethel, time passed without demand; I could hear the hands of her grandfather clock tick. We shared whatever activity the moment brought and whatever conversation felt natural.

Back in the house, we sat at the dining room table and each had tea from our own ceramic pot. I chose a tea that smelled like peppermint candy; Ethel's choice was named after an earl. I had seen a teapot only in the pages of *Alice and Wonderland;* I smiled to myself, imagining that I'd gone down the rabbit hole. Ethel saw me smile and remembered to bring out cookies from a fancy package I'd never seen in Safeway. Because they looked like they belonged in another time, I was afraid they would be stale but bit into them anyway. They were crispy and fresh. I savored the cookies while Ethel smoked and watched me eat. She showed me pictures of Henrietta, who lived in Nebraska. I had to ask a total of seventeen questions to learn that Ethel had left her home state when her husband, who was in the military, had been stationed in our town. He'd passed away a decade before, and she'd never left the house they shared. Like Ethel, Henrietta did not have children and felt she was too old to travel. Because nothing ever happened in either of their lives, they did not write to one another but called each other at least once a week to check in.

I left Ethel's house with treasures: a framed photo of a cartoon poodle, a small, wooden jewelry box, and a hand-painted figurine of a turtle. Once home, I turned each present over and over in my hands, imagining Ethel and Henrietta playing make-believe or decorating fancy dollhouses as children.

I began to visit Ethel twice a week. Like Nanay, Ethel liked to sit back in her chair, overlooking her domain. Ethel's was still and formal, like a museum preserved from a livelier time, where the paintings and furniture were now at rest. Ethel, too, was at ease in her home. I no longer saw it as a place beyond the rabbit hole but one of nurturing beyond my family circle, like a classroom decorated by my schoolfriends' artwork or a church swelling with the congregation's singing. Ethel gave me presents each time I came—black and white photographs, laminated pictures of saints, and little knickknacks that she had owned since she was a girl. We'd have our tea in separate pots, and Ethel would bring out a new package of cookies that I had never seen before, smoking while I ate them and apologizing for not being a baker.

"Henrietta," she said, "makes her cookies from scratch."

With each visit, Retta came out of her shell a bit more, peeking tentatively at me and finally, letting me stroke the top of her leathery head. Sometimes at Ethel's, I thought of Nanay and wondered why she never joined us. Then I'd go home to find her at the card table playing tonk with aunts and uncles, on the sofa watching my parents sing karaoke out of tune, or at the head of the dining table as family members buzzed around her, refilling platters of barbecue or ox-tail stew and talking in loud voices. Then it would be the other way around. I'd watch Nanay surrounded by loved ones and worried about Ethel all alone.

Nanay encouraged Irena, Jay, and Manuel to visit Ethel too, and once or twice they did. Between them, Jay and Manuel devoured the entire package of cookies before I could finish two, and Irena could not leave Retta's side. Ethel gave us a tour of the cacti in her front yard. She'd given each one a name. I noticed that while the rocks in Ethel's yard didn't change color, together they resembled a river that transformed each time you looked at it. We spent that day dressing up the cacti: Jay put a cowboy hat on Henry, Manuel placed Jazz in sunglasses, and Irena dressed Rita Hayworth in a Route 66 T-shirt.

When I told Kurt and Gina that Ethel was my friend, they looked bored. Their faces showed no expression; their mouths straight lines. Kurt made a joke about checking her refrigerator for bodies. Neither of them asked any questions about what Ethel was like or what I did at Ethel's. They continued to walk in a gigantic arc away from her house when we passed it. When my driveway was blocked by relatives' cars, they bounced the playground ball next door to slam it against Mr. Chang's garage. Then I came up with another idea. I asked my dad to move our car to the street so we could play against our own garage door. Gina hit the ball halfheartedly and Kurt tired of wall ball after a few rounds; I realized that for them, the fun was in anticipating Mr. Chang's wrath. After that, Gina and Kurt stopped coming by, as if they'd gotten bored of me too.

Just when the routine of living with Nanay grew comfortable, my parents started packing things into boxes and buzzing around like bees on a mission. Just as before a party, there was a flurry of movement and a sense of anticipation in the air. But something felt different, and I found out we were moving to a bigger house. Once I'd confirmed Nanay was coming with us and not being passed to an aunt or uncle, the move should've been exciting. We were going to have a more spacious backyard and move closer to the park. But I worried in a way that only Nanay would understand.

"The pigeons will keep coming for a while," Nanay said when I met her outside that Saturday. "They will wait, and when time passes and we stop coming for them, they will stop waiting. Soon after that, they will forget us. They will go on just as before. Ganyan ang buhay."

Ganyan ang buhay—*that's life*. This was supposed to help me feel better, but instead I felt worse. In addition to the pigeons, I worried about Ethel. The happy pair strutted before me, collecting scattered grains in close proximity to one another, and an idea struck. I thought Nanay would surely call me "gaga" when I told her about it, but to my surprise, she nodded in approval.

The next week, we threw the rice from a few houses down. The pigeons followed, racing over each other to get to their meal, each attempting to swallow more than the next. Some birds, in their confusion, flew away simultaneously, together forming erratic movements across the sky, only to land back on our street. Nanay and I walked even further down the block and joined Ethel where she was waiting on her driveway. From there, the three of us offered the pigeons the rest of the rice. I watched my favorite black bird peck away in Ethel's front yard, enjoying his fill without a care. Soon, I thought, you will be feasting on fancy tea cookies instead of hard, uncooked rice.

The next week, Nanay and I did the same thing, leading the pigeons to Ethel's, and the week after that, some of the birds were already waiting at her house instead of ours, including the happy pair.

After we moved, I asked for a ride to visit Ethel across town, but no one could take me. I didn't persist in asking. When I felt especially sad remembering her, I comforted myself with thoughts of Ethel outside her door on Saturday mornings, feeding her flock where Nanay and I had been.

NOELLE Q. DE JESUS is the author of *Cursed and Other Stories* (Penguin Random House SEA 2019) and *Blood Collected Stories* (Ethos Books Singapore 2015), Winner of the 2016 Next Generation Indie Book Award for the Short Story. She has an MFA in Fiction from Bowling Green State University and has won a Palanca Award. She is married and has raised a daughter and son, both of whom she considers her best work.

THE IMAGE OF FILIPINAS IN THE EYES OF THE WORLD

Growing up is tough enough. This challenging dynamic is not specific to the Philippines or Filipinos. However, Filipino Americans coming of age and finding and claiming their identity must also face the images and stereotypes associated with Filipinas in the world, all due to the extreme poverty in the country. The fact that the Filipina has become synonymous with domestic helper is likely the most dominant one. But there is also the inescapable image of the Filipina as a sex worker. Unable to eradicate poverty, so much so that its own government is unable to provide jobs at home, it has all but encouraged women (and men) to leave it to be OFWs (Overseas Foreign Workers). In Europe, North America and certainly, the Middle East, you will find Filipino domestic workers because this is their ticket to giving their children a better life. Growing up Filipino in the US/Canada or Europe or Singapore or Australia means contending with this, and due to the nature of some of that work, daughters have a special burden. Throw in family secrets, the attitudes that prevail in culture, and you have the makings for deep tempest in the coming-of-age teapot. This is the conflict in my piece here, which happens is the opening chapter of a novel-in-progress.

24

THE SECRET

Cassie was skipping school. There was no point going.

"The secret...to life...is confidence." That's what Cassie's mother, Leila, always said. "You can do...anything, even things you think you can't do, things you shouldn't do or are afraid to do...with confidence. It carries you through...anything." Cassie had to hand it to her mother, for all her flaws, she had almost too much so-called wisdom to share. Leila said this when Cassie was twelve, shortly after she got her first period.

"I made some...decisions, and if I had only known what I know now, I tell you, I would not have made...many of them."

The pauses were the thing. This Cassie knew well. You had to pay attention to the pauses, sometimes, even more than the words. But the truth was, it was a long time since she'd listened to her mother that closely. In fact, for some time now, she wanted to turn her mother off. Her mother was a piece of work. It seemed to Cassie, Leila spouted a lot of shit.

In fact, she didn't know how Frank could take it. And what the hell would they have done without him? Thank God for Frank Lubrano, was all Cassie could think, sometimes. He stood between mother and daughter, keeping them from driving each other mad. The tardy but integral third to their family unit, essential to their mother-daughter team. He was the bridge that connected them.

And Leila came from a completely different world, one Cassie had never even seen. But she was, and would say it ad nauseum, always a good student. Grades are all that count. Straight As. And then learn...all the rules. Like I did...like I still do. Cassie knew Leila meant the rules that belonged to this world. The world that was America.

"Here in America," Leila said to Cassie when she was nine "You need to learn to listen before you speak, see how they sound, and then speak the way they speak."

When Cassie was ten, Leila said, "Here in America, you must work harder than everybody else, but always stay quiet. If you are too loud, they will see you. If you are quiet, they will not be...afraid of you, and think you are out to get their stuff. You don't want them to notice you...you want them to only see your work..."

Cassie was 13 when her mother's voice started to grate on her ears. Who will see me? How will I ever be loud when you're always talking? Leila's voice, what she said, made Cassie flinch with annoyance. It was like that clicking sound the peeler made when her mother skinned potatoes for dinner.

"Here in America..." her mother only had to say, and the exasperation brimmed up in Cassie's soul. She felt she would soon be leaking it. "Where else?" Cassie stifled the urge to ask. "Where else have I been but here in America."

"Here in America— you must wear—" Leila said when Cassie was 14, but by then, Cassie had perfected shutting her ears to almost all of it. And sometimes, even answering back.

"Shouldn't you be saying, 'Back in the Philippines' instead of 'Here in America'?" Cassie allowed herself to retort.

Leila gave her daughter a sharp glance with narrowed

eyes. "Don't answer back to me! We...don't live in the Philippines."

"And why is that again, why did you leave?"

"What did I just say? You never listen?"

Their exchanges came to a halt because Cassie answered back. Even though all she wanted was information. She knew more and more, despite her mother's so-called mastery of the rules, it was Leila who did not belong. Her rules may have worked a long time ago, but not now.

Cassie finally got up out of her bed and pushed opened her bedroom window. It was still raining, soft but steady. She let the wind and the wet hit her face in cold, icy blasts. When she could no longer stand it, she returned to her haven on the bed and closed her eyes, but she did not go to sleep. This was the right decision.

Cassie was seven when Frank came into their lives. And instantly, she had fallen in love with him. But while she knew that Leila respected Frank, and liked him well enough, as a woman should her husband, she couldn't be sure whether her mother was in love. What was clear was Frank loved Leila. And how exactly had they met? Cassie was damned, if she knew. All she could remember was the day she met him; she played it in her head like a favorite song.

She was swinging her feet back and forth, fidgeting in her brand-new yellow sundress. Leila said her friend Frank was going to take them for ice cream, wouldn't that be nice? Mother and daughter had taken the path train into the city, and then, Frank appeared in his Volvo to pick them up.

"And who is this pretty little princess?"

Cassie had been too shy to say anything. She couldn't even find it in herself to try. She just looked into his striking blue-grey eyes—eyes so vastly different from hers or her mother's—blue like the sky in the late afternoon. She fell into his giant embrace, closed her eyes, and caught the comforting scent, a mix of menthol cigarettes, cologne, and mint. Then she raised her head again to look into those eyes once more, unable to believe them. For it was a relief to see love there, and acceptance so instantaneous, so freely given. But most of all it was a relief to be able to read those eyes, when she could never really read her mother's. She glanced quickly at her mother. Leila nodded and smiled with reassurance. Cassie sensed her relief as well. All of this, it was good. A good thing for all of them.

She was the princess. Frank was the king, and Leila was a small, slight queen with her long hair up in a bun, her strong jaw, and a kind of blank darkness in her eyes. Frank always made things right, and it was clear in the way he smiled, the way he shrugged like nothing really mattered, and the way he kissed her mother when they both thought she wasn't looking. It was always he who kissed her mother. Well, why couldn't they live happily ever after? They said that Cassie should call Frank, Frank.

"Why don't I have a Daddy?" She asked Leila. She was eight and Frank was away at work that night. Leila was taken aback, and took some time to answer.

"You…had a Daddy, but he…" Leila paused, "…At the time I knew him, he didn't have the focus for a family. He said that himself. He lived in the Philippines and was very busy. That's why he doesn't know you. And we live here, and we will be always OK without him."

"Why do you say, lived? Is he dead? Or does he have a family now?"

"I don't know. He stopped mattering to me once I had you. But if he knew you, he'd love you just like I do. Just like Frank does. You hear me?"

This was Leila all over, able to offer some joy, but you had to clear away the cobwebs of pain and the layers of darkness, first. That was the way she had always been. When her mother spoke, there was always something unspoken, like a falsehood in the words she offered as truth.

Gusts of wind whipped this way and that in whirling swirls outside so that the leaves on the lawn flew up in the air like pieces of red and orange paper. Even though it was only two o'clock in the afternoon, the sky was slate gray. It was a week till Thanksgiving. The clouds were swollen, gray and pugnacious, like every single one would spew black rain or slate snow or a freezing mix. Cassie felt justified. What would she miss at school today—nothing. She was pulling two As and three solid B pluses she knew she could tip over at finals. College applications for early action were posted. If all went well, they'd know by Christmas. What was missing one day going to hurt? She pulled the covers over her head and then rested the knuckles of both hands on her cold nose, a childhood habit.

There was Mike. He'd called once. Texted so often she had deleted the last few without even reading. Cassie stayed in her deep, dark, blue cloud. Just today. Just one day to set herself right. But she was afraid the next day, she would feel the way she felt this morning. Her eyes, glued grimly shut, fearing the waves of lowness lapping inside her would take monstrous shape and consume her.

Leila was at work in the city, where she was an administrative assistant to an advertising VP who had her working late, three or four days a week. Frank was on a sales trip upstate; he sold copiers. Being alone at home reminded Cassie that she didn't belong there. And that somewhere else, there was another world where maybe she might—a place she had never seen, air she had never breathed, city streets she'd never walked on. The pictures she had seen—beaches and rice fields and old Spanish towns did not fit the murky idea she had of it in her heart. Sometimes, Leila talked about it, or told a pretty story, like she was polishing a glass vase or a precious jewel, and then suddenly, almost willfully, she'd smash it with an offhand remark, "But it's not like that anymore. It hasn't been like that for years." Or, "But now the water is filthy and full of trash." Or "Oh that great green forested mountain is now flat and treeless. They've been selling it all, so China can make islands …"

The phone rang. Cassie let the machine pick up.

"Cassandra? This is your mother."

Cassie snorted.

"Are you asleep? Cassie?" The voice was shrill and piercing. Cassie turned over in her bed and glared at the phone. "I'm going to be late. There's… arroz caldo there. That's lunch and maybe you can make a sandwich for dinner. Throw in the chicken stock in the fridge and thin it if—" The phone beeped, cutting her mother off.

Cassie flung herself over her bed and made a retching sound. Minutes later, the telephone rang again, and Cassie reached to turn the volume all the way down.

"We will always be all right without him. But if he knew you, he would love you like I do."

Cassie's telephone buzzed a text. It was Mike, and she ignored again. She had been at his house the other day. It had been the second night in a row, and on a school night. Leila had not been pleased. Frank would have put his foot down, had he been home, but Cassie didn't care.

It wasn't as if she spent the night there. She always came home. And always by midnight, even if it meant making Mike drive her back.

"Don't worry, Frank." Cassie had said to him once, when he had driven up to school to pick her up one late night. Frank had caught her and Mike. Not caught exactly, Cassie thought, as they hadn't been doing anything. They were kissing, that was all. But Frank showed no visible reaction. Cassie actually made conversation, just to check.

"Just so you know, Mike and I aren't having sex, Frank. Not really."

Frank looked embarrassed at those two words and what they conjured up. "Yes, well. Whatever. Just be careful and safe, princess."

Cassie knew what he meant. Frank had two sons from his first marriage. One was married because the girl had gotten pregnant. The other wasn't, but he already had a child living with the mother in Philadelphia. He knew what he was talking about. And getting pregnant wasn't the only thing you had to be careful about—Cassie knew that, too.

Cassie must have fallen asleep, because the next thing she knew, she was awakened by another text. Cassie clicked it open, forgetting she didn't want to.

"I'm so sorry. It will never happen again. Please, can I come over?"

Cassie rolled over onto her tummy and propped herself up to thumb another text. Two letters. O. K.

She peeled herself off her bed, threw the pink top hanging over her chair, the one she hadn't bothered to toss into the hamper last night and slipped into black yoga pants, similarly not fresh. What a difference six months made. Back then Cassie took pains getting dressed even on the off-chance she'd see him at school. Now, no. A very definite switch had clicked on. Or off. She couldn't go back. Not after that night.

They were in his room. An old sit-com played on TV, and though they'd stopped watching it, having moved on to other more pressing things, the clever one liners and canned laughter continued to blare into the air. All through it, they were busy, their mouths speaking without words, their breath urgent. And then something happened. Without knowing quite why, Cassie found herself listening keenly to the older, white male character on the show make a terrible joke. It wasn't even funny. The punchline reverberated loudly in Mike's room, as if the two of them were right there in the live studio audience.

"Filipino women? Aren't they either maids or call girls?"

Cassie stiffened and stopped kissing him. Had Mike heard it? She looked up into his face, seeing his lips red and raw and a pimple on his chin had risen to the surface in irritation.

"What?" he mumbled.

Cassie pushed him away and raised herself up on her elbows to face the television set.

"He said women in the Philippines are either maids or prostitutes." Mike gave a nervous laugh.

Cassie looked at him in the dark. "Well ... I'm not a maid." Cassie heard herself say. She reached for the remote

317

and clicked the box off, so his room was completely dark except for a bit of light from the streetlamps outside. For the first time ever, she took off all her clothes. "So, maybe, I should get something for this …" she said, not even knowing why she was saying this, where it was all coming from.

"What…uh, okay, how much?" he said with a laugh, his voice low and husky.

"You can't afford it…"

"Wanna bet?" And he reached under his bed and pulled out a hundred-dollar bill and placed it on her tummy. And then turned to her. "Here's what I want…" he said as though she didn't know. She turned toward him, and the bill drifted to the floor.

"Are you…even…Filipino?" Mike whispered, almost absently, like he was finding words scattered amid all the wild thoughts in his head and he'd just managed to string them together. Cassie wondered if he had ever even said the word before.

"No…I'm not." Cassie murmured softly against his lips. "I'm nothing." And they continued. Afterwards, they just lay in Mike's bed, spent but not actually touching. Cassie could smell Mike in the bedclothes and started feeling acutely aware she did not belong here, either. She felt empty and alone, as though Mike was a complete stranger.

"I'm going." She whispered this into the cold still air of his room. Mike was sound asleep. Cassie slipped out of his bed, threw on her clothes, and tiptoed out of his room, and out of his house, not even bothering to put her on her shoes and socks.

That had been their first time. Not only that. That had been her first time, really. The first time she let it happen, without thinking, with no resistance at all. She let him do everything, an effort to erase what she heard on the TV show.

It felt like it happened yesterday. She had not spoken to Mike since. Suddenly starving, she went downstairs, turned on the heat on the chicken rice soup. Rummaging through the cupboards, she then made a sauce of soy and squeezed in some lemon juice, like Leila would have done. The scent of chicken and ginger filled the kitchen, and Cassie felt she could not wait. She stirred the chicken rice soup and took a bowl to fill as the doorbell rang. Reluctantly, she went to get it.

Mike looked like a little boy. A guilty little boy. For a split second, Cassie wondered what he had done.

"Can I come in?" She did not reply. She just turned back into the house, toward the kitchen, leaving the door ajar. Mike walked in. "Listen, Cas. I'm sorry." He followed her with his head bent in a mournful air of dejection. She said nothing, just nodded to the bubbling pot.

"You wanna eat?"

Mike mumbled, "I can eat."

They ate the rice soup without talking, going for seconds until there was nothing left the pot.

"I acted like a jerk, didn't I?"

"Maybe, but I…I made you."

"I'm sorry. Did I make you feel…Did I make you feel bad? Cheap?"

That's when Cassie heard herself speak in Leila's voice. "Nobody makes a girl feel cheap. A girl does that to herself."

Mike looked confused. He went near her, tried to reach for her hand, but Cassie pulled it away.

"I didn't know you'd never done it before."

Cassie suddenly felt sorry for him. She knew that he cared about her, but she also knew she didn't care about him at all. Not in that way. She thought she did, but it had been wrong from the start. Mike had been an idea she tried, like a pair of shoes or a French Poetry elective.

"It was wrong…" Cassie said.

"Yes. We won't do it again. I just want to be with you." Mike said in an uncertain rush.

"No, you and me. It's a mistake. I don't want to see anyone."

There was really nothing more to talk about after that. She made him leave, and he did, looking sadder and more confused than when he arrived. Maybe he would call back. Try to see her tomorrow. Cassie knew she would stand by her decision.

When Leila finally arrived, it was close to midnight, and she immediately started cooking a couple of dishes for the next few days. Cassie was drawn downstairs by the smell of onions and beef sauteing. The sight of Leila standing in the kitchen, still in her suit, was strangely comforting.

"Hey..." she said.

Leila looked up to see Cassie's disarray. The bed hair, the same clothes from the day before. She said nothing.

"Feel better now?"

"Some."

"Want to eat?"

"Yes." Cassie added, "Please."

Leila had started cooking even before taking off her work clothes. Cassie noted her raccoon mascara eye rings and the strands of hair falling out of her bun. Cassie thought, here they were, mother and daughter. What a pair of slobs.

Leila made her daughter a plate of beef and onions and rice.

"I thought you...would be with Mike tonight." Leila let her eyes meet Cassie's. "But I'm happy you're here."

"We broke up."

Leila's eyebrows rose, but she kept her tone even. "Really."

"I mean..." Cassie started to eat, without even waiting till her mother had made her own plate and seated herself at the kitchen counter. "I broke up with him."

Leila's eyes narrowed slightly before she looked down at her plate, though of course, she did not see it.

"Really..." Leila said, "...and how do we feel about that?" Leila said, before taking a spoonful. This is something else Leila did with Cassie. The We-ing.

"We feel nothing," Cassie said, shrugging. "We're graduating. There's really..." she hesitated, knowing full well she was using her mother's meaningful pauses. "There's no point."

Leila chewed meditatively, before making a very careful reply, "I see."

Mother and daughter ate in fairly comfortable silence. Leila knew that beyond this conversation, she could not press Cassie into saying more. She was just thankful Cassie told her. Leila watched her pretty daughter and resisted the impulse to stand up and hug her, unsure why she couldn't.

"You're right. You're going to have a whole new life. You need to be free for that."

As then, as though her mother had said nothing at all, Cassandra spoke up, brisk and breezy, saying out loud the thing she discovered she had been wanting to say for a very long time now: "I'm not going to college next year, no matter where I'm accepted."

Leila lost it.

"What? You can't. Here in America, nothing happens to people who don't go to college. You're going. You're not throwing away your future. End of discussion." Leila's voice rose higher and grew louder with every word, but Cassie's face only hardened.

"Mom, listen to me for once. I'm not saying I'm not going ever." Cassie stood up, realizing in that instant there was nothing her mother could do. She brought her empty plate and cutlery to the sink and then took her mother's. She started to wash both. Leila tried to keep calm. But she was bristling with some unidentifiable emotion.

"And what is your plan?"

"I'm going to the Philippines. I want to find my father."

Leila stood and took hold of Cassie by the shoulders. "Anak," she started out, "...you know he never knew I had you..."

"You don't think he ought to know?" Cassie asked, honestly curious.

"No, I don't."

"Well, it's not your decision."

Here in America, Leila opened her mouth to say, but stopped short. She knew it, and Cassie knew it, too. Here in America, Cassie finished the thought, you can't stop me.

All at once, she felt sorry for her mother. She saw Leila was afraid of the things Cassie might discover. But the truth was, she couldn't find it in her heart to care. Cassie couldn't even imagine Leila's next words. But she knew that whatever her mother said, whatever she did, even, it would only push Cassie on with certainty, more quickly and more fixedly, to some kind of end. With any luck, a good one. Cassie wished it would be the end of not knowing, as she had been looking for that her entire life.

OSCAR PEÑARANDA was born in Barugo, Leyte, Philippines, and moved to Vancouver, Canada when he was twelve years old in 1956, when his father and colleagues opened the first Philippine Consulate in Canada. When he turned seventeen, his father was transferred to San Francisco, where he has settled. An educator for forty years, a writer for even more, and a Filipino all his life, he received the prestigious Gawad Ng Unyon ng mga Manunulat sa Pilipinas for his lifetime efforts of his writings and community projects. He lives at the historic and legendary International Hotel in San Francisco.

WRITER AS A VERY YOUNG MAN

In pre-colonial times, fundamentals of Philippine leadership stood on four pillars: The Datu (Chief), the Panday (blacksmiths and other artists), the Bayani (warriors and protectors of the peace), and the Babaylan (shamans, interpreters of natural and unnatural phenomena, keeper of traditions, healers, reader of nature, unlockers of mysteries and histories). This story is a brief encounter between two people set against the backdrop of a San Francisco landmark's erasure, which itself was also a brief encounter with the people of the City, in which the narrator was one. The story also touches on a portrait of the writer as a very young man.

25

BABAYLAN IN PLAYLAND BY THE SEA

"Rosebud...A girl's name? *You wouldn't think that a man in his dying breath would mention someone's name out of the blue after fifty years, would you?"*

"Well...you're pretty young, Mr. Thompson. A fellow would remember a lot of things you wouldn't think he'd remember. You take me. Crossing the ferry to Jersey one late afternoon in 1896, I saw a girl with a white dress and a white parasol. Just for a second, it was. Don't think she saw me. But I bet that a month does not pass by that I don't think of her." ~ Mr.Bernstein in *Citizen Kane,* 1941.

The stupidest thing that the city of San Francisco ever did was to get rid of Playland by the Sea, with its Funhouse giant doll of a bouncing Fat Laughing Lady with freckles and red hair, its grand towering Ferris Wheel, and the formidable Salt and Pepper Shaker Loop, where he, as a teenager, once discovered too late, not to have anything in one's pockets because they will all fall down, coins, pens, whatever, when the ride turns you upside down violently and fearfully. Hot dog stands steaming in the night and the carnival atmosphere everywhere and all around, various sounds and barks of laughter floating in the air. It was a mini-Disneyland right across the misty Pacific Ocean, the Great Highway and the Cliff House, a turn of the (twentieth) century Restaurant made of brass and dark wood. Unfortunately, Playland was swallowed up by the waves of greed. Speculation, they called it. So they closed it down, built apartments and condos instead to make more money. Joy subsided quickly like the foams from among and along those silver-crested waves. No more mermaids beckoned from the sea. Where once it shimmered in the summers of the City, the area now is a very quiet place and deserted. Lonesome winds frequent it. Condominiums and apartments were put on the site where Playland used to be. Those apartments and condominiums have never been fully occupied. In due time, desolation took over the place and no children were ever seen near it. That was the day the magic died in Playland by the sea. Songs and stories will be the only remnants of those days. This is one of them.

*

Priday Night Walker called his trusted friend Amador one day during prom season and told him to get ready for a double date that he, Priday, is arranging.

"You gotta go on a double date with me, pal." He said with his phony Texas (Filipino) accent. Priday Night Walker was a Filipino mestizo whose white U.S. citizen father was in the military and found himself growing up mostly right in the heart of Texas, of all places. His father was transferred to San Francisco only six years ago. He got to know everybody fast. He was a very social guy as you can tell by what folks called him.

"I don't got a 'date,' Amador reminded him.

"I know that," answered Priday quickly. "I don't know why; you're kinda cute. Look at me…Pry-day Night Walker…"

"No thanks."

"I just don't know what it is they see in me, but …"

"Could it be that Chevy Impala of yours? It ain't the looks, that's for sure."

"But I always got a girl, right? And seein' that I knew you wouldn't have one, and seein' that the prom is already this Sarday nat ... I got you one."

He was right, the fucker. Compared to Priday's social life, Amador felt at times that he would languish in obscurity the rest of his life.

It seemed that his (Priday's) date's parents won't allow the two of them on a date alone. Amador did not know whether the parents had heard of Priday's reputation or not. They would, however, permit her to go on a double date with her girlfriend (and family trusted companion), who hopefully would be *his,* Amador's, blind date.

"We'll spend for everything," Priday told Amador. "I'll take care of expenses," he said.

"What about for the date?" Amador asked.

"Not the expenses that don't involve me, pare. You gotta cough that up yourself, brother. I'll just provide the merchandise; you gotta pay for the maintenance. Don't be kuripot, man. C'mon, you gotta fork out *something.* Show some class, man. You're buying her a corsage, right?"

Amador, the ever-accommodating (in his mind) young man of seventeen that he was, said, "Yes, of course." Amador himself had just graduated. His graduation celebrations and activities were nothing to brag about. In fact, it was nothing at all, period, even though he made dean's list again. Just a kiss from his mother and a controlled smile from his father. He was not really planning to go to his school prom, though Father Becker, his Saint Ignatius High School English teacher, had offered him a couple of names from his list of Mercy High School girls. The same priest had procured him one before on the Sadie Thompson Dance. Her name was Anne Farmer and her straight, long, red hair still had him remembering. The truth is that Amador had hinted to his mom about going to the prom, but she picked up on it right away and said, "Nating doing! No money for all dis kalokohans. It's not enough that you go to the most expensive school in San Francisco. You have to pick the most expensive event pa!"

"Ma, this is the prom. And I didn't pick the school. You guys did."

"Not me," she said, pointing her lips toward his father who was reading the newspaper while watching the news on the television in the sala, as he, with his Giants baseball cap on, was listening to the baseball game on the radio in the kitchen.

"They're paying for the whole thing, Ma."

"Who are 'they', ha?"

"I guess their family, Priday's girlfriends' family, or her girlfriend's girlfriend's family. I don't know. All I know is that I, I mean we, I mean you, are not paying for a centavo, Ma. Wala. Libre lahat."

"Siyet," she curtly said.

And he kissed her on both cheeks, making gigil noises and grabbed her shoulder and started massaging it and shaking it until she wrinkled her forehead and started screaming for him to stop. "Hoy! Hoy!" And laughing he slowly let her go.

"Siyet", she said again, regaining some composure and fixing herself up.

The ride after the prom was rather quiet. He had danced with his date Maria a few times only. He should have danced more, he knew, but it was too late now. Priday pulled over by the diner with the big Dachsund hot dog on top of it by 48th Ave, near the Great Highway. Priday and his prom date quickly disappeared into Lover's Lane by the Laughing Lady's entrance gate, leaving the two alone. Amador and Maria sat down at a small eating place and as they were ordering the food, Amador started noticing Maria. And he started listening well to what she was saying, as he slowly chewed on his fish and chips with a sprinkling of vinegar. The jukebox was playing *"Sally Go 'Round the Roses"* and she was humming and oo-oowing a bit. They finished their meals and smiling at each other (as the Rocky Fellers were busting out *"Killer Joe"*), walked outside into the lights-studded mist. They walked somewhat awkwardly through parts of Playland to cross the Great Highway on to Ocean Beach, passing the Laughing

Lady, the dart and balloon games, the shooting galleries, and the cotton candy wagons, till they confronted the giant Ferris Wheel with all its lights and colors and slow, creaky turning. Everything must have been turning in Maria's inside, too, because she suddenly said:

"Someday, I'll have my name in lights. Keystone Korner, Black Hawk, Blue Note. You never know, right? Why not?"

"Sure, why not?" he said. "You're a good singer. I can tell by your humming you got soul. I can't sing, but I can tell soulful singing."

"To sing, I think, to really sing your own, you gotta do it with passion. But you gotta have a broken heart or two under your belt to have that passion. I think. I don't know what I'm saying." She looked up at him smiling a bit and took his arm to cross the street to the ocean's side.

"Rumi said you gotta let your heart break till it opens."

She was looking up at him and beyond him, at the sky, with white-edged clouds bathed and drifting by the silvery moon, seawind blowing, foaming waves pounding, her chiffon dress puffed billowing with the billows of the sea.

After they've crossed, he said, "Maybe you can teach me to sing. Think it's possible? Can anyone learn? I'm pretty hopeless. I might scare away all the mermaids by singing off tune."

"Nonsense. Anybody can sing. My niece is toned-deaf and I taught her to sing."

"Wow, you're a teacher, too. You're gifted."

"Thank you." She looked at him straight and clear and kindly. They were stepping on sand now. "But you're the gifted one." She was looking through him, beyond him, into the moonlit sea. "You'll write about us, and someday people will read them and, maybe, one will come to know someone like me. You're the gifted one." She moved a little closer to him and walked in his rhythm, taking bigger steps. "The waves, the ocean, the sea, will wipe them all out immediately, but the spirit of our footprints will still be in these sands because you will write about them; I can tell. I know a little bit about you before, from Priday and them. Research is good, right?"

"When before, or before when?"

"Before before pa."

"Wow! A budding private investigator, too. 77 Sunset Strip, Hawaii Five-O, female Poncie Pons!"

"More like Paoay Five-O. I'm Ilokana. My mother's Tagalog, though. She named me after the legendary Maria of Mount Makiling because I was born in the calm right after a storm. I like to know what I'm getting into, of course, before I jump into anything. With a practical and desperate friend like Priday, one has to excavate a little oral history on his double date choices," she smiled, her red lips accentuating her scarlet and gold shawl. With a slight change of tone she said, "You keep writing. You keep us alive."

"That's funny," he answered. "Everyone tells me to dream another dream, to stop writing. I'll be broke all my life, they say. No one is interested in reading about Filipinos, especially Filipinos, they all tell me. Don't know if I should even consider it now. My own family…"

"Consider it? You talk as if you have a choice. You don't. You're a bridge longer than the Golden Gate. And you're good. I read some of your poems that you write for your friends to the girl of their dreams, or the object of their lustful affection. Some are too good to send away. I hope you have a copy of all of them."

"Yeah, some of them won't appreciate the poems, huh?"

"Oh, they'll appreciate them all right. Every one of them. A girl appreciates those things. But not necessarily for the same reasons."

"Really? Do they know it is not from their aspiring suitors?"

"Of course, they do. C'mon, they all know they came from you."

"I'll make sure to keep them all from now on."

They took off their shoes and started laughing. He tried to carry her pair but she would not let him. "It's all right. I'll carry them. They're my shoes, after all." The night was all a-splash in spindrifts brought by the wind and waves. They strolled on the sands of the silver-ladened seascape. He noticed the moon, though not yet full, was bright and it made his gaze wander towards the horizon. It was during this gaze that a strange surge of romantic feeling overwhelmed him. It was prom night after all, and he suddenly swept Maria off her feet and scooped her up, carrying her as they both almost fell. Regaining his balance, he continued carrying her, trying to keep up a conversation. He noticed the silveriness of things as the moon momentarily got in his eye. It took his attention for a split second and then that was all because a wave, a gigantic one, rose like a monster from the sea and it was heading straight for them. Terror-stricken and instinctively obeying the most formidable human urge, that of self-preservation, he forgot everything and ran away from the great wave, toward the Great Highway. But of course, he forgot, too, the bundle he had in his arms a few seconds ago, the object of his romanticism. He looked down at his empty arms and looked back and saw Maria squirming to get up from the water's edge like a cockroach on its back trying to get right side up. Coming to his senses, he rushed to her, shouting apologies before he even got to her and picked her up.

"Not just our footprints, now," she said laughing in her surprise, "but my body prints, too," brushing off the sands and water from herself. "I was shaking like a cockroach out there."

"Or a mermaid," he said.

When he had gathered her in his arms safely and things started to look right-side up again, he clumsily added, "You're a wise one. With a hell of a sense of humor."

"But you," she touched both his hands and turned them palm up, "through these soft hands, your gift will flow. Remember that."

"C'mon. Let's get outta here. You're all wet?"

"Just a little."

"Wanna go back to the diner and change in the bathroom?"

"Change to what, my slip or shawl?" she jokingly said, and then she thought for a while. "Why not? I'll just put my coat over it. C'mon. No. Let's go in the Cliff House. I'll change there."

When she came out of the Cliff House, she came out all colorful and babaylan-like. She looked like she belonged in the richy, classy Cliff House (by her carriage and posture) yet she did not belong in the Cliff House (by her splash of many colors), too bold to neatly fit the ambiance. Biblical yet pagan. Folkloric, yet modern.

He never saw her again. And to this day, hard as he might try, he cannot remember an iota of whatever happened to Priday and his date that prom night when he used him as an excuse to satisfy his (Priday's) concupiscence, bursting from his lustful, teenage loins.

The only thing he remembered clearly of the actual prom itself was that he had bought her a lavender corsage which reminded him of that corny song of which the only thing he liked was its title: *Lavender Blue*. They both had trembled at his pinning the orchid above her left breast. They must have driven home that night to end the date, but he has no memory of her at all after that night she came out of the Cliff House. They must have said goodnight but he does not remember if he kissed her or not, nothing, that unmentionable, for some, that dreaded moment, the prize of the prom—that good-night kiss. No recollection of it at all. Just the ocean, the beach, the moon, the wind, the Cliff House, the steaming smell of hot dogs, burnt cotton candies, and Playland by the sea that disappeared into the mist and recesses of San Francisco history, but not from memory, at least not from his.

ACKNOWLEDGEMENTS

All stories in Growing Up Filipino 3 *are copyrighted in the authors' names. All rights reserved. They are reprinted in this book by permission of the authors.*

Cecilia Manguerra Branard: "The Dead Boy" was first published as "The Altar Boy" in *Philippine Graphic*, March 23, 1992; it was also published in *Fern Garden*, National Commission of Culture and Arts, 1998; *Acapulco at Sunset and Other Stories*, Anvil 1995; and Brainard's *Selected Short Stories*, University of Santo Tomas Publishing House 2021.

Linda Ty-Casper: "Happy" is part of Ty-Casper's collection, *A River, One-Woman Deep: Stories*, PALH, 2017 & University of Santo Tomas Publishing House 2018.

Noelle Q. De Jesus: "The Secret" is part of a novel-in-progress.

Migs Bravo Dutt: "On Becoming Victoria" is part of a novel-in-progress.

James M. Fajarito: "The Goat" was first published in *Anak Sastra*, Issue 18, Kris Williamson, January 2015, online, Kuala Lumpur, Malaysia.

Angelo R. Lacuesta: "Nilda" was first published in *White Elephants: Stories*, Anvil Publishing, 2004, Manila.

R. Zamora Linmark: "Kalihi in Farrah" is part of the author's book, *Rolling the R's,* Kaya Press, 1995.

Veronica Montes: "Beauty Queens" is part of the author's book, *Benedicta Takes Wing and Other Stories*, PALH, 2017.

Dom Sy: "Then Cruel Quiet" was first published in *A Natural History of Empire*, Bughaw, 2019, Quezon City.

Eileen R. Tabios: "Negros" appeared in *Contemporary Fiction by Filipinos in America*, Anvil 1997 & PALH, 2021. It is part of *PAGPAG: The Dictator's Aftermath in the Diaspora*, Paloma Press, 2020, San Mateo.

John Jack Wigley: "The Fancy Dancer" is part of Home of the *Ashfall: A Memoir*, University of Santo Tomas Publishing House, 2014, Manila.

www.ingramcontent.com/pod-product-compliance
Lightning Source LLC
Chambersburg PA
CBHW031104030726
47496CB00002BA/379